OPS POPULI
INCEPTION

Mike Lieber

ISBN Number: 978-0-615-26500-1
Record Number: 1485875

Astute Publishing Company
4121 Plank Road, # 427
Fredericksburg, VA 22407
(800) 295-7594

For more information on the book, or to participate in an on-line discussion of the concepts discussed herein, please visit the Ops Populi web site:
www.op-usa.org

Acknowledgements

First, I wish to thank the love of my life, Jan, without whose unremitting support and boundless enthusiasm, this would not have been possible. My affectionate and heartfelt appreciation goes to Sheryl Hull, who selflessly critiqued and polished a rather raw manuscript in the midst of the final stretch of her master's program. And last, but by no means least, I wish to express my profound gratitude for the numerous and invaluable contributions of Elizabeth DeVita, William Erskine, Joyce Goforth and Laurie Roche.

To all who love America,

We mustn't let her perish;

Let us cast aside our differences,

And join as one people, one voice.

For despite her imperfections,

She remains:

A perpetual reservoir of hope,

The bastion of freedom,

A champion of liberty and justice,

To humanity and its posterity,

The world over.

The Cycle of Democracy

"A democracy cannot exist as a permanent form of government. It can only exist until the voters discover they can vote themselves largess from the public treasury.

"From that moment on, the majority always votes for the candidates promising them the most benefits from the public treasury, with the result that a democracy always collapses over loose fiscal policy, always followed by a dictatorship.

"The average age of the world's greatest civilizations has been 200 years. These nations have progressed through this sequence:

"From bondage to spiritual faith;
from spiritual faith to great courage;
from courage to liberty;
from liberty to abundance;
from abundance to selfishness;
from selfishness to apathy;
from apathy to dependence;
from dependency back again into bondage."

Dr. Alexander Tytler, a Scot professor, wrote a scholarly tome, called "The Athenian Republic," from which this concept comes. It was published shortly before the thirteen American colonies won independence from England.

"Every government degenerates when trusted to the rulers of the people alone. The people themselves are its only safe depositories."

—Thomas Jefferson

CHAPTER 1

The private jet's only passenger gazed out the window as the pilot started the final approach to Burke Lakefront Airport situated on the shore of Lake Erie in the Northeast part of downtown Cleveland. It had been nearly four years since he was here, but the last time, his pilot had been diverted to Cleveland's primary airport, Hopkins International, which did not afford the great views of downtown he now enjoyed. Martin Lochridge quickly moved to the left side of the cabin as the plane set its final approach so he could take in the many changes he knew were part of a major, multi-year urban revival plan to transform the infamous "Mistake by the Lake" into a healthy, vibrant city.

Lochridge's financial investment in Cleveland's revival was now well over a hundred million, and though he never had lived here, he had personal bonds to the city as well. His wife's family had its roots firmly embedded here, and he was about to visit one of his closest friends, the matriarch of a family from Cleveland's gilded industrial age.

Ahead in the skyline, he identified the erstwhile ornate Terminal Tower as his point of reference. The landmark was now dwarfed by newer and taller skyscrapers but was still distinguished by its many embellishments. He grinned at the sight of Jacobs Field—"the Jake"—a new retro-urban baseball park, and Gund Arena, the new home of basketball's Cavaliers, which were the heart of the $300 million Gateway Center. Then, along the shore of Lake Erie, there was the $92 million Rock and Roll Hall of Fame, and its neighbor, the modern Great Lakes Science Center, both overlooking Northcoast Harbor.

As the limousine rolled along Euclid Avenue, Lochridge scoffed at the ascendant commercial development proudly touted as "progress" by Cleveland's reigning political and civic leaders—progress, which in this case like so many others, had come at the incalculable expense of cultural gems destroyed by the perennial and iconoclastic assault of advancing civilization. His eyes instead scanned for the lucky survivors, the few remaining mansions that had once lined "Millionaire's Row" in 19th century sepia-toned photographs of international travel guides, which pronounced the elm-lined avenue "The Showplace of America," and designated it as a must see for travelers from abroad. Many years had passed since his hostess, the owner of the limousine in which he was riding, had showed him the old photographs, while telling him about the unparalleled concentration of wealth along "the Avenue." In the late nineteenth century, she had explained to his astonishment, the tax valuation of its mansions had far exceeded the valuation of New York's Fifth Avenue. Its residents included the families of John D. Rockefeller, John Hay, personal secretary to Abraham Lincoln and Secretary of State under William McKinley, Jeptha Wade, Cleveland benefactor and founder of Western Union Telegraph, and many other prominent citizens of the time, such as Sylvester T. Everett, George Worthington, Horace Weddell, Marcus Hanna, Ambrose Swasey, and Amasa Stone. Most of the few remaining estates of the industrial titans were now the property of institutions with the financial wherewithal to care for them; the few remaining in private hands, as in the case of his destination, were owned by tenacious "old-money" descendents who had persevered through the Great Depression and the subsequent and protracted decline and decay. In many ways, Lochridge reflected as the gates to the long drive swung open, Cleveland's fall from grace represented a microcosm of what was about to befall the entire country—unless he, his hostess, and the other members of the secret group could achieve their aim, to set into motion something that had not been done since the founding of the United States of America.

"Marty, Marty, Marty!" the effusive Marian T. Satterlee gushed as soon as he stepped out of the car. "Billie," as she had been known to him for the better part of two decades, had appeared coatless from the house's great double doors just as the limo came to a stop.

"Hello, Billie!" he yelled up to her while he waited for the driver to fetch his overnight bag from the trunk.

"Oh, don't worry about that right now," she said, "Jimmy will get it for you."

"Thank you, Jimmy," Lochridge said with a deferential bow to the driver. An icy, damp, bone-chilling breeze greeted him when he turned to face the house, and the barren elms, and heaps of dirty snow dotting the property meant Cleveland was already firmly in winter's grip. Lochridge walked up the few stairs to the portico rubbing his hands together, then grabbed Billie in a warm embrace.

"It is so good to see you!" Billie said into his ear. "C'mon, let's get inside."

The house was a virtual museum, loaded with precious antiques, and a testament to the skilled craftsmanship of a bygone era. Billie's grandfather, William Satterlee, who had made his fortune as the founder of one of the nation's iron ore companies, had spared no expense in the construction of the 30-room mansion, evidenced by plentiful Italian marble, English oak and Japanese rosewood throughout. On the way to the library, Lochridge hesitated just long enough for a quick peek through a narrow slit in polished double doors that led from the hallway into a spacious center room holding a magnificent old pipe organ. Centered on the rear wall, the organ was situated on a raised platform beneath more than one hundred gleaming pipes artfully arranged to form three convex arches that crested just below the two-story ceiling. Her father had purchased it in the 1940s from a war-ravaged Italian theatre, Billie had explained while guiding him on his first tour of the stately home so long ago. The elder Satterlee had taken great pleasure in operating the unique instrument, which played music programmed on large paper rolls.

As they walked into the library, the silver-haired Lou Jenkins rose to greet him. A retired network news anchor and now a best-selling historical author, Jenkins was among the most well-known personalities in America. He was certainly one of the country's most trusted journalists, with a reputation for being fair and impartial in his reporting. Lochridge felt his heart skip a beat as the surprisingly short, but fit Jenkins walked up to offer his hand.

"Mr. Jenkins," Lochridge said taking his hand in a firm grip. "It's a pleasure."

"No, sir, the pleasure is mine," Jenkins replied in his signature baritone. "Please call me Lou."

Billie, ever the consummate hostess, offered them refreshments, which they both declined. Lochridge's stomach had been bothering him lately, and although he maintained his characteristic poise, the tension leading up to this meeting had his insides in tight knots.

It was Billie who had arranged the meeting several weeks ago, calling on her old friend, Jenkins, to consider suspending his retirement for something of tremendous significance to the country. Years spent working on various philanthropic causes together had resulted in a genial, yet mutually respectful relationship, much like the one she had with Lochridge, himself. What they were about to ask him to do was no small favor, and Lochridge knew he must be very careful not only for Billie's sake, but for the sake of the other 18 people whose commitment to the cause and its eventual outcome he carried squarely on his shoulders.

"It's been a long time since I've been to Cleveland," Jenkins said as he sat down. "I understand you haven't been here in awhile yourself, Mr. Lochridge."

"Martin, please," Lochridge said, raising his hand. "No, the last time I was here was for a Cleveland Tomorrow meeting in 2001." Founded after Cleveland's financial default in 1978, Cleveland Tomorrow, was a coalition of 500 businesses and the chiefs of the city's old capitalist families, with surnames like Gund and Rockefeller. The group had galvanized the city's political, civic and corporate leaders and had provided millions of dollars in seed money to rebuild the downtown.

Billie nodded, adding, "Marty and his business partner, Erik Frese, gave us a proposal to develop some vacant land in the Hough neighborhood, above Cleveland Clinic. It's one of the best things that has happened to this city," she beamed.

Eying the empty glass on the end table next to Jenkins, Lochridge surmised that Jenkins had been here for quite awhile already. His plan had been to arrive first, but the FAA had kept them on the ground in Washington while a potent weather front passed through the region. By now, he was sure Billie had told Jenkins why he was here.

"Lou, I hope you don't mind if I get straight to the point of why we are both here today," Lochridge said with resolve. "Unfortunately, my pilot told me we might have to fly out tonight, depending on the track of this storm."

Billie frowned at the news Lochridge might not stay, but said nothing.

"I understand," Jenkins said. He reached into his breast pocket and pulled out a note pad and paper.

Lochridge shot a wrinkled glance of concern at Billy, who immediately leaned forward and gently tapped Jenkins on the arm. "Off the record for now, okay?"

"Sure." The notebook was quickly put back where it came from.

Billie, who had always taken great interest in observing interpersonal dynamics, was fascinated by the vibes she felt as her eyes alternated between these two powerful men in glints of circumspect observation. She caught a glimpse of Lochridge sizing up Jenkins with his steel-blue eyes, something she had watched him do many times in their nearly twenty-year relationship. It was 1988 when Lochridge, already a successful Washington-area businessman, assumed a seat on the board of the United Way of America. She had been on the board since 1980, as had her father and her grandfather before him, when the organization was still known as the Community Chest. From day one, it was obvious to all that he was a leader, having a keen intellect, boundless energy and intensity—qualities the organization would soon find indispensable when confronted with a disastrous national scandal brought about by the untoward actions of its chief executive. Yet, an engaging charm and dry wit eventually broke through his no-nonsense façade, winning not just their respect, but also wide admiration. She could tell he was a man genuinely concerned about improving the human condition, unlike many other businessmen she had met who sought out and served on prominent boards for less than altruistic reasons. As the heiress of the massive Satterlee family fortune, Billie was well-connected in philanthropic circles, and within a few years had Lochridge involved in numerous social causes, seeing him as often as three or four times a month.

Almost ten years his senior, Billie had no illusions about anything more than a platonic relationship with this very desirable man. She was well-aware of Lochridge's happy marriage, his devotion to his family and deep love of country, traits that made her more than happy to be able to call him a good friend. When he became interested in real estate ten years into their relationship, she brought him and his young business partner, Erik, to Cleveland to show them the ambitious plan for reviving her beloved hometown, and to sell them on the potential it offered to someone willing to take a risk. It was a fortuitous moment for Cleveland when Lochridge committed his money and energy to the city most had written off, for he not only brought his millions, but multiplied his own investment many times over through what he called "leverage." The city had been saved, and now Billie stood by his side, giving him her full support in what he persuaded her and the others—whom she did not even know—was the most important work they would ever do: rescuing their country.

The meeting with Jenkins was a calculated risk, Lochridge had explained to her several weeks before. Jenkins was retired, under no obligation to report anything they chose to tell him. To minimize the inherent risk, they would tell him only what was absolutely necessary; if he wanted to leak it, then the damage to their cause would be minimal. Jenkins was *her* friend, though, so if she preferred not to involve him in this, the group would understand, he assured her. But she had been just as reassuring, telling Lochridge that her friendship with Jenkins was strong enough to withstand any philosophical disagreements that might arise, deep enough to trust him implicitly.

"Lou, we need your help," Lochridge told him, his tone solemn, steady. "Our country is in deep trouble, and we want to do something about it. Billie has told you of our group, its plans?"

Jenkins nodded thoughtfully, his chin resting on his folded hands.

"You are no doubt still closely watching events, though I hope with plenty of time off for well-deserved relaxation. What is your candid assessment of the state of our country?"

Jenkins lifted his chin off his hands, let his arms fall to his side. "On the surface, the economy seems pretty healthy. We have an unpopular President, and even more dissatisfaction with Congress. And of course, the war. But, as a country, we have had these problems before, have always managed to pull through. I guess, I remain optimistic, but I take it from talking to Billie, you aren't?"

Lochridge shifted in his chair, now wishing he had something to wet his throat, which he cleared before he spoke. "On the surface, I, like most Americans would probably agree. It is what is under the surface that is most concerning to us."

"So I gather from Billie, but she didn't elaborate."

Lochridge knew Jenkins was not merely an accomplished journalist, but a master of the face-to-face interview, and highly skilled at formulating probing questions. He and millions of others had watched Jenkins work for decades—his subjects, the famous, the rich, the powerful—almost effortlessly, or so it appeared to the untrained, extracting information deemed important to his story or to support its conclusions. Undoubtedly, he had been deftly working on Billie, who, as Lochridge knew from observing her at many charity media events, could be equally adept at equivocation when she wanted to. But today was no time for ambiguity; it was time to take the first bold step forward in implementing a plan many years in the making, to take a great leap of faith, to trust a man he didn't know, but had every reason to believe had the intellect to comprehend the gravity of the complex problems that threatened to destroy the country and to understand the need for—perhaps eventually champion—the decisive action they were proposing. If Billie's and his own instincts were right, their cause would soon have an invaluable ally in the crucial struggle that lay ahead.

"As a country, we are approaching the point of critical mass—when our reckless actions begin to have catastrophic implications for our long-term viability as a nation," Lochridge began, his voice keenly penetrating. "We are on a ruinous course, with the federal government running roughshod over our Constitution, bankrupting our treasury, and neglecting its sacred responsibility as the stewards of our most precious asset: our country."

Jenkins shot a quick glance at Billie, who sat in quiet diffidence, hands folded in her lap. "We have always managed to overcome our problems, come back strong."

"True," Lochridge agreed. "This time, though, the dynamics at play have an ominous portent for the very essence of our society, our cherished freedoms, our way of life."

Billie unclasped her hands, lifted one to emphasize her words, and turned to face Jenkins. "Lou, you know as well as anyone that our government is failing its people. Just look at New Orleans. We have emergency responders who don't respond, regulators who don't regulate…"

"Which is the principal reason we are on the verge of the biggest global financial meltdown in history," Lochridge added, leaning forward in his chair. "This time, I'm afraid we will not be able to muddle through the problems we've created for ourselves."

"This supposed financial meltdown…" Jenkins started, "I just don't see it."

Lochridge rubbed his chin as he formulated his reply. "I'll have plenty of time to explain it in detail, show you the data. It is the biggest financial scheme ever concocted, and our banking system is squarely at its core." He shook his head as his face took on the pall of utter contempt. "It's a pernicious disease that the bankers—with the active support of the U.S. government, I might add—have spread throughout the world. But I—we—have to warn you, what we are contemplating is not without its risks."

"What kind of risks?" Jenkins asked.

Billie shifted in her chair, knowing what was coming next. Since the 9-11 terrorist attacks, it had been the topic of many conversations and now was so menacing, Lochridge felt compelled to warn him of the potential danger.

"Lou, we have evidence our government is actively engaged in an on-going program of domestic spying, using equipment and technology I, uh, well, that is under the control of the National Security Agency." Lochridge cocked an eyebrow before asking, "In the eighties—when you covered the Iran-Contra hearings—did you come across something called 'REX 84' in your research?"

Jenkins shook his head. "Don't believe so, at least not that I recall."

"An acronym for Readiness Exercise 1984. In April 1984, President Reagan signed Presidential Directorate Number 54 that authorized FEMA to engage in a secret national "readiness exercise," code named REX 84, to test its readiness to assume military authority in the event of a 'State of Domestic National Emergency.' Over the years, FEMA's powers have been expanded, its mission re-defined—perhaps explaining its abysmal response to hurricane Katrina. As I understand it, FEMA's elaborate plan now calls for suspending the Constitution, assuming control of the federal government, appointing military commanders to run state and local governments and, most disturbing of all, declaring Martial Law." He paused, his eyes glumly focused on his folded hands. "Our government has now built over 600 prison camps here in the U.S., all fully operational, surrounded by guards, and ready to receive an estimated 12 million prisoners. More are planned for closed military bases, as I understand it."

"Unbelievable," Jenkins said, his eyes fixated on Lochridge's face.

"The Presidential Executive Orders to implement it are right in the Federal Register. So, you see, what we are contemplating could be fraught with perils beyond the imagination of most Americans. On the other hand, it could very well be the pinnacle of your stellar career."

"I see," Jenkins said quietly, as he absorbed the words. He looked at Billie, who simply nodded, her face sullen. His eyes darted randomly for a moment, as though searching for answers, but found their way back to Lochridge, who waited expectantly for his next words. "What is it you would like me to do?"

CHAPTER 2

"Get down! Down! Down! Down!" the voice of the Sergeant Major boomed over the intercom. Major Sean May stopped dead in his tracks. No sooner than the familiar voice had stopped shouting, the sirens started wailing, sending everyone scrambling for any shelter they could find.

His first instinct was to dive for cover like everyone else. It wasn't the sirens that concerned him; he had heard them so many times before, they had become as easy to ignore as the blaring horns that announced the passing of a freight train within a few blocks of his house back home. No, this was serious business. The tone of the Sergeant Major's warning thundering over the intercom told him that; in fact, it had almost stopped his heart.

He darted out into the lobby and dashed across the corridor to the suite of offices housing 28 officers and enlisted men and women, including the Sergeant Major and his boss, Colonel Donna Bouchard. As his hand made contact with the door handle, he heard glass shattering, followed immediately by an explosion. The building shuddered, knocking May off balance and causing him to fall face-first into the door. He instinctively clutched the levered handle to break his forward momentum, but the lever offered no support; it simply depressed as it was designed to do, releasing the latch and allowing the door to swing open as he fell hard onto the floor inside the room.

Screams and cries rang out from all directions. As he struggled to his feet, he saw a flash of bright light through the window followed by another—closer—blast under his feet. This time the building shook more violently. The intense concussion hurtled him backwards, slamming his head on the steel doorframe. First, there was darkness, then his legs buckled underneath him. Then, total silence.

"Sir! Sir! Are you all right?" came a mayhem penetrating shout from behind.

He felt hands shaking him as he came to.

At first, he was oblivious to the pandemonium around him. The searing pain in his neck and head overwhelmed all other senses. Gradually, he became aware of the sensation of hands shaking his shoulders.

"Medic! ASAP!" someone close to him shouted.

May raised his arm. "No, I'm okay." He opened his eyes. As he struggled to focus on the face in front of him, the voice said, "Sir! Are you sure?"

The face was that of his boss's assistant, Spec-4 Juan Cortez. "Um, how long was I out?"

"Just a couple of..." His answer was cut off by a crash in one of the offices along the outside wall.

As May sat up, the shrill scream of a woman's voice pierced his ears. He and Cortez looked at each other for an instant before Cortez sprang from his crouch and darted toward the office.

May surprised even himself with his alacrity as he jumped to his feet. His own pain was obliterated by instinct as he spontaneously fell in behind Cortez, dashing headlong toward his boss's office. Cortez had barely made it through the door, when a large chunk of debris came down on top of him with such force, May knew he wouldn't be getting up. "Medic!" he yelled as loud as he could.

As soon as he reached the door, he saw the blood making a steadily expanding stain on the beige carpet. Cortez was lying on his stomach, covered in what appeared to be masonry debris and a white, chalk-like powder. He couldn't tell where the blood was coming from—only that it was from Cortez—and it was quickly forming a pool on the saturated carpet around his motionless body.

From behind, May heard the voices of several others approaching. He gingerly stepped around the mess in front of him, while pointing to the heap that buried Cortez. "See if you can get some of that junk off him, while I check on the colonel," he bellowed, as he caught a glimpse of the gaping hole in the wall to his right.

"Sir, don't go back there!" one of them yelled.

May ignored the warning, shouting in earnest as he navigated through the rubble. "Colonel! Colonel Bouchard!"

Hearing no response, he gradually made his way to Bouchard's desk, which was situated parallel to the windows lining the back wall of her office but facing the door he had just entered. He maneuvered through the dusty room with great care, stepping gingerly to keep his footing on jagged and uneven lumps of debris littering the floor. With his peripheral vision, he noticed the colonel's printer resting undisturbed on the credenza behind her desk, along with her computer and a few plants. Then, as he rounded her desk, eyes on the floor, he saw her sprawled, face-down, the lower two-thirds of her body buried in debris that had been blown in from the wall beside her. Chunks of masonry were strewn haphazardly all around and atop her normally tidy desk, which he surmised she had tried to crawl under but not quite made it. Her head and shoulders were protected, but most of her back and the lower half of her lifeless body remained exposed. Dropping to his knees, he shook one of her legs gently. "Colonel?"

Still no reply. Her body was limp to the touch but still warm, her shallow breathing evident by the faint wheeze he could hear as he drew in closer. "Medic! Medic!" he shouted again, as he lifted the chunk off her back and threw it aside. The flat piece of concrete had not broken her skin, but it was heavy enough to do some damage. May didn't want to move her, so he looked toward the door to see if help had arrived. A couple of the enlisted staff were hovering over Cortez, clearing the debris. One of them had removed his shirt, no doubt intending to use it as a bandage or tourniquet. It was then he saw the gaping hole in the ceiling. "Watch out!" he screamed, as another chunk of concrete crashed on the desk in front of him. He ducked to avoid being hit by the breaking pieces.

A quick glance at the hole in the ceiling showed jagged edges of concrete with a web of cracks radiating out in all directions. He quickly surmised what had happened. A projectile of some sort had entered through one of the large windows in the corner conference room adjacent to the colonel's office. Its trajectory had taken it through the wall separating the two rooms and up through the ceiling just inside the doorway. The ruptures and the subsequent explosion had made the structure of the building around them unstable, with gravity pulling all the weight from the compromised concrete floor above down on top of them. Through the opening, he could see into the room that was used for mail and copying, and the end of a large table used for sorting and assembling documents was perched precariously near the edge of the hole. He knew that he could be crushed at any moment if the combined weight of the objects on the floor above him—including the large copy machine directly overhead—and the floor itself caused it to give way and collapse.

"Major, are you all right?" called one of the soldiers helping Cortez.

"I'm okay. Watch out above you. The ceiling is coming down on top of us!"

"Roger that, sir! Those cracks up there…they're growing!"

May crawled under the desk on top of the Colonel. "Colonel?" he shook her gently.

"Uh…ummm," she moaned.

Relieved that she had responded, but alarmed by the danger they were in, he knew he couldn't wait for medics. He had to get her and himself out of there now—before any more of the ceiling caved in on top of them. With much of her body exposed, the desk afforded her precious little protection. And even if it could withstand all the weight crashing down on top of them, the only way it would protect him at all was if he crawled on top of her. "Your legs—can you move?"

"Fla…flash dr…"

"Colonel, we've got to get out of here. The ceiling could cave in anytime!"

"Get…get flash," she gasped. "Drive!"

"What?" He didn't understand. "Flash? Drive?" Her breathing was becoming more labored as she tried to speak.

"Compute…computer…Flash drive!"

"Uh, oh, flash drive!" he stammered when he finally understood. While he considered what to do next, he pulled himself out from under the desk, crouched on his knees, and in one fluid motion reached around to the credenza where her notebook computer sat, now covered by the settling dust. He grabbed it with his left hand, yanked the flash drive out of the USB drive with his right and stuffed it deep into the pocket of his battle-dress trousers.

He had to act. His head was throbbing now, but the circumstances he found himself in, the adrenaline coursing through his body, made him oblivious to the pain. With a deep breath, he bent at the waist, grabbed the colonel's legs and…

All he heard was a loud crack. Spontaneously, he fell forward, but total silence and complete darkness expunged all sensation as the blunt weight of a falling object propelled him uncontrollably down on top of her.

CHAPTER 3

The execution of the final document completed one of the largest personal transfers of wealth in history. With a stroke of his pen, Martin E. Lochridge directed approximately $19 billion in cash, stock, bonds and real estate into the hands of the trustee for *Ops Populi*—United to Save America, Inc., or OP-USA. He stood, shook the hands of the three attorneys, and said with uncharacteristic emotion, "Thank you all very much. This is my gift to our great country. Let's hope the American people choose to unwrap it and, more importantly, relish its contents."

Jerome Hunnicutt, the firm's senior partner, nodded in the direction of his two subordinates, who took the cue and left the room, closing the door behind them. He looked down at the stack of documents they had spent most of the day reviewing, revising, re-reviewing, signing, witnessing and notarizing. In a matter of hours, they had dismantled years of his finest work—an artfully constructed edifice of business entities and off-shore accounts designed to conceal the massive fortune from prying eyes and shield it from excessive taxation. Were it not for his diligent efforts, the name Martin Lochridge would have figured very prominently on many popular lists of the wealthy, something Lochridge had been willing to pay dearly to avoid. Now, acting on his behalf, the lawyers of Hunnicutt, Fagan and Hall would begin the process of converting everything to cash and discreetly moving the money to OP-USA's newly created corporate account.

"Marty, you have my word we'll do our best to keep this below the radar, but you know I can't stop the animals from digging." He closed his briefcase with a thud and clicked the locks. "There are too many media and government rats with nothing better to do than follow money around."

"Just make it as hard on them as you can. With a little luck, by the time they find out how the money will be used, it will be too late for their reports to make any difference." Martin looked at his watch and bowed his head to look at the table. "I want you to know how much I appreciate all the help you've given me over the years, Jerome. We've been through the best of times and the worst together. You helped keep me straight through it all."

Jerome looked into the eyes of the man who had helped make him one of the wealthiest corporate lawyers in the country. For nearly two decades, Martin Lochridge had always been courteous, if not friendly, to him, but never had such an outward expression of gratitude passed through his lips. Nor had one ever been expected. The handsome fees, which had flowed liberally and with increasing frequency until Lochridge had abruptly left the country—at the same time, sharply curtailing what had been a fairly consistent pattern of complex businesses and real estate acquisitions, mortgage securitizations, patents, and so forth—had been gratitude enough. It did not take long for him to reach the conclusion that this was goodbye—it would be the last time he ever saw Martin Lochridge. He knew better than to ask for confirmation of his conclusion, so he simply grasped Lochridge's arm with his right hand, looking him directly in the eye, and said, "Thank you. It has been my pleasure."

Lochridge reciprocated the warm gesture with a gentle tap on the shoulder with his free arm, then set about the task of gathering his belongings, while Hunnicutt stood, arms folded, watching.

"You're really going to do this, aren't you?"

Lochridge dropped a stack of papers into his briefcase and looked at him. "Absolutely. Very soon," he said with certainty, his eyes narrowing. He knew—after years and years of on and off debate—what was coming next. "And don't tell me I'm crazy again. I don't want to hear it."

Hunnicutt nodded, but didn't move, his arms still folded across his chest. "I won't, Marty," he said apologetically. "In fact, I'm starting to think you have been right all these years."

Lochridge showed no trace of surprise at the confession, but softened his expression slightly, then he grinned. "You're giving up? You? The debate champion of UVA law?"

"I admit, I thought you were nuts when you started talking about *Ops Populi*, and all these years, I was pretty hard on you—"

"Ruthless," Lochridge interrupted. "But I'll remind you, I was a good debater, too. It's easy when you're right."

Hunnicutt accepted the swipe gracefully, holding up a hand in surrender. "Guilty as charged. What is the penalty for blind optimism?"

Lochridge flashed a smile at him, then leaned forward, resting his hands on the table. The smile faded and his expression turned serious. "The penalty is death—death for the United States of America, unless the people act decisively—now, before it's too late."

"I see it now, didn't see it before," he said humbly. For years, Lochridge had been trying to convince him, accurately predicting the progression of events that together were beginning to signal a cataclysmic reversal of fortunes for the country. "What you are about to attempt is so incredible—so utterly fantastic—it's beyond comprehension. Dangerous as hell, too."

Lochridge stood up straight, hands on his hips. "No, what's dangerous is doing nothing—letting the politicians and appointees wreck our country and our way of life." He pulled his coat off of the back of the chair he had occupied for many hours and slipped it on. "As I've said many times, I don't pretend to have all the answers, but I'm confident there are people out there who do; people who are shut out because they don't have enough money or the right pedigree to get in. I have to try to unlock the iron gates keeping them out. Doing nothing when I have the wherewithal to act is not acceptable."

Hunnicutt's reflex response was automatic, uncontrollable. He dove back into the debate headfirst without even thinking: "There's a good reason we don't have Joe Six-pack in government—"

Lochridge slammed the briefcase closed with a thwack, while shaking his head. "You know damn well I am not talking about Joe Sixpack, Jerry, not your demeaning concept of him anyway. But I'm willing to take the chance that somewhere out there—" he made a sweeping motion with his arm—"some otherwise normal folks just might have some solutions!

Look at the evidence, man! Don't tell me you believe our current political system naturally attracts or guarantees the selection of the finest minds to run our nation."

"No, but—"

"Look at James Madison," Lochridge continued unabated, yanking his briefcase off the table. "A shy, sickly little man who didn't have the charisma or public speaking ability of his contemporaries, but he had the genius to give us the framework for our republic and our Bill of Rights. He was the type of person we need—an unlikely hero that stepped up to help rescue a country on the verge of failure." His tone took on a stinging sarcasm as he continued, "Do you think maybe—in our nation of 300 million—there might be just a few otherwise modest, apolitical, but brilliant people with some answers?"

Lochridge marched quickly toward the door, but Hunnicutt moved to cut him off. He grabbed the handle before Lochridge, looked into his strained eyes, took a deep breath.

"Okay, okay. I'll try to think more like a citizen, less like a lawyer." Hunnicutt sighed heavily, then somewhat meekly said, "What can I do?"

"Sell your stocks, buy gold—and pray." Lochridge straightened, took a deep breath of his own. "Now, if you want to get involved, *Ops Populi* would love to have your help. We need all we can get."

"What you are contemplating makes me nervous, but so does the *status quo*."

"Don't think for a moment that I'm not nervous," Lochridge said in a much softer tone. "You are a good advocate, but I don't need a Devil's advocate any more. I've had years to consider all the pitfalls, Jerry, and now it's time to act." He arched his eyebrow. "Help us?"

He nodded. "Yes. I will. Call me." He pulled the door open, and then added, "Thank you, Marty, for—well, everything."

Lochridge nodded, held his hand up so Hunnicutt could see his crossed fingers, and walked through the open door.

With that, the meeting was over and the next phase of the carefully conceived plan was about to begin in earnest.

CHAPTER 4

"Wh…where am I?" she asked the nurse adjusting her IV drip.

"Welcome back, colonel," she said, "you're at Landstuhl Regional Medical Center. Germany."

Donna Bouchard looked up at the ceiling, trying to get her bearings. The light stung her eyes as the objects around her slowly came into focus. Her body ached, but the pain was not sharp or severe. She carefully stretched her limbs, just a little at first. So far, so good—everything felt like it was there, working.

"How long…have I…?" she could hear her own slurring speech. Drugs, she thought.

The nurse walked to her feet and lifted a rectangular case chained to the end of her bed. She opened it, and scanned the admission form. "You were MEDEVACed from Baghdad on the second, admitted on the third. Six days," she announced as she removed the clipboard from the case, which she then let fall to its hanging position.

"We…we were…attacked." She tried to shift slightly on the bed, but it felt like there was something holding her down, like a dead weight on her upper body.

The nurse just nodded. "You are going to be fine, ma'am. I'll get the doctor to come in and check on you shortly." She walked up to the side of the bed, took pulse, blood pressure, made some notes on the chart…

Bouchard's mind drifted. That horrible moment in her office. Sergeant major's voice on the intercom. A crash. A hole bursting in the wall and the ceiling above her door. She tried to dive under her desk, hit by something hard on her back. She had so many questions. Who could tell her more about the attack? Had any of her staff been killed? What about May? Oh, and her computer. Did he get the flash drive? Would he hold on to it, try to look at it? Would he give it to her commander? Not to worry, she tried to reassure herself, it was password protected, its contents encrypted by some fancy-sounding software.

All of a sudden, she had to fight to keep her eyes open. The nurse had given her more drugs. "No—wait!" she begged. There was so much she didn't know. Where's the doctor? Did anyone here know anything about the attack? Maybe there was someone here with her who had answers…

Everything went dark as she fell into a deep sleep.

CHAPTER 5

Things generally slow to a crawl when the nation's capital receives a few inches of snowfall, and today was no exception. Although the storm had raced northeast toward New England, it left Washington in an icy, snow covered funk, as its residents, commuters and tourists did their best to cope and function normally.

Sean May was buffeted by a stiff wind as he walked southeast along Pennsylvania Avenue. The borrowed field jacket was zipped and buttoned up to his neck, while all his worldly possessions were either in his pockets or on his shoulder in his army-issued duffel bag. A handful of quarters he had been given to do his laundry jingled in his pocket as he strode past the seats of power and affluence. For the moment, at least, having less than five dollars to his name wasn't of concern to him. He was out of that terrible place and that was all he cared about.

This morning after breakfast, he had showered, dressed and walked to his re-scheduled appointment with the psychiatrist. Nearly an hour of waiting and no doctor; he had failed to show for this one, too. May fumed on his return walk to his room. He'd had enough of Walter Reed. They were not helping him, and in fact, he was sure that, mentally, at least, they were doing him more harm than good. Physically, he was fine, with the exception of the on and off pain in his neck and shoulder region. What he needed now, Walter Reed either could not or would not help him with: his memory. Missed appointments would get him nowhere, so it was time to help himself. How he would do this, he did not yet know.

"Where are you going?" his roommate and new friend, Tony Nelson, asked. Nelson was an infantry captain who had been injured when a roadside bomb blew while his company patrolled the streets of Fallujah. He watched May uneasily as he closed up the duffel on his bed.

"I don't know. Maybe I'll take in some sights. I just want to get out of here, that's all I'm sure of."

"They won't let you just leave," Nelson said with conviction. "This isn't the Holiday Inn."

May looked around. "Who's going to stop me?"

"I'll be the first one to admit that this place sucks. But they're not going to let us walk out of here when we feel like it. Besides, you don't even have your wallet or any money. You don't even have any ID."

He pulled the quarters out of his pocket. "This will get me downtown on the metro. Look, I just need to get out, think."

"Looks like you're not planning to come back," Nelson said, looking at the duffel.

May sat down on his bed, looking intently at Nelson. "Don't you see what this place is doing to me? Doing to us?" He rubbed the back of his aching neck. "We both have done our duty. We need help, but they aren't helping us. We have brain injuries which go way beyond their expertise."

"You think you are going to find help on the streets of D.C.? With no money and no idea who you are? You're nuts. I've never been to D.C. before, but I hear it's rough out there."

May reflected on his friend's concern for his safety. Oddly, he thought, he had not even considered it. Somehow, he felt perfectly at ease with the notion of getting on the subway, going downtown to the Mall. One of the stops on the Metro Pocket Guide had a ring of familiarity. Was it just the unusual name, Foggy Bottom, playing tricks on his mind? Or had he been there sometime in his past? Maybe, maybe not, but he wasn't the least bit intimidated by the prospect of a subway journey to Washington.

"So we're just supposed to sit here while they figure out what to do with us? Hanging around waiting for the shrinks to blow off our appointments?"

They sat there looking out the window at rows of shivering enlisted soldiers standing in formation. It was pathetic, May thought, making these soldiers stand in the snow in the freezing cold. Some were leaning on crutches, many were missing limbs, had bandages wrapped around their heads, and eye patches suggesting the loss of eyes. He recognized Pat Stillwell, a staff sergeant he had met while waiting for one of his follow-up medical appointments, who had absorbed the full force of an IED explosion from a tree next to his armored personnel carrier in Karbala. "It kind of detonated in my face," Stillwell had explained. "The combination of the heat and the compression took out my right eye. My left forearm was completely shattered at the elbow and my right hand is full of plates, pins, screws, rods, and wire."

"Look at them," May said, without moving his eyes. "Our nation's bravest men and women being treated like a bunch of children."

"They are just playing the army game because they don't have anything better to do," Nelson said, softly.

"Then they get to go back to their rat-hole and wait, and wait…and wait." May felt rage burning inside him as he remembered how appalled he was by the stories he had heard about building 18, the old hotel across the street from the entrance to Walter Reed, where many of the enlisted outpatients lived. Soldiers told of black mold all over the place, rat and mouse droppings, belly-up cockroaches, stained carpet, cheap mattresses. They complained about the smell of stale urine, torn walls, holes in the floors and ceilings.

"No, I've had enough, Tony. I'm not spending another day here twiddling my thumbs."

Seeing May's determination to leave, he pulled out his wallet. "Here." he said, holding out a few dollar bills. "It's not much, but it'll help."

It was nearly 10:30 in the morning when he boarded the Metro at Takoma Park, near the Maryland border. The throngs of commuters were all safely ensconced in their offices or businesses, so the trip to Foggy Bottom was quiet and comfortable. Beginning at Union Station, he had the odd sensation of comfortable familiarity, and the scenery in his window provided a constant source of stimulation, glimpses of sights that reinforced his notion that somehow he had ties to the area.

By the time he arrived at Foggy Bottom, he was fighting a growing ache in his neck and the urge to swallow a painkiller for relief. But he fought off the temptation, fearing he might miss an important clue to his past with drug-dulled senses. As he exited the dark metro station, he was assaulted by another in his doctor's lengthy list of common complaints from traumatic brain injury patients: sensitivity to light. He was so blinded by the bright sunlight, he had to stop walking. Looking down did not help, since the snow was reflecting it right back in his eyes.

Using his simple pocket map, he headed east on I Street toward Pennsylvania Avenue. Seeing the campus of George Washington University on his right gave him the same nudge of recollection he had felt at Union Station, but the connection just wasn't there. Were these places he had seen as a tourist? Did he live here?

He passed large office buildings that looked almost deserted, even though there were people busily entering and leaving them. Were they important government officials? Consultants? Lobbyists? Was he one of them before?

He found himself walking through heavy posts in the asphalt which brought an end to vehicle traffic on the road. To his right was the multi-pillared Eisenhower Executive Office Building. He continued toward the White House, dodging though a hodgepodge of security shacks, parked police cars, and tourists. On his left, he was being yelled at by a dozen or so bundled-up protestors in Lafayette Square waving signs and sipping hot coffee.

It wasn't long before the road came to an abrupt end. He asked a uniformed secret service agent for directions.

"Turn right, go past the Treasury, and then turn left after you go past Hotel Washington," he said, pointing south.

The Capitol Dome visible in front of him told him he was back on Pennsylvania again. He passed the Department of Justice and Federal Triangle to his right; to his left stood the Navy Memorial, the Canadian Embassy and the J. Edgar Hoover FBI building. All so strangely familiar, yet so distant.

Once again, he approached a dead end, this time into a parking lot. He followed Constitution Avenue around the Capitol and then turned right on 1st Street. As he made his way south on 1st Street, he saw the Supreme Court on his left and then—he stopped suddenly.

Before him stood the Thomas Jefferson Building, which was the oldest and most ornamental of the three buildings housing the Library of Congress. He was a sure as he could be that he had been in it before. He closed his eyes and opened them again, hoping for some recognition that went beyond dim familiarity. He slowly walked around the structure gazing at it from all angles. Maybe if he went inside, its significance to his past would be revealed. Cold and tired from the walking, he was ready for a break anyway.

CHAPTER 6

A few blocks away, an intercom startled a newly sworn Congressman. "Wade, I have a James Hewitt on the line holding for you. From KPH."

"KPH?" It took him a moment to place the name. "Are they one of our contributors?"

"Yes, sir."

He knew nothing about the company but, of course, had happily accepted its campaign contribution. He tried to place Hewitt. Had he ever met him? He couldn't recall. So many names and faces to keep track of. "I'll take this one," he told his assistant.

"Good afternoon, Mr. Hewitt," he said in his formal tone. "How can I help you?"

Hewitt grinned. This man was a prime target for KPH's overtures, and a special one, at that. Once upon a time, when the utopian business school notions of ethics, fairness and integrity still lingered in his short-term memory, making a call like this would have been intensely unpleasant, almost nauseating, forcing him to do battle with a conscience that told the American in him this was not the way it was supposed to work—influence should not be bought and sold in such an unseemly fashion. Like most of his fellow citizens, he was once disgusted with all the scandal, false promises, and machinations the media seemed to take great delight in reporting. But his assimilation into the Washington game had been swift and complete; he never looked back to the exalted ideals of the education that gave him his ticket to get through the gate. Dispensing money and artful manipulation were acceptable practices inside the beltway, and indispensable to a successful government contractor. Now, after years of seasoning in the ways of Washington, he actually looked forward to these calls. In particular, he enjoyed the opportunity to administer a healthy dose of humility to a characteristically self-absorbed, egocentric, professional Washington politician.

"It is a pleasure to finally speak to you, Congressman," he said with rehearsed diplomatic balm. "Let me offer my congratulations on your successful campaign."

"Thank you, sir," he replied, sure that he was about to be finessed, asked for a favor of some kind. Since his special election to fill the remaining term left vacant by the untimely death of his predecessor, Wade King had received many such congratulatory calls from contributors who wanted to make sure he understood early on in his career that generous campaign contributions might be accompanied by dangling strings. He was new to Congress, but not the chess game of politics; his first move was always guarded courteousness sprinkled with skilled indifference

"I know you are filling an un-expired term, but as I'm sure you are aware, you will have many advantages if you decide to run as an incumbent in the fall. I want you to know you can count on our continued support."

Promises of future money were always nice icing on the cake, King thought to himself. At the same time, they often signaled forthcoming requests for reciprocal munificence, so he braced himself. "The support of your—" he glanced at his scrawled note, "of KPH is much appreciated."

Hewitt laughed out loud, taking genuine pleasure in the shock he was about to deliver. "Congressman, our support is but a drop in the proverbial bucket. Perhaps you are not aware that I and my partners are involved with a couple of dozen organizations that contributed to your election?"

King thought about the reams of paper his staff compiled to document contributions to his election campaign to report to the Federal Election Commission. The detail—who, when, how much—was all there, but it would take hours to go through it all to even attempt to verify what this Mr. Hewitt was claiming. Then, there were organizations that had spent money on his election independently of his campaign, primarily running ads or sending out direct mail. He could have records identifying these groups, but he seriously doubted he would have any documents identifying all the individuals involved or how much money they had spent. For the moment, he would have to accept what he was being told at face value.

"A couple of dozen? You and your partners must be very busy, Mr. Hewitt," he said coolly.

"Indeed, I am, Congressman," he said, careful to keep his own tone even, "as I'm sure you are, so I will try not to take too much more of your time." Hewitt had no doubt that he would be a subject of intense interest in the office of the Honorable Wade King as soon as this conversation had ended, but King had been a subject of his for many months.

The dossier of Wade Russell King open on his desk said he had been a star in the part-time Florida legislature for many years, while starting and bankrupting several companies, most recently a luxury touring business. King fit right into the mold that typified the Washington power elite—white, protestant, law school—and far away from home, removed from the stabilizing sphere of family. At forty-six, he was in deep debt, thanks not only to his multiple business failures, but also three kids in private schools and a lifestyle he could not afford, not even on his new six-figure Congressional salary. Though King ran unopposed in his special election to serve out the remaining term of Stanley Gililand—an eleven-term career Congressman, who had dropped dead of a heart attack at a holiday party in his Tallahassee home—KPH had lavished prodigious support to his campaign. What made him special was not his financial gullibility, or even Gililand's prized seat on Appropriations King inherited. It was his older brother's position as deputy commander and chief of staff for the Joint Contracting Command for Iraq and Afghanistan—responsible for doling out billions of dollars in federal largess—that made him so attractive.

"Have you had the opportunity to meet Tom Drysdale?" he asked in a friendly tone. Drysdale, firmly in the pockets of KPH, was a four-term Ohio House member, also on the Appropriations committee.

"I have met him—shaken his hand—but that is about all," King replied, curious as to where this was going. "From Ohio, I think. Why?"

"Congressman Drysdale is a good friend," he lied. "He would like to meet you and discuss the potential for an alliance on future legislation."

Smooth, very smooth, King thought. Intrigue and mystery. Contributor calls were nothing new, and dispensing political favors came with the territory of politics, power, and influence. But being persuaded to meet with another Congressman? This was the last sort of thing he had expected. With suspicion growing by the second, he made a mental note to find out more about Drysdale—his background, contributors, committee assignments, legislative agenda.

"I, well, sure. Getting to know some of the other representatives is a priority for my first few weeks in Washington," he said with as much enthusiasm as he could muster.

"I agree. He is very highly regarded both within the party and across the aisle, and he is a fellow member of Appropriations. I'm sure he would be happy to introduce you to others with whom you might form, let's say, mutually beneficial relationships." Hewitt knew without a doubt that the prospect of networking with other Congressmen would have great appeal to King. The expertly prepared dossier told him King had been in legislative politics long enough to have learned that ultimately, his success or failure would depend on forging alliances with others.

"Perhaps," King said, feigning skepticism. He didn't want to give Hewitt the impression that he was a patsy.

"Once you have the opportunity to meet with him, I'm certain you won't regret it." He paused for a response, but hearing none, he added, "Give him a call. He is hoping to hear from you." *This one's in the bag,* he said to himself, with a grin. After King was on the KPH payroll, he would gladly sing its praises to big brother followed shortly thereafter by a larger slice of the federal contracting pie.

No sooner had King placed the phone in its cradle—after once again kindly thanking his benefactor and bidding him good bye—than he had his staff looking into the business activities and partners of KPH, and in particular, James Hewitt.

CHAPTER 7

Bright sunlight reflecting off the fresh coat of snow blinded her, making it almost impossible to read the display on her phone. Virginia Burress raised her sunglasses, but not only was the glare worse, now she was virtually blind. No matter how much she squinted, the tiny words and numbers were invisible in the brilliant light. She tried cupping her hands around it. No luck. So she stopped walking, turned her back to the late afternoon sun, and waited for her eyes to adjust.

"Dinner @ Belge" the display read. The text was from her friend, Kate, a legislative aide to the Honorable DeWitt Hill, Congressman from Denver. Once every two or three months, they tried to meet for dinner at Brasserie Belge, just a short walk from the Capitol, for some great authentic Belgian food and beer, and to catch up with each other. E-mail and text messaging were great, but no substitute for a relaxing evening together in the cozy confines of the brasserie. The sudden blast of arctic air passing through the nation's capital made tonight perfect for some tasty Belgian ale and a hot bowl of stew.

With a stiff, cold wind blowing in her face, she ran up the stairs of the Thomas Jefferson Building. Warm air greeted her as she entered the small lobby, and enveloped her in its warm embrace. "Awful out there," she said to the police officer as she dropped her purse on the conveyer belt to be scanned. As she waited for him to wave her through the metal detector, out of the corner of her eye, she noticed an olive-colored duffel bag sitting next to the wall behind the guard's station.

"Having a big dinner tonight, Jack?" she asked with broad smile.

"Huh?" He looked up at her questioningly. "Oh, hi there, Ginny!"

Giggling, she pointed to the duffel bag behind him. Jack, in his early-sixties, retired military, had been a Library of Congress policeman and the guard at the southeast entrance of the Thomas Jefferson building since her first day at the Congressional Research Service and had been there to tease her every single day since. Without fail, he was at his post each morning dispensing cheerful greetings to all who passed—mostly bleary-eyed, commute-strained federal employees at this entrance—lifting moods with his kind smiles, his ancient black metal lunch box and thermos full of coffee perched on the little guard stand. Within her first week on the job, he pegged her as a candidate for some playful teasing, and it wasn't long before she started giving it right back to him. Before long, if he wasn't busy, he would tell her jokes, and they both grew to enjoy their daily banter. Once, in a more serious moment, he had told her how much she reminded him of his daughter, Tasha, who lived in Seattle and who apparently was too busy, too absorbed in her own life, to visit. With uncharacteristic sadness in his eyes, he told her his daughter had been to see him just once in the ten years since moving out west. He spoke warmly of the days playing with her when she was a child—but then she had suddenly grown up, left him. Teasing and joking with a young woman who bore a strong resemblance, both in physical appearance and in demeanor, to "his girl" seemed to give him great fulfillment. It was obvious that he missed terribly this kind of interaction with his daughter and Ginny was more than happy to oblige.

"Oh, no," he joked. "I decided to go back in the army." He was standing behind the walk-through metal detector, pushing buttons on the cross bar over his head. Then he walked through it a couple of times and shook his head, reaching up to the control panel again.

"Seems like you are having a lot of problems with that thing lately" she said, watching him puzzle over the delicate settings.

"Something's definitely outta whack," he said in agreement. "Actually, if they don't fix it pretty soon, I may give the army some serious thought." He walked through again, threw up is hands in disgust and stood to the side, waiving her through. "I give up!" he huffed.

The alarm went off as soon as she passed under it.

"Damn!" He jumped in behind her and reached up to silence the shrill warble. "It has been giving me fits today. In fact, it started when the fella that owns that duffel bag came through couple of hours ago—the same thing happened to him." He patted his holster with his right hand. "But when I walk through it with my gun, sometimes it works, sometimes it doesn't."

"It looks like it's been here awhile," she observed. Maybe it's worn out"

He stared blankly at the panel. "Damned temperamental, that's for sure. Like Rex," he snickered.

"Who's Rex?"

"My old tabby cat," he answered over his shoulder. "Tasha's actually. She promised to take him when she moved out, but—well, I got suckered. Spoiled him rotten, then left me holding the bag."

Ginny giggled.

"Rex's worst problem is getting on the other side of a closed door," he said, rubbing his right hand on his shirt. He stood aside, waved her through while looking up. This time, it seemed to work.

"I'm clean?" Ginny asked, turning to watch him follow her through.

Jack nodded, then shook his head in disgust when it failed to detect his holstered pistol as he passed under the arch. "I've complained to the chief, but I guess he figures since it's mostly used by staff and you CRS researchers, it's not a big deal. Sure is aggravating, though. Getting worse, too."

"If you think it would help, I'll say something to him. I'll act annoyed," she contorted her face, "like I'm being inconvenienced by the delays."

With an exasperated sigh, he shrugged in resignation. "Yeah, sure. It couldn't hurt."

"Besides, I don't think the army will take you back." She smiled at him.

"From some of the stuff I've been hearing in the news, they're taking guys in their forties. I bet I could run circles around most of them," he said, winking at her.

She looked at the bulging duffel bag again. "I'm surprised someone tried to walk in here with that. Not your typical tourist bag."

"Guy seemed nice enough. I told him to walk around to 1st to use the carriage entrance, but he's wearing an army field jacket, tells me he's a vet on his way home, just wants to come in and warm up a little." He shrugged, his expression almost apologetic. "I guess I have a soft spot for vets. Anyway, I told him to come on, but he couldn't bring his duffel bag with him. They'll have to fire me, I guess, but I told him I'd watch it for him as long as he was planning to leave by the end of my shift. Can't turn a fellow vet away, out into the cold. Besides, he looked pretty tired, almost shell shocked or something. When this thing went off," he pointed at the detector, "I thought he was going to jump out of his skin."

"Did he have something metal on him?"

Jack shook his head resolutely. "Nope. I ran my wand over him. Nothing."

Her destination was the European Reading Room on the second floor to copy some old treaties for the Senate Foreign Relations Committee. "Well, I'd better get upstairs so I can get out of here at a decent hour tonight. Kate and I decided on Belgium tonight—meeting up at Brasserie Belge at seven."

He nodded recognition at the name of one of several popular international restaurants located around the National Mall. "Kate was just in here a few days ago." He turned his back to her, under the cross bar of the detector. "Have fun. Oh, and have one of those good Belgian beers for me."

"Your wish is my command. See you tomorrow, Jack."

He already had his hand above his head, pushing buttons again.

CHAPTER 8

"He's just vanished," duty nurse First Lieutenant Brennan explained to his superior officer, a slight shudder in his voice. His moist fingers stuck to the medical records folder of Major Sean May held in a tight grip at his side. "The staff has searched everywhere. He's just—gone."

"You gotta be kidding me," said Lieutenant Colonel Julie McCool, the chief nurse, whose official title was deputy commander for nursing. Frowning, she slammed a pile of medical folders onto her desk hard. Her day was not going well. In fact, it had been a tough couple of weeks, with everyone crawling all over the place digging for dirt, asking questions, and interfering with her over-taxed staff. Some recent patients had blogged and blabbed about deplorable conditions at one of the country's most preeminent medical facilities. It wasn't long before reporters with camera crews appeared at the facility's main entrance. Pentagon brass and Congressional entourages showed up shortly thereafter with demands for information and to just generally poke around. Earlier in the day, she had conducted a congressional aide with a notepad and tape recorder on a tour, and her interpretation of his comments and facial expressions made her believe he was probably giving his boss a juicy report at this very moment. And now, they had lost a patient!

"So what, he just walked away?" she asked.

"It would seem so, ma'am." Brennan said. This is not the way he wanted to start his army career. After finishing nursing school, the army had offered him a first lieutenant's commission, which at the time, seemed to promise opportunities for travel and a stable career path for a newly minted nurse. He had been at Walter Reed—his first duty station—for only a few months since completing his officer basic training. Now, with beads of sweat forming on his brow, he was standing rigidly in front of the person who would write his first efficiency report—who literally had his army career in her hands—having to explain the mysterious disappearance of a patient.

"The duffel with whatever clothes and personal things his Baghdad people threw in it is gone, too," he said

"He was one of our TBIs, right?" Walter Reed was one of the army's principal facilities for treatment of traumatic brain injury patients and soldiers with post-traumatic stress disorder. Ironically, advances in protective gear worn by soldiers in Iraq had improved survival rates for those directly involved in or close to explosions from mortar, artillery, rockets—and the infamous IEDs—but the price of survival was a larger proportion of casualties due to PTSD and TBI than in previous wars. Her dilemma was that there were far too many of these cases coming in lately for her staff to handle. In many ways, these patients were more difficult for the nursing staff to deal with than those suffering purely physical injuries. Although many of them had physical injuries to treat, PTSD and TBI patients could be free of visible wounds but suffering severe psychological problems. Her staff was up to the task of handling physical trauma, but she was learning that the unique challenges presented by the growing number of PTSD and TBI patients—the special attention they needed—was something Walter Reed was not prepared to deal with properly.

"Yes, ma'am. Outpatient. Assigned to building eighteen."

"Oh, great!" she said sarcastically. "The media hounds will love this."

"Ma'am?" he asked, raising his eyebrows.

"Never mind, lieutenant." She stared blankly out the window onto the grounds, saying a silent prayer to herself that this problem would go away. Maybe he was out there somewhere just taking a walk.

"Memory loss?" she asked.

"Yes, ma'am, RA"

"So, we have managed to lose a soldier with retrograde amnesia—someone who doesn't even remember who he is—and he could be wandering the streets of Washington as we speak!" She clenched her teeth. "Dammit!"

Brennan was visibly uncomfortable. He stood rigid, but shifted his weight from one foot to the other. "We have everyone we can spare looking for him right now," he said defensively.

"Lieutenant, this installation sits on 113 acres with over 60 buildings. Assuming he is still on post, I think it is going to take more than a few tired nurses to find him!" Her head was beginning to ache, so she opened her drawer and pulled out a bottle of aspirin. "If he's out there on the streets…" she started before tossing one, then another capsule into her mouth.

"Maybe that's where he wants to be," he said, not thinking.

She slammed the aspirin bottle down hard. "TBI patients have no business wandering the streets of D.C., especially one who doesn't remember his past. He could get mugged. If he becomes disoriented, he may hurt himself, or God help us, hurt someone else." She felt a twinge of guilt as her concern for May was temporarily overshadowed with worry about the damage to her career. A patient with amnesia she is responsible for wanders off. Freaks out. Is hurt or killed, or worse yet, hurts or kills a civilian bystander.

As if reading her mind, Brennan tried to reassure her. "He's had several appointments with the psychiatrist. And no problems or incidents since his discharge from the hospital."

She picked up her phone. "We need to make damn sure he's not here before we report him AWOL and alert the authorities." God, she prayed in silence, let him be just wandering around the grounds or in one of the other 65 buildings. But the fact that he had taken his duffel bag did not give her much hope. Maybe, just maybe, he went to do laundry and got sidetracked somewhere. She would ask security to conduct a thorough search of all buildings and common areas before reporting him missing to the commanding general.

"Get back to work. I'll handle it from here."

"Yes, ma'am."

A thought suddenly occurred to her, so she put the phone back in its cradle. "Lieutenant?"

Brennan stopped in the doorway and turned to look at her. "Ma'am?"

"Do we know how much money he has?"

"Well, let me see." He opened the file he was holding, flipping past the first few pages. "Says here that they secured his wallet at Landstuhl because he had almost seven hundred dollars in cash in it, some credit cards, ID, the usual." Landstuhl Regional Medical Center in Germany was a first stop for seriously injured soldiers being sent back to the U.S. from Iraq. Just a few miles from Ramstein Air Force Base, Landstuhl administered whatever treatment they could and arranged for specialized or long-term treatment at U.S. facilities. Because of his brain injury and amnesia, May was sent to Walter Reed on an air force flight to Andrews Air Force Base. Brennan flipped through a couple more pages, read May's admission form, and raised dumfounded eyes to meet McCool's hard stare.

"He doesn't even have his wallet, it's still in Germany!"

"Oh, for Christ's sake!" She grabbed the phone and began dialing.

CHAPTER 9

"It's time for us to make our move. The ti– –nev– –bet–" the voice broke into fragments.

From his study in Frederick, Maryland, Erik Frese squinted at the 4-inch screen on his desk. When it was first made less than ten years before, the rectangular shaped gadget, a little larger than a Kleenex box, was a technological marvel that had substantially increased the already hefty fortune of the man whose slightly distorted face it displayed. Now in its third production generation, its size had been reduced by nearly 40 percent, while its weight was less than one-half of the original model. A camera no larger than the tip of a ballpoint pen beamed his face in high resolution over a distance of several thousand miles with a delay of only a few seconds. At the moment, though, parts of the image were frozen, while the remainder continued to move in real time. Like most technology, it had its flaws. But, it was the most advanced mobile, secure, satellite video conferencing equipment of its kind, a quantum leap forward in battlefield technology that the Pentagon decided the military couldn't live without.

"You're breaking up a bit," Erik said.

"Let—try—There. Is that any better?"

"Seems to be," Erik replied.

It had been awhile since they used the sat-phone's voice or video capabilities—since Lochridge's retirement, communication had been infrequent and conducted in person when he was in the States or through the sat-phone's proprietary encrypted messaging and data relay function—

but today, Lochridge had them in a three-way video conference to discuss something of great importance to them all.

For her part, Sally Sexton, who was currently sitting by her pool in St. Augustine, Florida, had heard just small bits of dialogue with no video at all. Suddenly, Martin's face appeared on her screen. "Much better," she said, her eyes fixed on her screen. She thought his face, one she knew so well, looked odd somehow, gaunt.

"OK. Sorry about that. I think there is a big storm moving down into western Germany from the North Sea, so we'll use another satellite for the moment. As I was saying, from what I'm seeing in the media over here, I think the time is nearing for us to finally move into the next phase of our plan. I can assure you, I'm not alone in my assessment." He grinned widely. "After 10 years of waiting, I hope you two and the others agree with me."

Erik leaned forward, folding his hands in front of him. Apparently, Lochridge had talked this over with other members of the group before reaching his conclusion. "I, for one, definitely agree. There are some disturbing indicators of things starting to unravel economically. And politically?"—he snorted loudly—"deep division. Judging by the latest poll numbers, I think we would be able to find a lot of support quickly."

"It looks like Wall Street is taking another three percent haircut today, too," Lochridge observed.

"No doubt, there are a whole lotta people ready for a course correction," said Sally. "A new direction,"

"Yes, a new direction," Martin agreed, Looks to me like things are going to get worse, much worse in fact, before they get better, too."

"So now that the time has come, how do you propose to proceed?" Erik asked.

"As I've always said, step one is for all of us to get together," Lochridge said without hesitation.

"That will be no small feat," Sally said. "Twenty busy people scattered all over the world. Could we…can this gizmo handle all of us at once?"

Lochridge chuckled at her use of the term "gizmo." "Oh, sure—the Pentagon is very demanding of its gizmos," he said with a laugh. "But in all seriousness, I think we need to meet face to face, maybe several days of concentrated, uninterrupted time together." He was walking as he spoke. The background behind him shifted to reveal a large set of wooden double doors. "I don't want to use battlefield commo gear for something this—well, you know, a moment we have all been anticipating for almost 10 years!"

"Again, I agree," Erik said. "This is too important to rely on, um, fragile technology for…no offense intended."

"None taken." The scene behind him had shifted to what looked like a moat. He was standing on a bridge.

"So where do you want to do this?" Sally asked them, her thumb on the red "X-mit" button.

"I guess somewhere in the mid-west would be the most central location for everyone—except, of course, you, Martin," Erik said.

Martin's grinning face appeared on the screen. "Actually, I was thinking of having all of you and any family members you want to bring over here as my guests. We all have nothing short of a monumental task ahead of us, so think of it as an opportunity to relax a little, charge your batteries. A celebration. And I'm buying first-class tickets to fly everyone into Cologne, which is about an hour and a half's drive from here. How about that?"

Neither Sally nor Erik responded immediately while they considered the idea. They both knew from his tone of voice that he was counting on them to try. Last year's Christmas card contained a photo of a smiling Martin Lochridge standing in front of *Berg Segur*, a German castle set in the middle of a picturesque valley in the Western state called *Nordhein-Westfalen*, not far from the border with Belgium and the Netherlands. In his note, he explained that he had purchased the Castle from the last surviving descendant of the Von Segur family, who had owned it since the 12th century. Based on Lochridge's description, much of the structure was comfortably modernized over time, and maintained well. It would surely be large enough for their purpose, with its nearly 50 rooms that been built over a span of 400 years.

"You want to show off your latest real estate acquisition?" Erik asked, with a chuckle thrown in for good measure. It was a rhetorical question, of course. He knew full well that this was to be the culmination of a decade of painstaking effort and the legacy of a man who had enjoyed tremendous business successes—and spectacular failures, too—in technology, real estate, and finance. Sadly, the publicly affable, but intensely private Lochridge had no family to share the fruits of his long career, a substantial fortune that he would now try to use to change the country he loved but temporarily abandoned, mostly out of disgust for the ruinous path its leaders had chosen for it. The group of people who would now help him were, in a sense, his only family in what otherwise was surely a very lonely existence.

"You know, Erik, that I have never been one to flaunt my money or achievements. But this place is one of a kind, and yes, I would like you all to see it." A skilled advocate, Lochridge was always prepared to justify his position. "And I think all would agree that we could use a few days together to review our implementation strategy without worrying about technical glitches." He looked intently into the camera, his eyes relaxed, but intent. "I have more than enough room, and we definitely won't have to worry about being disturbed." He turned to look behind him, "I could even stock the moat with some flesh-eating beasts to protect us!" he added with a laugh. "Agreed?"

Erik nodded, determined to give it a try. "No argument from me," he said in a sudden burst of enthusiasm, which was just as quickly neutralized by practicality. "But the others? Well, we'll soon find out," he said in a muted tone, as though thinking aloud.

"I'll start making some calls," Sally said, signaling her agreement as well. As Lochridge's executive assistant for much of his career, she had learned much from him, and capitalized on the knowledge to make her a very wealthy woman in her own right. He had rewarded her not only with money, but also by treating her more like a peer than a subordinate, treatment, it was understood, that was expected of all with whom she interacted on his behalf. Comfortably retired with a horse farm in Middleburg, Virginia and her winter home in St. Augustine, she and her husband of forty years stood ready to put their joint retirement on hold for her former boss's last—and greatest—undertaking. True enough, the circumstances in the U.S. were favorable for the group to finally take action, but as his closest confidant, she knew something the others did not: Martin Lochridge was dying, and likely would not live long enough to see the results of what had been nothing short of a private crusade.

Steadfast devotion had earned Sally his unequivocal trust and confidence, and he knew he could entrust his dream to her, that she would do her utmost to see it through to the end.

"Good, good!" Martin said with enthusiasm. "I hope everyone else is as ready to do this as I am. We're going to need a lot of energy and some good luck, too."

"How soon?" Sally asked.

"The sooner the better. Let's see if May works for everyone. Early May," Lochridge replied.

"May, um, don't you think—" Erik started.

"I realize that we are dealing with some very busy people," Lochridge interrupted, "so I will try not to be too impatient. But, I'm sure that when everybody stops to think about it, when they look at how quickly things have deteriorated this past year, they will agree with me. We've all been waiting patiently for this moment to come, and it's finally here. Honestly, I can't imagine that anyone would disagree."

"If we need your, uh, persuasive talents, we'll call on you," Erik said with the hesitation of one who was skeptical.

With a perceptible change in voice from the relaxed tone of a retiree to one of a task master, Sally said, "We each have about a half-dozen people to contact, so let's get to work. Let me suggest that if anyone says they can't make it in May, we get a commitment for the earliest date they can."

"Agreed, "Lochridge said. "Oh, Erik, one more thing. You remember telling me about your army buddy—May, I think his name is? You know, the one who wrote the doctoral thesis?"

"Dissertation. Yes, Sean May."

"We certainly could use his expertise in our implementation effort. We're about to venture into uncharted territory and he's one of the few who have studied the terrain. You think you could get him to come over here, too?"

Erik glanced at the smiling faces in the picture taped to the front of his computer. He and Sean had their arms around each other in a warm embrace, celebrating one of the few times they had managed to get together over the years. Although the picture was more than 20 years old, he remembered when it was taken like it was yesterday. They had parted ways after high school, but remained very good friends, talking to each other at least once every few months. "He's on active duty, I think. In Iraq. If I can get in touch with him, I know he would be intrigued by what we are about to do."

Martin frowned. "Maybe, I can call in some favors from my Washington friends to get him a leave—if he's willing."

"Too bad he doesn't have one of these," he said, pointing at the screen in front of him. "I'll see if he's still over there. If I need some help, I let you know."

CHAPTER 10

Oh, great. Another one of the district's homeless begging for money. Why was it, in the capital city of the richest nation on earth, there were so many people languishing on the streets?

As she made her way toward the elevator that took her to her office, his image tugged at her conscience. The alarm bells in her head rang loudly; she had been warned often by her father and others to ignore the pleas of DC's homeless. Don't give them money, they said, they will just blow it on booze or drugs. Certainly don't strike up a conversation with them unless you want to get mugged—or worse. Yet, she saw this kind of thing almost daily as she walked around the hub of democracy, and it gnawed at her. Maybe it was her Catholic upbringing, or perhaps it was just feminine nature to want to help people. Maybe, just maybe, one small act of kindness or good will could make a meaningful difference in a life, provide that little push to get back on track.

The elevator doors opened for her, but she just stood there looking into the empty chamber. Something about this one is different from all the rest, she told herself, not the typical down-on-your-luck, homeless type. She could tell by his demeanor. Besides, although not unheard of, homeless people usually didn't panhandle in the Library of Congress. And she would be safe here.

She turned on her heels and headed back the way she had come.

"Excuse me," she said to May, whose face was hidden behind a newspaper.

He closed the newspaper, and looked up at her. "I didn't mean to harass you before, I just want to get some coffee, maybe a little something to eat," he said in an apologetic tone. "I just need to buy a little more time to sort some things out."

As she looked at him, she felt as though her skepticism was obvious. Amazing, she thought, I'm about to hand this person money, but I feel uncomfortable. Her face couldn't conceal the fight raging in her conscience, between mistrust and suspicion on the one hand and tender compassion on the other.

"Are you, um, okay?" she asked. Right away, she felt stupid for asking the question. Of course he wasn't okay, or he wouldn't be asking strangers for money.

He was too tired and hungry to mince words, so he just let them roll off his tongue. "Other than not being sure who I am, not having any money, and not knowing where to go, I guess I am fine." He smiled to soften the sarcastic tone of his answer, but it was, after all, the plain, unfortunate reality of his present condition.

She didn't want to pry, but she also didn't want to come across as cold and uncaring. "You don't remember who you are?"

"No, I don't remember anything about my life beyond the last couple of weeks," he said, lowering his eyes to the crumpled newspaper in his lap. "I know I was injured in Iraq, which is why I was at Walter Reed, but the first thing I remember is waking up in the hospital."

The mental connection was instantaneous: the duffel bag Jack agreed to watch was his, an injured and confused soldier. What was he doing here, of all places? "You're not far from Walter Reed. You want me to get you a cab?"

"No!" Again, he realized the tone of his voice was harsh. "No, thank you," he said a little more softly. "I'm sorry—my nerves are a little frazzled right now."

She looked at him with obvious sympathy. "If there is something you are looking for here," she made a sweeping motion with her arm, "in the library, I mean, I work here, so maybe I could help you."

He looked at her, running his fingers through his hair. "No, I'm not here for any particular reason, other than to get warm." He turned his head, looking around. "It's funny, but this place seems very familiar to me, like I've been here. Comforting somehow, you know?"

She nodded.

"I was walking down Pennsylvania Avenue earlier, thinking, I've been here, I know these buildings. This one in particular."

Her eyebrow arched displaying her intrigue. "Maybe there's some connection to your past here," she suggested.

"It's anybody's guess at this point. Maybe I was here as a tourist, maybe I worked in Washington at some point. Of course, it could just be my imagination, too."

"Shouldn't you go back to the hospital? Shouldn't you be getting help?"

"All they've done for me since I woke up there is jerk me around." He looked down at his feet. "I don't want to go back."

This revelation struck her as odd. Walter Reed, after all, had the reputation for being one of the finest military hospitals in the world. "Maybe they are trying to find someone, a professional, who can help you get your memory back."

He shook his head. "No, there are a lot of guys there with injuries similar to mine—worse even—who have been there for months." Encouraged by her softening expression and more relaxed posture, he continued, "They just wander around, play games, eat and sleep while waiting for appointments with the shrinks. Half the time, the appointments are cancelled, and the ones that are kept don't seem to be helping anyone." They both turned to glance at a noisy tour group walking down the hall. "After being around them, talking to them, I'm convinced they don't know how to help us."

"As long as they are trying, what else can they do?"

"Well, for one thing, they could make it a little more pleasant to be there. You've got guys who have given their all for their country—lost arms, legs, eyes, ears, you name it—living in conditions that you wouldn't let your dog live in. One guy I got to know told me the building he was living in has holes in the walls, mold all over the place. And rats." He sighed, rubbing his face. "He said the mattresses are filthy and the place smells like urine. Is that any way for our country to be treating people who sacrificed so much?"

She nodded in compassionate agreement. She was taking it all in and analyzing his words. Even though his description conflicted with the stellar reputation of Walter Reed, what possible reason would he have for making this up? He seemed reasonably articulate, and although he appeared tired and a little haggard, it was understandable if what he had been through were true.

She shrugged her shoulders and said, “What are you going to do?”

“I don’t know,” he said with a quick shake of his head. “But I’m not going back there if I can avoid it.”

She considered just handing him some money and going back to work. On the other hand, her reason for being here in the first place—having this weird conversation with a complete stranger—was to try to help him. She might actually be able to make that meaningful difference. Perhaps she could use the library’s resources to help him get his memory back, or at the very least, figure out where his family lived.

“Maybe I can use the computers to find some records that would help you. You know, family, addresses, phone numbers, things like that.” She saw the look on his face become hopeful. “We know you are in the military, that’s a good start.”

“Anything I can find out would be more than I know now. If I could get in touch with someone who knows me, maybe they could help me get my memory back.”

She glanced at her watch. “It’s getting late, and I know you are hungry,” she said, flipping her cell phone open. “I have a little work to finish up here, but I’m meeting a friend of mine for dinner a few blocks from here at seven. Would you like to join us?”

“I’m famished,” he said, eagerly, “but, I’m not exactly spruced up for dinner out, either.”

She looked him over quickly before saying, “You’re fine—this is not a fancy place. When was the last time you ate anyway?”

“I walked out of Walter Reed this morning when everyone else was eating breakfast, so dinner last night.” He stood, stretching. “Are you sure your friend won’t mind?”

She found Kate‘s number in her phone’s contacts list. “Oh, no, Kate loves meeting new people. Very sociable. She works for DeWitt Hill, a congressman from Denver.” Ginny selected Kate’s number, then abruptly snapped the phone shut when it occurred to her that she didn’t even know his name. Surely, he would at least know his name. “Can I tell her who is joining us?”

He nodded, a smile cracking his lips. "Sean. Sean May. At least I know that much!"

She held out her free hand. "Hi, Sean May. I'm Virginia Burress, but my friends call me Ginny. As soon as I talk to Kate, I'll tell you how to find the restaurant."

May let his hand fall to his side as soon as he felt her grip relax. "Your restaurant probably won't be happy with me if I walk in there with my duffel bag."

"Oh, right," she said, opening her phone again. "We can put it in my car—it'll be fine there." With her free hand, she pulled a few bills out of her purse and held them out to May. "This will get you that cup of coffee to tide you over till seven."

CHAPTER 11

A blast of warm air welcomed him as he walked through the 11th Street steel and glass entry entrance of Brasserie Belge. The mosaic floor of the anteroom led him to a leather tufted hostess stand, where he was invited to wait in the bar for the arrival of the other members of his party. May nodded and took the short walk toward the raucous crowd of Washington's hip and hustling who were unwinding from the work day.

He took an empty stool at the long bar directly in front of a wide-screen television displaying news footage of a chaotic scene of panic-stricken people—many of them bloodied by injuries—running haphazardly through debris-strewn urban streets against a backdrop of billowing smoke, fire, and wholesale destruction. When the image shifted to U.S. soldiers atop rolling armored vehicles, May averted his eyes. It was the last thing he wanted to see right now, and he was grateful the background noise drowned out the audio.

Loneliness overtook him as he absently glanced around at the smiling faces of business-clad revelers, sipping from glasses of many shapes and sizes, struggling to be heard amidst loud chatter punctuated by occasional outbursts of boisterous laughter. In this high-charged atmosphere of the Washington movers and shakers, both his casual appearance and the keen awareness he was the only lone person in the bar were unsettling.

"May I get you something?" someone shouted above the din.

He turned to see a harried bartender in a neatly pressed white shirt, bow tie, and black pants. Unwilling to part with the quarters in his pocket—which he was certain would be insufficient in any case—he decided to stall.

"Menu," he mouthed rather than yelling back at him.

While waiting for the welcome distraction of the menu, he studied his surroundings to avoid looking at the television. The long, marble-topped bar, its front paneled in rich walnut, was embellished along its entire length by a row of iconic beer tap towers, which displayed the names and logos of an immense variety of Belgian ales. At the far end sat a raw bar, which showcased a tempting array of seafood. Adjacent to the raw bar was an area dedicated to a barista offering an assortment of hot beverages to a more restrained clientele, who congregated around classically styled café seating.

The bartender handed him a menu and busied himself drying glasses within earshot while May began scanning through it. Although it was larger and thicker than most of the menus he had ever seen, he was amazed to see this one contained nothing but page after page of different Belgian beers.

"There must be a hundred beers here," he said, in disbelief.

"130 at last count," the bartender replied, looking at May with pride. "11 draft, 119 bottled."

"Amazing. All of them Belgian?"

"Every last one. If you need any help choosing one, let me know. I've tried them all."

"Hopefully not all at once," May quipped, as he continued flipping through the pages casually. Suddenly, one caught his attention. "Brugse Zot," he said quietly—or so he thought. He stared blankly at the page, bemused by the cartoon drawings of a jester and a half moon crossing his mind at that very instant.

Within seconds, it seemed, the bartender placed a glass on the bar behind the menu and began pouring. "Good choice," he said.

"Oh—oh, no!" May stammered. He glanced at the price on the menu, then at the bartender, horrified. He had less than half of what it cost.

The bartender reflexively ceased his pouring in reaction. "I thought you said—"

"I was just reading—to myself—thought I remembered," he babbled, his face flushing from embarrassment.

Without any hesitation, he resumed his pour. "My mistake. It's on me if you want it."

May looked at him sheepishly. "I couldn't. I'm really sorry about this."

"Don't worry, it happens once in awhile." He placed the bottle on the bar, with a label containing a colorful, animated clown above the words Brugse Zot. "It'd be a shame to pour it down the drain. Enjoy it."

Feeling pangs of guilt, May shrugged, looking at the wide-rimmed glass imprinted with an exact duplicate of the bottle's label. A bright white froth sat atop the light, golden liquid. "I know it may sound—well, I think I've had this before."

The bartender had resumed drying glasses, but stopped at the question. "Quite a nice blonde ale. I've actually been to the brewery. Took a tour." His attention shifted to a group congregating behind him, several of whom were holding up empty glasses. He nodded and walked to the large cooler that ran the length of the back bar.

While other hustling servers rushed about in front of him, May, still determined to avoid the television, raised the glass to drink. A strong fruity aroma caught his attention before the glass touched his lips, so he paused to pass the glass under his nose before taking a small sip. He tasted hints of lemon, orange, and some spices he couldn't identify all of which were balanced nicely by a faint, malty sweetness. It was a delightfully complex sensation to his palate. Mindful of his empty stomach, he put the glass down, while lifting the empty bottle with his free left hand. The print was in a foreign language, so he turned the bottle to study the jester, again drawn by the glimmer of recognition.

"Flemish," the bartender said returning to his former spot. "A mixture of French and Dutch, I'm pretty sure."

"Great tasting stuff," May said, raising the glass in a mock toast. Just then, it hit him: a vivid image of an old town as seen from a vantage point like the top of a hill—a jumble of medieval buildings crowned by multicolored tile roof tops and chimneys broken apart by deep green canals, narrow stone paved streets and gothic church steeples sprouting up at random—flashed through his mind.

"It's brewed in the city of Bruges. A little old brewery in the middle of the town called de Halve Maan—the half moon. Great place for beer—and chocolate. Bruges has a reputation for that, too."

May raised his eyebrow, in reaction to the queer feeling that somehow he already knew this.

"Supposedly, the brewery has been around since the sixteenth century, but the building I toured was built around eighteen fifty. The tour I took shows you how they used gravity to move the grain and liquid through the process." He pointed to a barely visible snapshot tucked into the corner of one of the mirrors. "That's a picture of me and the owner standing on the roof of the place."

May had to raise himself slightly on the stool to squint at the distant photo, which showed the two of them standing in the sun with a brick wall behind them.

"There's a lady over there waving at you," the bartender said pointing toward the hostess stand. May looked to his left past a growing throng of merrymakers to see Ginny and her friend had just arrived. "Enjoy your dinner—I'll send your beer over to your table."

May stood to leave, but hesitated. He leaned forward on the bar to get a better view of the photo. "I'm pretty sure—well, I think I've been there, too. Anyway, thanks," he said, with a partial shrug at the odd look the bartender was giving him.

By the time he made it to the host stand, they were already squeezing through the crowd in single file, toward their table. A smiling Ginny said a quick "Hi" to him as he fell in behind her.

Before long, they had left the noisy crowd behind and entered into a much quieter, more intimate space containing lots of nooks and crannies. The dining area was styled like a grand old train station with high ceilings, walls decorated by rich, dark wood tones with touches of blue throughout, and lacelike curtains on the windows. He was amused as they passed by more than a few old-fashioned wall-mounted clocks, each the current time in different cities throughout the world. About midway between the front and the rear along the right wall was an open kitchen, visible from three sides, and surrounded by clear and textured glass, framed by steel and cobalt blue tiles. Across from the kitchen was a unique family-style chef's table paired with a dozen leather Medieval-style chairs. Just past the kitchen along the same wall, a glass covered wine cellar, capped with another series of the elevated angled mirrors like those in the bar, showcased neat rows of what was sure to be a vast selection of fine wines.

When they arrived at their table, he and the waiter stood while Ginny and her friend removed their coats. He held Ginny's chair while she was seated then took his seat in view of two private dining rooms, which like the kitchen, were set off by steel and glass in a solarium style.

"This is quite the happening place," May said, looking at Ginny's friend. "I'm Sean—Sean May," he said, extending his hand.

"Kate Fowler," she said, reaching toward him, Her cold hand was soft and feminine, her handshake gentle, but firm. "This is one of my favorite restaurants, but I could do without all the wild jubilation up there," she said pointing toward the front.

"I'm sorry you two," Ginny said with a contrite expression. "I didn't have the chance to introduce you. It's a madhouse in here tonight."

"The more people find out about it, the less I like coming here," Kate observed. "Next time, let's try the middle of the week."

While their waiter took their drink orders, another appeared with May's glass, which he placed on the table, nodded, and walked away. Ginny looked a little surprised that someone who had no money to feed himself was drinking a beer that cost more than most fast food meals, so May briefly explained the accident that occurred at the bar.

"Hey, maybe I should try that!" Kate joked as she opened her menu.

For what seemed like several awkward minutes, they looked at their menus while May, who had already studied one, wondered how much Ginny had told Kate about him—his condition, his situation. He decided to keep his mouth shut as much as possible, figuring it shouldn't be too hard with two females, who were apparently good friends, as his companions.

"So I hear you walked Pennsylvania Avenue all the way from GWU today," Kate said, unfolding her napkin.

So much for his plan, he thought, as they both awaited his reply. "I was, um, sort of taking in the sights." As soon as he had said it, he realized how ridiculous it sounded—walking miles by himself through DC in the freezing cold. His eyes shifted to Ginny, who sensed the uneasiness revealed in them. Kate looked down at her menu, shifting uncomfortably in her chair.

"I told Kate about our meeting at the Jefferson Building. Our conversation," she told him. "I hope you don't mind…"

May shook his head, relieved. "No, I'm glad you did." Turning back to

Kate, he said, "I was hoping to spark my memory. I'm fairly certain I've spent some time here."

"What did you discover?" she asked. "Were you successful?"

Seeing the waiter approaching out of the corner of his eye, he refrained from giving a serious reply. "Well, for one thing, America's grand boulevard is so chopped up, you need a map just to stay on it," he quipped.

Without a word, their server carefully placed a basket of steaming hot bread on the table, which smelled delightful to the famished May. He hoped it would help counter the onset of a serious buzz produced by the strong Belgian ale on an empty stomach. At Ginny's urging, and while munching on a generous helping of the bread smeared with garlic butter, he summarized the roughly two-week experience at Walter Reed, with all of its attendant anxiety and frustration for Kate's benefit. No, he did not know where he was going, but he'd rather live on the street than go back.

Their meals were brought out by a different waiter carrying an oval tray balanced precariously on his fingertips. Having no idea who had ordered what, he pulled each plate from the tray, cheerfully announcing the name of the dish, which he delicately placed in front of its claimant. Apparently, his sole purpose was to deliver food, as he simply nodded and walked away carrying the empty tray.

"Well, Sean, let me tell you what I discovered before I left the office," Ginny said, while helping herself to more bread. "I did a quick search on news from Baghdad in the last month. I found a short story about a rocket attack on a building that killed several soldiers, one civilian contractor and seriously wounded over twenty."

May looked at her intently with a raised eyebrow. "Good. What else?"

Ginny took a folded sheet of paper from her purse and unfolded it to reveal the two-paragraph story under an ABC News banner. "Not much really useful, I'm afraid. No names." She looked down briefly before handing it over to May. "Says that it was believed to be an insurgent attack with an Iranian made HM 20-something rocket. The building housed over 120 military and American civilians—military police, contract officers, public affairs people and some private contractors."

"You aren't a military cop, are you?" Kate asked May before wrapping her lips around her fork.

"I doubt it," May said, cutting into his steak. A sudden realization caused him to abruptly drop his hands heavily onto the table. Both Ginny and Kate stopped what they were doing as well, their faces displaying bewilderment.

"What's wrong?" Kate asked.

May leaned in toward the center of the table, his expression thoughtful, weighty. "It just occurred to me that the MPs could be searching for me," he said softly, careful to keep his voice low enough to be barely audible. "I'm AWOL—you know, absent without leave."

Ginny waived her hand dismissively. "You've only been gone, what, nine or ten hours?"

Kate nodded her head in agreement. "They might not even know you're g—"

"Oh, they know I'm gone alright," May cut her off. "Question is, how bad they want to find me."

Defying expectation, he was destined to be the center of attention for the evening. Ginny and Kate took turns quizzing him about different phases of his life, career, family, hobbies, and so forth. His ability to clearly recall memories ended in his early twenties, shortly before finishing his undergraduate degree, though, he had his vague and disconcerting interludes of déjà vu on his journey through Washington. Somehow, he managed to finish his meal before either of them despite what seemed to be endless talking.

"So what are you going to do?" Kate asked him.

May pushed his plate aside and leaned forward, resting his elbows on the table. The question forced him to confront the obvious; no place to sleep, no money for food, nobody other than these two virtual strangers to turn to for help. "I'll probably try to find a shelter or a church—somewhere to spend the night. Then, tomorrow, try to find a library with public computers, see if I can find out where I live, family connections."

Ginny and Kate watched him with expressions of forlorn doubt mixed with pity as they slowly chewed their food. An awkward moment of silence ensued while they all contemplated his prospects of surviving a cold winter night alone on the perilous streets of the nation's capital city.

Visibly uncomfortable with the silence, May leaned back, reached into his pocket, and pulled out the flash drive. "Maybe this will help me," he said looking at the device in his hand hopefully.

"A portable hard drive." Ginny observed.

"I have one of those," Kate said with perceptible surprise at seeing the black rectangle with its short wire dangling from the hand of a man who seemingly lacked everything but the clothes on his back. "Do you know what's on it?"

"Not a clue," May said, shaking his head. "It was in my duffel bag, so maybe it has something to connect me with my life—you know, names, phone numbers, bank accounts. I'll take anything I can get at this point."

Ginny took the final sip of her beer and placed her napkin on the table with a quickness and firmness indicating she had reached a conclusion. "Spending the night on the streets is not a good plan. I'll check you into a hotel. You can pay me back later."

Kate's eyes perked up immediately. "Let me see if I can get him a room at the Wiltshire." She reached for her purse on the empty chair between her and Ginny. "Congress keeps a few on indefinite reserve for VIPs and I doubt they are being used during recess."

May held up his hand. "Please, you don't have to—I can't pay—"

Kate, with her phone already in her hand, waved him off, saying, "Don't worry about it. By the time my boss gets the bill, I'm sure you'll be in a position to reimburse the taxpayers. But I do have to get his approval first."

Ginny reached out, laying her hand on Kate's arm. "Maybe he could make a few inquiries at the Pentagon. If Sean could get his wallet—"

"No, no," May said with a hard shake of his head. "Not yet. I'm AWOL, remember?"

Kate paused, resting her hand and the phone on the table. Looking at May, she said, "He's a vet himself—he'll probably want to help." She resisted the temptation to tell them about Hill's opposition to the war, or the quiet investigation he and several of his like-minded colleagues had already undertaken to look into the many challenges confronting its veterans. "Maybe he could help, get you transferred to a different hospital or something."

May looked at Kate gratefully, then at Ginny. "I really appreciate your help. Just give me a little time to think this all over, okay?"

Ginny nodded, Kate shrugged indifference. "The Wiltshire is just a few blocks away. They have a couple of computers, I think, for their guests. Do you want me to see if one of the rooms are available?"

For a moment, May hesitated, but the alternative was certainly not attractive. The streets could be brutal, perhaps deadly, and he was tired, his neck and shoulder were aching.

"If she can get the room, Sean, why not?" Ginny urged.

"You could probably stay there at least through the weekend I would think," Kate added. "Who knows? Maybe longer. Congress is back in session Monday, but I wouldn't expect any dignitaries to be flying in for a while."

May nodded, visibly relieved. "Yes, thank you. Thank you very much." As Kate stood to walk outside to call Congressman Hill, he added, "tell your boss he can take the cost of the room out of my army pay if he wants."

Kate smiled at him. "I think we all know you're good for it. Be right back."

"He'll go for it," Ginny assured May. "Kate's his right arm. And then some." She picked up the flash drive, examined it casually, and said, "Maybe this has some answers for you."

Neither of them could ever imagine that the innocuous little black box on the table before them was an omen of fantastic opportunity and adventure, but at the same time, was fraught with wretched terror—and death.

CHAPTER 12

Bright morning sun gleamed through her hospital room window, mercifully pulling her out of an awful dream. Sleep had been fitful since learning from her commander that two of her staff had died in what was assumed to be an insurgent rocket attack on her Baghdad office building. During the night, she had twice refused sleep aids offered to her, believing that whatever natural sleep she managed would be more refreshing than the artificial, drug-induced kind.

This was the beginning of Bouchard's eighth day at Landstuhl, which she had found to be a well-run, clean hospital with excellent staff. Although she would never describe it as a pleasant experience, given the circumstances that resulted in her being here in the first place, she was as comfortable as could be expected.

The prognosis for a full recovery was good. Chunks of debris had come perilously close to crushing her lower back and left leg, which, while not broken, was fitted with a thigh cast after surgery to repair damaged tissues. A regimen of physical therapy would be necessary once the cast was removed to restore normal mobility. Time would heal the numerous cuts and bruises, the swelling and soreness would diminish gradually, life would go on. Her glass was half-full: Had the rocket's warhead exploded on impact, that would more than likely not be the case.

"I thought I should wake you," said the first-shift nurse, who was busy tying back the curtains, "so you wouldn't miss breakfast." It was nearly 8:30 a.m. local time, and the sun was just above the winter horizon in western Germany.

"Thank you," she said, raising herself to a sitting position. She was delighted to see the box on the table, which she hoped contained some personal items she had asked her assistant to ship to her from Baghdad. Of all the things that it was supposed to contain, it was the cell phone that she wanted most. The call she needed to make to the states was not one she was looking forward to, but it had to be made quickly, in private, and on a line she could trust to be reasonably secure. After seven full days, she could not escape the realization that it may already be too late.

"Is that my package?" Bouchard asked, ignoring the breakfast tray just placed in front of her.

"Yes, ma'am. Came in at oh seven hundred." The nurse adjusted the tray in front of her. "But please eat first. Doctor's orders."

"I will, I will," she said dismissively. "I just want to make sure they sent everything I asked for." She shoved the tray away while the nurse retrieved the box, which she tore open with vigor. A handwritten note that she did not read, make-up, toiletries, purse, planner, personal address book—and yes!—her cell phone. No charger, but it should be charged. It was rarely used.

With the nurse out of the room, she stood, stretched and hobbled to the door, closing it until it made a heavy metallic click. After a couple of deep breaths, she sat down on the chair beside the window, pulled a special phone card from her wallet, and entered the number. Eight rings, nine, ten…

"Uh…hello?" the quiet, groggy voice answered.

"It's Bouchard," she said. We have a prob—"

"Do you know what time it is?" he said cutting her off.

Of course, the time difference. It hadn't even occurred to her that it was 3 o'clock in the morning in Virginia.

"Sorry," she said without conviction. "This is important."

"Just a minute," came the voice she knew only as Lee, as he moved quietly away from the bed and his sleeping wife.

She heard static come and go as he moved to a different room. She had never met Lee, and did not know whether Lee was his first name or last name, or whether it was his name at all. They had spoken to each other only twice before, the conversations brief and cryptic. Their normal mode of communication was electronic, though not by e-mail, but rather through a removable flash drive, sent and received by a civilian courier, American, no doubt well-paid, that he—or his employer—had selected.

"What is it?" he asked, after a minute or so. The irritation in his voice was punctuated by a loud sigh.

"Our building was attacked last week. By rocket. My office was badly damaged, I was hurt." She waited for a response, but hearing none, she continued. No sympathy, all business. "One of the staff who came to help took the flash drive."

"Why?"

"My office was a wreck, I couldn't move. I told him to grab it to keep it from falling into the wrong hands."

"Did you get it back?"

"No, he still has it."

"What the hell—are you out of your mind?"

For the first time ever, she heard some genuine emotion in his voice. "I didn't have a choice at that moment," she snapped defensively. Be careful—stay cool—she told herself. "It was a choice between someone who I know and trust, or whoever they sent in later to clean up the mess."

"Who is this man?"

"I told you. He is on my staff. A major." She considered how she would tell him the rest of the story. But it was obvious he was already agitated, so she might as well just speak plainly and to the point. "He was hurt also—while trying to help me."

"Good," he said, his voice cold. That meant that he wouldn't be trying to look at the drive's contents. Everything was encrypted and password protected, but he knew there was always someone who could figure out encryption algorithms and break password protection schemes. "So, get it back."

"It's not going to be that simple," she said. "I'm in a hospital in Germany. He was sent back to the U.S."

Silence was all she heard for perhaps half a minute. "Where is he, exactly?" Lee asked, finally.

"Walter Reed Hospital. Washington."

"We'll deal with it," he said in a shrewd, incisive tone. He was wide awake now, and he was already calculating, formulating his plan.

"Wait!" She blurted into the phone. "I'm not even sure he has the drive with him." She knew from her own experience that personal items didn't necessarily get sent with a wounded soldier; however, it was likely that anything on his person would have been shipped with him as long as the Baghdad combat support hospital staff had done its job.

"We'll find him," he said, the impassive tone again in his voice. He would need this major's name. And a photo would certainly be helpful. He also had to consider the possibility that the drive was still in Iraq. "When will you return to Iraq?"

"I don't know exactly. Maybe tomorrow or Saturday."

"Get back there quick," he said, in a commanding tone. "And give me his name."

Bouchard frowned. What bothered her was not so much the abrasive nature of Lee, or whatever his name was. As a career army officer, she was used to abrupt, even harsh language from the gung-ho males the military seemed to attract. No, for the moment, she thought only about May and the danger she had put him in. As much as it had disturbed her on a professional level, her admission to herself months ago that she found him interesting, attractive, desirable even, was now fleeting through her mind, interfering with her normally pragmatic thought process. She knew nothing about Lee or what he was capable of, but considering his cold, ruthless tone and all the money at stake, she felt certain that violence was not out of the question. She closed her eyes tightly, blocking out the sunlight, and hoping also to somehow slow the racing of her mind.

"May. Sean May."

"Call on this phone when you are back in Baghdad," he said, curtly, before the abrupt click that ended the conversation.

CHAPTER 13

As soon as she was able to walk on crutches without suffering excruciating pain, Bouchard visited a wounded clerk who was working in the room above her office when the rocket had blasted through the concrete and who had been evacuated to Landstuhl with her. The large hole in the floor—in Bouchard's ceiling—had given him a clear view of events unfolding in the office below, a view that allowed him to observe the chaos occurring below. The chilling account was only made more horrific by his battered and bruised appearance, just a stub where his right arm should have been, his physical being totally shattered.

Her plan had been to call Walter Reed when she returned to Baghdad to check on May and to thank him. From what she could remember of the attack and based on the details she had learned from the clerk and her own staff, the powerful HM23 rocket had killed five, injured twenty-six, and severely damaged several floors on the north side of her building. May had probably saved her life, and whether or not she would have been killed without his intervention, she felt indebted to him.

The disturbing conversation with Lee, however, had changed things. If she could talk to May, she would simply ask him to return the flash drive to her by Federal Express and that would be the end of it. Lee could leave him alone, everything would be fine.

The Landstuhl operator who gave her Walter Reed's Public Affairs number had offered to connect her directly through a military DSN line. She declined the offer with thanks, preferring to keep the conversation as private as possible. She chose to use the company-provided cell phone, which Lee had assured her was far more secure than any land-line phone.

Ten minutes later, after being lectured on HIPAA medical privacy laws, regulations and procedure, she demanded to speak to the commanding officer. "I'm sorry, ma'am, but the general is currently unavailable. I'll put you through to the deputy commander for nursing."

"Lieutenant Colonel McCool. How can I help you colonel?"

"Colonel, one of my staff—a Major Sean May—was sent to Walter Reed last week from Landstuhl." She tried her best to conceal her frustration, but at this point her impatience was audible. "I have spent the better part of ten minutes trying to reach him. No one has connected me to his room or given me any information whatsoever."

McCool had prepared herself for a call like this and was actually surprised that it had not come sooner. They would not be able to conceal the fact that May was missing forever; the army's strict system for handling casualties would soon require them to file an official report. She was buying all the time she could, and for the moment at least, she believed she could hide behind the bureaucracy for a little longer.

"Colonel, we do not disclose patient information over the phone due to the medical privacy—"

"Yes, the HIPAA privacy laws. I've already heard that, Colonel. What I need is to speak to Major May, not lectures on procedure."

"We would be happy to provide information on Major May's condition once his next of kin has been notified of his injury and we authenticate your identity and need to know through chain of command," McCool said with authority. "Your adjutant or local support hospital can give you the exact protocol."

"Why don't we just dispense with all this BS and just connect me to May directly."

"I'm afraid I can't do that, colonel. His condition is—"

"His condition is, or at least was, good enough for him to talk when he left Landstuhl," she interrupted. Her patience all but gone, she no longer attempted to mask her impatience. "How do I know that? Because I am sitting in a room at Landstuhl myself and I just spoke to the doctor who signed the transfer order sending him to you. Now, like I said, enough bureaucratic crap. Let me talk to him." She clenched her jaw. "Now!"

This caught McCool completely off guard. May had still been unconscious when he was flown to Ramstein from Iraq, so they had counted on using the HIPAA restrictions and next-of-kin notification requirements to give them a little more time to find him. She was a career military officer and an accomplished nurse, but artful deceit and duplicity were not among her talents.

"He's not here," she said. "May walked off the post two days ago."

CHAPTER 14

At her insistence, she was discharged from Landstuhl on Thursday morning, two weeks to the day after the rocket attack had splattered her with debris. Her battered body was mostly concealed by a baggy battle dress uniform and its bulky field jacket as she was helped aboard the shuttle bus to Ramstein Air Force Base for the flight back to Baghdad.

Her doctor had urged a few more days, perhaps a week, but Colonel Bouchard would have none of it. Physically, she was feeling well enough to resume her duties, which were for the most part, performed behind a desk; psychologically, though, she was anything but stable, her mind clouded by pain medication, nightmares and emotional distress. Yes, she was very lucky to be alive, as she was constantly reminded, yet that was not enough to alleviate the persistent anxiety about how this event would affect her future.

Once back in Baghdad, she discovered that her office and small staff had been relocated to a heavily sandbagged compound of trailers, which she discovered were actually converted cargo containers. The old apartment building that had been modified to serve as offices was already being repaired, although it wasn't clear when, or even if, they would ever move back into it.

Within the bounds of military decorum, her staff threw a party to celebrate her return, all quite happy to see that she had suffered little discernible damage, recovered so quickly. As head of an administrative, non-combat operation, she chose to conduct her relationships with subordinates in a relatively casual fashion, reasoning that a relaxed atmosphere would lead to higher morale and better performance. In her eleven months as its leader, her unit, technically an ad-hoc logistics detachment created specifically for the re-construction effort, had performed superbly. The lack of discipline problems or perceptible tension among its staff of 5 military, including herself and Major May, and two civilians, was confirmation enough that her leadership style was working. The surprise party in celebration of her return, though, was clear indication that they had grown to like her as well.

Her excuse for abandoning the party in her honor was valid enough: the six-hour plane ride from Ramstein to Sather Airbase on the west side of Baghdad International Airport had been uncomfortable, and had left her entire body aching. Her true motive was to conduct the obligatory search for the flash drive in the unlikely event it was still here, although news of the hastily undertaken repairs of her former office dashed what little hope there was considerably. In all probability, May had the device—and her destiny—with him somewhere in Washington, D.C.

"I think I'll take my laptop back to my quarters," she said to the group after thanking them for the party. "Does anyone know where it is?"

PFC Mead, her young clerk, pointed to a neat stack of boxes in the corner of the office. "I labeled all the boxes for you, ma'am. Let me get it for you."

"Thank you, private," she said.

Mead retrieved the laptop, power cord and mouse and brought it to Bouchard, who remained in her favorite high-backed leather chair, which inexplicably had escaped any perceptible damage in the attack. As expected, there was no flash drive in the laptop's USB port. With a casual voice, she said, "Has anyone seen my flash drive?"

They all looked at each other and her, shaking their heads. "I don't remember seeing the flash drive in it when I cleaned out your office," Mead said. "Was it in the computer when we were hit?"

Bouchard nodded, frowning. "Can we still get in there, you know, to look for things?"

One of the two civilians on her staff, Allan Grant, a Department of Defense logistician, three years into his second career after 24 years in the army, shook his head while swallowing a piece of chocolate cake, perhaps the best thing ever created by an army cook to cross his lips. "I went back Wednesday afternoon to see if I could get our network laser printer, I thought maybe I could try to fix it. Anyway, everything is gone, hauled off to the desert dump."

"That was quick," Bouchard said dourly, her hopes all but shattered.

"Yeah. One of the contractors told me that the engineers told them to gut the place." He looked at his plate and scooped up another bite of cake. "Concerned about the structural safety, I guess."

"The damage must have been pretty bad," she said with a wan face and a voice devoid of interest. She looked away in despair, forced to confront the hopelessness of her situation. If May had dropped the flash drive on the floor, it was long gone, most likely in a landfill. It could have fallen out of his pocket anytime between the time he was hurt and evacuated, or been taken from him by a medic, or a nurse. It could be lying on the street, in an ambulance, in Germany, or…

Before leaving her new office for home, she halfheartedly picked through the unpacked boxes, which contained mostly books and files left to her to organize—just to be certain that the drive hadn't been tossed into one of them by someone who happened upon it by accident. The staff continued to party, oblivious to her dejection, occasionally offering help when she visibly struggled to maneuver the heavier ones. In a box that contained some miscellaneous items taken from her desk, she discovered a photo long since forgotten of her entire staff taken at a Thanksgiving dinner and party held in honor of the troops. The powers in Washington had decided to "stand down" and provide a traditional turkey dinner to every soldier in the country as a morale booster, which had been a huge success, if just for a day. At over six feet, May stood in the back row with the tall ones—Grant and Captain Bramhall, who had since rotated back to the states—but his head and smiling face were clearly visible. She had the picture Lee wanted, she thought, as she slipped it into her laptop case. No flash drive, but at least she had the photo.

CHAPTER 15

"Our source tells us that Bouchard has returned to full-time duty," said Prather, one of the firm's principals, as they sat in the luxurious cabin of the corporate jet. This was Scott's second meeting in a week aboard Prather's private Gulfstream G550, known for its comfort and long flying range, both of which served Prather well in his frequent trips between the Northern Virginia corporate headquarters and Baghdad. Prather spoke quietly even though they had the plane's 50-foot cabin to themselves.

Scott nodded. "I'm more convinced than ever that the residence complex is our only option," he said, as he studied a plat of the complex Prather had given him.

"Hers is number 28, third pathway to the right of the entrance gate." He took a sip of his drink. "Sunset Strip I think is what they call it."

"I see it," he said, momentarily focusing on the "KPH" company logo stamped onto the plat. Scott's employer, Krug, Prather and Hewitt Inc., had been one of the U.S. firms involved in the design and construction of the complex on the grounds of Saddam's former Republican Palace. He knew of at least a half dozen large projects in Iraq alone KPH had its hands in, hands that were also busy pulling strings in Washington and counting money, lots of money. It was definitely a growing company, but for the moment, all KPH hands were quite full.

Scott looked at his boss. He guessed that the man had about 15 years on him, give or take, but he still had Special Forces written all over his face. Scott was taller than him—perhaps a little quicker—but any advantage he had in height was lost to Prather's bulk and obvious muscular power. He had learned by accident of Prather's prowess on the army's boxing team when Krug, the other half of the special forces pair in the executive suite, referred to him as "champ." After their one and only meeting—he had never seen nor talked to Hewitt, the only non-military principal—Krug had showed him a framed photo of Prather standing in the ring, looking down at an opponent sprawled on the canvass. He remembered thinking how the man's upper body looked like it was carved from stone. "Most were knock outs—he called them 'good old country ass whippins'—only 3 decisions, I think, before he quit."

Scott stated the obvious. "The only other alternative is to wait. We could watch her. She'll leave the zone sooner or later."

"We cannot wait and we cannot fail," Prather said, looking out his window at the runways of Baghdad International. "That rocket attack shook her up badly. We've been monitoring her personal e-mails. Her e-mails to her mother are particularly disturbing, with references to 'conflicts of interest,' 'ethical dilemmas,' and so forth. In one message, she says 'There is nothing for you and dad to worry about. There's plenty of money for all of us now.'" His eyes narrowed as he took another drink from his glass. "I'm afraid she may be about to bail. She's been useful, but we can't risk her compromising our operations."

Scott did not know—nor did he care—what information his boss was worried about her divulging. At this moment, his only concern was carrying out Prather's wishes. "My plan will work," Scott replied with confidence.

Prather turned his head to look at him. "Your method concerns me," he said. "Wouldn't a—let's say—more conventional weapon be more prudent?"

"Security's too tight. They've sealed up the entire zone. It's like a fortress in there—crawling with MPs, multiple checkpoints, metal detectors, dogs, body scanners, you name it." He shook his head and gestured with his hands for emphasis. "Carrying any kind of weapon in there is a 'no go.'"

"What about C-4?" he asked, referring to the powerful plastic explosive.

"Won't work. They're using sniffers at all the checkpoints." One of his old platoon mates had told him about the new hand-held devices that had started appearing at checkpoints at the end of 2004. Desperate to thwart terror bombings inside the Green Zone, the military had purchased a new device on the market designed to scan for particulate and vapor signatures of explosives. "They supposedly can sniff out just about anything—TATP, plastics, nitrates and black powder." He shrugged. "Who knows if they work, but I don't want to find out."

Prather nodded. It was unfortunate that this was the only option—or necessary at all, for that matter. Innocent people would suffer, probably die. "Get it done."

Scott stood to leave. "I need Luttrell for this mission."

Robert Luttrell was a former special forces officer hired by KPH soon after being unceremoniously forced out of the army for being passed over for promotion a third time. While working together on one of the company's security projects, Scott had learned that Luttrell had been one of the army's experts in nuclear, biological, and chemical warfare after leaving—or being transferred out of—the special forces. One of the most bitter men Scott had ever met, Luttrell blamed the premature end of his army career on an injury sustained in a motorcycle accident that occurred while he was on leave. The injury had resulted in a permanent physical "profile," the military term for an official medical determination that a soldier is physically unable to perform one or more required duties. Because the special forces no longer wanted him, the army gave him a branch transfer from the infantry to the chemical corps, but neglected to tell him that his upward mobility potential would be much reduced because of far fewer available "slots" for higher ranking officers. Nonetheless, he had assumed his new role with as much, if not more, vigor than he had the special forces, taking advantage of every educational opportunity he was offered. This expertise had proven invaluable to KPH when, in 2004, it had discovered a small, but potent cache of chemical projectiles carefully stored in an underground vault connected to a building they were restoring near Mosul.

"He is in route as we speak," Prather said, draining his glass. He stood and pulled a key from his pocket and handed it to Scott. "When we were setting up the shipping containers, we had these masters made. This should open all of them."

Being handed a master key that operated all the locks in the complex would definitely simplify his job.

"As long as it opens 28, we're in business," Scott said, looking first at the key, then at Prather. "And the weapon?" he asked, with a raised eyebrow.

"Luttrell is handling it."

CHAPTER 16

After a couple of glasses of wine and a relaxing bath, Bouchard pulled the cell phone out of her purse. Lee would be waiting for her update and the photo, which he would definitely need before attempting to find May. The picture was sitting on the end table beside the half-empty wine glass. She had looked at the photo many times since returning to her quarters in yet another complex of trailers housing mainly army officers and civilian State and Defense Department personnel. As a lieutenant colonel and a female, she had one all to herself to the envy of the junior males, who generally had a roommate.

The hot bath—a luxury bestowed on her by the grateful company to which she had awarded a lucrative contract to transform cargo containers into habitable spaces for living and working—not only soothed her aching body, it gave her time to consider her predicament. Lee was very concerned about the whereabouts of the flash drive, which contained sensitive data potentially injurious to him, her and others. It had been chosen as the method of transmitting documents and financial information above all others precisely because it was the most secure—at least, so she had been led to believe. Overseas e-mail could be snooped, faxes intercepted, and paper was out of the question. The password-protected, encrypted flash drive, couriered back and forth, was simple, efficient and afforded maximum protection. Lost, it would likely be harmless, if not inconvenient—surely, Lee had the data backed up, since he had rightly insisted that she not make any copies. If it somehow fell into the wrong hands, well, that's why it was encrypted, right? In any event, there was little she could do at the moment—except try to force herself to relax.

Try as she might, as she lounged, with eyes closed, her mind drifting, she could not repress the vision of Sean May, nor the wild speculation about his disappearance from Walter Reed. The handsome, chiseled features, engaging smile, and bright hazel eyes invaded her conscience, dashing her feeble attempts to conjure diversions. The price for her single-minded focus on her career since her commissioning as a Second Lieutenant from ROTC at Florida State, though producing the desired professional results, had been a huge void in her personal life. Now in her mid-thirties, she had no romance in her life, no one with whom to share her innermost thoughts and dreams. Then May had been assigned to her contracting office through the National Guard Bureau's auspices. He had already been in Iraq twice with his own Ohio-based unit, but had agreed to one last tour on special assignment to assist her with the complex re-construction efforts underway throughout the country. In both coordination and advisory roles, he brought a special set of skills to the U.S. team, being a former civilian Defense Logistics Agency technician and contracting manager, and a political scientist with renowned expertise in western democratic government. This knowledge proved invaluable to the State Department in advising the Iraqis on establishing new institutions for self-governance through its Provincial Reconstruction Teams. Undoubtedly, there were few with this unique set of skills in the regular army, leaving the Pentagon to look deep into its reservoir of available manpower until it found what it wanted in Ohio, in Sean May.

Their relationship had been as it should be: that of a senior and subordinate. He was very competent in executing the tasks he was given and, although he was National Guard, had a good military bearing. But within several weeks of his arrival, she found herself being drawn to him, wanting to be around him, and finding reasons to do so.

Perhaps it was the wine, she thought, or maybe her relaxed state. The forced separation from her work for a couple of weeks had certainly given her more time for introspection than she had allowed herself in years, introspection that was painful in many ways because it forced her to confront the disturbing aspects of her existence, all too easy to deflect when engrossed in work.

Yes—she finally had to admit to herself—she found him attractive and stimulating.

Her mind wandered into the more pleasant future. His junior rank would only be an obstacle for as long as he was here. After his final tour, he would be a civilian again, just Sean May—professor Sean May, she reminded herself.

No, she had never even considered the possibility of giving up her career. Her meteoric rise relative to her peer group gave her a fair chance of making it to general, although the officer promotion process was very competitive above her rank of Lieutenant Colonel. The rude irony in her otherwise stellar tenure was that she had risen so quickly it was conceivable she could be forced out of the army altogether before reaching the minimum twenty years to retire. But money was no longer a consideration. She had seen to that.

In another of life's ironies, it was her mother's sudden and crippling stroke that had led her to a desperate search for money. Her father, himself in failing health, would not be capable of caring for her, and it was only a matter of time before he would need professional care as well. So, the burden fell to her, their only child. Not until she had completed her education and embarked on her career had Bouchard begun to fully appreciate how much her parents had sacrificed to give her opportunities that they themselves never had. She called and wrote often, visited whenever possible, but, as a career army officer, there was little opportunity for her to be there. At least, not as much as—nor in the ways—she had convinced herself that she owed them. So she tried to compensate by providing some financial support, just as they had done for her until she had finished college. For years, she had been sending money to her parents to supplement their meager $1,050 monthly Social Security income, her father's reward for 33-years as a house painter. Once he had been diagnosed with colon cancer, his days on a ladder were over. Her mother had been in good health until recently, managing their family home and caring for her father, but now an invalid, clearly, there would be no alternative to round-the-clock institutional care. Her army salary would not be enough, especially when she returned to the states and this temporary hiatus from having to pay the normal expenses of daily living was over.

Her position as chief of contracting had given her principal authority and control of phenomenal, seemingly limitless sums of money for reconstruction projects—had provided the opportunity—and she had taken it. With all the time for contemplation, she had resolved the ethical dilemma quickly; given the same set of circumstances, she would do it all over again. Take care of your own. No qualms. Period.

She pushed the button to speed-dial Lee's number. Morality was for philosophers, and she really didn't care how she would be judged. In her mind, the right decision was to put her parents—her only family—above all else, just as they had done for her. Now, she not only could pay for the care of her ailing parents, she had more money for herself than she would ever need.

"Colonel," he answered, "I've been waiting for your call. Back in Baghdad, I presume?"

"Yes, I returned this morning." This time, at least, his voice did not have the sharpness of being irritated by her disturbing his sleep. It was ten o'clock in the evening Baghdad time, two in the afternoon on the east coast of the U.S.

"What information do you have for me?" he asked in his characteristically stoic tone.

She looked down at the photo, having by now rehearsed her reply numerous times. She had enough money, and she would not put May in any more danger than she already had.

"I'm afraid I have nothing for you," she lied. "The flash drive is not here and I have been unable to find a photo of Major May."

"The photograph has been handled," he said coldly, "compliments of the Denison University web site."

Of course. She had not considered his civilian life as a professor and published author, both of which certainly would result in an internet presence. She made a mental note to so some searching herself, to learn more about the man whom she was trying to protect, whom she hoped might again be a part of her life someday.

"What will you do?" she asked, trying very hard to keep an indifferent tone in her voice.

"We will find him," was all he said before the line went dead.

CHAPTER 17

The two officers were inconspicuous as they walked through the quiet compound. Most of the military and civilian personnel housed in the trailer complex were working in the city at this time of the afternoon. Had anyone paid close attention to them, they would not have been recognized; the faces were new, but there was nothing unusual in seeing new American faces in Baghdad, particularly with so many additional U.S. troops coming into Iraq.

They looked dirty and tired. To the military police at the security checkpoints they had passed through—and to anyone else who saw them—their appearance was common in Baghdad, typical of soldiers returning from the field, perhaps a day of patrolling the nearby suburbs. They wore fully loaded web gear, gas masks strapped to their hips, light brown scarves around their necks to shield their faces from blowing sand and dust. The captain, whose collar insignia was that of a tanker—an M-26 tank, gun slightly raised, superimposed on two crossed cavalry sabers in scabbard—also had a field satchel slung over his right shoulder. The major, wearing the crossed Springfield muskets of an infantryman, walked to his right, hands to his sides, eyes shifting left and right under his dark sunglasses. The disguises were perfect, right down to the security passes and fake military IDs in their wallets.

On both sides of the gravel walkway, four-foot wide sandbag walls lined the sides of the identical trailers up to just below their flat tops, with openings for the individual entry doors or air conditioning units, or where an intersecting path caused a break in the long continuous rows. Each of the modified shipping containers was configured to house two, a private room on either end, each having a separate entry door, and a shared bath in the middle. The two officers were headed for a trailer with a single occupant, one of the fortunate few who did not have a roommate.

"This is it," the Major said, stopping, "Twenty-eight."

"Check," the captain said in a standard military reply. Nearly a year after his discharge, Luttrell felt comfortable in his old battle dress uniform, even as an impersonator. Different name tag, different branch insignia, same uniform. He slipped into the opening between the walls of sandbags while his fellow imposter, Scott, stood watch, his back to Luttrell.

Luttrell pulled the key from his pocket and quickly slipped inside her trailer. A glance left, then right, confirmed he was alone.

He pulled the gas mask out of its carrier, while slipping the satchel off his shoulder. He flipped open the top of the satchel and pulled out the factory bag containing a MOPP suit, the army's acronym for "Mission Oriented Protective Posture." It had been re-packaged to look brand new, both to facilitate easy passage through security and to provide an extra barrier between them and the deadly weapon inside. As expected, the MPs ignored the vacuum-sealed plastic bag during the perfunctory security checks. He laid the rolled up suit on the floor and carefully unrolled it. A MOPP suit included butyl gloves, jacket, trousers, and boot covers—with a separately issued M17 protective mask to complete the ensemble. In the center of the roll, he found a small resealable butyl bag, which he pulled open to reveal the laboratory applicator containing the organophosphate nerve agent VX.

Before doing anything else, he patted the cargo pockets on both legs of the pants until he found the pocket containing MARK I injector, which carried a large dose of atropine and 2-PAM Chloride, antidotes that could save his life if anything went wrong. Touching VX with bare skin would be lethal without fast decontamination and medical attention. Even a drop would cause severe symptoms, such as convulsions, vomiting, difficulty breathing, and if not soon treated, eventual death. There was zero margin for error, he knew, and his training made error very unlikely. Still, knowing the antidote was within reach gave him extra confidence to work quickly.

With practiced efficiency, he first donned the mask, properly clearing it as he had been trained, then, he slipped into the outer garments. He was now adequately protected from a certain and painful death from contamination—protection his target, an unknown female lieutenant colonel, would not have.

Three taps on the door was the signal that he was about to break the seal, releasing the liquid agent into the applicator. Scott was not an expert—his real military job had been special forces infantry—but he knew from his training that VX was one of the most lethal agents ever made. He said a silent prayer to himself as he looked left, then right. No one around.

Luttrell took a deep breath through the mask's filters, let it out slowly, and began his nasty work. Officially banned from offensive use by the United States, first by the 1925 Geneva Protocol and then the Chemical Weapons Convention in 1993, tons of VX and other lethal chemical and biological agents remained in the inventory of the U.S. arsenal, officially for the purposes of deterring their use against the U.S. and for in-kind retaliation. And though all service men and women were trained in defense against nuclear, biological and chemical weapons that potential adversaries were known to possess or to have the capability to acquire or produce, only a small cadre of highly trained specialists ever actually handled them. The army was the service charged with the management—and now the mandatory destruction under the 180-plus country 1993 Convention—of these horrific weapons, stored in cartridges, artillery projectiles, rockets and mines in nine sites throughout the U.S. Luttrell had been to them all—places like Aberdeen Proving Ground, Maryland, Pine Bluff Arsenal, Arkansas, and the former home of the Chemical School at Ft. McClellan in Anniston, Alabama. His favorite posts had been out west in Colorado, Oregon, and his next to last duty station, Johnston Atoll in the Pacific, about 800 miles southwest of Honolulu, where he had supervised the destruction of all the weapons on the island in preparation for its closure in 2003.

He did not know for certain how his employer had come to possess VX, nor did he really care. Still he suspected that while working around Iraq, they found the VX and God knows what else hidden in secret storage somewhere. He was as certain as he could be it didn't come from the

U.S., not with the impregnable security guarding its arsenal. Besides, he, like the rest of the world, had been told convincingly that Saddam had chemical weapons—he used them on his own people in the nineties, after all. But if his theory was correct, no evidence would ever be found because the weapons had been found—and probably sold on the black market—before the UN inspectors ever arrived.

Hidden behind the mask was the ruthless sneer of a remorseless killer who reveled in the irony. Yes, many thanks to the U.S. Army's Chemical Warfare school for all the fine training that had given him the skill to do this job, he thought, as he applied the oily, colorless and odorless liquid to the kitchen faucet handles. The army also deserved credit for his willingness to do this job—to do something that would have been repulsive to him until last year. The bastards had screwed him out of his career after he gave them the best years of his life and 110 percent of his effort everyday. Outstanding efficiency reports, honor graduate from every school he attended. He moved to the bathroom, carefully squeezing the applicator while quickly brushing the handles with its saturated sponge. Well, who would have the last laugh now? Now he got to use all that training to make multiples of his former army pay.

Within five minutes, he was finished, the applicator, MOPP suit, and mask in the butyl bag, which he sealed and put back in the satchel. He pulled a trash pack from his cargo pocket, in which he placed the satchel, his web gear, scarf and mask carrier. As soon as he opened the door, he nodded to Scott, who removed his web gear and tossed it into the open trash bag, before beginning his walk back toward the complex gate. As agreed, Luttrell would give him a head start by circling around the perimeter walkway, where he would find a couple of KPH workers in hard hats—ostensibly inspecting utility connections—whose mission was to take the trash bag to a nearby incinerator.

As soon as she came home for the day, the lady colonel would be the next American added to the ever-increasing body count in Iraq.

CHAPTER 18

"Jim Hewitt," he said in an impassive tone to the receiver, while still staring at the TV screen. Reflexively, he had grabbed the phone from its cradle, but he did not look at the caller ID.

"I have some valuable information for you."

Hewitt recognized the voice, one of the select few who had his private number. "Hold on…just one second." The network news anchor was finishing a report about 5 American soldiers killed in a brazen attack by Iraqis impersonating American soldiers, who had apparently simply driven onto a secure government compound in Karballa, just outside of Baghdad.

The anchor's seriousness was palpable. "In an unrelated event, the Pentagon said today that a high ranking army officer was found dead in a secure residential area inside the heavily fortified Green Zone earlier this week. The army is withholding identification pending notification of relatives and would say only that an internal investigation into cause of death is under way. When we come back…"

"I'm terribly sorry, Congressman," Hewitt said, as he pressed the button on his remote to silence the TV. "I was listening to the rest of a news story."

"Quite alright," he said. Congressman Thomas Drysdale was not accustomed to being put off, even for a few seconds, but for a golden egg like KPH, he concealed his irritation. "As I said, I have just learned something that you will find interesting from one of my staff."

"Oh?" he asked, with genuine interest.

"I am fairly certain the individual you mentioned in our last conversation—the one you are seeking in connection with our…arrangement—has befriended a female Congressional Research Service employee." Raucous voices in the background were a blessing and a curse at the same time. At least no one was going to be able to overhear him. "In fact, he is probably with her as we speak."

Hewitt jumped from his chair. "Where, exactly?"

"I don't know at the moment, but as of last night anyway, he was still here in Washington—he had dinner with a CRS employee at a restaurant behind the White House."

"Really," was all he could manage in his momentary state of shock. His partners were practically tearing their hair out in a frantic effort to find this missing major, and he falls right into their lap by some fluke.

"Yes, indeed. I, uh, overheard a conversation…turns out this CRS staffer is an old friend—college roommate, I think—of one of my colleague's legislative assistants. Apparently, the she—the CRS gal—brought him along to a dinner they had planned."

Incredible, Hewitt thought, as he scratched his head. Was it possible that this was their major, that he had just fallen into his lap? Hewitt knew very little about the major, couldn't even remember his name, for that matter. It was the flash drive and its contents that were important. When Prather had explained the missing drive was most likely in the possession of this injured major at Walter Reed, Drysdale, with his Pentagon connections was the first call he made. As a ranking member of the defense appropriations subcommittee, Drysdale would be able to cut through bureaucratic red tape; as a beneficiary of KPH corporate largess, he would be motivated to do so.

"Anything else? Anything that might be important?" Hewitt heard his own anxiety as he spoke. His role in the KPH partnership—dealing with contracts, finances and negotiations with the power brokers in the relative safety of Washington—did not often require his involvement in what he considered to be the grunge work of company operations. The messy details of execution normally fell to his partners, especially the driven, if not ruthless, Prather. He was KPH's brains; the ex-special forces guys were the brawn. But this time was different because of the very real threat the contents of the missing drive posed to the company and the three of them personally. With both Krug and Prather out of the country, it was time to roll up his sleeves.

"No, not really. As I said, I just overheard a brief conversation while waiting to go into a meeting. One of my aides was making casual conversation with his staff and one of them mentioned a major who walked out of Walter Reed. That's all I heard before I went into—" A high-pitched beep interrupted him. "Call waiting, sorry. Look, I need to get back to the floor. I'll call you later."

"Wait! Who is she—what's the CRS friend's name?"

Drysdale was on the move, as evidenced by the sounds heard in the background, the uneven signal. "Ginny, I think is what she called her… don't think I heard a last name."

"Can you get a name, a number for me? Or better yet, tell your assistant I want to help him if she can find out where he is. Give her my cell number, whatever." Hewitt frowned at the transparent desperation in his voice.

Hewitt heard voices echoing in the background. He guessed Drysdale was walking through the Capitol toward the House chamber.

"I'll do my best. I have to handle this…discretely."

"Just ask your assistant to call her friend!" Hewitt blurted into the phone. "That's all."

There was perhaps half a minute or so of silence from Drysdale. Then in a barely audible voice, he said, "These are smart ladies, Jim. If I suddenly take an interest in the subject of an overheard conversation, they might get suspicious. Let me handle this my way. Now, I really have to go."

Hewitt stood there behind his desk, mind running full speed, wondering when Drysdale would call again. Of course, Drysdale was right to be cautious with his aide, he thought. If there was one thing he had learned in dealing with politicians, it was not to act impulsively, and in his moment of shock, he had forgotten that. Patience, he said to himself as he returned to his seat. They would find the major and get their flash drive soon enough.

Sooner than he expected, as it turned out, for not too long after their conversation had ended, Hewitt received a cell call from a very friendly, young, unsuspecting, gullible Blanche Martin from Congressman Hill's staff. Kate Fowler was on her way to National Airport to fly home to the Congressman's district office in St. Louis, but could she help? No match for Hewitt's adroit coaxing and finesse, Martin was putty in his hands. We want to help him, we are veterans, we have money and contacts. No, she wasn't at the dinner, but she made the arrangements for Major May to stay at the Wiltshire as a guest of the Congressman, had heard the entire story from Kate this morning.

"I see," Hewitt said. "The Wiltshire." He knew the five-star hotel by reputation, as did most of the Washington inner circle. "Oh, by the way, do you know the Congressional Research Service employee—you know, the one who brought Major May to dinner last night?"

"Ginny? Yes, of course."

"Can you give me her last name? Just in case we can't find the Major."

"Burress," she said cheerfully. "Virginia Burress."

"Thank you," he said to her with genuine sincerity. "We'll do what we can for him."

CHAPTER 19

Any fear he had experienced in the military paled in comparison to Friday afternoon rush-hour traffic in northern Virginia. May had to force himself to relax his anxious grip on the armrest, as Ginny boldly darted in and out of mile after mile of snarled traffic. Not only was she weaving in and out, crisscrossing six lanes jammed with sundry vehicles, so was everyone else, including the 18-wheelers.

"I don't think we're being followed—at least not that I can tell in this mess." Ginny said, looking in her review mirror.

He wondered. Neither of them yet understood how it was that two federal agents had inquired at the front desk of the Wiltshire about his whereabouts earlier in the day. Fortunately, having been offered nothing other than a glimpse at their badges and identification cards, the seasoned clerk held fast to the hotel policy of divulging nothing about its guests to the public. It was fairly simple to conclude that Kate Fowler or Congressman Hill, himself, had divulged he was staying there; the question was, why? Until Ginny's message to Kate was returned, they could only speculate, assume it was accidental, since it was their belief Kate intended to ask her boss to help him. Meanwhile, May was not ready to turn himself in just yet, at least not until he had examined the contents of the flash drive to hopefully recover some contemporaneous memory—regain the strength and stability of knowing himself—where he stood, what resources he could draw upon. He was also not ready to dismiss the possibility that the feds were now onto him, perhaps tailing them as they raced down I-95 and away from Washington.

"Ever heard of the infamous mixing bowl?" she asked. "This is it." She had been pointing out landmarks as they passed them, hoping to spur his memory.

As far as the eye could see, a mass exodus of impatient commuters and trucks of various sizes staggered toward the Virginia suburbs and beyond in a perpetual cycle of spurts and clogs. Ginny was among the many not content with the agonizing pattern of acceleration and braking, constantly shifting lanes in an attempt to escape it. When a semi cut in front of her, it was all he could do to keep his eyes open. Unfazed, she hit the brakes hard and jumped over into the right lane. At least she kept her eyes on the road while talking to him.

"Unbelievable," was all he said in response, his hand once again clutching the armrest.

"Used to make this commute every day when I lived in Occoquan. Ever hear of it?"

"Doesn't ring a bell," he said. "But then, not a lot of my bells are ringing these days, are they?"

"Well, thanks to the internet, at least you know a lot more now than when I met you." She gunned the engine to pass a couple of slow moving identical trucks and came up right on the tail of a Porsche Cayenne.

"Yeah," he said, his muscles tensing. "How much farther?" he asked, hoping that the thrill ride was nearing its end. His neck and shoulders were aching again, but getting to his medication would require unfastening his seat belt, something he thought unwise at the moment.

"Not long." She pulled in front of the two trucks, close enough that the driver of the one in the lead blasted his horn. Traffic was thinning a little, as cars peeled off to get into the HOV lanes. She turned her head toward him and asked, "I'm curious. Did the doctors at Walter Reed tell you anything more about the amnesia you have? What did you say it was, retro-something?"

He wished she hadn't done that, for as soon as she did, someone in an old silver Cadillac Seville with smoke pouring out of the tailpipe crossed two lanes in front of her. She hit the brakes, causing the car behind her to blow its horn at them. May turned to shoot the driver a nasty look. "Grade. Retrograde."

"How is it that you remember your childhood, but nothing about the past 15 years? It seems very odd."

Traffic flowed smoothly now, so he felt his body relax. "To tell you the truth, I really don't think the doctors know much about what is wrong with me, which might explain why they blew off so many appointments. There were other guys there with amnesia, too, and they were in the dark as much as me. It's obvious the functioning of the mind is still way beyond the capabilities of medical science."

"It is fascinating, though. You told me you remember high school and college. Well undergraduate school, anyway. Then you go blank until you are in Walter Reed. Your language skills are intact, which I guess is not surprising since you remember the period when they were developed. But you don't seem phased by things that you've seen that are new in the period you can't remember. Like cell phones, or this GPS." She pointed to the LCD screen on the dashboard, where a small electronic map displayed an icon showing their present location on I-95 along with their exact coordinates. "Neither of these devices was common until recently, but they seem familiar enough to you."

"I can't explain it, Ginny." May rubbed his chin thinking about what she had just said. It did seem strange that even though he had no recollection of events for a good portion of his adulthood, the modern technology—the things all around him now—did not feel foreign at all. He looked around at the cars. The newer models should stand out—strike him as novel, if not futuristic—if he couldn't remember them. Cars look quite a bit different now than, say, the late 80s Seville that just cut them off. But his wasn't the experience of Rip Van Winkle, not like he fell asleep to wake up to a transformed world. It was more surreal, like he lost the connections to his past selectively. Then he remembered something he had been told by the psychiatrist.

"'Islands of memory' is what they call this in psychobabble."

"Interesting way to describe it, I guess." She looked in her review mirror nervously. "Your islands are pretty small when it comes to the last decade or so."

"All I know is what the doctors and nurses told me. I've never had any reason to learn about amnesia before, so all I know has been learned in the past week." He reflected a moment on how well he was able to recall the events of the recent past, starting at Walter Reed.

"Did they at least give you a prognosis? Or any ideas about how to recover your memories?" She flipped on the intermittent wipers as a thin mist began to form on the windshield. The clouds ahead of them were thickening, turning deep gray.

"Like I said, I don't think they really understand it too well. They told me that this injury—TBI, or traumatic brain injury—has been occurring quite a bit with soldiers in Iraq. Of course, I don't remember exactly what happened to me," he reached behind his neck and rubbed it, "but apparently, I took a lick on the back of the head. They said the amnesia I have is somewhat rare, or at least used to be, until now. With all the improvements they've made to body armor more people can survive explosions that would have killed them before." It was sleeting, the drops pelting the car like fine gravel. Thankfully, Ginny backed off her speed a little, although he would have preferred that she slow down even more. "Some forget things going back a few weeks or months, some, like me, lose years. Some get their memory back in days or weeks, for others, it can last much longer. So, to answer your question, no prognosis—nothing definitive."

"At dinner, the night we met, you told Kate and me certain places in D.C. felt vaguely familiar, like déjà vu. Did you feel anything happen—in your mind, I mean—at the moment I showed you your bio on the Denison web site?"

"No, not really. For the moment, anyway, it just confirms that I am not crazy." He focused on a white BMW that just zoomed by weave in and out of a pocket of congestion ahead of them. "If I was in grad school at GWU for a few years, it makes sense. I probably rode the metro to Foggy Bottom to get to school from wherever I lived. When I saw the Thomas Jefferson Building the day we met, I just knew I had been there. Maybe I spent time in there doing research for school. The psychiatric specialist told me all my memories are still there, the connections to them in my brain have been broken. For most people, though, they come back over time."

"I'm certainly no expert, but it was a shock that resulted in your losing them, so maybe a shock will bring them back. Not like a blow to the head or anything physical, but—well, maybe there's something on the flash that will trigger your recollection of some major events. Maybe some names, or pictures…"

"Associated contextual cues," he announced with a hint of sarcasm.

"Huh?"

"That's the language they used when they described the therapy I need. Give me some specific information about events that occurred during the time period I can't remember, and it may help re-establish those lost connections." The pain from sitting in the seat and being tense was getting worse. "Let's hope so," he sighed. "I just wish I could remember the damn password."

"If anyone can break it, it's Cybil. She's been working in computer security for years."

"Fort Belvoir," May read from a sign. "Hmmm. I'm getting that peculiar feeling again. Damned frustrating." His head jerked when she abruptly braked, sending a wave of pain down his neck to his shoulder region. Traffic was completely stopped ahead.

Barely moving now, she looked at him. "Do you want to take a look? Maybe seeing it will spur something."

"We won't get through security. I don't have any ID, remember?"

"Oh, right," Ginny said.

"Just driving by might…well, maybe on the way back." May squirmed, trying to shift in his seat to make himself more comfortable. "Let's try to find out what's on this flash drive first. Who knows? It may bring it all back," he said hopefully. "Besides, I'm more than ready to get out of this car."

Twenty painful minutes and six miles later, they crossed the Occoquan river bridge. On May's right, the little historic waterfront town was shrouded in a misty haze. To his dismay, but not his surprise, he did not recognize it.

"Did you live on the water?" he asked.

She laughed. "No, we lived a thousand dollars a month away from the river. Above one of the stores in the town."

"We?"

"Cybil and I. I guess I didn't mention it, but we were roommates for a couple of years. She kept our place after I moved up to D.C." Shaking her head, she breathed an audible sigh as she pulled onto the exit ramp. "Making this trip reminds me how thankful I am for the metro. I hate I-95."

CHAPTER 20

Cybil's apartment occupied the upper floor of what at one time had been a grand old Occoquan home. The bottom floor was divided into two shops, one a used book store, the other, a small antique shop. In keeping with its Victorian-era style, the living area was tastefully furnished with antiques. Having provided ample room at one time for both her and Ginny, it was quite spacious for just one person.

After introductions were made, May complimented her on the apartment and immediately pleaded for a drink to wash down his pain medication. Ginny had insisted they park several blocks away on the main commercial street in town, which paralleled the Occoquan River. Although May had been happy to finally be free of the confines of her car, the pain had made the walk uphill to Cybil's apartment an arduous task. As much as he wanted to stretch his legs, he found himself ready to collapse on her sofa.

"Thanks for giving us some of your time on such short notice," Ginny said with genuine sincerity.

"Let's have a look at that flash," she said to May. Her voice was gruff with a deep, tenor tone.

Ginny nodded in his direction, while he pulled the drive from his pocket. As he handed the flash drive to her, he took notice of the stark physical contrast between the two of them. Clad in jeans and a Hard Rock Café tee shirt, he guessed she was in her early to mid-thirties, about the same as Ginny. But she was noticeably shorter—perhaps a full foot shorter than him—and had a thickset frame. She wore her hair short, calling attention to a full, round face, devoid of the artfully applied make-up common to most women her age.

"Ginny tells me you are a computer security expert," he said to make conversation. He noted the rough appearance of her hand as she took the flash drive. By her casual appearance on a Friday afternoon, he surmised that she either had the day off or worked from home. "Where do you work?"

"Here," she said, smiling while she looked at the flash drive. "Actually, I'm an independent contractor. I spend most of my time right down there," she crooked her head toward a short hallway leading from the dining area, "in Ginny's old bedroom. Right this way," she said, leading them. "How was the drive down?" she asked, her voice echoing slightly in the empty hall in front of her. The naked hard wood floors squeaked beneath their feet.

"Awful, as usual," Ginny replied. "I swear the traffic gets worse every time I come. Either that, or I'm just getting more spoiled by living on the metro."

"I don't know how you did it every day, Gin. I'd rather dig ditches than deal with ninety-five," she said with conviction.

Ginny's former bedroom was large—nearly as large as the living room, in fact—with dark, thin stripped oak wood floors like the hallway's. Valences and heavy drapes adorned the tall Victorian-style windows, which on a sunny day, would afford plentiful light and warmth. An antique cherry desk with a large plasma monitor, keyboard and mouse sat on a plush Persian rug. Belying the tasteful décor, were five other beige desktop and two notebook computers haphazardly placed on folding tables that sat below an eclectic mix of art work, prints, diplomas and certificates neatly arranged on the plaster walls

"Duke," May said, looking at one of them. "Good school."

Ginny turned to look at him, her eyebrow raised. "How do you know that? I mean, are you remembering things?"

A vexed expression came over his face, as he turned from the wall to look at her, then at Cybil, whom he assumed knew something of his condition. "Yes, but nothing new—my grandfather got his engineering degree from Duke just before the U.S. got into the first World War. I considered going there myself, but tuition was way out of my league." With his hand on his chin, he looked up at the diploma again. "Childhood, early adult stuff."

May quickly concluded that idle chit-chat was unnecessary, for Cybil did not even acknowledge him. She snapped the flash drive into the back of one of towers on the table closest to her desk, and took her seat behind her desk.

"Definitely not military hardware," she said with authority, eyes on the monitor. "Just a standard off-the-shelf office supply store job." She typed in some commands and leaned back in her chair.

"What do you have to do exactly?" Ginny asked her.

May ignored them and instead looked over Cybil's head and through the window. From his vantage point on the second floor of a building situated above the center of the town, he could clearly see the several blocks to the main street where Ginny had parked her car. The weather deterred what May assumed would normally have been a town busy with browsing tourists in search of food and local treasure. He watched uneasily as two husky looking men in overcoats crossed Cybil's street at its intersection with the main road. Despite the falling sleet, neither carried an umbrella, giving him a clear view of identical short, close-cropped hair styles. One of them pointed to the opposite side of the main street—the river side—before disappearing from his vision.

"I'm going to run some hacker code against the flash password prompt." Correctly assuming that May knew little about her work, for his benefit, she elaborated. "Most of my work involves building and maintaining security systems to protect sensitive data—mostly federal government, but some of their private contractors, too—so I am in constant test mode. I have to anticipate what a hacker would do to break through my protection schemes, so I have to wear a hacker's hat, so to speak, to develop the shields against them." She leaned forward, typed a few key strokes and leaned back, looking straight at May. "So, like a good hacker, I have several programs designed to generate passwords and run them against my systems for testing, you know, quality control."

May nodded, struggling to avert his eyes from the window while she was talking to him. "Sounds interesting. Has anyone ever been successful breaking through your, uh, shields?"

She snorted. "Are you kidding? Happens all the time." The computer beeped, drawing her attention back to the monitor, freeing May to look out towards the town. "This is a cat and mouse game. Even if I was a genius—which Ginny can tell you I'm not—I couldn't write enough code to stop every determined hacker in the world. I try, and I'm sure I make their lives more difficult, but no security protection is impervious. Just ask Microsoft."

"She's good," Ginny said. "But she definitely has good job security."

"You got that right, lady," Cybil said, the keyboard clattering as she typed. She opened one of the drawers and pulled out a sheet of paper, which she laid on the desk and slid toward May. "Now, I'm going to ask you to write down things that are significant to you—things that you might use to create a password. Like your birthday, social security number, stuff like that."

May retrieved the piece of paper which was actually a form with a fairly comprehensive list of prompts with blanks to fill in to supply the information. May frowned as he scanned the list. "I don't know if Ginny told you, but I don't know—remember—a lot of this information."

"That's okay. It's not crucial anyways. It just makes the job easier and faster." She slid the mouse in the desk, clicking while she talked. "It's common practice for hackers to gather any information they can on their intended victims. Since most people tend to use words and numbers already familiar to them to create passwords, a good hacker will plug whatever information they can find—like names, birth dates, ages, social security numbers, phone numbers and such—into programs like this one to generate as many combinations and permutations as possible. Their success rate is pretty high because people just don't realize how sophisticated they are."

May pulled a chair up to her desk and busied himself filling in all the blanks he could. While sitting, he no longer had a view of the town or the streets below, and it bothered him. Should he say something? Ginny knew they might be followed, but he didn't want to alarm Cybil, especially if he were wrong about the two men he saw in town.

"If Sean leaves some blanks on the form, do you think you can still get into the drive?" Ginny asked her.

"Oh yeah, it might take longer, that's all. With store-bought, civilian hardware, it's pretty easy to find out how the manufacturer defined the password field." She clacked away at her keyboard, eyes glued to the monitor. "Things like how many characters wide the password can be and the type of characters that are accepted by it are stored in hacker databases all over the net. Some manufacturers use only numbers in passwords, while others allow letters and numbers, still others permit special characters, like asterisks and tildes. The passwords can be case sensitive, too. All of these factors are criteria that I supply to a randomizer program up front, so it will try the permutations of the most likely characters and numbers first."

"All of a sudden, I don't feel too computer secure," Ginny said. "You make this all sound too easy."

"It is, especially for this civilian stuff." She clicked a few times with her mouse. Her eyes grew wide. "Here it is!" She jotted some notes on a piece of paper and returned to her keyboard. "Sometimes, they even have the actual encryption algorithms posted on these sites, but no luck for this drive. Too new, maybe."

"So once a hacker has figured this out, he might put it on the internet for the whole world to see?"

Cybil looked up at her. "Back when you were living here, hacking was still the domain of relatively isolated eccentric geeks who holed up somewhere to do their dirty work. As the internet has matured, whole communities of hackers have formed, colluding with each other online, sharing information, software, techniques—all their dirty little secrets. If you know where to go and can get accepted as one of their peers, you can get just about anything. I used to spend tons of my time trying to figure all this out. Now it's just a few clicks and keystrokes away."

"So, they think you are one of them?" May asked, sliding the form to her. Though he would have preferred to stay sitting, he stood to restore his unobstructed view of the town below.

"Anonymity is the beauty of the internet. In a way, I am one of them. I speak their language, participate in their discussions, even try some of their methods once in awhile. I contribute very little, and most of what I do contribute is completely bogus. But they don't seem to notice."

The sleet had changed over to mostly just rain. No sign of the two guys in town. Was it paranoia or just prudence? If they were federal agents on the hunt for him, May guessed they were checking the businesses, looking store by store, restaurant by restaurant, block by block. His intuition told him that they were relatively safe for the moment, since with only the two of them and many businesses to look through, their search would be an endless process until they realized the futility of it and gave up. The weather, though, was a wild card; if the temperature dipped below freezing after sunset, they would have a treacherous, and for him as Ginny's passenger, he feared, a harrowing return journey ahead of them. He walked back to the front of the desk to be in Ginny's field of vision. Cybil's wide eyes were fixed in rapt gaze at her monitor; Ginny was standing behind her, peering at the animated screen expectantly. When he was able to catch Ginny's eye, he shot her a concerned look.

"Might take some time, huh?" she asked over Cybil's shoulder after a furtive nod at May.

"Depends. It could be worse, for sure. The manufacturer has provided for an eight-character-wide alphanumeric password, but it's not case sensitive, and does not accept special characters. That's 26 possible letters and 10 digits." A few keystrokes and a mouse click later, she read from her monitor: "Basically, 2.8 trillion possible combinations."

May looked at her, frowning. "That's trillion with a 't'?"

"Trillion, indeed. But I'm used to dealing with hundreds of trillions of permutations in my work with military applications, government databases, network operating systems and such. This little flash drive is a piece of cake."

"That's astounding," May said, glancing out the window.

"If I have to use brute force, it could take quite a few hours even if I sic all my puppies on it." She gestured toward the computers on the folding tables. "Chances are, a hybrid dictionary attack will work—it usually does with something as simple as a peripheral device."

May raised a curious eyebrow.

"I think you just lost us," Ginny said. Brute force? Hybrid dictionary attack?"

"Sorry, hon. The two basic methods hackers use are brute force and dictionary attacks. Brute force is the slowest because essentially, you are trying every single combination. By dividing the work among 6 very powerful processors, I can generate perhaps 30 million passwords a second," she turned the flat-screen monitor to face the front of the desk, "which my software tells me here could take a little over 26 hours of computing time with almost three trillion. It never takes the maximum, though. A dictionary hack takes a fraction of the time. You throw a database, or a list, of simple words at your target." She grinned widely. "You'd be surprised how many people use the word 'password' as their password. Anyway, even with, say 40 million or so words, it's too fast not to try before anything else. With a hybrid attack, the computer takes the dictionary and appends random characters and numbers to each of the words. It takes longer than a straight dictionary attack, but has a very high degree of success since this is exactly how 99 percent of people form alphanumeric passwords."

In less than the time it took her to explain the hacking methods, the monitor displayed "Dictionary Attack Failed…Executing Hybrid Attack." Cybil stood and stretched.

"Anyone hungry?" she asked. "There's a nice bistro around the corner."

"No!" Ginny and May exclaimed at the same time. They looked at each other, wearing expressions of consternation.

"Cybil," Ginny said, "there's something I need to explain to you."

CHAPTER 21

After learning that May and Ginny were most likely being followed by government agents, Cybil offered to let them stay with her as long as necessary. If she was anxious about being put into this situation, she did not show it in the least. Instead, she cheerfully offered to fix them something to eat while they waited—she had plenty of food and a comfortable sofa bed she assured them. If the hybrid attack failed to open the flash drive, then she would start the brute force attack and hope that there was a hit sooner rather than later.

To their delight, May and Ginny sat down to a steaming bowl of homemade chicken and dumplings and fresh, hot crescent rolls.

"I had almost forgotten how good a cook you are, Cybil. This is quite a treat."

"I made a big batch last night. Lucky for us I didn't get around to freeze—"

A loud beep from the bedroom stopped everyone dead.

"Bingo!" Cybil dropped her spoon in her bowl and they all rose from their seats, to see for themselves.

The screen reported a successful hack in 74 minutes, 23 seconds, and in large yellow letters, displayed the password. After verifying the password actually worked to open the drive, they returned to their meal.

"Now what?" Cybil asked after polishing off her food.

"I guess we'll have to sneak out of here somehow," Ginny said. If the guys Sean saw were following us, they're probably watching my car now that it is dark."

"My invitation stands. Stay here tonight. They can't stay out there forever."

"There are plenty more of them where they came from. Shift change," May said, pointing out the obvious.

"I have an idea," Ginny said.

Within 30 minutes, Ginny and May were headed south on I-95 toward Fredericksburg, the home of Ginny's alma mater, Mary Washington College. While in school, she had lived with her widowed aunt who owned a house in Spotsylvania about 10 miles west of campus. The arrangement had been ideal, since her aunt was a snowbird who spent every winter in Florida. The empty house would give them a refuge to explore the flash drive, rest, and most importantly, elude the agents. Ginny's plan hinged on Cybil's willingness to give up her car for the weekend.

"It's parked back in the alley," she had said, pulling the key off her key ring. "I planned to be home working all weekend anyway, so it's yours."

Ginny predicted her car would be ticketed, maybe towed, since it was parked on the street, but she left her keys with Cybil anyway.

"Take my laptop, too," Cybil had offered. "In case you don't find a computer in your aunt's house."

A shroud of fog surrounded the street lights as the BMW exited the interstate about 40 minutes later. Fortunately, the temperatures remained above freezing, which May's frazzled nerves appreciated. They were headed west now on Plank Road, which was also marked as State Route 3, first passing through a heavily commercialized area with a mall and strip shopping centers before reaching an open, but dark, stretch of road leading them into the countryside.

"How long has your aunt lived out here?" May asked her.

"All her life. Spotsylvania is my family's ancestral home going way back to the eighteenth century. The house she lives in was built on land owned by my family for over two hundred years."

"Do you have any other relatives here?"

"No—well maybe some distant cousins, but I don't know them. I'm an only and my aunt and uncle never had children. My grandmother had an older sister who died when I was in elementary school, so I never really knew her or any of her family."

"How about your uncle?" May asked, as he scanned the darkness.

"Killed in a hunting accident somewhere out here about twenty years ago," she said, adding, "not before he had a chance to sell out to the developers."

"The family property, you mean?"

Ginny nodded, frowning. "It's a sad tale. My uncle and my mother inherited hundreds of acres from my grandparents in the eighties. Since my mother was happily married and living in Boston at the time, she sold her half to my uncle who was, of course, living here. Over the years, he gradually carved it up and sold it to developers and blew most of the money on a variety of failed businesses. All that's left is this house and the 25 acres or so it sits on."

"A shame," he said, reading a sign on the side of the road that said "Entering the Chancellorsville Battlefield." An image of an old black and white photograph of a bearded Civil War soldier suddenly flashed in his mind's eye. He stood erect with one hand on top of his sword in the uniform of a Union cavalry officer, young and fit. May rubbed his chin, struggling to find the significance of this image in his memory.

The white, two-story colonial was built on a cleared knoll in the midst of thick woods. Crunching gravel beneath the tires was the only sound around them in the damp, heavy night air as they made their way up the long driveway toward the faint halo of light glowing from the house ahead. They continued past the point where the driveway split into a circle at the front of the house to the detached garage that became visible only when they had gone past a stand of trees.

May followed Ginny into a screened porch at the rear of the house, where she retrieved a key hidden beneath the cushion of a white wicker rocking chair. As soon as the door was opened, she flipped several switches that simultaneously threw bright light in all directions, revealing a large kitchen closed off from the adjacent room by French doors.

"Looks the same as it always has," she remarked as she sat the laptop onto the counter. She rubbed her hands together. "First order of business is heat."

May followed her through the French doors into an elegantly appointed dining room, where more lights illuminated most of the rest of the first floor, giving him a sense of the woman who lived here. Although much of the furniture was covered in sheets, he could see enough to tell that this was not just a home, it was a treasure trove of family heirlooms and antiques. A shiny black baby grand piano in the front parlor caught his attention, and he walked over to it, touching it lightly with his finger tips.

Ginny had retrieved Cybil's laptop from the kitchen and stood watching him through the partially opened pocket door separating the living room from the parlor. May shot her a glance.

"Do you play?" she asked him.

"No, not unless I learned…I don't think so," he stuttered. "My great aunt had one exactly like this in her house. An organ, too. With foot pedals to pump air through it and all kinds of knobs that pulled out to change the tone." He reached down with his right hand and hit a chord. "I just played around with it a little as a kid. The trombone was my instrument." He touched his temple with his index finger. "Memories. They're definitely up here—just need the rest of them."

Ginny patted the laptop case dangling from her shoulder. "Let's have a look at the flash drive. Maybe we'll uncover Sean May's recent past in here."

CHAPTER 22

A spacious office occupied what had once been a family room on the side of the house. According to Ginny, her uncle had spent much of the latter part of his life in this room, squandering the Burress family fortune, which evidently had started with finishing this room. Ginny removed several sheets to reveal a marble topped, antique mahogany desk with Queen Anne legs and feet, with a deep burgundy leather executive desk chair. An attractive oriental rug ran the length of the room between large Palladian windows painted jet black against the dark night outside.

While Ginny set up the laptop, May walked around the room examining the carefully hung assortment of hunting trophies, artwork and certificates on the birch paneled walls. In the center of the longest wall, a sheet covered a large frame that sat beneath a wall-mounted lamp.

"Here we go," she said, after the laptop had booted.

Making a mental note to ask her about the frame, he walked behind the desk to look over her shoulder, while she typed the password. The screen displayed a meaningless listing of perhaps 50 file names, their sizes and dates, arranged in alphabetical order. She turned to look at him.

"Looks like it's mostly word processing documents. A couple of spreadsheets, too."

He shrugged. "Go ahead, try to open one," he said.

"Here. You do it," she said, standing. "I'll go fix us some coffee."

May sat his tired body down heavily, and chose one of the files at random. He quickly scanned through the document, and repeated this process with another, and another. He scratched his chin, glowering in dismay at the irrelevance at what he saw.

"Well?" Ginny shouted from the kitchen.

"Contracts," he shouted back. "Just contracts."

He decided to open one of the spreadsheet files and was presented with appeared to be a list of transactions, involving some fairly large sums of money.

Ginny returned carrying two mugs and wearing an inquisitive expression. "What kind of contracts?" she asked, placing one of the mugs in front of him.

He leaned back in the chair, rubbing his neck. "So far, a couple of construction contracts and a contract to provide security at a supply depot." He stood and pulled a plastic prescription bottle from his pocket. "I don't remember any of this. And look at this spreadsheet." He slid the laptop to her on the smooth marble. "Some big money changing hands here."

She studied the screen for a minute. "You're not kidding. What do you suppose it all means?"

He tapped the bottle on his outstretched palm. "I'm too tired for this right now. You think we could get a little sleep? It has to be late." He swallowed the pills and chased them with a sip of the coffee.

She looked into his red eyes. "Sure. Do you want to take this upstairs with you?"

He shook his head. "Tomorrow." He pointed to the covered frame on the wall. "That frame. What is it?"

"Oh, that," she said, walking toward it. She carefully lifted one corner of the sheet, while May walked over to it. The frame was so large, that she had to wait for him to lift the other corner for its contents to be visible. "A painting that includes a relative of mine." He lifted his corner, revealing a group of seven gray-clad confederate soldiers in a small clearing amidst a stand of trees. Surrounded by a night sky and background, the setting was lit by a small campfire. Two of the soldiers—one an older man with white hair and a thick, white beard—sat on wooden boxes conversing, while another looked on as he smoked a pipe.

"Lee?" he asked, suddenly feeling more confidence. Yes, the older officer seated on the box must be Robert E. Lee. "Is a relative of yours?"

"No, the one smoking the pipe. A.P. Hill. Heard the name?"

May took a couple of small steps backwards, lifting the sheet above his head. He stood there, transfixed by the painting, struggling to make sense of the garbled facts and images it evoked from the fringes of his memory. He knew the actors, but the context of the scene it depicted was a blur. Was it exhaustion? Pain medication? He felt certain that he should be able to understand its historical significance, yet the jumbled fragments would not coalesce in his mind.

"A.P. Hill, yes, of course," he said after couple of minutes of gawking. "And that must be Stonewall Jackson sitting next to Lee."

"Yes, that's right. This is an artists rendition of the final meeting between Lee and Jackson the night before Jackson was shot—mortally wounded—by his own men a couple of miles back in the direction we came from." From his facial expression, she sensed a change in him. "You must have studied some Civil War history when you were younger, right?"

He nodded, eyes still fixed to his front. "I know I took military history when I was in ROTC as an undergraduate. I remember studying Jackson's famous flanking maneuver at Chancellorsville. But on our way in, I saw the sign for the battlefield visitors' center and I remembered the image of a soldier—a Union cavalry officer—out of the blue. In ROTC, we studied tactics, battles, maps, but I know I didn't see pictures like this or the one that popped in my mind in our textbooks."

May took a couple of steps back, then Ginny, and they let the sheet fall to once again cover the famous meeting in the Spotsylvania wilderness. "Do you think this Union officer might have fought in the battle?"

May shrugged. "Possible. Who knows? Maybe I've been here and just can't remember. How about we drive to the battlefield in the morning? I would like to see it—again perhaps."

"Worth a try," she said, nodding. "You've been having these sensations, these vague connections to places. If there's a chance this may help you, I'm all for it."

CHAPTER 23

Sean May awoke a little after eight the next morning, a brilliant late February sun streaming through the windows and the sound of wind gusts rustling the trees outside. Ginny was apparently still sleeping, as he found the downstairs deserted and quiet. He warmed his coffee leftover from the previous night in the microwave, and went to the office to continue exploring the contents of the flash drive. Feeling more rested and refreshed than he had in many days—and, thankfully, free of pain—his only wish was for a hot shower.

While he waited for the laptop to boot up, he walked over to take another peak at the covered painting of Robert E. Lee's last meeting with Stonewall Jackson, gently pulling the sheet and letting it fall on top of his head so he could look at it while sipping his coffee. His senses honed by a full night's rest and a blissful jolt of caffeine, he simply stood there as he had the night before, transfixed by the confederate generals, their battle-hardened faces illuminated by a small camp fire, congregating in the Spotsylvania wilderness.

"What a sight!" Ginny exclaimed, as she walked up from behind. "You must really like that painting to be standing there staring at it with a sheet on your head."

"Take me to Chancellorsville," he said, with excitement. "I feel pretty sure I've been there."

She insisted on a cup of coffee before doing anything that required much movement. As they stepped outside, they were greeted by a bracing breeze—rudely announcing that the temperature had turned much colder overnight—interspersed with strong gusts. Cybil's BMW had not even had time to warm up before they were on the driveway leading up to the battlefield visitor's center.

"What are you thinking, Sean?"

"My memory of the Union officer I saw when I read the Chancellorsville road sign last night—and now your aunt's painting—have me convinced that there is some link between this place and my past. I'm hoping if I see it, it will come back to me."

"I hope you're right."

The single story brick visitors' center was nestled deep in the woods on hallowed ground that had witnessed some the bloodiest fighting of the Civil War. In the first days of May 1863, Robert E. Lee's Confederate Army of Northern Virginia squared off against Major General Joseph Hooker's Union Army of the Potomac in what ultimately would be a tactical triumph for Lee, though at great cost to his army. Nearly 22 percent of his army—13,000 men—were killed, wounded, or missing, including the legendary General Stonewall Jackson, who was shot by his own men, and would die within days of complications. The butcher's tab for Hooker's army was 17,000, or 13 percent of his force, making the battle the costliest in human terms up to that point in the war.

Ginny followed May patiently as he explored the numerous exhibits throughout the building, watching his face closely for any discernible reaction. When they reached the end of the exhibit pathway, he asked a ranger for reference material containing photographs and names of noteworthy Union soldiers who had fought in the battle. For her part, Ginny had very little interest in the war or its personalities, so she observed from a nearby bench, sipping her coffee while May flipped through a series of books.

"I knew it!" he exclaimed loudly, drawing not only her attention, but that of everyone around them. Embarrassed by his outburst, May looked around while awkwardly raising his hand to his mouth. Ginny rose unabashedly while he walked to her, the book held open in his hands.

"Hiram Berry," he said, shoving the book at her. "Once I saw the caption, it came to me—I was here in this visitor's center right before I graduated from GWU." He excitedly snapped the book closed on his finger before she had even looked at the picture, grabbed her wildly and kissed her on the cheek. "We had this old black and white photo in one of our family albums, and my mother always told me that the family lore was that he was an ancestor of ours who was killed at a place called Chancellorsville in Virginia. Before I graduated, she mailed the photo to me with a letter encouraging me to come down here to see what I could learn about him. No one could remember his name, only that he was from Rockport, Maine, where my grandfather was born." He sat down on the bench and Ginny joined him, listening intently. "So one day, I drove down here and spent some time with a Park Service historian."

She was excited about the flood of memories, but not too interested in the substance of what he was saying, yet she felt compelled to ask him why Hiram Berry was a notable figure in the battle.

He placed the open book on her lap, pointing to the photo of Berry, a semi-profile pose, the fingers of his right hand stuck into his uniform coat just below his chest. "In the photo at home, he was a little younger than this, but he looked pretty much the same. He was a brigadier general, shot dead right out there—while crossing Plank Road." When he looked up at her, her face betrayed her indifference to the exploits of Hiram Berry. "Anyway," he said, "I remember one of the rangers walked me out to the road to show me the spot where he was killed." He snapped the book shut triumphantly.

"That's great! Anything else?"

He gave her an odd look, his eyes alternating between her and a stream of people emerging from the theatre. "I remember I came back a couple of weeks later to see the other battlefields."

She knew he was referring to the Fredericksburg, Spotsylvania Courthouse, and Wilderness battlefields, all just a short drive from Chancellorsville. "No, I mean do you remember anything more recent, like what happened in Iraq?"

He frowned. "No. Not yet, anyway. Islands of memory, the doctor told me. Maybe I get my memory back in pieces. Maybe a stimulus is necessary." He tapped the book, smiling again. "But, thanks to your bringing me here, I know the amnesia is not permanent. What a relief!"

They decided to drive a little further west—less risk than heading toward Fredericksburg, she reasoned—in search of breakfast food. She knew there were some restaurants and a grocery store in Locust Grove, just over the county line in Orange County. Along the route, May gleefully pointed out Wilderness Church, part of the Wilderness battlefield, and the location of the Confederate field hospital where Stonewall's arm had been amputated. She did her best to conceal her revulsion as he explained that the arm was buried at Elwood, a home just to the South.

Over a fast food breakfast, May celebrated his breakthrough, joyfully recounting details from his years at GWU. He did in fact ride the metro to Foggy Bottom to attend classes, and, yes, spent quite a few hours doing research at the Library of Congress. Other than the common affliction of most students, meager finances, his time in Washington had been an enjoyable experience.

They agreed to spend another night at her aunt's house to give him some uninterrupted time with the flash drive. Ginny would get in touch with Cybil to check on the status of her car, which she felt certain would be towed if left on the streets in Occoquan. A quick run through the grocery store to grab sustenance for the remainder of the day and the morning, and they were on their way back toward Chancellorsville.

"What if it's the flash drive they want?" Ginny asked out of the blue.

"Huh?" His eyes, which had been fixed on a battery of cannon resting atop a grassy knoll, their muzzles carefully aligned to point toward Chancellorsville, caissons at their rear, suddenly grew wide as what Ginny had said struck him. He snapped his head to look at her.

"You mean…it's not…I'm not supposed to have it? Of course! Why didn't I think of that? Maybe it contains classified documents. That would explain the encryption, the password—but wait! Cybil said it was civilian—"

"Maybe the army bought civilian flash drives—you know, before they had them specially made. Or maybe it's not army equipment at all."

"What do you mean, exactly?" May asked, staring out her window.

Ginny shrugged. "Doesn't the army ever improvise? What if there is something it needs that isn't available in the supply chain?"

"Well, sure it does," May said in reply. "Happens all the time. Body armor, sunglasses, even weapons—if it isn't available, or the military issue isn't as good as the comparable equipment available to civilians, troops will get it, use it." He turned to look trough the windshield as they passed under a thick canopy of oaks, the remnants of trenches visible on either side of the road. "If I'm not supposed to have it, why didn't someone take it before I was evacuated?"

Ginny shrugged. "Maybe you should just hand it over and be done with it," she said impulsively.

Not that easy, he thought, his muscles tensing as the onset of dread shattered what just moments before had been sheer jubilation that attended the recall of his memories from graduate school. Although not encouraged by what he had seen so far—some contracts and financial legers—May tenaciously held on to the remote chance the flash drive might yet contain important clues in the many files he hadn't seen yet. Ginny's plausible suggestion and their speculation notwithstanding, was it not reasonable to believe the drive was his? Why else would it be in his possession? If the remainder of the files proved useless to him, so be it. But, for now, he remained hopeful that he would uncover something—anything—he didn't care.

"I don't know if it's that simple, Ginny," he said, looking at the speedometer. For the first time since last night, he tuned into her manic driving again, as they cruised through Spotsylvania at 70 miles per hour. "If that drive has classified information on it, they are unlikely to just let me hand it over and walk away." He returned his gaze to the beautiful, sunlit rolling terrain ahead of them. "Not to mention the fact that I am AWOL from the army right now," he added.

"Good points," she agreed. "At the same time, you must realize that you can't run forever."

"I know, I know." He stroked what was fast becoming a full beard on his face, his mind racing as he pondered the different scenarios. "I know one thing for certain—I am not going back to Walter Reed. Especially not now."

CHAPTER 24

"Ginny," May yelled from her uncle's office. "You should see this."

She walked into the room rubbing her hands on a dish towel. "Chili's cooking," she reported. "What's up?"

"Part of a letter," he said, pointing to the laptop screen. "I changed the folder's display settings so I could see the dates on the files, and it just appeared. It has a weird name and it was a dim gray color, so it made me curious."

"Sounds like a temporary file," she observed.

"Temporary file?"

May stood so she could sit down to read the document. "When you're working on a document, most software will make a back up copy every so often in case there is a crash or a power interruption. Maybe you were composing this message when—wait a minute." She began reading aloud, "dear mom…I may be in some trouble. Who's Donna?"

"Donna Bouchard, Lieutenant Colonel, U.S. Army. Her name is on all the contracts. Don't you think it's strange that the letter has a closing before she even finished writing it?"

The letter abruptly ended mid-way through the first paragraph. It was dated, addressed and had the words "Love, Donna" in the closing.

"Probably just a template. I use templates for letters all the time," she said, brushing off his comment. "Do you know this Donna?"

"No—I mean, I don't know. I still can't remember Iraq. It's hard to explain, but I see images of places and people in uniform—images that could very well be from Iraq—but there is no context, no cohesion," he said shrugging.

They looked at one another, seemingly coming to the same realization together. "I don't think this is even my flash drive," May said. "I'll be damned!"

"You know what else occurs to me?" she asked, nodding. "The letter, the contracts, the spreadsheet—I'm getting the feeling that this woman was up to no good."

"On the take?" He looked at the screen again, a blank expression on his face. "I hadn't even gotten that far in my thinking, but you're right. It fits."

"And what if those guys who are after you are not federal agents at all? They might be trying to get this drive back. Working for someone who is trying to cover their butt."

May walked around to the front of the desk and plunked down in an armchair directly in front of Ginny. She was a step ahead of him in brainstorming the possibilities, but he had to admit her reasoning was sound. "You're good," he said, his expression turning dour, "maybe too good."

"Putting pieces of a puzzle together is what I do in my job, remember?"

He bent over and put his head in his hands. "A fine time for my head to start hurting again," he mumbled.

Ignoring him, she continued with her train of thought. "If they aren't federal agents, they probably aren't too concerned about protecting your civil rights."

"Danger," he said, looking at her again, his face blank.

"Exactly." Sensing from his blank stare that she should take the initiative, she stood, placing the dish towel over her shoulder, her hands on her hips. "I have a plan." She found a notepad and pen in the drawer, placing it beside the laptop. "If you write down any names you find on those contracts, I'll poke around on the internet to see what I can find. First, I'm going to check in with Cybil."

While Ginny recounted the events since their leaving Occoquan and her hypothesis about May's predicament, Cybil munched and crunched in her ear. For her part, she reported that in her jaunt to her favorite café for lunch, she had indeed discovered an empty space where Ginny's car was supposed to be. The streets were crowded with tourists today, so it would be hard to tell whether the agents—or whoever they were—were still hanging around in the town. More likely, they followed the car to where it was impounded and were waiting for them to show up to claim it.

"What are you going to do now?" she asked Ginny.

"First, I'm going to do some searching on the net to find out what I can about this colonel and the other names on the documents. I'm reasonably sure we are safe for the moment, so if it's okay with you, I'm going to keep your car and computer another night."

Cybil had no plans to use her car or the laptop, she assured her. "If you think there's danger, don't risk it. I'm okay."

"Sean is dead set against going back to Walter Reed. I can't say I blame him, but we're going to have to come up with a plan very soon."

For the first time, Cybil brought up the issue of her own safety. "It wouldn't take too much effort to connect you to this apartment. If these people are dangerous, maybe I should get out of here myself."

"Yeah, I thought about that. Hang in there—I'll call you back shortly."

CHAPTER 25

Ginny's internet searching revealed nothing of use to them with respect to Bouchard. Being a lieutenant colonel apparently did not merit a lot of attention in cyberspace. With little effort, she discovered that Krug, Prather and Hewitt was a small private company founded in 2003 by two former army special forces soldiers and a tax lawyer, who was also a registered lobbyist. The company's web site touted its "World-Wide Operations," naming the government, military, and educational institutions among potential users of its services. Over two hundred employees and independent contractors were available to provide construction management and security services, it said.

After a feast of chili, salad and garlic bread, May excused himself to take a shower. As she returned to the computer, it occurred to her that she had never finished her search on May himself, having stopped at her discovery of his bio. They had both been so consumed with what they believed was his flash drive and now the tangent it had led them on, they hadn't explored the web for anything that might shed light on his recent past.

The first search engine hit brought her back to the faculty profile on Denison University's Web site. A professor of Political Science, author of numerous academic articles, several political science textbooks on the judiciary. A nice photograph of him appeared in the column above his academic credentials and experience.

Next, she was taken to the Granville Gazette, its small-town stature made apparent by the lack of sophistication relative to the major newspaper sites she regularly visited. Ginny was quite impressed to find two pages containing links to articles mentioning Sean May, beginning with the most recent piece announcing his wounding in what was thought to be a Shiite insurgent rocket attack. The building in which he was working on special assignment to a logistics detachment had been heavily damaged, with twenty-six total wounded, five killed. May had been evacuated to Walter Reed Army Medical Center in Washington, DC for specialized treatment, it said.

A March 2005 article reported the re-activation of the 373rd Combat Support Battalion, including its Newark-based headquarters company, for a second deployment to the Middle East. May's unit was bound for Camp Arifjan, Kuwait, a large army installation about ten miles from Kuwait City, to provide logistical support and security to a huge industrial area surrounding the Seaport of Debarkation, or SPOD. Its men and women would travel 20 hours and cross eight time zones en route to the highly strategic SPOD, used by the U.S. for the transport of personnel, equipment and material to and from Iraq. Accompanying the story were several photographs of soldiers in formation and embracing family members at the local armory.

In a November 2004 article, Sean May was listed among the five Granville residents mobilized in the unit's first call to federal service for a June deployment to Baghdad International Airport in support of Operation Iraqi Freedom.

Even though Ginny had been reading in reverse chronological order, she decided to skip ahead to the next page to scan the earlier "hits" for his name. As she scanned through the short list, she was momentarily stunned by the next to last headline:

Denison Professor's Wife and Daughter Killed in Auto Crash

May had not said much about family since they met. Ginny had assumed his amnesia had robbed him of family memories like all the others since his young adulthood; if not, he would certainly have contacted them, gone home to them. Now, reading this tragic account of the death of his wife and two-year old daughter at the hands of two teenagers, drunk, and driving recklessly on icy country roads, she realized the tremendous irony of the amnesia, of forgetting what must have been devastating memories to have to carry around with him. She couldn't begin to imagine the anguish he must have endured—perhaps still was feeling up until his injury. For her, the decision to not remind him of this tragedy was an easy one; he would have to contend with it soon enough.

The very first article announced May's appointment as an associate professor at Denison University. Its author had evidently done some homework, discovering that May had lived here as a child up until the age of ten. He had lived in Columbus for a decade, working as a civilian employee of the Defense Logistics Agency, before attending George Washington University in Washington DC to pursue his doctorate. Now, having recruited him from the prestigious University of North Carolina at Chapel Hill, Denison, and the town of Granville were happy to have him home, and to welcome his wife Lorraine and three-month old daughter. Ginny grinned at the monitor. Headline: Professor Stolen from UNC Chapel Hill. Only in a small town newspaper, devoid of the daily litany of murders, rapes, robberies, and other human tragedies, would such an article be published, she thought.

Back on the first page, she found a brief article about his volunteering for a third tour in Iraq on special assignment to a logistics detachment responsible for administering the U.S. part in rebuilding areas destroyed in the war. Ginny considered his volunteering to go back to the Middle East yet again after having been away from home so much. With the death of his family, she imagined him living alone in an empty house, surrounded by constant reminders of his wife and little girl. Perhaps he had been trying to escape the awful memories pervading what had been an ideal small town life, but in which he now found himself trapped.

In her attempt to prevent him from seeing the auto crash article, she decided to feed him the information she had found later—when they didn't have access to the computer. Ginny felt a twinge of guilt for concealing information that might aid him in recovering his memory, but her conscience convinced her the information about his family would do more harm than good at the moment. Besides, she reasoned, background and biographical information might be helpful to him, but he seemed to be affected most by visual stimuli—his actual physical presence in places he had been before.

It was his connection to the people in his past that was sorely missing in his life right now. In the near term, he might be better off staying here in her aunt's house, but in the long-term, he would need help from people who knew and, hopefully, loved him. As a practical matter, she could be of little additional help to him. With little clothing and none of the other basics of everyday life—access to money, identification, transportation—he needed the help of someone more intimately involved in his life before Iraq to put the pieces back together. Her challenge was to help him connect with that someone as soon as possible.

"Find anything interesting?" she heard him ask from the kitchen.

"A few things," she said. She joined him there to fix coffee and fill him in on the basics of KPH, and the apparent absence of anything relevant on Bouchard. "I'm certain I could get more detailed information on her at work. KPH, too, for that matter. We have access to tons of data that is not available on the internet."

Feeling rested, refreshed and well-fed, his mood nonetheless turned glum as he pondered his tenuous circumstances, the imminent return to Washington and all the uncertainty and danger in would entail. He stared at the coffee swirling in the cup as he stirred it. Ginny had sacrificed much for him and inadvertently put herself in danger in the process. Of course she had to get back to work, and couldn't be expected to put her life on hold indefinitely for him. On the other hand, if her suspicion about their pursuers was true, surrendering himself to the army would not necessarily take her out of harm's way. One thing was clear: for her sake, he needed to sever the tie between her and the flash drive in particular, and separate her from his problems in general. But how?

Sensing his uneasiness, she revealed the plan she had been mulling over in her mind. "I think you should stay here for a couple of days while I go to my office, use the resources I have access to there to find someone who is in a position to help you. You know, family, a good friend—someone you can trust."

"Go into work? You can't be serious. What if they ran your license—"

"I will rent a car" she interrupted. "Or keep Cybil's for awhile longer if she doesn't need it. I can go into the office after hours. There is nothing unusual about that—I do it all the time. There's a lot of security at night, so no one will bother me while I'm there and they even escort me to and from my car. I'll come directly back here after I find out what I can."

He leaned on the counter heavily, sipping his coffee. "I suppose the only other alternative is for me to turn myself in." Even as he said it, he bristled at the prospect of returning to Walter Reed or the equally unattractive possibility of being arrested and prosecuted as a deserter.

"If nothing else, you need the support and advice of someone you can trust." She shrugged at the absurdity of what she was about to say, but at the same time, wanted him to acknowledge the foolishness in it. "You know I could help you get back to Granville, but that is precisely where anyone who wants to find you would look. I think you are safer here." May opened his mouth to protest, but she had anticipated it. "And I will be very careful, I assure you."

He knew she was right. Mentally, he wasn't ready to give himself up just yet. A whistleblower, a psychiatric patient, a deserter. Whatever he was, he needed a more solid foundation under him to take on the United States Army.

She seemed to be reading his thoughts when she added, "A couple of more days for your memory to come back."

CHAPTER 26

Cybil was astonished by Ginny's story. She had called her on the way to the grocery store to buy more food and rent some movies to tide May over while she was in Washington. Keep the car, Cybil had assured her. She would be okay without it for a couple of more days. They made tentative arrangements to meet at the old abandoned Lorton Prison a couple of miles from Occoquan early Tuesday. Cybil would take her to pick up a rental car for her trip back to Spotsylvania.

Ginny's drive to Washington on a Sunday evening had been uneventful and free of congested traffic. There would be no worries until she arrived at the Thomas Jefferson Building, which quite possibly, was being watched by the agents or KPH goons, whomever they were. She called ahead to have security meet her at her car, which, she explained, was not her old Saturn, but a new BMW borrowed from a friend. In her office, she prepared for a sleepless night by making a pot of coffee, then set to work.

Much of her initial searching was public records information. It was a fact of modern life that one would have to expend significant effort to avoid leaving an electronic fingerprint in the numerous public and private databases scattered throughout cyberspace. For virtually anyone except the small minority who took the time to conceal or deliberately obfuscate their personal information, all the basics were readily available. So much so, in fact, that entire businesses were built around aggregating and re-selling it to others for marketing, security, collections, and research. The U.S. Postal Service, state motor vehicles departments, the Social Security Administration, county recorders' offices, credit bureaus—and others, to be sure—all housed massive amounts of data, which, despite laws enacted to ensure privacy from prying and illicit eyes, were accessible to those who knew how to find it.

On a legal pad, Ginny captured every piece of data that might prove useful to May in his quest to reestablish himself. It came as no surprise that his Granville home was indeed the same house he had purchased with his wife before she and their daughter had been killed. Had he sought to escape by volunteering for additional duty in the Middle East? Perhaps he had been suffering from depression—something she did not pretend to understand on anything but the most basic level—making him especially vulnerable to losing his memories of this painful period of his life. It seemed at least plausible, then, that he could be subconsciously blocking out his memory in instinctive self-preservation.

Her next task was to gain access to his army personnel records, something she had never had any reason to do. A quick web search revealed that the army maintained the emergency contact and beneficiary information on form DD 93, the Record of Emergency Data. Starting in 2003, each soldier's personnel data was stored in a system known as eMILPO, or the Electronic Military Personnel Office. She was fairly certain that the Congressional Research Service would have no official access to the individual personnel records of military members, but she also remembered that Cybil had been involved in the development of the system's security.

"Hey," she answered, after one ring.

"I'm sorry to call you so late," Ginny said in a sympathetic tone. "I may need your help with something."

She yawned loudly. "I was watching a movie and must have fallen asleep. You still at the office?"

"Yeah, me and my pot of strong coffee," she said as she eyed her empty cup. "Didn't you do some work on the military's web app for personnel?"

Cybil sat up, stretching her legs. "Ah, yes, eMILPO. I worked for the subcontractor for the security and a couple of other modules back in 2001 or 2002 I think, and I've been working on its replacement for it, too. Something called DIMHRS. Why?"

"I want to get into Sean's army personnel file to get the emergency contact data."

"You would have to have his password and something the army calls an AKO code. The security on their system is tight—thanks in part to yours truly."

Ginny frowned. Her hopes for an easy way to find someone close to May faded fast. "No way for you to get into it?"

"There's always a way to get into any online system, it's just a risk I can't afford to take right now. This DIMHRS contract is going to pay my bills—wait! I know the people who are working on the data migration!"

"Data migration?"

"Whenever you change software that manages massive amounts of data, you have to move it all from the old system to the new one. I have an old friend—you met him once I think—Paul DuMont?"

"I can't place the face…" Ginny replied, her voice trailing off.

"Anyway, he's one of the people working on the programming to move the data over to DIMHRS, so he undoubtedly has access to the eMILPO database." She took a gulp of her drink. "He owes me a favor or two."

Suddenly, she remembered. "Oh, yeah! Was he the guy with the tattoos and the earring? A stutter?"

"That's Paul, alright. Prefers to work at night, but I don't know if that includes Sundays. What the hell, I'm willing to try. What is it that you want exactly?"

An effusive Ginny gave her May's Social Security Number and told her to ask Paul to pull everything he could find on Sean's DD Form 93. She briefly considered asking for whatever he could find on Bouchard, but decided against it, reasoning that data from her personnel file would be useless to them. The clock was ticking for Sean and time was drawing near for Ginny to pack up and leave before her co-workers started arriving for work.

"I hope Paul comes through for us," she said looking at her computer's clock. "I'll see you at seven. At the Lindsay house."

"Got it," Cybil replied. "I'll have the cabbie drop me off on Lorton Road."

CHAPTER 27

In 1910, the U.S. Government acquired land along the Occoquan River to construct the Occoquan Workhouse, later adding a reformatory and penitentiary for the District of Columbia. Reflecting the philosophy of the time that criminals should be rehabilitated, the facility that would become known as the Lorton Prison was designed to transform its inmates into productive citizens. The workhouse complex initially included a 1,200-acre farm the inmates operated, raising cattle, hogs, chickens, and they later built additional structures to house the dormitories, dining hall, laundry, bakery, a hospital and even an ice plant. By the 1950s, Lorton had grown to encompass nearly 500 buildings on over 3,000 acres, while housing more than 8,000 inmates at one time. Over time, its mammoth size became too much for the District to staff and maintain, so it fell into disrepair and was eventually closed in 2001.

Among Lorton's most famous inmates were the 170 woman suffragists, arrested in 1917 while marching on the White House to advocate women's voting rights. News accounts of their poor treatment at Lorton—including physical abuse, filthy living conditions, and force feeding—ironically increased public support for their cause, eventually leading to the 1920 ratification of the 19th Amendment.

Ginny pulled up to the historical marker honoring the suffragists, turned off her lights, and turned the car to face the steady stream of Northern Virginia commuter traffic passing her on the busy State Route 123, also known as Ox Road. It was just after 6 am, with barely a hint of daylight beginning to break on the eastern horizon. She waited, watching anxiously, and when she was satisfied that she hadn't been followed, bolted onto Ox Road through the commuter rush, making a quick right onto Lorton Road before turning on her lights.

She and Cybil would meet at Laurel Hill, the abandoned 18th century home of revolutionary war patriot Major William Lindsay. While living in Occoquan, Ginny had discovered the structure by accident during a long morning run. Finding it had been quite a surprise, surrounded as it was by an abandoned prison complex and a large tract of undeveloped acreage, unusual in the concrete jungle of Northern Virginia. Situated on a two-lane road, its entrance was flanked by brick gateposts and a gatehouse. A 250-foot long, four-foot high masonry wall with a pointed triangular cap course, lined the lane in front of the house. After researching the history of the old house, she and a curious Cybil had together explored its grounds, where they discovered the Lindsay family cemetery surrounded by an iron fence, a weathered white marble tombstone marking the grave of Major Lindsay. To the south and east of the house, they found what had once been an elegant terraced garden defined by a short wall—now overrun by weeds—which contained a series of stairs leading to shaped earthen terraces and benches constructed entirely of brick.

About 15 minutes later, Ginny saw the approaching figure of Cybil against the backdrop of the cascading dawn sunlight. She had been dropped off on Lorton road, opting to make the short hike to the house rather than revealing its location to her cab driver. She watched her friend approach the car, her breath visible in the frigid morning air. As she walked up to the driver's side door, Ginny scooted over to the passenger seat.

"Cold out there," she said as she climbed into her seat. She immediately reached down and a motor whirred to life, moving her seat closer to the steering wheel. "Now, where are we headed?"

Ginny had reserved a rental car at Dulles airport. From there, she would take the back roads down to Spotsylvania. "Dulles," she answered, looking at Cybil in anticipation. "Well? Did your friend get the army form on Sean?"

Never one to carry a purse, Cybil retrieved a piece of folded paper from her bulky coat pocket and laid it on Ginny's knee. "Paul wasn't too happy with me for calling him in the middle of the night, but he came through."

"Thank you!" she exclaimed. "I owe you a lot for this—for everything you've done," Ginny said, grabbing the form.

She eagerly unfolded and scanned the two-page DD Form 93, Record of Emergency Data. In the first block labeled "Emergency Contact," was the name Erik Frese of Frederick, Maryland. Further down the page—in the spaces designated for spouse, children, mother, and father—each of their names were typed with the word "deceased" in the space reserved for addresses. The remainder of the form contained just two names: his only beneficiary, a sister, Laura May-Cooper, address listed as a post office box in Montreal, Canada; and an uncle, Richard Gilgar, with a post office box in Boothbay Harbor, Maine, as the person authorized to direct disposition of his remains. Ginny found an interesting notation in the "Continuation/Remarks" section: "Sister is research scientist in Antarctica. Direct all communications to her husband, Robert Cooper, in Montreal."

CHAPTER 28

Erik paced restlessly, holding the phone to his ear listening to dead silence. His wall clock told him he had been on hold for nearly ten minutes waiting for an intelligent being to explain to him why he was not able to talk to his best friend. He had just about reached his wit's end with the army's endless bureaucratic red tape. It had taken him days and innumerable phone calls to learn Sean was in fact not in Iraq where he was supposed to be but was, in fact, in the U.S., at a hospital in the "Washington area." His first guess, Bethesda, was wrong. Now, this.

For the second time, the call waiting tone broke the silence. This time, though, he cussed under his breath and pushed the button.

"Hello," he said, defeated.

"Mr. Fres—um, I'm sorry, I'm not sure how to—"

"Freeze, like a freezer" he said, rolling his eyes. Great, he had traded a ten-minute hold for a telemarketer.

"Yes, thank you. My name is Virginia Burress, and I—well, this is more awkward than I—I'm calling about Sean May."

Erik was at once relieved that he didn't have to listen to a sales pitch and stunned. "Yes?" was all he could manage.

For the last hour or so behind the wheel of her rental car, Ginny had rehearsed this conversation in her mind, trying to decide how much to trust this man, a perfect stranger, who, for all she knew, was an army acquaintance obliged to help hunt him down. She spent the next 5 minutes convincing herself she was being too cautious, if not paranoid. If Sean had listed him—not his own sister or even his aunt—as an emergency contact, Erik was more than likely a close friend who would want to help him. Probability, she concluded, weighed in favor of her making this call, of fulfilling her promise to help him.

"Sean has been injured in Iraq," she said, neither prepared for, nor entirely surprised by his reply.

"I know, Miss Burress. I have spent the better part of a week trying to find him."

She swallowed hard, weighing her next words carefully. Of course, she thought, the army had followed its procedures for duly notifying the emergency contact, probably eliciting his help in finding one of its newer deserters in the process. She briefly considered hanging up on him, but decided instead to ask a pointed question. She had little to lose at this point.

"If I told you he was in trouble—needed help—could he count on you?"

Tired from the experiences of the past few days, he was in no mood to play games. "Look, Miss Burress, I don't know what this is about, but I happen to know Sean is in the hospital, exactly where he should be if he's hurt. Now—"

"He's not in the hospital, he is with me," she interrupted.

"What the—let me talk to him." He sat down, rubbing his temple with his free hand while he digested her words.

"He's not with me at this very moment," she corrected herself. "He's—safe." This wasn't going as planned. She felt herself getting rattled, the lack of sleep and caffeine withdrawal affecting her. Thankfully, the traffic on U.S. 29 was light. "So, could he count on you for help?"

"Of course, I would do anything for him. He's my best friend," he said without hesitation. "Where is he? Is he okay?"

For several minutes, she recounted the events of the previous 10 days, still carefully measuring her words and revealing only that May was in Virginia. When she was describing his peculiar, but gradually improving amnesia, Erik interrupted her.

"I'm a little surprised he hasn't at least mentioned me. I've known Sean since high school. In fact, we enlisted together the summer between our junior an senior years."

"I don't pretend to understand the amnesia or what is going through his mind. I am a government researcher, not a psychiatrist."

"It has been hard to keep in touch," he admitted, "especially in recent years. Our lives have gone in different directions."

Ginny could hear disappointment in his voice. "With all he has been going through, there are many possible explanations. Maybe, it is something as simple as he doesn't want to bother you."

"Possible," Erik agreed.

"At this point, he has nothing except some clothes and a f—" she cut herself off, not sure of how wise it was to get into the flash drive—"you know, some personal items. No wallet, no money, and apparently no family nearby. He has a sister in Ant—"

"Antarctica. I know. She hasn't been around in years. His parents, wife and kid are all dead—he really has no one, Miss Burress."

"Please call me Ginny." She was growing more comfortable with the conversation now. "Yes, I can't imagine what he's gone through, and now this."

Erik wondered to himself why the army had not contacted him. Until now, he did not know he was Sean's emergency contact, although it made sense with his sister out of the reach of civilization. He knew the army did not routinely hunt for deserters unless they had committed a crime, so the other plausible explanation was they were trying to cover up his disappearance in the hopes of finding him before their snafu became public. After all, there was no wife or close family hounding them, so time was on their side. Only when they were ready to give up—fess up—would they contact him.

"I have room for him here. I will drive down and pick him up. Help him get back on his feet."

Ginny felt a sense of relief sweep over her. She mentally crossed her fingers hoping that she had done the right thing by calling him, hoping that Sean would approve. "I will be back, um, with him shortly. I'll have him call you."

"Where is he, exactly?" he demanded, too impatiently.

Not one to be easily intimidated, she dug in her heels reflexively. Was there some reason Sean hadn't called him already? Some reason to fear him? "I'm going to leave it up to Sean to tell you that, Erik," she said firmly. "I will ask him to call you."

CHAPTER 29

"The address, Miss Clancey!" he shouted, after striking her across the face so hard, she saw flashing white stars.

She fought back the tears, tightly clenching her eyes. "I told you—I don't know her aunt's address!" she screamed, praying that someone had showed up early to open one of the shops below.

"Aunt, huh? Now, we're getting somewhere," he grinned, sticking his face close enough to hers that she could smell stale cigarette smoke. "Turn this place inside out," she heard him them say to the other one. "Start with the room that has all the computers."

"No! Wait!" Pain clouded her mind. No computers, no income. Thousands of hours of work gone. She couldn't let that happen.

"Spotsylvania," she sobbed in resignation. "She lives in Spotsylvania."

She cringed when in one fluid motion, his large hand tightly grasped her face, his muscular arm encircled her neck. The violent and forceful twist ended her pain.

CHAPTER 30

"I don't understand it," Ginny said, shaking her head, after listening to the voice mail greeting for the third time. "She always answers her phone—she has it with her everywhere she goes."

"Maybe out of battery?" May guessed.

"No," she said with certainty. "I told her I would call her when I got here. She told me she was going to swing by the grocery store and go straight home." She frowned. "Something's wrong."

"Don't jump to conclus—"

"Sean, I've known her for years. She's into her techie gadgets, especially her mini-computer cell phone. She even carries a spare battery around with her!"

He looked at her blankly. "What do you want to do?"

She had spent the first five minutes or so filling him in on the form DD 93 and, apologetically described her conversation with his friend Erik. May didn't seem at all bothered by her decision to call Erik. Of course, he instantly recognized his friend's name from his youth—remembered him well, he told her—but like everything else in his recent past, did not recall specifying him as an emergency contact before his latest deployment.

"Why didn't you call him?" she asked, in astonishment.

"To be honest, it didn't occur to me," he said with a shrug. "I can think of a lot of people from school I would call friends, but that doesn't mean I'm going to call them right now. I don't even know which ones I've stayed in touch with, you know?"

She studied him, an odd expression crossing her face as she digested his reply, trying to imagine how she might react with most of her adult life suddenly erased from memory. Other than family members, what relationships could be taken for granted? Were the bonds of friendship different for men than women? Would she feel comfortable pleading for help from someone whom she may not have seen or talked to since then? Her expression changed to one of sympathy as she reached the conclusion that there was no way to know—to truly comprehend—what it was he was experiencing, what was going through his mind.

Ginny stuck her hand in the pocket of her jeans, sliding her fingers across the smooth paper of the folded form. She knew that to avoid the topic of his dead wife and daughter, she would not show it to May. For the umpteenth time, she reassured herself she was doing the right thing by concealing the tragic deaths from him. Although she despised lying, she feared what the information might do to him if she revealed it. Would it put him in shock? Render him incapacitated? She couldn't afford the risk, not now.

She walked over to the kitchen sink and began washing dishes so she would have an excuse to not make eye contact with him.

"Let me see it," he said. "The DD 93 form."

"Oh, Cybil has it," she lied to the window in front of her. "She gave me Erik's information on the phone." Thinking ahead and looking for an excuse to end this line of discussion, she said, "I'll go out to the car and get his number."

Resigned, May sat down in one of the breakfast nook chairs and watched her walk out the back door. "Why him?" he asked himself. "Why not family?"

His thoughts turned to his family. He remembered his first meeting with death as a boy, looking down in disbelief as his father laid in his coffin, still and cold, even younger than Sean was now. The memory of his mother being consoled by grandparents and his aunt—his father's sister—rubbing his back while he cried. Was his mother still alive? Ginny had found nothing on the internet, no listing with the phone company. His last memory of his sister was at her college graduation in Boston, pride beaming from her face, as well as his mother's. There had to be an explanation for not listing one or both of them as emergency contacts. Could it be that his whole family was dead?

The door slamming drew him back to the present. He looked up to see Ginny with the phone at her ear, looking unhappy. "Still no answer," she said, handing him her hastily contrived note with Erik's address and phone number. "I'm really starting to get worried."

"Do you know the people who run the store on the first floor? Maybe they could check on her."

"Yes, good idea," she said, as she touched 4-1-1 on her phone's keypad.

May stepped into the mud room to retrieve his clean clothes from the dryer. Erik would certainly be able to shed some light on recent years, but how close they had been lately, he just did not know. Together, they had gone through basic training at Fort Knox, Kentucky, the summer before their senior year in high school. Then, after graduation, they spent a couple of weeks in Florida before heading to Texas for their advanced training at Fort Sam Houston. It was in Texas that Erik made the decision to go to Germany and, since May would start his freshman year at the University of Wisconsin in Madison, they parted ways. His last memory of him was at Erik's wedding. Held on an early spring day of May's senior year, the setting was a conservatory, where they were surrounded by a seemingly infinite variety of flowers…

"Oh my God!" Ginny's voice rang out.

May dropped his clothes on the dryer and ran to her. "What happened?"

She held up her hand, and let it come to rest on his chest, her face contorted with trepidation. "Will you call me as soon as they tell you something?" she asked whomever was on the other end. She slowly spoke and then repeated her phone number, then looked at him, shaking her head, as she promised to say a prayer before saying good bye.

"Something has happened. Judy—the owner of Cybil's building and the shop—smelled smoke when she came in to open her store just before ten. The fire department broke down her door, and told her that it was just some food burning in the oven. But then the paramedics went up, the police came—and…and—" she hung her head, letting out a sob, "only would say that it was now a crime scene."

"Jesus," he mumbled, pulling her into him.

For a moment, she rested her head on him, then abruptly stepped back, wiping her eyes on her sleeve. "Call Erik. We need to get out of here, quick!"

CHAPTER 31

From his office in the castle's *hohen turm*, or high tower, he could look out upon one of the most beautiful scenes his old eyes had ever beheld. Simply by swiveling in his chair, the grand panorama of the snow-covered valley displayed ever-changing vistas produced by frequent, but subtle changes in the angle the sunlight illuminated the valley. At this moment, however, Martin Lochridge reclined with one foot draped over the corner of his desk, eyes fixed in an empty stare on the Von Segur family coat of arms carved into the mantelpiece above the dancing flames, listening attentively to Erik recount the incredible events happening in the life of his friend, Sean May—a man whom Lochridge very much wanted to meet in person and whose assistance he and *Ops Populi* were eager to obtain. It was through an ironic stroke of good fortune and detective work that May's new lady friend had discovered Erik on the army emergency contact form. Afflicted with amnesia and with no other family to turn to, Erik's friend was reaching out to him for help.

Many questions flashed through his mind while Erik talked, but now was not the time to ask, nor was Erik likely to have the answers. Not one normally given to emotional responses, Lochridge nonetheless was deeply moved by the tragic deaths of May's wife and daughter, an uncanny parallel to his own grievous losses of a wife and son in the prime of his life, and a blow that had caused him such anguish, he had for a time been suspended in a living hell, depths of despair no living soul should ever have to endure. That the army had failed this man and was taking advantage of his lack of close family to cover it up was an outrage. Exactly who was pursuing May and his lady friend was not clear, but his pragmatic side told him that if the flash drive contained incriminating data, if lives were in danger, quick and decisive action was needed.

When Erik had finished, he spoke clearly and resolutely. "Mister May's well-being is of prime importance to our group and its aims. Anything I have is at your disposal—money, transportation, refuge—name it."

"My concern is that my name and address are linked to Sean through this form and maybe other places, like his university job, estate documents and so forth. He may not be safe here in Frederick—at least not for long."

"What about you and Linda? And May's friend—Ginny was it?"

"Yes, Ginny." Erik breathed a sigh into the phone. "Martin, there is a lot about this situation I don't understand, but she definitely has herself involved in it. Based on the crime scene at the apartment of Ginny's friend, I'm going to assume they are both in danger. Linda and I—well, we can bug out for a little while if we need to."

"You're both welcome here any time," Lochridge offered, "but right now I'm sure you want to help your friend." He readily agreed with Erik's assessment of May's and Ginny's plight. The worst part: lack of knowledge. Lochridge quickly considered the available options, mindful nothing could be taken for granted until they learned more about the pursuers—the extent of their resources and capabilities.

"I'll send a plane to Frederick," he suggested. "My house in Camden is always vacant in the winter. They can be out of the DC area by this afternoon, in Maine in time for dinner."

"Good," Erik said, feeling relieved and grateful to have received this offer without even having to ask. "I'm not sure about the long-term, but at least they will be safe."

"Know thine enemy," Lochridge said.

Erik paused briefly to ponder this truism. "Agreed. I will get as much information as I can. Let me get them to the Frederick airport, first."

CHAPTER 32

Lochridge had his property manager, Marjorie Ott, meet them at the airport to drive them to Camden. The utilities were on, the refrigerator and pantry were stocked with basic necessities, and a car was available for their use. It was after dark when they pulled in the driveway of the nineteenth century saltbox. A crisp breeze carrying the fragrance of the sea and the soothing sound of waves crashing against the rocky Maine coastline greeted them as soon as they opened their car doors.

Exhausted and hungry, Ginny asked Marge, as she preferred to be addressed, for restaurant recommendations, but instead of a name or two, she was given a whole spiel about Camden's reputation for good food. Oh, she would love to join them for dinner before getting them settled into the vacation rental. Too tired to offer resistance to her company, Ginny and May left their sparse belongings in her car and they all walked a couple of blocks to a small restaurant in the village, where within minutes, they were devouring steaming bowls of fresh chowder in its cozy confines. Ginny and May said little, only occasionally trading restive glances as they engaged their hostess in polite, superficial conversation. Thankfully, Marge had plenty to say, freeing them to concentrate on the unfamiliar task of extracting juicy white meat from their lobster tails. She gave them a healthy dose of local lore, highlighted the popular tourist attractions—though warning that many would be closed for the winter—suggested some day trips they might want to consider. They learned how the housing boom of the last few years had resulted in many of the homes along the coast being gobbled up as vacation properties. As a real estate agent, Marge had ridden the wave, made good money, and then figured out how to capitalize on the trend by transitioning into property management. The lower stress and steady income that came with her new profession were a welcome change.

After she had let them in, given them her 10-minute orientation spiel, and handed over keys to the house and the promised car waiting for them in the garage, Marge bade them good bye and left.

"I feel disoriented, like I'm dreaming," Ginny said to him as she closed the door.

"It's not everyday you get whisked out of town in a private jet for an impromptu vacation."

"Is that what this is? Maine, in the middle of winter? Being chased around by thugs? I don't think so." She could hear the sharpness in her own voice, but fatigue was drowning all other sensibilities.

May hung his head. "I'm sorry, I didn't mean—"

"No, I'm sorry for snapping," she interrupted and waved her hand dismissively. "We both should go to bed."

"Sounds good to me." He walked toward the stairs, then stopped suddenly and turned to face her. "Did you check your voice mail for news about Cybil?"

"I almost forgot," she said, reaching into her purse. "I turned it off when we boarded the plane," she paused while listening to the voice prompt, "and we've been going non-stop." With the phone to her ear, she nodded to him, a signal that there was a message.

Standing with his hands in his pockets, May watched as she listened—but said nothing—to what seemed like a very long message. In fact, he gathered there was more than one when she jerked the phone away from her ear to push a button. Suddenly, he saw her eyes roll back in her head. He lurched in her direction, but his dulled reflexes prevented him from catching her as she fell.

"Ginny!" He shouted. Fortunately for her, the living room sofa broke her fall, though her collapsing body produced a sharp thud as she made contact with it. Her phone wasn't so lucky, shattering into several pieces as it struck the edge of the coffee table.

His training as a medic as well as numerous first aid classes made his next action almost instinctive: He shoved the coffee table away from the sofa to make room to position himself in front of Ginny's limp body.

Adrenaline surged through him as he lifted her onto the sofa, elevating her feet above her head. Then, he placed his hands on her shoulders and gently shook her, saying her name repeatedly.

"Wha…what happened?" she whispered within a couple of minutes. She opened her eyes and started to sit up, but May gently restrained her with his hands.

"Just lie there couple of minutes," he said. "You fainted while you were listening to your messages."

She raised her right hand, placing it over her eyes, and began sobbing. "Oh my god, Sean. They killed her—broke her neck. She's dead."

CHAPTER 33

Although KPH was flush with cash and enjoyed a fairly robust array of talents among its staff, hacking into the army's personnel system was beyond their capabilities. Instead, Prather had opted for a low-tech option for finding leads to May's probable location. A couple of plane tickets to Columbus and a 40-minute drive to Granville later, he had two employees rummaging through May's house with instructions to search for address books, estate documents, computer media—anything that could prove useful in hunting this heretofore elusive major down.

From his condominium high atop Crystal City, Prather skimmed through a stack of papers that FedEx had just delivered to his door. The job had been fairly easy, he was told the day before. May was well organized, with all the important personal documents in a desk drawer in a spare bedroom. A simple break in. In and out in less than 10 minutes. Nice work, he said. He would see to it that the next payroll included a little something extra for each of them.

Marriage license, birth certificate, transcripts, all useless, but he set the multi-page "Last Will and Testament of Sean Christopher May" aside to scan later. As he lifted the next file folder, the small jacket cover slipped out onto his lap. It was a microfiche copy of his "201 file," the army's nomenclature for personnel records, which would be useless to him without the special reader. He tossed it aside. If need be, he would take it to the library later, but he hoped that a paper copy of the DD Form 93 was in here somewhere.

Less than 5 minutes later, he leaned back in his chair, the form in his lap, to formulate his next move. A large picture window displayed the spectacle of planes taking off and landing on the busy National Airport runway below, the mighty roar of the jet engines suppressed by the structure's clever soundproofing. His concentration had him looking without really seeing the few boats dotting the frigid Potomac River beyond. Although the novelty of the view had long since faded, he was not about to trade it for a six-by-nine jail cell, would not relax until the flash drive was back in his hands. May had been lucky, he told himself, but that luck was about to change. The silver and blue of an approaching Airbus cut off his gaze, and he averted his eyes to the phone long enough to dial. Without uttering a greeting of any sort, he began barking instructions to the person on the other end. "Leave Kernan and Woods in Ohio to watch his house. I want you and Tyner to drive over to Frederick to pay a visit to an Erik Frese. I'll give you an address when you're ready to copy. Pull Hopkins and Moore off whatever they're working on and put them on a flight to Maine." He paused to give his employee time to get pen and paper, and glanced at the form before continuing. "Yeah, Maine. His uncle is in Boothbay Harbor, but all I have is a PO box. His name is Richard Gilgar. The address for Frese is…"

CHAPTER 34

Whether it was the adrenaline rush produced by Ginny's fainting or the shock of learning of Cybil's murder, he wasn't certain, but the memory recall had hit him like a ton of bricks in the middle of the night. To be sure, he was exhausted, but it was not the physical type that led to an easy, deep sleep, rather it was mental fatigue that resulted from the cumulative effects of the stress and strain of the past two weeks. This time, it wasn't the sun that woke him, but a full moon gleaming through the window that roused him from a fitful dream. All the memories came crashing on him at once—so intense was the experience, he was unable to move from the bed. He lay awake for what seemed like an eternity, crying more than not, as the crushing emotions that accompanied the death of his wife and daughter relentlessly swept over him like waves breaking on a beach. At the moment he learned of their deaths, living had become devoid of purpose, had become meaningless; life since then had been simple existence.

Then came his guard unit's first mobilization for Iraq. His unit needed him, there was purpose again. The first tour had been a success, but after returning to Granville, unrelenting desolation once again swept over him. His attitude toward the tedium of his civilian life became one of disdain, with no desire to play the silly games of faculty politics. His heart was not into teaching, so he withdrew as much as possible from daily interaction with people, preferring the company of Jack Daniels and the solitude of research and writing. Indifference and cocooning did not stop Denison from rewarding him with tenure after his publication of a third American government text received nationwide acclaim.

The second mobilization and deployment of his unit was a relief. Once again, his sense of purpose was renewed, but this time, the enthusiasm waned as it gradually became clear to all who were paying attention that Operation Iraqi Freedom had been based on faulty intelligence at best, or outright deceit at worse. It was not just the American press arousing suspicion that the administration had perpetrated an egregious fraud on its people. Prominent and respected leaders and academicians throughout the world were questioning America's pre-war posturing, especially since there was never any link established between the Hussein regime and terrorists—al-Qaeda in particular—no weapons of mass destruction found, and therefore, no direct threat to American security from Iraq. The majority of Iraqis, themselves, viewed the occupation as nothing more than American imperialism; they felt the reasons given for the invasion were mere pretext for the true motive of ensuring a stable oil supply for itself and its western allies. As time went on, morale sank, more men and women were killed and maimed, and his bitterness grew. He dutifully performed his job, but only for the sake of his unit, not out of any sense of noble purpose or grandiose patriotism.

When he returned home, he fell back into his rut of apathy and reclusion. A couple of months later, the call came from Washington asking him if he would consider a special assignment to an ad-hoc detachment charged with overseeing the rebuilding of Iraq—or at least America's substantial role in the effort. He was under no obligation to accept the assignment, he was told, since he had spent two out of the last three years deployed with his unit. He accepted, indeed embraced, the opportunity to play a role in redressing his country's ill-founded aggression, to help rebuild the country he was firmly convinced he and the U.S. had unjustly destroyed. He could not undo the deaths of so many brave Americans, restore to health the injured, or recoup the fantastic sums of world treasure that had been wasted, but conscience would permit his eager participation in an effort to make amends.

As the moon faded and the aurora of the new day became visible, May's sadness became anger when he thought of the aftereffects of the Baghdad rocket attack. The non-treatment, if not maltreatment, of those fine men and women at Walter Reed. How could the administration justify its profligacy—dumping literally billions of dollars per month into an occupation doomed to failure, as any student of history would attest—yet fail to provide adequate care for those who did its bidding? Then, while trying to help a senior officer, to be given evidence implicating her in a scheme of corruption and fraud—ultimately resulting in the death of an innocent bystander, and placing both him and Ginny in harm's way.

Determined to repulse the melancholy, he willed himself out of bed, into the shower. Once dressed, he ambled into the village in search of a strong cup of coffee with the little money left in his pocket. Although the sun had risen, thick fog had descended on the little village, still deep in its slumber. Even without a caffeine crutch, he was invigorated by the damp, chilly air and the fresh smell of the sea, which in combination with the hot shower, had the welcoming effect of clearing his head. He stopped walking at the corner of what appeared to be the intersection of two main roads, but not a single car could be seen within the thick haze, nor, he concluded, was he likely to find any open restaurants or cafes. So he turned back the way he had come to peruse the contents of his host's kitchen. As soon as he walked through the door, the delightful aroma of fresh coffee filled his nostrils, accompanied by the distinctive gurgling sound of a drip coffee pot echoing from the kitchen. But it wasn't until he walked into the kitchen, invigorated and with a broad smile on his lips, that he heard Ginny's soft sobs and sniffles coming from the small sun porch in the rear of the house. He paused briefly, surprised to see the fog-shrouded shoreline of Camden Harbor within 50 feet of the porch, then sat down beside her on the white wicker love seat, gently placing a consoling hand on her shoulder.

"Last night, it came back to me. I remember everything now," he said softly, as the tears welled up uncontrollably, "and I am sorry." He lifted his eyes to meet hers. "I am so sorry."

Ginny said nothing, instead, simply grasped his hand tightly in hers. Together, they sat silently gazing out at the bay through teary eyes, watching the fog slowly yield to the sun's relentless assault. Gradually, the mask was lifted to reveal Camden harbor, its vessels resting peacefully in their moors, then, the quaint seaside village beyond was slowly unveiled to complete the vista.

CHAPTER 35

"Do you remember the name Martin Lochridge?" Erik asked May in a tentative tone.

From the sun porch of Lochridge's Camden home, May now had a crystal clear view of the harbor and even the lonesome Curtis Island lighthouse off in the distance. After sitting together most of the morning, Ginny had left him—planting an unexpected peck on his cheek, their spirits uplifted by coffee, conversation, and the natural beauty of the spectacle they had just witnessed—to shower and dress. In a flash of instant recall, the name came back into his consciousness from a conversation with Ginny the day before, but certainly Erik didn't know about that. Then, from the more distant and latent reaches of his mind, he retrieved Lochridge's association with Erik, and as the information coalesced in his mind, it suddenly dawned on him whose house he was in, whose plane had brought him here the day before.

"He's one of your investors, right?"

"That's right," Erik answered. "He's been a major money partner for years."

"I heard the name yesterday, but I didn't put two and two together until..." His voice trailed off as he tried to comprehend why this man would be helping him.

"I know, your amnesia." Erik assumed—correctly, as it turned out—that his friend had been through an emotional roller coaster over the past several weeks. Now was not the time to burden him with something else, something as intense as what Lochridge had in mind for him. On the other hand, Erik expected his friend to be mystified, at the very least, by such magnanimous gestures from a total stranger, if not outright suspicious that Lochridge's motivation might not be purely altruistic.

"But, why—" May scratched his head, perplexed.

"Why would he want to help you and Ginny?"

"Yeah. I don't even know this man, and he just blew a big wad of cash flying us over here, putting us up in this house."

Erik cleared his throat while he formulated his reply. "You may not remember this, but years ago, I told you the story of an investor who came into my office and recognized your picture—one of us together at your wedding—from a lecture of yours he had attended."

"No, not really, but go on." This lapse in his memory had nothing to do with amnesia, but was just the product of a middle-aged brain crammed full of too much useless information.

"Well, it was none other than Lochridge himself. This lecture was actually somewhere close to where you are now. He was vacationing there, in the house you're in, when he heard about a talk you were giving as a guest lecturer for some institute—"

The word 'institute' was all it took to make the mental connection. "Oh, now I remember you telling me about that!" It was a lecture he had given in 1995 for the International Institute for Ethics In Public Administration and Government. In his early thirties and with plenty of idealism still driving him, the tour of half a dozen or so Northeastern colleges and nonprofits was one of the few times in his professional career that he had drawn on his dissertation as the nucleus for a lecture.

"Rockport," he said. "About a five-minute drive from here. Years ago, when you told me about all this, I remember thinking it was just one of life's little coincidences. That was the end of it for me, I guess."

"I know, I know. No big deal." He knew May wasn't attuned to the world of business the same way he was, probably had no idea how prominent—or wealthy—Lochridge had become since then. "The lecture topic. Do you remember it?"

"Of course, but try not to fall asleep on me, ok?" he said jokingly. "America's Democratic Irony and the Need for Constitutional Reform." More than a few times in the past, he had described to Erik the principles underlying his dissertation and the blueprint he envisioned for modernizing the great document, but he was never sure if Erik grasped its importance or appreciated its implications for the country. Erik was less an abstract thinker than he, and as a businessman, more focused on the realities of the present than the ideals of the future. "Why?" he asked.

"Lochridge was in the audience that night in Rockport, claims to have introduced himself to you at the end of it. Anyway, you made quite an impression on him, and through him, a number of others, myself included."

"You? Really? I never thought you gave two hoots about my work!"

Erik grinned, remembering some of their youthful escapades. Lots of partying, loud music, girls and generally reckless behavior. May had grown up, settled down, become serious much sooner than he. While May had his nose in books as a broke college student, he continued the party they started in high school while stationed in Europe. After his discharge from the army, Erik took the advice of his father and plunged head-first into a career in real estate, going to parties, making deals, and going to parties to make deals. Lots of money, expensive toys, and women.

"You're right, Sean, at least up until I married Linda and finally settled down enough to start paying attention to the little bits and pieces Lochridge had been feeding me for so long. He would bring these things up out of the blue—ask me a question like, "What do you think about the gridlock in Congress?" or the war, the national debt, a Supreme Court decision, you name it. To be honest, I thought he was a little off his rocker at first, but he liked talking about it, so I humored him."

"You were good at that with me, too," May said with a snort.

"No offense, but I was never really interested in government, except when it took my money or made my life difficult. Lochridge got my attention, though, when he started talking about how the U.S. was on its way down the tubes. When I stopped working so much, I read, listened, studied what was going on in Washington, and, well, I basically fell in line right behind Lochridge."

May couldn't help but be a little flattered that his best friend had taken an interest in his professional work, but there was more to this, and he knew it. "So he spent all that money on Ginny and me because he's a fan of my work?"

"He wants to meet you, Sean." Erik scratched his head, deciding on the spot to give his friend Lochridge's ulterior motive. "He wants your help to implement your plan."

"What plan?" May asked reflexively, not quite getting Erik's drift.

"Your plan for revising the Constitution, you know, in your thesis."

May laughed out loud. "Not likely, man. Do you know what you're talking about? All of that stuff is pie in the sky—written when I was much younger and not smart enough to realize that it would take an army and a king's ransom just to even get started. And that would probably not be enough, either."

"The king's ransom part has been taken care of," Erik said with sincerity. "As to the army—well, I am trying to recruit one of the generals right now."

With a fresh cup of coffee in hand, May resumed monitoring Camden Harbor from his wicker perch, noting signs of life on the patchwork of docks arrayed around him. It had been at least several years since he had talked to his friend at any length, and their present conversation would have interested him more in a different time and place. But right now, he had more urgent problems on his mind than some wildly idealistic notion of his youth. On the other hand, he owed Erik—and Lochridge—for his present comforts and relative safety, so he would try to humor him a little and avoid sounding too dismissive or patronizing.

"Did you hit the lotto and not even call me?" he asked facetiously.

Fearing he had made a mistake bringing all of this up now, but also realizing that it was too late to change his mind, Erik wished he had Lochridge's persuasive powers, which were far superior to his own, and the almost viral optimism he exuded. It didn't help that he had always felt somehow intellectually inferior to Sean, although it hadn't ever really mattered since their interests were so different. Was his friend simply distracted by the chaotic events of the past few weeks, or had the passage of time and his assimilation into mainstream culture subdued, perhaps even extinguished, his passion? Maybe both. For the time being, he was satisfied they shared a common intellectual interest—whether or not the flame could be re-ignited would have to wait.

"No. It's Lochridge. He's giving all his money to the effort—setting up a trust—"

"You don't understand, Erik. I wasn't kidding about needing a king's ransom. It would take millions—no, tens of millions at today's prices—to fund a sustained PR campaign just to get the word out to enough people to even hope to attract enough donations to—"

"About twenty billion, Sean. Maybe more. He's loaded," he said in a level, serious tone of voice.

"You gotta be kidding me," he said, astonished. "It's obvious he has some money—that Dassault Falcon I flew on cost a few bucks—but billions?"

"Yes, billions." Erik considered his next words carefully, wondering if he had said too much already. "Sean, I can't tell you too much more—not right now. But I want you to know he has been planning this for a while—has a group of people he put together who've been waiting for the right time to spring into action. He thinks that time is now."

"Now, huh? Hmmm…" During his recent deployment, May had lost touch somewhat with the political and economic conditions of the country. Under normal circumstances in his civilian life, he was analytical, accustomed to reading the major daily newspapers, listening to network news, and regularly visiting the web sites of other major media outlets. But army life in the Middle East had left little time to read anything in depth or think critically about goings on back home. Still, he knew enough to agree that all was not well in the United States of America.

Erik surmised correctly that Sean was taking this all in, along with everything else he had to think about. "It was just a few weeks ago that Lochridge made this decision. He called me to get in touch with you and well, all this happens to you—and Ginny."

"It's intriguing, Erik, I have to admit. Once I get my life back together, I'll meet with him. It's the least I can do to re-pay him for all of this."

On the spur of the moment, Erik blurted out a suggestion: "Why don't you talk to him now? He wants to help you, Sean. And Ginny, too. With all of his resources and contacts, why not let him"

With nothing to lose and everything to gain, he agreed.

"I'll set it up. He's in Germany—"

The loud clang of a doorbell interrupted him, followed instantly by incessant barking as his dogs raced toward the door. "I've got company. I'll call you later."

CHAPTER 36

Erik was a dog lover, had always had at least one all of his life. With a few acres and a large house in suburbia, he was now up to three, despite Catherine's tepid protests. They stink, she constantly told him and, at least twice a week, there were murmurs about fur all over the house. Occasionally, he would gently remind her that his dogs came with the package when she decided to marry him, and besides, she loved him anyway. They were great watchdogs, he cajoled her when her protests became acute, good protection for her when he was away on business trips, which was rare, but it sounded nice anyway. The ferocious barking of several dogs would make any would-be intruder think twice, and, as she had learned many times, wake her from a deep sleep.

The two-story foyer was the center of the traditional colonial floor plan, living room to one side, dining room to the other, with a hallway leading to the kitchen at the rear. Rather than blocking all three to keep the dogs out of the foyer, he had trained them to mount the stairs, which he then blocked with a portable gate Catherine picked up at one of the baby super stores. With a clap of his hands, they stopped barking and obediently followed him to the stairway. Once behind the gate, they sat, waiting patiently to re-new their barking once the front door was opened.

"Mr. Frese?" Two men in dark business suits—their stocky builds and shortly-cropped hair cuts suggestive of a law enforcement or military affiliation—stood before him. While they both shot furtive glances at the cacophony of barking behind him, Erik noted the giant black suburban that would block Catherine from getting up the driveway when she returned with their lunch.

"Yes?" He replied, looking at his own frown in their dark sunglasses. Living in a gated community with hefty homeowners' association fees to pay for private security was supposed to prevent this type of intrusion.

"Army CID," the one said, flashing a badge from a leather case he had been holding in his left hand. He snapped it shut, and placed it in his pocket in a fluid motion, eliciting some agitated grumbling from the dogs. "We are investigating the disappearance of a Sean May, who listed you as his emergency contact."

He had barely seen the badge long enough to distinguish it as a badge, let alone to read it. Being former army, himself, he knew the acronym stood for criminal investigation division, a shadowy military police force that combined elements of police detectives, Secret Service agents and forensic investigators. Most soldiers would never interact with CID or see one of its agents. Erik certainly never had. He cocked his head, raised his eyebrow, questioningly. "Disappeared?"

"Yes, sir. He had an unfortunate, uh, incident recently. Has he contacted you?"

"What sort of incident, Mister—what did you say your name was?"

"My apologies, sir. I'm special agent Chambers, this is Watts," he lied, nodding his head to his partner. "Yes, sir, he has walked away from a military hospital in Washington. He was injured. We are trying to find him."

"For his own safety," Watts added, responding to Erik's contrived expression of grave concern.

"Is he all right?" Erik asked, feigning ignorance.

"Sorry, sir, I have no information about his medical condition. Only the obvious—that he was well enough to walk."

Erik briefly considered asking to see their identification again, but knew this might cast suspicion on his intended denial of knowing anything about May's whereabouts. It should be fairly easy, he surmised, to verify their legitimacy later. If they were CID, Sean, though safe for the moment, now had a bigger problem; for the arm of federal law enforcement was indeed a long one, and Maine was within its reach.

"I'm sorry, gentlemen, but I haven't talked to Sean—Mr. May—for a very long time." As though on cue, Catherine pulled into the driveway and came to a stop behind the black suburban.

They both turned to look at her, then back at him. Chambers reached into his vest pocket, too suddenly for the dogs, and retrieved a pen and notepad. As the dogs clamored—Erik made no motion to stop them—he quickly scribbled a phone number, tore it off and held it out to him.

"Thank you for your time, sir. If you hear from Mr. May, please contact me immediately at this number."

The lack of a formal business card only solidified his misgivings about the two.

"What was that all about?" Catherine asked him, as she walked through their garage entrance carrying a brown bag and a bottle of wine. "Chinese," she answered the question on his face.

He kissed her on her cheek as she placed the wine bottle on the counter. "That—I'm pretty sure—was a big crock of shit."

CHAPTER 37

It was nearly 11 p.m. local time when Martin Lochridge placed the call. The six-hour time difference was sometimes advantageous, but more often than not, it proved inconvenient, if not annoying. From conversations with Erik and through his own research, he now knew quite a bit more about May's predicament than he had earlier in the day. With May's blessing, Erik had told him about the flash drive and its incriminating contents. The visit from the bogus CID agents led them both to the conclusion that Ginny and May had successfully eluded their pursuers for the time being. It was obvious this firm, KPH, was running scared, desperate to protect its golden egg of government largess and the continued freedom of its beneficiaries, both of which hinged on a device about the size of a deck of cards in the possession of an injured national guard major. The probability of their being found in Camden was low without sophisticated investigative techniques, which by all appearances so far, KPH did not possess. But the federal government did have many techniques and resources available to it to find fugitives, and, although there was no direct evidence they were treating him as one, their continued safety in Camden was by no means assured.

Lochridge knew too much about telecommunications technology to feel secure about having an extended international phone conversation with May and was especially uncomfortable with knowing he would be using a portable phone, the only phone in his Camden home. The less said, the better, he reasoned. So after some perfunctory introductions and the expected expressions of gratitude for his help, he steered the conversation to its purpose.

"I know Erik has filled you in on what transpired earlier in the day and the fact that your home in Ohio has been burglarized, which is more than likely how they obtained a copy of your emergency contact data form. I think it's safe to assume your home is being watched."

May was parked where he had been all day—on the wicker love seat overlooking the harbor. Sounds and smells of a meal being prepared wafted into the sun room from the kitchen, as Ginny engaged in what she termed therapeutic cooking. Although Lochridge was a stranger, by his actions, he had demonstrated trustworthiness, which, of course, had been reinforced by the encouraging words of his best friend.

"Yes, and safe to assume that they have all of my other personal documents, too," he agreed.

"I know one of your immediate concerns is having no identification, no access to money, so—"

"Actually, my immediate concern is for the safety of my uncle, whose contact information was also on the form. He hasn't answered his phone this afternoon."

Erik spoke for the first time. "The retired Miami cop, who lives on a houseboat, right?"

"Yes, the one and only" May answered. A hard-drinking, gambling, thrice-divorced, battle worn cop, who had gone to Miami in the 1960s when it was a thriving tourist mecca, only to watch it decline throughout his career. The houseboat had been purchased on a whim when he elected to receive a partial lump-sum pension distribution, and two months later, hurricane Andrew took aim at the city. Unable to afford the expensive insurance on his new floating home, his only option was to leave, slowly cruising up the intracoastal waterway until reaching Maine. "I think he's still living in Boothbay Harbor—at least, that's where he was the last time I talked to him."

"When was that?" Lochridge asked.

"When I was here for the lecture you saw me give. I stayed with him."

That, they both knew, had been nearly ten years before, so with the mobility of a houseboat, he could very well be living anywhere accessible by such a craft. "Erik, let's get the local cops down there to check on his uncle. Sean, whatever you do, don't drive down there. Unfortunately, our friends may be a step ahead of us on this. As an ex-cop—well, let's hope he can protect himself if necessary."

His allusion to "friends" they all understood to mean the fine folks at KPH, who—they were also aware—were quite capable and willing to murder.

"He's protected, all right," May assured them. "And probably drunk as a skunk, which could make for a big mess."

"Let's see what the sheriff comes back with, then we'll figure out where to go from there. Now, Sean, as I was saying, you will be receiving a package—a small box—by Federal Express tomorrow morning. It is addressed to me and the sender is Regency Holdings, LLC in Alexandria. In it you will find $5,000 in cash, a cell phone, and applications for an emergency birth certificate and passport. Ignore these for now—I'll explain later."

"Mr. Lochridge, that's—"

"Martin, please," he interrupted.

"Yes, well, Martin, that's not necessary. Ginny and I are fine—"

"Ginny needs to stop financing you with her credit cards. She's leaving records everywhere you go. No ATMs either. As to the identification, that's completely up to you, but I suggest you do it now if you're going to do it at all—before Uncle joins the chase, if he hasn't already."

May inferred the reference to "uncle" was to Uncle Sam, the army, the feds. "Thank you," he said meekly, and let out an audible sigh without even realizing it. For Ginny's sake, he was going to have to confront his dilemma head-on and quit avoiding the inevitable. They could not continue to run and hide indefinitely. As undesirable as his two alternatives were, the only practical one was to turn themselves in to the authorities, who could offer protection, deal with KPH, allow Ginny to return to her life. Despite his misgivings, the army would have to do with him what it chose, which in any case, was preferable to being dead.

Lochridge and Erik were discussing how to stealthily extract his uncle from his boat and transport him to safety.

"We need to find him, get him away from the coast," Lochridge said.

"I know a guy from high school, an ex-cop who got hurt on the job and started a private detective agency. I'll ask him to do a skip-trace on Sean's uncle to find him," Erik suggested.

"Good," Lochridge said. "As soon as we find him, we'll—"

"I have to turn myself in," May interrupted. "This is crazy."

"I would advise against it, at least for now," Lochridge replied immediately. Mindful of the government's liberal stance towards eavesdropping, he chose his words carefully. "There is something that I discovered earlier today that I haven't told you, either of you, but it will have to wait until tomorrow—when things are a little more secure. Sean, for tonight, just hang in there and try to get some rest. I'm sure you could probably use it."

CHAPTER 38

"What can I do for you, Mr. Krug?" Drysdale asked in his customary telephone greeting.

Krug was in no mood for polite chitchat, so he lit into the unsuspecting Congressman in a harsh tone. "It's time for you to call that hunting buddy of yours. We both know the Deputy AG is the one who runs things in the Justice Department, so take him out to lunch, have a few drinks, whatever. I don't need to remind you your retirement plans are in jeopardy, and if we don't get some help, we may all be in prison very soon." Making no pretense at discreetness, any deference Krug normally would have shown him was subdued by the urgency of their predicament. "We need some help and we need it now."

"How dare you speak to me in that manner!" Drysdale shot back, outraged by the insolence "And how in the hell do you know he and I are friends."

Krug, a former drill instructor and an old-school noncommissioned officer, was certainly not the partner chosen to routinely interact with politicians, bureaucrats or anyone else who required diplomatic balm. Originally from West Virginia, he had enlisted to escape the abject poverty of his youth, rising to the rank of Sergeant Major in a 24-year career that had educated him and made him more worldly than was readily apparent by his demeanor. Still, he was more in his element on the front lines, getting dirty and sweaty, making things happen. Hewitt had tried unsuccessfully to coax Drysdale into action, and the three partners had concluded the time for coaxing was over. It was do or die, and a hard-ball approach was warranted.

"Oh, I know a lot more than you think I do, congressman," he said in his thick drawl. "I learned a long time ago that this accent of mine makes people think I'm not that bright. Use it to my advantage. I know something else, too. You're on the ropes same as me, so you'd better stop draggin' your feet and get with the program."

"You want what, specifically?" he asked, making no attempt to mask his indignation at Krug's abrasive mannerism.

"Hewitt told you what we want before. We can't wait until our major is AWOL a full 30 days for the army to classify him a deserter. We need him declared a federal fugitive now, so the nice folks at the U.S. Marshals Service will lead us to him. Then we nab him."

"Oh, it's that simple, is it?" Drysdale spoke in what for him was a characteristically condescending tone, though in this conversation it was made more poignant by his low regard for Krug's gruff, unrefined manner. He was accustomed to dealing with Hewitt, who was polished, articulate, and adept at stroking his ego. It had been easy to rebuff Hewitt's appeal the week before with the reasoning that law enforcement involvement at this stage was imprudent, premature, and inherently risky. His political chips were far too valuable to cash in on foolishness that could very well backfire in his face. That was a week ago. Now, thanks to the inept blundering of KPH the situation was becoming dire.

Exasperated by the imposition, Drysdale stroked his thick, white beard and scowled. "Dammit, you can't even catch an unarmed, injured national guard officer, with amnesia and no money?" Silence from Krug made him realize that chastising him for what they both knew was an embarrassing failure was useless, so he softened his tone. "What happens if this, uh, material falls into the wrong hands—of someone who is motivated, has the expertise to probe its contents?"

"We have friends in the law enforcement community. Let us worry about that. You just tell your buddy that this man is mentally unstable, a threat to national security, whatever. The fact that he's got amnesia, went AWOL and is nowhere to be found should be persuasive enough."

Drysdale was too pragmatic to be comforted by this "trust us" assurance, particularly since it was being offered by one whose competence was in doubt. Hollow assurances might appease someone whose perception and reasoning abilities were not as keen as his, but for him, this approach was fraught with too many risks to ignore. What if this flash drive came into the possession of an entity beyond their collective sphere of influence—some sophisticated big city or state law enforcement agency with the capability to analyze and interpret its contents? Why take the chance, particularly if the major didn't even understand the significance of what he was carrying around with him? On the other hand, though, what if he did?

"The material has been out of your control for nearly two weeks. You can't be certain—"

"It's encrypted and password protected. Look, I've never even seen it myself, don't know exactly what's on it, but Prather said it's useless to anyone who doesn't know the password. Chances are, if he has it on him when he's caught, the damn thing will just be thrown into a safe along with his other personal belongings." Krug paused just long enough to let this sink in. "Nobody has a reason to look at it at all, but if they did try to, they couldn't."

The more Drysdale considered their quandary, the more it became clear this dark cloud would hang over them until the disposition of the drive was certain, and they were absolutely sure that its contents had not been compromised. It was a choice between allowing the nagging uncertainty to continue indefinitely while KPH tried to find May—all the while running the risk that its contents would be exposed or it would fall into the wrong hands—or to use the power of the government to bring this to a swift conclusion.

"For all you know, it may have been lost, or disposed of at this point," Drysdale said very quietly, almost to himself.

"We have to assume he still has it and we're all better off knowing where it is than we are now."

Point well taken, although without knowing who would ultimately apprehend him—it could be anyone in law enforcement from a federal Marshal to a park ranger—there was no way to be assured that this would end their problem.

"I told Hewitt and I will tell you. It is highly irregular for a congressman to intervene in the operation of an executive agency. Yes, the Deputy AG is a friend of mine, but he is very perceptive and this may very well arouse his suspic—"

Krug had grown tired of the patronizing tone of the congressman. As long as he believed the flash drive contained data incriminating him, he had no choice. "Just do it, congressman. Or you're going down along with all of us."

CHAPTER 39

The package arrived a little after nine in the morning. It contained $5,000 cash in $50s and $20s, what appeared to be a common cell phone, and the forms. The handwritten note said "Please call when received, press and hold # 1 on the cell," so May obliged, aware that it was mid-afternoon in Germany, but not knowing Lochridge was now in a different time zone, in route to the U.S.

Erik had called him back with the good news on his uncle late the previous evening. His houseboat was no longer in Boothbay Harbor. A little more checking revealed he had pulled up anchor the previous fall, opting to spend the winter months in warmer climes. His mail was being collected and forwarded to him by a private company specializing in mailing and shipping services, but they would not divulge the forwarding address to him or anyone else, he was told. Whether May's uncle was planning to return or not was anyone's guess, but for the time being, it was reasonable to conclude that finding him would not be easy.

Lochridge had obviously been talking to Erik, since his first words were about his uncle's unknown whereabouts, and his belief that this was actually good news, albeit only temporary. A skilled investigator, he told May, would sooner or later pick up his trail—the inevitable footprints one unwittingly leaves behind wherever they go, whatever they do.

"Now to the really bad news. Yesterday afternoon, your name was entered into the FBI's National Crime Information Center by the Army's Desertion Information Point at Fort Knox. Unfortunately, you are now considered a deserter and a federal fugitive."

"Oh, shit," May said, regretting it immediately. So much for eloquence.

And so much for the good mood he had been in this morning. His first inclination was to reject this news as false or mistaken, and he briefly considered asking Lochridge how he knew this information, but on second thought, it hardly seemed important at the moment. What was much more relevant was that his hand was being forced—he would have to surrender now or be hunted down and arrested like a common criminal.

Lochridge ignored May's epithet and continued in a smooth level voice. "Normally, they—law enforcement—would just wait until you revealed your whereabouts either by getting stopped by the police or by applying for a passport or birth certificate, which, by the way, is why I told you to ignore the forms in the package. It's too late. But your NCIC record is coded—annotated with a special code indicating you are a potential threat to national security. What this means is—"

"A threat to national security! Are you sure?" he asked in disbelief.

"I'm afraid so. As I was saying, what this means is they will be proactive in their searching. They will monitor bank and credit card accounts, watch your house, tap your phone—well, you get the idea. I'm still fairly certain you're safe in Camden, but the more people who see you, the more likely you will be found, particularly as your name and picture are disseminated down to the local level."

"What about Ginny? She's used her credit card here."

"Nothing on her. Of course, the only reason they would have to be interested in her would be aiding and abetting, but the army's desertion people apparently do not know about her—at least not yet."

May was silent, truly at a loss for words. Perhaps he had made a mistake by walking away from Walter Reed, but he felt justified in doing so, given what he saw and experienced there. And the damn flash drive. If it weren't for his amnesia he would not have supposed it contained information potentially useful in restoring his memories, would not have been so eager to view its contents. Yes, all of this could have been avoided by just handing it over to someone at the hospital to be sent back to Baghdad. Was it the source of the supposed national security threat? He had no secret or classified information that could remotely be construed as threatening. Of that much he was certain. No, it was time to end this insanity before anyone else was hurt—or worse.

"Martin, I'm going to the police station to turn myself in. I've waited too—"

"Don't, not yet!" he urged.

"But I've put people in danger. Ginny, Erik, even you. There's one person de—"

"Sean! Sean! Say no more!" Lochridge, ever mistrustful of telecommunications technology, blurted into the phone. After hearing that May had stopped talking, he said, "I am over Newfoundland, on my way to Camden as we speak. I have some things I want to share with you—in person—before you do anything. Just hang in there for a few more hours, okay?"

"Here? Now?"

"I'll be there in about an hour. Just give me a chance to explain, that's all I ask of you."

May uttered a heavy sigh, but after all this complete stranger had tried to do for him—and Ginny—it was the very least he could do.

CHAPTER 40

When he told Ginny that Lochridge was going to be there in person in an hour or so, her reaction surprised him. Rather than saying anything, she simply nodded, squeezed his hand, gave him a friendly tap on the cheek and walked away. It seemed she was beyond words now. Having spent several hours discussing and rehashing their situation, they reached what seemed the inevitable conclusion: turning himself in was the only viable alternative. She would ask for police protection as well—was willing to sit in jail if necessary—until her safety could be assured. First, a shower, then a few phone calls to let people know what they were about to do and she would be ready to go. But after hearing of the conversation with Lochridge and his imminent arrival, she seemed to be relieved, almost welcoming the delay.

From the living room, May carefully peeked through closed blinds for any approaching cars. Theirs was not a through street—the house was at the end of a waterfront dead end—so he expected Lochridge to drive up in about an hour. When a yellow cab crawled up toward him from the main road 20 minutes later, he yelled to Ginny and moved to the side of the window so he could look through the natural gap between the blind and the window's frame unobserved. His nerves were on edge, his palms sweaty, and the last person he expected to see get out of the cab was his best friend, Erik

"I can't believe it!" he exclaimed after a long embrace. "What the he—"

"Martin was supposed to tell you I was on my way," he said, reacting to the surprised looks from both of them.

"I guess I didn't give him a chance. I tried calling you after I talked to him, but—"

"He called me in the middle of the night and asked me to come. Said he would be here," he glanced at his watch, "well, anytime now, I guess."

"In a half hour or so," May told him. "He was over Newfoundland while we were talking to each other about 30 minutes ago—wait a minute!" His expression suddenly became apprehensive as he peeked through the closed blinds. "How did you avoid?—"

"Being followed?" He snickered while he removed his heavy overcoat and scarf. "It started about three this morning with me jumping the fence in my back yard. I borrowed a neighbor's car, drove to Dulles, bought a commercial ticket to Vegas for insurance, then took a cab to Union Station."

Dumbstruck, May took his coat.

"Then I rode the MARC—you know, Maryland's light rail—up to BWI. And here I am." He took a bow just as Ginny walked into the room, toweling her hair dry.

After exchanging greetings with her, she offered him some coffee, before returning to the bedroom to finish her hair.

"What's going on?" May asked, looking at him quizzically.

Erik shrugged. "I don't really know much," he confessed. "If you haven't already noticed, Martin doesn't trust telephones very much. He's worked in the telecommunications industry long enough to know how easy it is to eavesdrop on civilian phones, and he thinks it is being done a lot these days, as part of the war on terror."

May nodded. "He all but told me to shut up a few minutes ago."

"Anyway, I do know that he doesn't trust our government much, which is just the result of knowing too much, I suppose. Frankly, his distrust—no, disgust is more like it—with our government is the reason he's been living in Europe."

Ginny, who had been listening from the other room, blurted, "He's obviously willing to do more than just complain about it like most of us."

"True enough," he said loudly with a nod toward May, realizing that he had told Ginny about their constitutional reform plans. Of course he had—how else would he have explained all of this to her? "As I mentioned before, Martin has been working on this for years, putting together a group of committed and influential people—present company excepted, of course—" he grinned, "and quietly amassing a fortune to make it happen."

With coffee in hand, Ginny joined them in the living room to wait for Lochridge.

"Billions," May said, staring out the window. "That's the kind of money it will take for it to work." He turned to look at Erik and Ginny. "What about family? Lochridge, I mean. Aren't people waiting in line to get his money?"

"He's got one son who he doesn't seem to get along with very well, but knowing Martin, I'm sure he's taken care of him financially. No one else that I know of. Some people leave money to their schools, some to churches, foundations, whatever. He's decided that helping his country is his legacy."

"Incredible," Ginny said, looking at something off in the distance.

"That's why he wants you, Sean. He wants to do everything possible to make this succeed. Any good executive will tell you it's who you surround yourself with that makes the difference between success and failure. He considers you an expert—and he wants you to join him."

May had been much too preoccupied to give Lochridge's ambitions much consideration. As to its possibility, his gut told him yes, it might work. With this much money and the groundswell of popular fervor it might produce, a sustained movement with enough traction to withstand fierce resistance from the entrenched and equally well-financed champions of the status quo was certainly feasible. Whether any meaningful constitutional reform could be achieved was an entirely different story. The founding fathers had erected substantial political and institutional barriers against revising the country's most sacred document, proven by the fact that it had been done only 27 times in over 200 years, a mere 17 if the first 10 amendments comprising the Bill of Rights were excluded. Martin Lochridge no doubt understood it would take a Herculean effort to overcome the inertial resistance and generate enough momentum to call a new convention, achieve consensus on revisions, and finally, have them ratified by 38 states.

Was reform needed? Absolutely. The legislative process, as he had observed during the interludes separating his Middle East deployments, was even more gridlocked than it had been when he was in graduate school: paralyzed, locked in the stranglehold of fierce partisanship. In a perverse departure from the original intent of the Framers, Congress was dominated by career politicians, whose tenure was unassailable and often measured in decades. They were primarily accountable to a cadre of wealthy and influential special interests, free to disregard the popular will of their constituencies. As severe problems confronting the country were largely ignored, the public confidence in their government's capacity to solve them rightly waned.

Was now the right time to appeal to the patriotic sensibilities of Americans? Perhaps. But one thing was without question: having a twenty plus billion dollar benefactor willing to finance the attempt was an opportunity he and the United States of America would not likely have again.

"Here comes another cab!" Ginny nudged him into the present.

"Whatever you are thinking," Erik said with a nod toward the approaching cab, "whatever your impressions of him, just remember, it was your lecture that was the catalyst. You told him it was possible—he believed you."

As is so often the case, the physical appearance of Martin Lochridge did not match the mental image formed during their several phone conversations. That he was older was no surprise. His hair was white and thick for a man who must be pushing seventy; his frame, gangly; his gait, somewhat tentative. The strong baritone telephone voice, on the other hand, had suggested its source was a man with a more formidable physique.

"Travels light," May quipped at the absence of any luggage.

"Is he ill?" Ginny asked, as he paid the cab driver.

Erik did not answer, rather, he simply stood at the open door, taking in the shocking appearance of a man in decline, who had aged considerably since they had last seen one another less than two years before.

Erik made the introductions. Dressed in a charcoal gray business suit, up close, his presence was impressive enough, evidenced by steely eyes and the firmness of his handshake. Yet, Ginny's perception was right; May sensed there was something ailing him, weakening him prematurely.

Ginny offered coffee, which he declined, instead, privately offering his condolences to Ginny for the death of her friend while Erik and May refilled their mugs in the kitchen. Some ensuing genial small talk included a discussion of Ginny's job with CRS—something of unmistakable interest to Lochridge—compliments to him on the house and surrounds, a profusion of gratitude for his help, and an apology from Lochridge for not informing May of Erik's imminent arrival. For his part, Lochridge made no effort to steer the conversation towards the inevitable topic for which he had traveled across the ocean, apparently willing to let it progress naturally to that point in relaxed fashion. Erik's presence, May was certain, was intended to make him feel more at ease, and it was he who led the conversation to the business at hand.

Erik pulled a folded stack of documents from his vest pocket. "Sean, I printed out the files for you before I left—definitely, some very interesting reading." Erik had been the one to suggest copying the files from the flash drive to his notebook before putting them on the plane to Maine. He reached out to hand them to May, but May signaled to hand them to Lochridge instead. "Martin has a copy already."

"Good," May said, praising his friend's initiative. "The cops will have fun with this, don't you think?"

Lochridge, who had been admiring the view of the harbor, turned to look at him. "Sean, I have some very real concerns about your plan to turn yourself in to the authorities—at least in the short term."

"So I gather," May said. "I don't see any other alternative. The only way to eliminate the threat to Ginny's safety and allow her to return to normalcy is to turn this matter over to law enforcement. Ask them for protection."

All eyes shifted to Ginny, who was obviously moved to hear that May's primary concern at this point was for her well-being.

"I agree with your conclusion," Lochridge said, again making eye contact with May, "just not the timing."

They all looked at him in anticipation of expected elaboration.

"You see, I have been observing all of this from afar—objectively, you might say." He rubbed his chin thoughtfully as he formulated his explanation. "Erik has probably told you by now that I have been involved in government contracting work for many years primarily in technology, and more recently, as a landlord for federal agencies in and around Washington. You need only watch the news or pick up a paper to see that corruption is pervasive, and our current Congress and administration both seem especially predisposed to questionable influences from private interests." He leaned forward, tapping the printouts on the coffee table. "I have suspicions that there is someone inside the government feeding information to—this firm…"

"KPH," May and Ginny said in unison.

"Yes, KPH. After looking through these documents—well, of course I can't be sure, but my intuition tells me with this much money at stake and now with this trumped up desertion charge, some high-level people might have their fingers in this pie."

Ginny raised an eyebrow. "Are you implying that we can't trust law enforcement to protect us?"

"Until we know who's involved in this, I would trust no one if I were you. One of those spreadsheets shows many disbursements—amounting to several hundred thousand dollars over a span of about a year and a half. All the coding is beyond me, but I'm sure some of them are account numbers—probably at foreign banks—while others most likely identify the recipients. "I—we," Lochridge nodded to Erik "searched for a code listing, but not surprisingly, found none." A small lobster boat on the harbor drew his eyes away. "No, this thing is much bigger than a little government contractor and an army lieutenant colonel."

"How big?" May asked.

"I didn't add it all up—" Ginny began.

"Millions," Erik said.

"Tens of millions," Lochridge corrected, again turning to look at May. "When you mentioned turning yourself in, my first thought was NCIC desertion entry and the obviously fictitious national security threat code. Somebody with government authority is responsible for putting that on that system. And it most certainly was neither KPH nor your former commander."

Erik leaned forward, looking at the floor, folding his hands in front of him. "Usually, it takes a minimum of 30 days for a soldier absent without leave to be removed from the roles and reclassified as a deserter. But, in Sean's case, it hasn't even been three full weeks yet." He shook his head in disbelief.

"Yes, even under normal circumstances, this would be unusually harsh treatment. In Sean's case, though, you have a brain-injured National Guard officer, with amnesia, on his third deployment to the Middle East—as a volunteer, no less."

Ginny, who had been quietly taking this in, took May's hand in hers. "I agree with Martin. We all know you are not a national security threat. Therefore, the desertion thing is not legitimate." She looked at Erik, then Lochridge. "If we surrender to the authorities, we very well could be in as much danger as we are now."

They both nodded, grimly.

May looked at Erik with a helpless expression. "So we are damned if we do, damned if we don't. But we can't hide forever."

"I came here not just to introduce a problem, but also to offer a solution," Lochridge said, turning to May and Ginny.

May saw that Ginny looked hopeful, but he, himself, was skeptical. "We're open to anything at this point, I think," he said.

"I propose to have a friend of mine deliver a copy of the flash drive, along with a detailed explanation drafted by either one, or both, of you with any and all information you feel comfortable divulging, to the Department of Justice." When he saw May's contorted expression, he held up his hand, signaling to let him finish. "Although I know the FBI director personally, I think it best to keep your connection to me hidden as long as possible, which is the reason I don't just deliver it to him myself. The person I have in mind is a Senator I have known for many years and who owes me a favor or two." Grinning, he paused to take a drink from his water glass, and then continued. "In any event, my Senator friend ranks high enough that he should command the personal attention of the director to your case. While the FBI investigates, you two can be my guests in Germany until such time as your safety in the U.S. is assured."

Ginny and May exchanged uncomfortable glances, while Erik, who was as surprised by this as they were, shot Lochridge a look of astonishment. "But they don't have passports," he said, hands outstretched.

"Which explains one of the main reasons I am here. The idea came to me out of the blue—as Erik will attest, some of my better ones do." He cleared his throat, and clapped his hands together before continuing. "Anyway, my home is in the far western part of Germany, very close to the border with Belgium and the Netherlands. The little single-runway airport I use is actually in a Dutch town, called Maastricht, which is hosting the European Fine Arts Fair, beginning tomorrow, and which attracts a fair number of notables from all over the world—most of who fly in on private jets. To please the VIPs and accommodate the 150 or so planes that fly in for the Fair, the manager suspends his normal rules and allows cars to drive onto the tarmac to pick up passengers. Door to door service. This is our opportunity to get into Germany without any identification—we go directly from my plane to a limo to my home."

"Very nice, Martin," Erik said. "But what about getting back?"

"We'll get the consulate to issue them temporary emergency passports. They do it all the time."

May and Ginny traded stunned glances, then May folded his hands and said, "That's quite an impressive plan, Martin." He looked at Erik for encouragement. "I don't know what else to say…"

Lochridge raised his hand dismissively. "Say you'll come. Stay until it's safe to return."

"Germany. Wow," Ginny mused.

May looked at her, his expression pensive. Pangs of guilt he had been experiencing lately were becoming more frequent and harder to bear. "Ginny, this could take a long time. I'm thinking of your job. Your friends. Your life!" he said with an almost apologetic tone.

She stared blankly at her feet as her mind raced. "Believe me, I'm thinking about my life—our lives—too. I think we should keep them. I'll worry about the job later."

CHAPTER 41

The Knox County Airport at Owl's Head Maine was a short five-mile trip from Camden. They dropped Erik off at the small terminal first—his plane was not scheduled to leave for another hour—then drove right up to the re-fueled Dassault Falcon. Two pilots greeted them all on the tarmac, and the younger one escorted May and Ginny on board. As they settled in for the long overnight flight, Lochridge had a brief word with the senior pilot. By the time they were airborne, it was nearly 7:30 in the evening. In a unanimous vote, they all had agreed to delay their departure long enough to consume a feast of lobster, hush puppies, cole slaw and French fries at a little waterfront place a short walk from the house. The owner, a former software engineer whom Lochridge had befriended years before, seemed startled by Lochridge's changed appearance, promising an extra helping or two of hush puppies to help fill him out. This meal, Lochridge explained, always made it easier to get some sleep on the eight-hour flight to Maastricht, which he had learned was crucial on the eastbound trip to Europe. A six-hour jump forward combined with the eight-hour flight, he told them, would put them in Maastricht at 10 o'clock the next morning, disrupting the body's circadian rhythms enough to cause a severe case of jet lag.

Despite the friendly travel advice and the large meal, May was still wide awake three hours into the flight, while both Ginny and Lochridge enjoyed a peaceful slumber. It wasn't for lack of comfort, for the cabin was furnished with fully reclining leather seats that, with a push of a button on the armrest, would provide their occupants with a warm massage. Each had a flat screen monitor mounted to a swivel arm for private movie and television viewing. The 25 by 6 foot cabin was only dimly lit and comfortably warm, but try as he might, May just could not turn his mind off.

He stood and stretched, looking fore, then aft along the length of the cabin. This Falcon was a little larger, a little newer, and quite a bit more luxurious than the one that had flown them to Maine. He walked up to the small galley where one of the pilots was fixing coffee.

"Trouble sleeping?" he asked, knowing full well the answer.

"A little." May started rummaging through the refrigerator for a caffeine-free beverage.

"Dramamine's in the middle drawer," he said, pointing at a birch burl cabinet behind him.

May opened a Sprite, and sipped slowly while he contemplated inducing sleep artificially. A hissing noise filled his ears providing relief from the pressure in his head. "How high are we flying?"

"Cruise altitude is 41 thousand, at 880 kilom—about 550 miles per hour."

"No wonder," he said, touching his right ear with his free hand. "Seems pretty high."

He nodded. "We generally try to stay above the commercial traffic. On a trans-Atlantic, most of it will be a few thousand feet below us."

"I see you've met my ace!" Lochridge said ambling up to them. "Telling war stories again, Chet?"

"No, sir," he replied respectfully. "Just after some mid-flight fuel." He nodded, smiling at the two styrofoam cups in his hands, then slid by May to head back to the cockpit."

"Flew Tomcats in the Navy," Lochridge said in answer to May's unspoken question. "Claims to have hit a couple MiG-29s and a Mirage F-1 in Desert Storm. I know he's a damn good pilot." He yawned.

May sipped his sprite, watching Lochridge as he tore into a bag of Oreos.

"Help yourself. I think there are chips and crackers in that cupboard behind you." He opened a carton of milk and took a long drink, looking at May's bloodshot eyes. "Guess you saw the beer, the hard stuff is out in the cabin. Oh, there's Dramamine and Benadryl in that middle drawer—if you need it."

Alcohol would just keep him awake unless he drank a lot of it, which was counterproductive. So he gave in and helped himself to a couple of Benadryl.

"This is all going to work out for you and Ginny," Lochridge predicted with a gentle pat on the back. "Meanwhile, you will be safe."

May swallowed the Benadryl and leaned back on the Formica countertop. "My head is spinning from all I've been through the past few weeks. I owe you more than I can ever re-pay—"

He held up his hand, shaking his head. "I expect nothing of you in return, Sean. Erik may have already told you, but I asked him to invite you to fly over to consult with our group a little later this year. Now, with all of this—" he fought back a yawn "well, I'm just glad I could help you. I have admired your work for years and would appreciate any assistance you would be willing to give us."

"Yes, of course. It looks like I will have plenty of time on my hands, it's Ginny that concerns me."

"She will be fine," he said with confidence as he glanced back at the cabin where she lay under a heap of blankets. "I will make certain of that."

May nodded, steadying himself against a ripple of turbulence and the anticipated punch of the Benadryl. He felt reassured by the assertive tone in Lochridge's voice, though he did not know its basis. That he was well-connected in Washington, he had no doubt, so perhaps he was thinking of using his influence to smooth over any rough edges with the CRS. Whatever he had in mind, there was not an inkling of doubt in his tone about its ultimate outcome.

"Let's sit for a minute," Lochridge said, teetering toward the two aft chairs behind the bulkhead. "With all you've had on your mind, have you been able to give our project any thought?"

"Just a little," May confessed. "I am definitely intrigued, particularly since I had reached the conclusion years ago that a second constitutional convention was just a fanciful notion—theoretically possible, but not realistic."

He tossed the last piece of the Oreo in his mouth and chased it with some milk. "You might think me foolish, or at least overly optimistic, but I have to think a well-implemented plan to reform our government will resonate with the American people. And with the exception of a little for my son, I'm ready to stake everything I have on it."

Twenty billion was enough to buy most countries, May thought. It was all too much to comprehend in his current state of mind, though his intuition told him failure was at least as likely as success. Maybe he would feel differently once the burdens of the flash drive and KPH were lifted and they were all safe. Without knowing more—much more—about the group, its plans, objectives, and so forth, he would be the fool for making a hasty and premature judgment, one way or another.

"Why take such a fantastic risk?" May asked him, without consideration for how the Benadryl might soon start to affect his comprehension.

Lochridge did not hesitate in the least before replying. "If nothing else, I hope you will come to understand and appreciate my motives." He looked at his watch, then at May, who, whether feeling it himself or not, definitely looked a little hazy.

"I admit it astounds me that it would ever occur to anyone to undertake something like this." May was in fact starting to feel the effects of the drug, but his intent facial expression begged for Lochridge to elaborate.

"I guess we all would like to leave some kind of legacy. I'm no different." A deep frown settled over his face, and he let out a heavy sigh. "Like most people, throughout my life, I have been involved with various causes and organizations, some of which I care about more passionately than others. Years ago, when I started thinking about my own mortality, I had several lengthy conversations with a lady who called herself a planned giving coordinator—"

May nodded his understanding of the term. "We have one at Denison," he said, "constantly after the alumni for bequests."

"Exactly. I think most larger charities, colleges and universities have one these days. Anyway, she came up with this complicated proposal to set up a foundation to give my money to all these different causes and organizations over time—charitable remainder trust, I think is what it's called."

Again, May nodded his understanding, sipping his Sprite.

"My business interests at the time were beginning to generate income I never imagined possible." Not one given to talking freely about his success, he looked down in a sign of genuine modesty. "I have never been frivolous, so I wanted the biggest bang for my buck, which made the trust idea appealing. A gift that would keep on giving to causes I care about. But the more I thought about spreading my money out over a fairly broad range of interests—who knows? some of them maybe conflicting with each other—the less practical it seemed, at least in terms of my bequest having an appreciable affect on any of them."

"I see your point," May agreed.

"Well one day as I was packing up my office to move into a new building, I came across some of my favorite political science texts—a collection I started in college and added to over time until it filled many shelves. By the way, I have everything you have ever written, or at least everything that I have been able to find."

May took this as a compliment. "Thank you."

"I re-read the classics—you know, Locke, Hobbes, Rousseau—and some of the modern philosophy, including yours. Then, one day, it just hit me. Why not apply the same principles to giving away money as I had used to make it? Principles such as leverage, concentrating resources for maximum impact, and control, to name a few of my personal favorites. Instead of a meager attack on a few symptoms of America's many ills, why not try to make the whole body as healthy as possible?" He placed his drink on the counter and gestured with his hands. "Of course, I am assuming you accept the premise that our country is sick, but you of all people understand the systemic flaws in our government."

"Indeed, I do," May said. "Partisan gridlock is the main culprit—it prevents the legislation we must have to address our problems in any meaningful way."

"In my opinion, the United States is on the fast track to ruin because of it. The waste of life and treasure has been nothing short of astounding. But it is the financial mismanagement that will soon create the very mass instability—if not hysteria—the Founding Fathers feared most. We will soon cross the line and begin our headlong descent into the abyss."

On the fringes of academia, May knew some alarms were being sounded about rapid deterioration of the nation's finances, which, according to many, would eventually result in either some very painful reckoning or a catastrophic failure. "I know there are many who agree with you," May said, unable to fight the urge to yawn.

"And many who disagree, too," Lochridge admitted. "If the evidence is presented to the American people and they are given the opportunity to take control—to correct the systemic problems that are hastening our decline—our country might make a transition from one dominated by economic elites, whose main interests seem to center around creating optimal conditions for production and consumption of material goods, to one that places the highest possible value on the human condition." Lochridge beamed at May as he reached his conclusion. "It is a calculated risk. The colonists took a huge risk in breaking with England, as you know so well—amidst much internal dissent among them—but the payoff was the greatest nation the world has ever known. If it can be saved and made to thrive, the potential impact on humanity is incalculable. It pales in comparison to anything I could hope to achieve by giving my money to a batch of charities."

"Impeccable logic," May said, nodding "for those agreeing with the premise of the idealists who believe that a rising tide lifts all boats. But as I'm sure you know, there are more than a few who feel that the cure could be worse than the disease—the dreaded runaway convention that throws the baby out with the bath water, turns the country on its head."

"As you and others have argued, that is a risk inherent in any convention initiated by the people."

"A risk that can be minimized procedurally," May added.

"True enough. But I think it unlikely that rational Americans would see any need to re-write the whole Constitution. It makes no sense to kill a functioning body to cure its ailments. The basic structure of our government and the Constitution that is its foundation are fundamentally sound. They only need some relatively minor tweaks, but the Congressionally-initiated amendment process and the Supreme Court are not up to the task."

May nodded agreement, then yawned. "A convention is the only recourse the people have."

"Yes, and we are fortunate to have a peaceful alternative to another revolution, aren't we?"

"Most fortunate, indeed," May said through another yawn.

Lochridge looked at his watch again and stood. "But I know we need some sleep. If nothing else, you can see how this all evolved for me, how my thought process led me to convince myself and a few others," he winked, "that the awesome potential of our country justifies an extraordinary risk to save it, hopefully improve it for the benefit of all."

"It will never be perfect as long as people are involved," May said, "but it definitely can be made more perfect."

"That is what I want my legacy to be, Sean. Ironic as it may sound as we fly away from it, my country is my fervent passion—has been all my adult life—because the more it thrives, the brighter the outlook for the world. Where would humanity be if those colonists had not taken the risk that they did 230 years ago? Is the world a better place because of it? I think you agree with me that it is. The way I see it, it's a win-win proposition for me. If I can help it survive, hopefully prosper, I have achieved success. Even if nothing is changed, many more Americans will have become engaged citizens involved in a critical assessment of their government. Either way, my life will have had a positive, enduring, and measurable impact."

CHAPTER 42

Lochridge's plan to get May and Ginny out of the U.S. was flawless. Landing at the tiny Aachen-Maastricht airport amidst the steady flow of the rich and famous, who were arriving on private jets from all over the world to attend the European Fine Arts Fair, made it easy for the chauffeured Mercedes to whisk them away inconspicuously and without delay. Tired, but stimulated by the novelty of the experience, May took in the stunning scenery along the short 20-mile route. Ginny, who had slept throughout the entire flight, appeared well-rested and refreshed, while Lochridge looked no different than he had at the moment he arrived in Camden the morning before.

May and Ginny listened intently as Lochridge introduced them to their new surroundings. They were in what was known generally as the Eiffel region in the German state of Nordrhein Westfalen, headed almost due South toward the village of Monschau. They were passing through the hilly forests of the High Fens that formed the northern edge of the Eifel Mountain Range. He pointed out the abandoned checkpoints as they crossed briefly into Belgium and then back into Germany, explaining that the European Union had rendered border crossings as seamless as passing from one state to another in the U.S. The further south they traveled, the more prominent the highlands in the foreground became.

The direct route to his home would take them around Monschau, but Lochridge asked his driver to take them through the village. Another picturesque town, Ginny proclaimed, though, unlike Camden, this one was tucked in a peaceful valley surrounded by dolomite cliffs. Craning his neck, Lochridge pointed up to two medieval fortresses above, then directed their attention down to the Rur river that bisected the town as it snaked its way through the valley. Left untouched by the ravages of war, the centuries-old town was dominated by well-preserved, half-timbered and quarry stone houses capped by high, slate roofs, many of which were richly colored and quite ornate. Smiling tourists ambled about its winding, narrow cobblestone streets and walkways, cameras dangling, as they took in the village's charming ambience.

"Monschau owes its wealth and prosperity to the textile industry," Lochridge said. "Cloth and Cashmere. A clothier named Heinrich Scheibler, who made drapes for the German-born Russian Tsar Peter III, helped it gain an international reputation."

"Wow, look at those!" Ginny exclaimed, pointing to a row of hedges that stood as high as the houses, with entryways, windows and archways carved from them.

"Those are the famous Beech hedges," Lochridge explained. "They can grow even taller, up to 100 feet, I'm told. The locals planted them to help shield their homes from the weather, especially wind. In fact, you can see the houses were generally built at a right angle to the West and North—the main wind direction—with hedges and outbuildings strategically placed upwind for protection."

They had left the village, once again traveling through the snowy landscapes of the rolling countryside.

"Monschau certainly is charming," May said, turning to look at Lochridge, "but what brought you here of all places?"

"My ancestry. And love of history."

"You have relatives from the area?" May asked.

He nodded, shifting in his seat slightly to give a thoughtful response. "When I was still very young, my maternal grandmother told me a story about a little town about a mile from the border with Belgium where her grandfather and her grandfather's parents lived. I was probably eight or nine at the time, so she patiently explained that they made a bubbly drink called beer, which was a very traditional and popular drink in the area. Her maiden name was Bierman, German for brewer or taverner. Anyway, by the time I took an interest in my heritage, all of my ancestors on my mother's side—at least the ones I knew about—were dead, so I began searching for a town in Germany that fit the description. It took me awhile—you know, before the internet, it was like looking for a needle in a haystack—but persistence paid off and eventually, I found Monschau." He pointed to a towering steeple in the town. "That's the church with the birth records. And I also discovered the brewery, the *Felsenkeller*, or cliff cellar in English—so named because it was built into the side of a mountain using dynamite—is still here and still making beer."

"Does your family still own it?" Ginny asked, intrigued

"Oh, no, it's been sold many times over, but I'm told my family's recipes and brewing methods are still used," he said.

"I'd love to try it," Ginny said. "I'm a big fan of good beer."

May nodded, thinking of his recent experience at Brasserie Belge in Washington. "Me, too. German, Belgian—it's all good."

"I'm not a big drinker myself," Lochridge said, "but the Belgians are known mostly for their ales, using all kinds of ingredients, especially sugar and malt. On this side of the border, most brewers still follow the old German Purity Law—the *Reinheitsgebot*—which limits the ingredients to just water, hops, barley, and yeast. I think Felsenkeller makes several different varieties, but it's the pilsner that they are known for."

"I think I read about the law when I was over here for my honeymoon," May said. Ginny thought she saw a slight wince at his recollection. "It's the oldest food quality regulation in the world, I believe."

"Oh, so you've been to Germany?" Lochridge asked.

"No, just France and Belgium. All we had time and money for in those days."

Lochridge nodded his understanding, then looked at Ginny questioningly.

"Me neither. A week in England is my only European experience until now."

As they turned on to a long gravel drive leading down a steep grade, the top of a high turret became visible after they passed through a small canopy of trees. A short distance further, they approached iron gates hinged on two stone stanchions topped with bronze lions positioned to face each other, each with one front leg raised. The driver touched a button on his visor and the gates swung open to allow the Mercedes to pass through and over a crest to reveal a magnificent medieval castle in all its splendor below.

May's jaw dropped at the same time Ginny gasped in awe.

"Oh, my! Is that—is that yours?" she asked Lochridge in total disbelief.

"Yes, indeed," he said, making no attempt to conceal his pride. "But very soon, it will belong to the German people."

May gaped in disbelief as Berg Segur came into full view down in the valley before them. "When Erik said you lived in a castle, I—well, I thought he meant—"

"Just another big house?" Lochridge chuckled. "Those are a dime a dozen, especially the so-called McMansions they are throwing up in the states. This is a priceless, timeless gem."

"And you plan to give it to the German government?" May asked, as they slowly crept toward the castle.

With a shake of the head, he explained, "No, not give, but I made a promise to the last surviving member of the Von Segur family who sold it to me. Apparently, the German government was not in a position to purchase it from him, so I promised to give them the option to buy it-and its priceless contents—from me in 5 years at the same price I paid. I wouldn't agree to such a condition for any other property, but this—this is an opportunity I couldn't resist. You can see why," he said with a sweeping motion of his arm.

A circular gravel drive took them around to the castle's right side, where they crossed a single lane stone bridge over the moat, passing what Lochridge called a garden house. Another gate opened to an ornate archway flanked by Tuscan columns, which led through the thick outer walls into a large, inner court, itself containing several structures, which Lochridge identified as a stable, a bakery, and a storage depot. As the car crept along a narrow stone-paved path through its center, Lochridge explained that the court formed the original farmstead for the castle, which in medieval times, had to be entirely self-sufficient. In the center of the court, they took a left turn, toward another archway that led them under a building that once housed a brewery into a much smaller second inner court. Directly to their front was the main building, with perpendicular wings flanking them on both sides. Like all of the outbuildings, the rear of the main castle was constructed of red brick on a quarry-stone foundation, while its front was covered entirely in stone. A covered walkway led up to the Castle's main rear entrance and extended to either side along its entire U-shaped periphery.

"Look behind you," Lochridge said to them as the got out of the car.

Over the archway they had just passed through, inset in the wall of the brewery was the gilded blazon of alliance of Von Segur, its coat of arms embellished by two mottos. The upper motto said *Amor Verus Nunquam Perit.* Set off by Roman Numerals on either side was the lower motto—*Sit Pax Inviolata Tibi.*

"I'm sorry, Martin, but my Latin is a little rusty," May said, shrugging.

"The top one says 'true love never dies.' The bottom is 'May untroubled peace be yours.'"

"What about the numbers?" Ginny asked him.

"From what I've been able to learn so far, it is the year—1640—that they started the construction of all the building in the outer court." His expression became reflective. "In 1640, the Von Segurs understood what was truly important in life, didn't they?"

The driver retrieved the meager baggage from the trunk and stood patiently waiting for Lochridge, who wanted to give his very first American guests time to admire the splendor around them.

An entranceway on the South wing led them into a portion of the castle he used for daily living. Amazingly, they were standing in a modern kitchen, equipped with late model appliances and cabinetry. French doors opened to a dining room dominated by a handsome black walnut table over which hung a crystal chandelier. They followed as Lochridge led them into a modest, but tastefully decorated living room, furnished in a modern Western European motif, and lined with built-in shelving filled with books. A small television and stereo occupied a corner cabinet. The room's center was dominated by a huge stone fireplace and chimney, which undoubtedly supplied ample warmth to all who gathered around it.

Lochridge pressed a button on a device sitting on an end table. "I'm sure you would like to freshen up after our long trip—I know I would." He glanced at his watch. "I'll have Karla show you your rooms. Let's meet back here at noon, eat some lunch, and if you feel up to it, I'll take you on a tour."

A few minutes later, a woman not much older than Ginny descended the stairway from behind them. "Sir?"

"Karla, these are our guests, Doctor May and Miss Burress. Please show them their rooms." He turned to Ginny and May. "I believe Wilhelm has already brought your bags upstairs. If you need anything at all, Karla here will take care of it."

Ten minutes later, Ginny was standing underneath a blissfully hot shower, while May was face down on his bed, snoring loudly.

CHAPTER 43

He was jolted awake by the screams of several wailing sirens and clanging bells. Still lying face down on the bed, he pulled himself up and looked around the strange darkened room. His watch read 5:42, but having been abruptly roused from a very deep sleep, he felt completely disoriented. Had he adjusted his watch six hours forward? He stood so fast, he had to grasp the footboard to steady himself momentarily, then he stumbled over to one of the windows to peek out through the heavy drapes. The view of the inner court revealed nothing out of the ordinary—the Mercedes was parked exactly where they had left it, no fires, no commotion of any sort. He dashed toward his door and out of the room, surveyed the long hallway for signs of anything unusual, and finding nothing, bolted down the stairs as fast as his still wobbly legs would carry him.

"It's all right, Sean!" Ginny said, as soon as she heard the thumping noise of his bounding footsteps.

He was able to stop himself—barely—before the momentum of his charge carried him crashing into her. She stood near the bottom of the stairway landing with both her arms outstretched, ready to meet his forward progress.

"What the hell?" he shouted over the noise.

"Martin said not to—," she began shouting, then it stopped as suddenly as it had started. "Worry," she finished in her normal tone.

He brushed the back of his hand across his eyes, thankful the racket had ceased, and feeling a semblance of composure returning. "I thought the world was ending," he gasped.

"It's some kind of intruder alert system. Martin said animals set it off once in awhile."

May walked over to a wing-backed chair and sat down heavily, waiting for the adrenaline rush to subside. His empty stomach growled. "I guess I missed lunch."

"It's almost time for dinner. While you crashed, Martin took me on a tour—this place is incredible."

"I can't wait to see it," he said, suppressing a yawn. After a minute or two gazing at the television without really paying attention to it, May stood, his equanimity restored. He walked up to one of the shelves and perused its contents. "I would be happy just exploring this room—did you notice all these old books?"

"I guess the artwork and the photographs caught my attention. Look over here—it's a picture of Erik and Martin in front of a big office building."

He instantly recognized his best friend, wearing a business suit and a hardhat, but he focused on the smiling Lochridge, who in his khakis and polo shirt, appeared younger, more vibrant than he did now. "Looks new—like something you would find in suburbia," he remarked absently, focused on the seeming anachronism in Lochridge's appearance. "Probably one of the projects they worked on together." Abruptly, he stepped back. "Anyway, I think I'll grab a quick soldier's shower while I have the chance."

Karla and Wilhelm served the three of them a traditional German dinner, which to May's and Ginny's delight also included the wonderfully crisp Felsenkeller pilsner. "Karla is a wonderful cook," Lochridge told them, "but most of the time, I end up just eating simple, American food. Believe me, preparing this meal is a joy for her."

"Does she speak much English?" Ginny whispered.

"Oh, definitely. Since I don't speak German, English is a pre-requisite for working here. I'm afraid my Latin didn't help much with German—it's a tough language to learn."

"This looks delicious, Martin," May said. "What is it?"

"Well, first, the meat is *Jagerschnitzel*, breaded pork cutlets, fried, and smothered in a mushroom and onion gravy."

"Mmmmm," Ginny hummed.

"The vegetable dish is *Rotkohl*, red cabbage sautéed in butter with apples and onions. The pasta is called *Spatzle*, and she mixed it with sauerkraut, onion, butter and spiced it with caraway. The bread is German Black Bread—basically a rye pumpernickel—but when topped with the *Plugra*, a rich, European-style butter, is quite tasty." He grinned widely. "I could make a meal out of this by itself. And for desert, a special treat: Karla's homemade *Apfelstrudel* with a scoop of ice cream. If you'd like something else to drink, we have cider, which is what I'm drinking, and I know we have American sodas, milk, and water, of course. Oh, by the way, we also have some locally made Riesling if you'd like to try it later. Believe it or not, there are some very good vintners down along the Rhine."

Lochridge apologized profusely to May for what he confirmed to be a false alarm caused by a wild animal. Although the system had been calibrated to ignore smaller animals, he explained, occasionally, a large beast would trigger one of the many sensors encircling the property. Extensive fencing made such occurrences rare, he assured them, but he had disabled the system until the breech was located.

Even though Lochridge had drunk no beer or wine, Ginny thought she sensed him becoming groggy, lethargic. Perhaps he was just tired from the traveling, she thought, but he did not look well. And it came as no surprise to her when he abruptly excused himself after finishing just part of his meal, inviting them to explore the castle if they wished and promising to disable the castle's interior alarm system before going to bed.

"I saw that coming," Ginny said softly after he left.

May emptied his glass, nodding. "I noticed from the photo you showed me how much older he looks now. That picture is fairly recent—you can tell by looking at Erik—but he looks 10 years older than he did when it was taken."

"Maybe he's ill," she said, savoring her last bite of Strudel.

"Maybe he's just tired. I slept all afternoon, and I'm still beat. Of course, this doesn't help," he touched his empty glass, "but it's good."

Pondering her next question, she emptied the remnants of the bottle they had been sharing into her glass. "What do think he has in mind for you, exactly?" she asked.

"The reform group?" he asked, caught off guard by her sudden shift in the conversation. He didn't look up from his empty glass, did not wait for her reply. "I'm not sure—exactly."

Feeling relaxed by the meal, the beer, the candle light, she took her glass from the table and reclined in her chair, fixing her gaze on May, who seemed lost in his thoughts. "We've had quite a time together," she said, in a quiet, thoughtful way. "It all seems so unreal."

He nodded, then finally moved his eyes off the glass to meet hers. "Yeah, quite a time." He sighed and closed his eyes. "My thoughts are so scattered right now. It's been so crazy—so much has happened—it has been hard to think, you know?"

She nodded slowly. "It has been terrifying and sad, very sad." Then, unexpectedly, she flashed a pleasant smile at him, before saying, "On the other hand, look at us! Sitting in a German castle tonight after eating lobster in Camden Harbor less than 24 hours ago. I have to admit, I've enjoyed parts of it—especially getting to know you."

May looked into her eyes, as a tidal wave of emotion swept over him. In all the years since his wife's death, he had never even considered the possibility of a relationship with another woman, but now he felt the tug of attraction drawing him to her. Perhaps the chains of guilt and grief that had bound him in a tight grip were beginning to loosen, set him free. In fact, quite suddenly, the future and the possibilities it held were exciting, arousing many long-dormant sensations and ideals that a week ago he believed were lost to him forever. Though danger was never far from his thoughts, for the moment anyway, it seemed quite remote; so for now, he resolved to adopt Ginny's attitude, to savor the moment he became reacquainted with living spiritually rather than simply existing in the shadows of his past.

"Thank you for all you've done for me" he said to her warmly.

A broad smile broke across her face, and she said, "The first time I decide to help someone down on his luck, and look what happens?"

CHAPTER 44

In the half hour or so that had passed since he opened his eyes, he had been motionless, listening to the unusual sounds of his novel environs, thinking about the strange twist of fate and the kindness of two people he barely knew that had brought him here. For Sean May, this new day brought a fresh outlook, a new lease on life. The irony of the moment was unfathomable to him, yet, he would not dwell on it: It was the first time in many years he felt truly alive, free of the melancholy that had crushed his soul, extinguished his passion.

It was still very early when he gently tapped on Ginny's door.

"Good morning," May said. "I didn't wake you, did I?"

"Good morning to you," she said, with a smile. "And no, you did not wake me. I've just been lying in bed, thinking." She stood to the side to let him enter. The aroma of fresh coffee snuck in behind him.

"Funny, that's what I've been doing for the last hour. I do some of my best thinking in bed and in the shower," he said, a look of relief on his face.

"We turned in early last night, I guess." She sat down on her sofa, tucking her legs under her robe.

"That's all right. I didn't really feel up to walking around a dark, eerie castle last night. Probably would have got lost anyway."

She chuckled softly. "What were you thinking about?"

"Oh, just a little introspection, I guess." He sat down on the edge of the sofa beside her. "How much I am looking forward to the future, how lucky I am that you came to my rescue in the Thomas Jefferson Building."

"Its' like I'm dreaming," Ginny said. "Any moment now, I'm going to wake up in my bed in Georgetown."

"I feel the same way," he said, "but I don't want to wake up. Nope, I like this dream." He slapped his knees and stood. "Are you ready to explore Berg Segur? I'll run down and grab some coffee if you want to jump in the shower."

Ginny stroked her bathrobe thoughtfully. "You know, I think I'm going to take a long, hot bath. Why don't you go on—I had a tour yesterday, while you were asleep, remember?"

He nodded.

"Besides, I'm willing to bet that Martin would like to have some time to talk to you."

As he had already discovered, Ginny's instincts were dead on most of the time, and this was no exception. Her absence from breakfast was attributed to fatigue from the trip, and after a light meal of *brotchen*, jam, juice and coffee, he and Lochridge, evidently reinvigorated and feeling better, began a tour of the castle.

"The main thing to keep in mind," he explained as he pulled open an old door in the kitchen, "is like most medieval castles, this one was built, changed and extended over many hundreds of years. We just don't have anything this old in the U.S., anything that has had to adapt and re-adapt to so many changes in function, style and ownership. The historical context can be very different from one room to the next."

A short archway led them into the older section of the castle. "To get the full affect of the splendor of Berg Segur, we would have to go outside and walk around to the main entrance on the ground level," he said. "Let's save that for a warmer day—you can't hear it in here, but the wind is howling, and it's very cold this morning."

The room they had entered had no furniture, but a large ornately framed painting depicting a hunting scene hung on the wall to their front. "That is the Roman goddess of hunting, Dianna," he said, pointing above his head at the woman overlooking the hunt. "She was also the goddess of chastity. This room used to be larger—it was a study—but I can't explain why there is no furniture in it. Maybe they took it out when they split part of it off to form the kitchen in the living quarters."

As May looked out the window at the beautiful terrain of the valley, he listened as Lochridge explained he was still discovering—researching and learning about the history of the building and studying the many timeless and priceless Von Segur family artifacts it contained. It was a painstaking process, he said, made all the more challenging by the fact he did not speak German. Further complicating his research was the close proximity to the borders with Belgium and the Netherlands, bringing into the mix elements of those cultures as well. But the time and expense was an investment gladly made to indulge in his love of history and to live in a priceless and timeless national treasure in his ancestral hometown.

From the study, they walked through a doorway into what Lochridge called the "Green Room," which wasn't green at all. "Right now, we are on the first floor of a four-story structure—with a ground floor and a basement below and one above—and we're still in the newest part, completed sometime in the late eighteenth century. Nobody seems to know exactly when it was started and when it was finished," he said, with a quick shrug. "When castles no longer had to function as a defensive works, additions to this and most other castles around here shifted from a Spartan, military character to the more luxurious, and this room is a good example of that transition. In the eighteenth century, this was the count's bedroom, and was named not for the color of the walls, but for the color of his green four-poster bed."

"A huge bedroom," May commented. "Even the master suites in the massive houses they are building in the States are tiny compared to this."

Lochridge nodded his agreement and walked over to a grand piano between two of the room's large windows, which revealed blowing snow and swaying trees in the distance. "Later, in the nineteenth century, the Von Segur family decided to take advantage of its size and views, and changed it to a music room. And it was also used for several weddings."

They continued into a hall with stairs on both sides. A small window directly ahead indicated they had reached the front wall of the castle. May followed as Lochridge took the short flight of stairs to the right, which brought them into an eerily dark passageway.

"You've seen the newest, now I'm going to show you the oldest—at least the oldest part still standing. This was built in the fourteenth century. Only a portion of the foundation from the original thirteenth century main building still exists, and we would have to go outside to see it."

They entered a round room, into what Lochridge called simply the old turret. "The older parts of the castle are very Spartan relative to the eighteenth and nineteenth sections. The German name for the room translates to the 'brick room,' and there are plenty of bricks in these walls," he said with a hand pat on the gray brick. "Three meters thick."

"Amazing," May said, as he looked around him. In less than two minutes, they had traversed 400 years of history, into a period of time defined by warring lords and vassals who were masters of these self-sustaining mini-communities that existed only to serve and protect them.

"You see what I was talking about before we came in here. Other than the small modernized section I live in, most of the Berg is suspended in an earlier time, a monument to 800 years of history through which it and civilization have evolved. Our context is so different in the U.S., we can't even imagine anything like this."

May listened as Lochridge explained the recesses in the wall, each having a wooden bench at its base. They were not actually in the turret, he said, but were small extensions hanging on the outside. One contained a loophole for observation and firing weapons, while the other contained a privy—or toilet—with a drain leading to the moat.

Down one more flight of stairs on the turret's lowest level was the castle's prison, set off by a thick door. A small shaft in the wall was its only source of light and air.

Lochridge placed a hand on the wall, as if to steady himself. "Damp down here, isn't it?"

"What are these?" May asked, pointing to two moldy beams on the floor.

"The one with the channel cut into it was a feeding and watering trough. That is an iron straightjacket for punishment bolted to the other one."

May looked thoughtfully at the beams. "What a contrast. From Victorian elegance and civility to the relatively barbaric dark ages of feudalism and fiefdoms."

"A bleak period for humanity, to be sure. This was the mode of living for hundreds of years until the enlightenment and the renaissance."

May followed Lochridge back to the spiral stairway. "The top of the turret will give you a good panoramic view of the whole property," he said, signaling for May to go first.

"I've only seen two people working here," May observed. "How do you keep this place up?"

"It takes a small army to maintain," he laughed, "but during the winter months, most of the housekeepers and maintenance people come just once a week. In the summer, though, this will be a very busy place."

With his relative youth and good health, May soon realized he was climbing much too fast for Lochridge, so he stopped to wait. Looking behind him, he saw Lochridge was on the verge of collapsing.

"Martin, what's wrong?" He quickly retraced his steps, reaching him in time to prevent his fall. He grasped both arms firmly. "Here, sit down."

Even in the dim lighting of the turret's narrow stairwell, he appeared pasty and red-eyed.

Seeing the concern on May's face, he held up a hand and said, "I'll be all right. Just give me a minute."

"Are you sure? Do you want me to—"

"I'm fine," he said, ignoring May's doubtful expression. He extended his arms to the turret wall on both sides for support and slowly rose. "This stairwell is only 60 centimeters wide for a reason," he said, patting the wall. Only one hostile person could attack up the stairs at a time—and the defender could just stand up there at the top and waylay each one. And this spiral design made it difficult to attack with their long lances and spears."

Lochridge seemed to have recovered, although May was now certain that Ginny's perception that something was amiss was accurate. "Maybe we can do this another time," he said, still not moving, just in case Lochridge began to teeter.

"I'll be all right," he reassured. "I'll wait for you where we came into the turret while you climb the stairs. The view is worth it."

Without saying a word, May seized his free arm and squeezed by Lochridge so that he could walk behind him in case he were to fall. Once they were again in the brick room, May shot a long, worried look at his host.

"Go on," he said. "I'm okay."

May climbed the stairs, wondering if he should have insisted on returning to the living area where help would be more readily available. He decided to feign needing to use bathroom as a pretense after seeing the top of the tower.

On the next level, May found an empty room with a hole in the ceiling, but no loopholes. The only light came from a hole in the ceiling above.

"The room you're in was used as living space in times of peace," Lochridge said loudly, his voice echoing through the stairwell. "The hole was used to hoist up items too large to be carried up the stairs."

"I would have had a bad case of claustrophobia up here," he said, looking up. "I'm headed to the top for a look around."

The spiral stairs led to a small chamber containing a steep set of wooden stairs—more like a ladder—which he followed to the top of the turret. Loopholes were cut at regular intervals all around, providing defenders a clear view and field of fire in all directions. May peered through each of them to get a good feel for the layout of the castle and its grounds. From the water level of the moat below, he guessed he was about 100 feet high, give or take, maybe 10 feet or so higher than the turret on the castle's opposite side. Perhaps he had been too exhausted to notice this yesterday, but the turret on the other side had been modified to include a hexagonal-shaped dome at its top, with arched picture windows in two of the visible sides, a brick chimney on the third. Rugged, but beautiful snow-covered hills surrounded the wilderness around him, with no other houses or buildings in sight. Interestingly, May spotted what looked to be several different sized satellite dishes in the clear-cut outer court below, land that probably had once been used by the castle's farm. He was certainly no expert in satellites, but these looked to be more sophisticated than those used for television—and why three?

A gust of wind blew an icy chill through the turret giving the coatless May incentive to descend the stairs. "You were right, Martin, a magnificent view," he shouted ahead. Hearing no response, he picked up his pace, being careful not to lose his equilibrium as he wound around the circular pathway. "Martin, you still there?" he shouted again.

There, on the floor, Lochridge lay in a crumpled heap, legs buckled, eyes closed. May rushed over to him, falling to his knees. Thankfully,

Lochridge was still breathing normally, as far as he could tell, so he carefully straightened his legs, while calling his name repeatedly. He felt a hand brush across his waist and turned to look at his face.

His eyes were open, though he did not—or could not—try to sit up. The fingers of his left hand were searching his waist and hip area. "In my pocket. A small radio."

The fall had left his pants askew partially blocking the opening to his pocket. Without hesitation, May grabbed his belt with his left hand and pulled hard enough to raise Lochridge's hip slightly and jammed his right hand as deep in the pocket as he could. He clenched his hand tightly and yanked hard, successfully retrieving the small radio, about the size of a deck of cards, before letting go of his belt.

"Transmit button. On the side."

May squeezed hard. "Help! Martin has collapsed!"

"Vere?" came the reply, which he assumed was the voice of Willhelm.

"Turret! First level!"

"Vich one?"

"Old!"

CHAPTER 45

Within a minute, Wilhelm dashed into the turret carrying a plastic bag. With May's help, they raised Lochridge to a sitting position, and while May supported him from behind, Wilhelm dropped a pill into Lochridge's hand, pulled a bottle from the bag and waited. No more than five minutes after swallowing the pill, he was back on his feet, talking and walking as though nothing had happened. He needed to lie down for a while, Wilhelm whispered to May, but Lochridge would be fine, he assured him.

An hour later, a revived Lochridge walked into the living room and asked May and Ginny to join him in his office. They walked through a long hall across the first floor of a wing built in the seventeenth century, passing by several small rooms that had been used as bedrooms for the castle's domestic staff.

"They used black sheets on the beds," Lochridge told them. "It says something about their hygiene. Back then, they bathed themselves an average of three or four times a year—more often was considered unhealthy."

To the right was another of the castle's twelve privies, though there was no door—not even a wall—to obstruct the view, indicating privacy was a luxury not available to domestic servants. "As I understand it," Lochridge explained, "having twelve of these in a castle this size was very unusual. Versailles in Paris didn't even have one."

At the end of the hallway, they stopped to look into the castle's small chapel. "This was built around 1650. It was used for private baptisms, marriages, funerals—in fact, there are some family members buried down below."

They entered the room across the hall from the chapel, which was furnished as a modest bedroom, with two canopied beds, two small chairs, a table and small wardrobe. "This was the bedroom for the senior domestic servants. They even got their own fireplace," he said, resting his hand on a fire screen."

Leaving the bedroom, they entered a small hall, which to May's and Ginny's astonishment, contained elevator doors. Lochridge pushed the lone button and the doors opened instantly, revealing a small car.

"The high tower was modernized at the same time the living quarters in the eighteenth century wing were done. This was also built in the sixteen hundreds, but sometime in the twentieth century, the Von Segur family decided to use the upper floor as a living area. Right below us, though, there is a perfectly preserved seventeenth century bedroom, and a storage cellar at its base. So, basically, they preserved half of it, modernized the other half."

The elevator doors opened to the large dome May had seen from the old turret earlier. Like its sister turret, it afforded dramatic views of the castle and surrounds, but this one was heated, carpeted and modernly furnished.

They all stood in the center of the dome, taking in the panoramic view. "I know the family entertained in here. What they did to modernize it seems a shame somehow, but I guess it was the views that proved too irresistible to them. I have to admit—it does make a nice office. I spend most of my time in here."

May saw that the room provided just about every modern convenience one would need. A kitchenette and what he guessed was a bathroom flanked the elevator shaft on either side. A television, stereo and some other electronic equipment rested in a built-in cabinet. A large L-shaped and glass-topped cherry desk sat by itself to the left of a very large stone fireplace, a leather sofa, chair and coffee table to its right. Above the Von Segur family coat of arms carved into the mantelpiece was the Latin inscription *Bene vivere et laetare*.

"Can you help with the Latin?" May asked, pointing.

"To live well and to rejoice," Lochridge answered, a smile breaking across his lips as he spoke. "They did, I'd say."

Curious as he was, May resisted the temptation to look around at the numerous wall hangings, instead following Lochridge and Ginny to the sitting area in front of one of the room's huge windows. Before sitting, he and Ginny marveled at the snow covered, sunlit valley which opened before them like an artistic masterpiece. Once seated, though, May's eyes were drawn to a small display case hanging on the wall behind Lochridge's chair. In the display, against a black cloth background, hung a Silver Star next to a Bronze Star with a bronze "V" and a Combat Infantry Badge underneath.

"Viet Nam," Lochridge said when he saw May's eyes looking over his head. "Two tours—sixty-nine and seventy-one."

May nodded, saying nothing, but thinking that there must be some interesting stories to go with the stars, which were awarded for gallantry and valor in combat. Maybe there would be time to swap war stories, though he was certain his experiences in the Middle East were dull in comparison to those that won honors among the highest the nation awarded to its military.

While May looked at his medals, Ginny discreetly observed Lochridge. Seated in his chair in the bright light of day, his skin and eyes had definitely taken on an unnatural yellow hue. He caught her eye, but rather than looking away, she rested her chin on her hand, waiting for whatever it was that he was about to say.

"There is something I want you both to know. Something I have not told anyone except my former assistant and close friend, Sally Sexton, whom I hope you will soon meet." Visibly uncomfortable, Lochridge fidgeted with his hands, his legs twitched. "I have terminal pancreatic cancer."

May and Ginny exchanged a quick glance. There was no surprise, just the tacit acknowledgement between them that their suspicions had been accurate.

"I am truly sorry, Martin," May said awkwardly.

He nodded, but there was no perceptible change in his facial expression, which was thoughtful, but not brooding. "Sean, I am the one who is sorry that you had to witness that—that episode this morning." He shifted uncomfortably in his chair. "I don't want to sound callous at all, but your reaction is, well, exactly what I have been trying to avoid. Up until this very moment, I was feeling as though I had been successful."

From the corner of his eye, May saw Ginny fold her hands in her lap. Neither spoke a word out of deference to his obvious aversion to expressions of sympathy, nor could either think of anything else to say to this man they barely knew.

After an uneasy minute or two of silence, Lochridge again spoke. "My health is deteriorating more quickly than I had anticipated. My doctors initially gave me 6 to 12 months, but the way I have been feeling lately, I think I will be lucky to see six."

Fighting her temptation to squirm, Ginny asked, "Is there anything I—we can do?"

Oddly, Lochridge's expression changed at her question, his body noticeably relaxing as though he were somehow comforted by her offer. "Indeed, there is," he said nodding. "Though, you may be sorry you asked."

Both of them perked up slightly in anticipation of whatever it was Lochridge was about to say. Looking at May, he asked, "Have you told Ginny about our discussions—our group and its ambitions?"

"Well, yes—a little," he said, with discernible apprehension in his voice.

"Good," Lochridge said, to May's visible relief.

"The constitutional reform group?" she asked, looking at May, then Lochridge.

Lochridge nodded, addressing her. "For about ten years, we have waited patiently for an opportune time to launch our effort. It is hard to know, of course, whether the conditions are the best they will ever get, but they are as good as they have ever been for a variety of reasons. Public dissatisfaction with government as measured by many different polls is unprecedented. The internet—the keystone outlined in Sean's thesis—has matured enough to offer a reliable foundation for mass participation. And money." He looked down at his feet in modesty. "Well, I don't know about the others, but I've been very lucky. My only regret is that I will not live long enough to do more—or see the results."

They all turned to look at his desk as the telephone began ringing. Lochridge ignored it.

"You two possess talents that would prove invaluable to our cause. Ginny, I had envisioned all along asking for Sean's advice and what I hoped would become active support, but you—well, obviously, none of this was planned—your presence here is another stroke of good luck as far as I am concerned."

She smiled. "Thank you. I'm flattered, but—"

"I would like you both to consider working for us," he interrupted. "I'm afraid I don't have the time to wait for better circumstances to approach you with this, but believe me when I say I would have preferred better—for all of us." He leaned forward, fixing his eyes on Ginny, and rested his elbows on his knees. "I have no idea whether you are interested in any of this or not. Again, all I can say is that you possess critical skills the group will need and my hunch—as a businessman—is you would rise to the challenge if you were so inclined."

May looked at Ginny, whose expression betrayed her bewilderment. Lochridge leaned back in his chair, clasping his hands. Anticipating more, he bit his tongue rather than giving into his impulse to speak.

"What I am proposing is what I believe is a fair exchange. I am offering each of you financial security for the rest of your lives," Lochridge said, looking at each of them for their reaction. "In return, I ask you give our group your time, your effort, your talents for as long as it takes, which, make no mistake, will most probably be a period of years. As you know Sean, this is a huge commitment, one which my intuition tells me you are amenable to considering, although I do not presume your agreement to it." Watching them closely for facial and body language reactions, he added, "I would have put this in writing had any of this been planned, but, as they say, I am flying by the seat of my pants."

Speechless with surprise, Ginny simply looked away and thoughtfully gazed out the window at the thickly forested hills in the distance.

May, who had been made aware of Lochridge's desire to have his help by Erik, nevertheless had been caught off guard by his overture, especially the promise of compensation. The prospect of implementing the framework of his doctoral dissertation was exciting enough—he had never expected to be paid for it.

Sensing that both of them were understandably stunned by his proposal, Lochridge stood and walked to the window, deliberately blocking

Ginny's view. "I am asking for a huge commitment, and I am offering one in return. But I certainly don't expect a quick answer. On the other hand, I don't know how long I can wait, either."

"Martin, you must know that I can't help but be interested in working on this. But I don't think I—" he looked over at Ginny "we—are in any position to commit to anything at this point. Particularly me. I might be on my way to Leavenworth—," he said, referring to the infamous Kansas federal prison.

Lochridge raised his hand to stop him, while also nodding his understanding. "I have people working on that as we speak. In fact, the phone call a few minutes ago might have been to report some news on that front." Still standing directly in front of Ginny, he put his hands in his pockets. "I know you both have your careers, homes, family and friends—all important considerations, of course. But trust me when I tell you that the only ones going to prison will be our friends at KPH."

"The flash drive?" Ginny asked.

"Erik took it—a copy of it—to Washington yesterday and personally handed it to my good friend, Preston Bachman, a—"

"You know Senator Bachman?" May asked in astonishment. Bachman, a four-term Washington Senator, was a nationally known, if not outspoken figure who had been elected to the Washington legislature in the late 1970s on a populist platform, fervently pledging to fight entrenched interests, eventually bringing that same fervor to the nation's capital as a Senator. Despite making enemies along the way, his unconventional political style and good looks commanded more than his share of media attention, with the occasional, if unflattering, reference to the nickname "Pretty Boy" an eager Seattle Citizen-Journal reporter had dredged up from his army days. No one had been able to mount a serious challenge to him and he steadfastly persevered through his first two terms. Steadily increasing seniority and growing popularity won him several key committee assignments in the 1990s, and with them, power and influence.

"I know him very well," Lochridge said, walking to his desk. May and Ginny adjusted their positions on the sofa to see him. "I served with him in 'Nam. He's got more metal hanging on his wall than I do. Well-connected family. His brother runs the family business—LaSalle Bachman Aerospace—which during the nineties, we developed into a world leader in commercial satellite communications. You might know of his brother in-law, Hugo Formato?"

May shook his head, but Ginny, craning her neck, said, "Deputy Attorney General, I think."

"That's him," Lochridge said with the receiver to his ear. "The rumor is he is on a short list for a federal judgeship. And, of course, my favorite Bachman is my long-time employee and confidant, their little sister, Sally."

"Sexton?" Ginny asked.

He nodded while listening to a voice mail message. About a minute later he placed the receiver back in its cradle. "That was Erik. He is already talking with the Department of Justice and Army CID. Let's give him a call."

May and Ginny stood and walked to his desk while he dialed the international call.

"Your name will be cleared, Sean. You both will be able to go home and get on with your lives—lives which I hope you decide will include working to save our country from itself. Just give it a little time."

CHAPTER 46

Krug stumbled into his girlfriend's kitchen, opened the refrigerator and grabbed a beer. With a quick twist of the cap, he leaned against the countertop and took a deep gulp. His eyes were drawn to the brightest object in the room: green numbers on her stove's clock, which displayed 1:49, with the colon between the one and four blinking rhythmically. Another sleepless night, he thought, shaking his head in disgust. As the days wore on, sleep was becoming increasingly sporadic, fitful, the antacid tablets no longer providing much, if any, relief. If they didn't get their hands on the flash drive soon, he was destined to find himself in a hospital before long.

He ambled into the family room, where he stretched out onto the sofa with his head propped up just enough to nurse the beer. TV offered nothing of interest, so he turned it off and studied the shadows created by the moon's luminous glow, but try as he might, his mind soon wandered to where it had dwelled far too long, into the trap of ceaseless brooding about his fate and that of his partners. Krug closed his eyes, tried to think pleasant thoughts, but to no avail. Between the two of them, he and Prather had brainstormed every scenario, considered every angle, taken every possible measure to find the elusive Sean May and Virginia Burress, but they somehow had managed to stay one or two steps ahead, then to simply vanish into thin air. KPH employees were watching their homes, the house in Spotsylvania, the lady's apartment in Occoquan, and to the extent possible, the Library of Congress, around the clock, yet neither of them ever showed. They had searched through May's house initially, then Burress's Georgetown townhouse, hired a private detective agency, all with no results.

The idea had come to him a week ago, while he was listening to one of the men watching Burress's townhouse describe a device he had fashioned from a plastic food container, fishing wire and a couple of wood screws, which he fastened to the door behind the mail slot to allow him to intercept her mail easily and quickly. Checking credit card statements for recent activity had been Hewitt's decidedly low-tech idea for May, but Prather had reminded him that as a deployed National Guardsman with no family, May's mail was being handled through the military postal service, probably still forwarded to Baghdad. But Burress was getting her normal mail delivery every day, and if they were together—the partners all agreed they were—then a credit card statement might be telling. The files in her bedroom office contained old statements from her bank, American Express, Discover, and Visa; the absence of anything recent was concerning, suggesting she was conducting all her banking business on-line. Several days effort at trying to get into her accounts had been fruitless, and no passwords or on-line IDs were found in her office or on her laptop.

So, on a whim, Krug had his girlfriend call American Express posing as Virginia Burress. He hated like hell to involve Lisa in this, to lie to her about why he was asking her to impersonate a woman she did not know, but the three partners had reached the conclusion that it was far less risky than using any of the few female KPH employees. It was surprisingly easy: With nothing more than the account number and the year of Burress's birth, a duplicate statement and a printout of recent activity was on its way—seven to ten business days were required for paper copies.

Day seven had come and gone, as had day eight, and nine. Nothing—except more fretting and dread. It was either prison or make a run for it—

"Matt! Matt!" Lisa's voice echoed through the house.

Krug was startled, having drifted off to sleep. As soon as he moved, he felt the cool liquid of the spilled beer seeping into his t-shirt. "Huh… What?"

Lisa stomped into the family room to find the bare-chested and bleary-eyed Krug dabbing the sofa cushion with his shirt. "Your cell phone!" she said, much too loudly. Then, in a softer tone, she continued, "I answered it when I couldn't find you. It's some guy named Smith."

"Smith. Oh yeah, thanks," he said groggily. He took the cell phone from her outstretched hand, then she turned and stomped away with a loud gasp of displeasure at having her sleep interrupted. "Krug," he said when she was safely out of earshot.

"We got a break," came Smith's nasal monotone.

Krug made a tight, hopeful fist, squeezing the beer from his t-shirt onto his bare leg. "Go on."

"The Amex printout. A couple of charges last week in Maine. Camden."

Krug let the shirt drop onto the floor as he said a silent prayer of thanks. "Good work," he said, snapping the phone closed.

It was Prather's turn to have his sleep interrupted.

CHAPTER 47

On a secure satellite link established through a device Lochridge promised to explain in detail afterwards, Erik gave them all a detailed account of his meeting with Senator Bachman. Apparently, numerous investigations of contractor fraud in Iraq were already underway, and, though Bachman mentioned no specific names, at the first mention of KPH and its principals, he thought he detected some recognition in Bachman's reaction.

"He said to give you his pat on the back, Martin," Erik's strong voice resonated from the speaker. "The numbers he rattled off were pretty amazing—all told, about $27 billion in alleged fraud is currently under investigation by several different law enforcement agencies. I had no idea—the media certainly haven't said much about it."

"Preston mentioned it the last time I saw him. Said he wanted to castrate the bastards." Lochridge looked at Ginny apologetically. "He really doesn't have any role to play, though. I think it's the House—the oversight and reform committee—something like that."

"Yes, he mentioned the committee. And there's a Special Inspector General for Iraq Reconstruction, but he's leery of his close ties with the President. So he went to the Department of the Army and Justice with Sean's disk and the story. Of course, I don't know what he said to whom, but he got results—they are all over it."

"That's what matters," Lochridge said. "The White House wouldn't give him the time of day, but he's got some allies in the bureaucracy."

"They certainly didn't waste any time." May said, imagining that the murder of Cybil, and the big numbers on the spreadsheet got some attention. "What about me? Are they asking about my whereabouts?"

"I asked him about that, and he said the subject of your bogus desertion charge hasn't ever come up. On the other hand, they were quite interested in the guys following us around, impersonating CID agents."

"Are those goons still watching you?" Ginny asked.

"I'm pretty sure they tailed me to Washington. Probably watching my every move. I don't see them around the house, but I live in a gated community. I have to think they're out there, waiting, hoping I'll lead them to Sean."

"Anything I can do at this point?" Lochridge asked.

"Nothing I can think of at the moment. All I—we—can do is wait. Let the pros do their jobs." Erik promised to keep them informed as the situation developed, then said goodbye rather suddenly when his dogs erupted in a cacophony of barking.

The remainder of the afternoon was spent touring more of the castle, led by the surprisingly sprightly Lochridge, who beamed at their reactions to the many elegant furnishings and priceless works of art.

"At one point before the reunification of Germany, three branches of the family lived here at the same time—the von Segurs of the Gold Lion, the Silver Lion and the Buffalo Horns. German inheritance law required possessions be divided among all heirs equally, so they all lived here together, collecting all these priceless items, renovating, building extensions. Then in the early twentieth century, the laws were re-written to allow for the castle to be brought back under the ownership of one branch."

It was in the "Great Hall" that Lochridge stopped to explain his ulterior motive for purchasing Burg Segur. Furnished with two huge tables, 24 chairs and pewter and silver place settings, it had been used primarily as a dining room, but also for dancing and general entertaining. To clear the floor, the tables could be quickly collapsed and hidden in specially designed cabinets behind the wainscoting against one of the long walls. There were two serving hatches, one leading from the kitchen, the other from the bottle room, where wine bottles and dishes were stored. A vomiting hole leading to the moat said much about the table manners of the time, when diners commonly ate until they could eat no more, after which they emptied their stomachs through this hole. The importance of the room was underscored by its many embellishments—its two ornate crystal chandeliers overhanging the cherry Rococo period tables, trimmed in gold and crowned with ormolu mounts, imaginatively laid floors, wider windows and doors, intricate plaster work adorning the ceiling and a smaller version of the blazon of alliance hanging over the impressive marble fireplace. Large portraits of counts and countesses who had lived here through the ages adorned its walls.

Lochridge had taken a seat in front of the fireplace, signaling his intent to stay for a while. Ginny and May both turned to look at him when he spoke. "I envisioned having our organizational and planning meetings right here in this room," a frowning Lochridge said in a heavy voice, laying his hand on the glistening wood of the table in front of him.

"Here?" May asked, surprised. "That sounds complicated."

"Ambitious, for sure. They are all very busy people, but they are fervently committed to our purpose, so I'm optimistic."

"How many?" Ginny asked him.

"Twenty original members," he said, staring at the table, "one already dead, soon to be two. Erik and Sally are trying to coordinate it all. I have faith in them."

"Why bring them all the way to Europe?" May asked, curiously. "Wouldn't it be easier to—"

"Easier, yes," Lochridge interrupted, looking up at him. "But not safer."

"Safer?" Ginny asked. "In what way?"

Still wearing a glum expression, Lochridge cleared his throat, stood and walked over to one of the large windows, looking out at the snow covered forest. "We are all prepared to be viciously attacked by our detractors, of which we expect many. They will accuse us of being subversives, promoting anarchy, fomenting insurrection, and many other similar aspersions, to be sure. We expect that those with the most to lose will resort to desperate measures when they realize the status quo is being seriously challenged. I'm sure either one of you could list many of them—the power brokers and stakeholders—without even trying."

He turned to face Ginny and May, the expression on his face steely and intense. "You two have experienced the cold-hearted ruthlessness of a single company whose livelihood was threatened. Multiply that many hundreds of times—add to it the government itself—and you can see the magnitude of the resistance we could face. What we are proposing to do will be viewed as a direct threat to some very formidable people—the Washington power elite, with their big egos, and voracious appetite for all the trillions of dollars that flow through our treasury every year. There is no doubt they will fight like cornered animals to protect what they have."

"So, you are expecting violence?" Ginny asked him.

"I would not say we expect it—we want to be prepared for it, that's all. Personally, I believe it's quite likely."

"From our own government?" she asked.

"Most especially our government," he said, with conviction. "I would not put anything past them, particularly our current administration, which seems to have a rather low regard for our civil liberties."

May had been listening to Lochridge attentively, all the while reflecting on how ironic it was that a German castle could be the site of such importance to the future of the United States of America. He agreed with Lochridge's assumption that a movement whose purpose was to strip power from the elite and give it to the people would meet with stiff resistance. To the novice, his concerns might be dismissed as mere paranoia, but he knew world history was replete with examples of established elites violently repressing mass attempts to seize their grip on power and control.

"So, you are concerned that the resistance might target the leadership? Try to stop the movement as early as possible before it gains traction?" May asked.

"Exactly," Lochridge said. "That is why we made the decision to keep our identities and plans completely secret. For ten years, we have managed to remain anonymous, communicating infrequently and only through an encrypted satellite transmission system I developed for the military, waiting patiently for the right time to unleash our blitzkrieg—a swift, surprise, massive coordinated media campaign designed to generate so much instant momentum that any attempt to resist by violent means would be difficult."

"The element of surprise," May thought out loud. "This meeting you want to host would be the first time you all have ever been together face to face?"

"And probably the last. *Ops Populi* is the match that starts the fire that eventually consumes the match."

Ginny's brow furrowed at the mention of the organization's name. "*Ops Populi*?" she asked.

"Ops Populi, United to Save America, to be precise," Lochridge said. "Power to the people."

At dinner, Lochridge barely touched his food, his appetite sharply curtailed by the cancer and the resulting nausea he felt most of the time. Instead of eating, he talked, explaining that the founders of *Ops Populi*, which he referred to simply as "OP," had agreed to this one meeting once there was consensus that the conditions were favorable—that the time to both finalize its implementation plans and formally approve the launch of the public relations blitz had finally arrived. Another crucial function of this core group was to reach out to anyone and everyone they could—to contact business and political leaders, give media interviews, participate in discussion forums, and so on. As the plan was designed, the shock of the media blitz was to be followed closely by a coordinated outreach effort, and it was the energy, talents and considerable influence of the OP members that were counted on initially for sustaining its momentum.

"Considerable influence?" Ginny asked, leaning back in her chair. "You haven't said much about the members, their backgrounds and so forth, but I'm getting the impression they are—"

"Elites?" May finished her sentence, smiling.

Lochridge also grinned, surmising what May was thinking at this point. In his lecture in Maine, May described his elitist theory of American politics, which was a direct challenge to the traditional notions carried around by most Americans that they were in control of their government. According to May's elite theory, nothing was further from the truth—the United States was dominated by a very small group of persons possessing uncommon social and economic advantages. These elites placated the masses by given them an illusion of control—the vote—while running the government, corporations, and other organizations in a way of their choosing to further their own interests.

"Yes, elites," Lochridge admitted freely, but not mentioning specific names or the positions they held. He fixed his eyes directly on May. "Necessary, but, as I'm sure you would agree, ironic. I assure you they are enlightened, and like America's founding fathers, willing to take risks and make sacrifices for the good of the country." He held up his hand defensively, as though to ward off an anticipated objection. "Also like the founding fathers, I'm sure they are not all motivated solely by altruism or noble ideals, though plenty of that exists, to varying degrees, of course. They know, as you and I do, that a healthy, vibrant, stable country is the tide that lifts all boats. It's good for business and in the long-term, their own well-being and the welfare of their families."

CHAPTER 48

Lochridge had once again excused himself from the dinner table early complaining of abdominal pain. The cancer was taking its toll on him, preventing him from eating, making him tire easily, he said. Tomorrow night, he was to fly to Baltimore for more tests and "minimal treatment" at Johns Hopkins, a trip that was wearing, but usually gave him temporary relief.

May and Ginny both declined the offer of dessert, but Ginny asked Karla if they could have a bottle of wine and a couple of glasses to take upstairs. She brought out a bottle of Riesling and they headed to Ginny's room looking forward to a relaxing evening.

Ginny worked on figuring out the TV while May poured the wine. Her room was much more spacious than his, with a small living room containing a sofa, reclining chair, coffee table, and an armoire holding a TV on top and a small refrigerator underneath. Pocket doors separated it from the bedroom where he could see a queen bed and a night stand against the wall. Thick beige carpet covered the floors. All relatively new, very comfortable.

He handed her a glass and they sat back on the oversized sofa, watching as a CNN International reporter with a heavy British accent described the day's plunging world-wide financial markets. "It all makes sense now. This castle. The alarm system. All the mystery and secretiveness. Amazing, isn't it?"

"A fortress on foreign soil. What better way to ensure the physical safety of the OP members?" She flipped the channel to BBC showing the reporter who was standing outside the United Nations complex in Manhattan.

"I have to admit, I was a little puzzled by how impractical it is for a single American man to buy a German Castle. I know he told us about his love of history, and his ancestral roots in Monschau. And his disdain for the current situation in the U.S. is pretty clear to me. But this—it just didn't make sense. He could live anywhere. If it were me, I would be on some warm, sunny beach somewhere, like Antigua."

Ginny nodded, sipping from her glass. Fragments of German, French, Dutch, Flemish and heavily accented English flowed from the TV speaker as she flipped through the channels. "After all of this, it seems unfair that he won't be able to see it through. I think he's hoping you will take this on."

May sighed, took a deep drink, draining half his glass. He let his head fall onto the soft cushion behind him, staring at the ceiling. "We—he's hoping we will take this on."

"Well, that's what he says, but it's you he really wants, and we both know it. So what do you think? Are you ready to give up your career?"

"I've gotta do this, Ginny," he said. "As a political scientist, I can't pass up an opportunity to be involved in something so, well, so momentous. For years, I've written and lectured about the systemic flaws in the structure of our government, and like everyone else, sat around waiting for Congress to make the necessary changes—which of course, they never did and probably never will do as long as they are vested in the status quo. In my dissertation, I was dreaming about citizens taking action, but reality soon set in. The obstacles were insurmountable. Now, there is a chance it can be done, and as long as there's a chance, I have to try to contribute."

"I know," she said, pausing her channel surfing to look at him. "I know this is right up your alley. So does Lochridge, which is why you're here. He's no dummy."

He shook his head slowly. "I'm beyond dumbfounded by what he's doing, what he's already done. I would end up being involved in a movement like this sooner or later anyway, so why not be part of it from the beginning? Besides, I really don't have anything back in Ohio I want to go back to—that part of my life is over."

"Don't you like your job? You have tenure, right?"

"Yes, but the way I'm looking at it, participating in this *is* my job. And my duty as an American," he added. "You heard him—no money worries, so Denison can put me on sabbatical, or fire me, I don't care. He poured the rest of the Riesling in their glasses, then he stretched his legs out in front of him. Though the possibility of being prosecuted for desertion flitted through his mind, he ignored it, shifting his focus to Ginny instead. "What about you?" he asked. "This whole thing has been such a whirlwind. Your friend is dead. What are *you* thinking—and feeling right now?"

She picked up her glass and sat back heavily, looking straight ahead. "I will miss Cybil—I think you could see, she was a great friend." She sighed, then said, "as to all of this," she made a sweeping motion with her free hand, "I guess I would have to say I'm in a sort of intellectual shock. I'm a normal city girl, you know. No grand aspirations. I was very happy with my life. I like my job—for the most part, it is fun, interesting work."

"It seems like it would be a great job. I probably would like working there myself, but it never crossed my mind as a career."

"It is kind of esoteric," she said with emphasis on the word *is*, "but until all this happened, the thought of a constitutional convention never even occurred to me, let alone helping to organize one." She sipped, and changed her position to face him. "I've taken my share of poli sci classes, had civics and social studies as a kid, but nothing like this was never even discussed—"

"Because it is considered by most to be virtually impossible," he interrupted. "Oh, it's theoretically possible, right there in Article V, but the obstacles are so great, the couple of serious attempts at it have failed."

"We were taught about amendments. Supreme Court opinions," Ginny continued her thought, adding, "I would imagine the average American would be shocked to learn a convention is even possible."

"Are you interested, though?" he asked.

Ginny looked down at her glass for a moment, then back up at him, her eyes soft, but serious. "I'll admit, the more I think about it and listen to you and Martin, the more I realize that it may be what our country needs. And I like challenges, and change. But you know what?"

May shook his head.

"I like the excitement I am feeling—and the idea of working with you."

Without hesitation, he reached over to her, taking her hand gently in his. "Thank you. Me, too."

She grasped his hand tightly, shaking it slightly to emphasize her next words. "Sean, it's pretty clear to me you're one of the most qualified people in the country for this type of project. But I—well, I am good at finding information, solving puzzles—I'm not sure how much I can contribute—"

"Lochridge seems to think your skills will be very useful. And so do I," he said with conviction.

"Let's face the facts, though. The only reason he offered me a role is because I happened to be with you."

He shook his head. "No, I think you are selling yourself short. You see, he knows—as I do—how vital your skills will be, not just now, but if and when a convention occurs. This whole process will fail without good information—and its organization, synthesis and interpretation are critical, which is why he offered you the same deal as he did me. It's going to be a big responsibility—and a lot of work, too."

She shrugged. "Hard work doesn't intimidate me. I would never want to get in the way, that's all."

He chuckled, giving her hand a couple of playful squeezes. At the same time the wine was working to relax him, he felt his enthusiasm build. "Are you kidding? We will be so busy, we'll have to schedule appointments to see each other. My guess is this will be like running a Presidential campaign, only worse—or better, if you like riding roller coasters. And boy, what a ride it will be! At least if we ride it together, we'll be able to hold onto each other."

She smiled, clutching his hand tightly. "I'll ride with you, but I'll be doing most of the holding on. So, it's settled?"

"It is for me."

"Me too. You only live once," she said as she let go of his hand and grabbed the remote again. "Maybe we can find something in English besides news. By the way, what was the grinning about—you know, when you were talking about elites?"

"Oh, that," he said. "A few years ago—well more than a few, now—I wrote and taught graduate students some, let's call them uncommon interpretations of American government—things that you wouldn't hear in most social studies or civics classes." He watched the TV screen while Ginny reclined, positioning one of the thick pillows to prop her head up against the wall. "Basically, the theory argues against the commonly held notions we all carry around with us—that ours is a government of the people, by the people, and for the people, as Lincoln said in the Gettysburg Address. Those words sound great, but in reality, the actions of our government—public policy—do not result from the demands of the masses of people, they reflect the self-interest and values of the controlling elites. The Founding Fathers never intended any real power for the masses. In fact, many of them were downright fearful of mass participation, and some of the fear was justified back then, I suppose."

"Why?" she asked.

"The average citizen was an uninformed, uneducated farmer—a freeholder, who worked his own land—deeply in debt relative to his income, barely able to eke out a living. Another 40 percent of the population was either indentured servants or slaves. So, the Founding Fathers feared the masses, seeing the potential for uprisings and wild swings in majority opinion based on whim, or worse—manipulation by demagogues."

"Afraid of another revolution, like what happened in France," Ginny remarked with a thoughtful nod.

"Sure. They knew social and economic inequality combined with little or no education could lead to instability. So they came up with a system of government that would placate the masses with a watered-down vote, but hardly any power."

"Watered-down?" she asked, her eyes alternating between him and the television.

May nodded, shifting his focus to her. "The people only had a say in choosing the members of the House—not senators, not the judges, not the President. As you know, they excluded women altogether, and many of the convention delegates wanted property qualifications attached for the men, but since they couldn't agree on how to define them, they left it up to the states. In the end, the Framers had crafted a government that isolated and protected themselves and their economic interests from mass influence and control. No referenda, no mass-initiated legislation like we now have in about half the states. That's the gist of it, but if you're interested, Lochridge has just about everything I have ever written up in his office. Anyway, he knew I would see some irony in the composition of *Ops Populi*. Just like our Founding Fathers, I'm willing to bet these folks are not your average working stiffs."

"But the Constitution and the government it created was radical for its time. Enlightened," she said. May raised an eyebrow, at once both surprised and impressed by her use of a term heard mainly in academic discussions of the eighteenth-century "Age of Enlightenment," a philosophical challenge to prevailing Western institutions, customs, and morals of the era.

"I'm not disputing that at all. In my writing and in my lectures, I tried like hell to avoid making value judgments—I wanted to challenge people to think critically, beyond the popular notions, or myth, as you call it, and then draw their own conclusions. It's all based on observations, historical accounts and supported by as much data as I could find."

She sat forward to take a sip of her wine without spilling it on herself. "So, what is your conclusion, professor?"

"I believe my observations are right. The Constitution was not ordained by the people, as stated in its preamble. It was written by a few extraordinary men—wealthy, well educated, and representative of the most powerful economic interests of the day. The masses did not participate in writing it or ratifying it, and probably would have rejected it if they could have. It was America's elites who were its main beneficiaries and they made sure it was adopted with some artful political maneuvering. But," he lifted a finger, "in the context of the time, they did a truly remarkable job, there's no question about it. As a nation, we no longer need to depend on elites to govern—at least, that's a question its citizens need to ask themselves."

"What strikes me is the illusion—that the people have the power—persists. I guess you could call it a great popular myth."

As he lightly ran his index finger over the rim of his glass, Ginny continued her channel surfing, stopping when she landed on the Armed Forces Network in the middle of an old *I Love Lucy* rerun. "It comes from our schools, our parents, the elites themselves, like Lincoln, and it has worked for over two centuries. We'll soon find out whether Jefferson's words that government relies upon the consent of the governed have any meaning in reality or we're all just suffering from a delusion," he said.

They sat quietly for a couple of minutes, watching and chuckling as Lucy got progressively drunker while trying to film a commercial for a vitamin concoction. Then Ginny rolled her head on the pillow to look directly at him. "Like you said, our government has worked for over 200 years. Aren't you at all concerned about, well, you know, breaking it?"

"Anyone who is paying attention can see it's already broken—that's the point. Look at what is happening—has happened in just the last decade or so. A President, chosen not by the majority of the voting public, but by a single Supreme Court Justice, commits the U.S. to an undeclared, ruinous war. Meanwhile, economic inequality between elites and the masses is increasing sharply, while popular trust and confidence in governmental leaders plummets. Short-sighted corporate and government actions are tearing apart the stability and integrity of our great private and public institutions, slowly eroding the country's competitive position in the world. We have saddled future generations with debt that they cannot hope to pay. Congress spends more energy trying to win elections—catering to their fat-cat contributors to protect their perks and insure their tenure—than governing. The serious long-term problems go unsolved, while we pile on debt to confer short-term windfalls to a privileged few." He stopped, looking down at her with resolute eyes accompanied by a slightly self-assured grin. "Need I go on? There's more, plenty more."

"Okay, we have a lot of problems," she quickly conceded, "But I haven't heard solutions. How does tinkering with the const—"

"Not tinkering, Ginny. I don't think that's what this is all about—getting more of our citizens engaged in solving the nation's problems is. Simply pulling a lever in the voting booth every couple of years to approve or disapprove of a slate of elites, whose selection is carefully orchestrated and controlled by the political establishment is not going to work anymore."

"I'm just playing devil's advocate, Sean," she said somewhat defensively. "The assumption is that a new convention will be good for the country—I'm just thinking that it could get out of control, could end up doing more harm than good."

"You're right—it's called a 'runaway' convention, and that scares the hell out of a lot of people. It can be prevented, though, by setting some limits at the beginning to keep its purpose narrowly focused. There is no need to re-write the whole Constitution—although that is exactly what the Founding Fathers did when they got together for the ostensible purpose of revising the Articles of Confederation."

"I forgot all about that," she said, bending forward for another sip.

May looked blankly at the credits flashing on the TV. "All we need are minor changes to shift some power and control to the people, to recognize and take advantage of the twenty-first century context of our country—over 200 years of social, economic and technological evolution."

"The internet," she stated, working the remote.

"The internet is huge, it makes mass participation practical. But that's not all. Think about how the population has changed since the eighteenth century. Education is a big one. There might be some solutions to our problems floating around out there, better ways of governing our nation. Elites don't have a monopoly on brains."

Ginny again turned her head away from the TV to look at him, and with a snort, said. "Lochridge fits the definition of an elite—talk about economic inequality. But yet, he's doing this."

May drained his glass and stretched to place it on the table. "Yeah, but what strikes me is that it seems he made most of his money *after* he decided to do this, or so says Erik. Ginny, you know I don't know Martin very well, but I think Erik was right: He was motivated by this cause to make as much money as he could, otherwise, he could have just stopped working billions of dollars ago and enjoyed the rest of his life. He told me that he was already planning to give all his money away before he made most of what he has now—he had an advisor who wanted to set up this elegant plan to give it to all his favorite causes."

"Did he tell you what made him change his mind? About giving it to charity, I mean. Just think how many needy people could be helped with all that money."

"He had an epiphany of sorts. First, he decided it makes more sense to concentrate his money in one area rather than diminishing its effect by spreading it around. He used the term *impact*, I think. Then, his reasoning led him to weigh impact in a short-term versus long-term calculus—you know, do you give a man a fish or teach him to catch his own? Anyway, since he believes that the U.S. is in big trouble, especially in the long-term, he came to the conclusion that trying to save it from imploding is the best thing he can do with his money. Achieve the biggest impact for the good of humanity—help the most people in the long run."

"Humanity? Or the people in the U.S.?"

"No, he's thinking globally—he's convinced a healthy, thriving U.S. will be able to pull the rest of the world up with it. I'm not so sure about pulling up the rest of the world, but I do agree with his assertion that we have the greatest country in the world. It's worth saving and it is definitely capable of doing a lot of good at home and abroad—history proves that."

She focused on the ceiling, thinking. "I suppose if you think in terms of potential, he's right. One thing's for sure: the decline of America will be a disaster for at least 300 million people. It's hard to believe the elites, as you call them, are consciously driving the country in reverse."

"Yeah, and not even looking in the rearview mirror to see where they are going." He leaned forward, resting his elbows on his knees, folding his hands under his chin thoughtfully. "Of course, it's not deliberate in the sense that they are making a calculated decision to run the country into the ground. It's our system that encourages myopic policy choices whose cumulative effects are going to eventually be our undoing as a nation. Maybe, though, within a few years, the people can take back their government and make it work again. If it's ever going to happen, now is the time."

CHAPTER 49

The next morning, Ginny and May found Lochridge seated behind a barely-touched plate of scrambled eggs, bacon, and toast. Holding the front section of the Washington Post, he was shaking his head, a look of disgust on his face.

"*Guten morgen*," he said, when he saw them enter the room. He laid the paper down, and took a bite of his toast.

They looked at him with quizzical expressions as they were seated.

"German for good morning. I'm learning—a little at a time."

"Bad news?" May asked him looking down at the newspaper.

"Isn't it always?" Lochridge said, taking a small sip of his coffee. "Another example of our President ignoring the law with a signing statement." He slid the paper to May.

Signing statements were Presidential opinions that were written in conjunction with the signing of a bill into law, generally to express the President's views about the constitutional validity of the law and to give guidance to executive departments on its implementation. May knew the current President, who was well on his way to surpassing the 600 or so signing statements written by all the previous 41 Presidents combined, had been using them frequently to modify and limit the Congressional intent of laws with which he disagreed.

"He seems to like those," May said, glancing at the story. "He's done this hundreds of times."

Lochridge snorted. "Up until Ronald Reagan's administration, only 75 of these had ever been used. Now they are being misused—no, abused. Shifting the balance of power to the executive."

May nodded his agreement and handed the newspaper to Ginny. Karla brought them coffee, and May asked for the same thing Lochridge was eating. Ginny asked for cereal.

"*Muesli*?" Karla asked her.

"Sure," she said, then asked, "that is the mix of cereal and dried fruit, right?"

Both Karla and Lochridge nodded. "We have some American cereals if you would prefer," Karla said.

"No, I'll try some *muesli*."

As soon as Karla left the room, Lochridge smiled at them and asked, "sleep well?"

"I know I did," May answered, looking at Ginny, who nodded her reply. "You've made us very comfortable here. Thank you."

"You're welcome," he said, with a warm smile breaking across his lips, "though, unfortunately, I will have to leave you tonight. I know you can appreciate how important my appointment is, and, of course, I wasn't expecting guests when I made it."

"We'll be fine, Martin, Ginny assured him. "We're safe. That's all that matters."

"You will be in good hands," he said, looking at Karla as she placed Ginny's *muesli* on the table. "You'll have use of the car as soon as Wilhelm drops me off in Maastricht. And I want to make sure you know how to get into my office to use the phones and the computer."

"Oh, God!" Ginny rolled her eyes. "I dread looking at my e-mail—I probably have hundreds."

May made eye contact with him and said "Martin, Ginny and I want you to know we are with you. With *Ops Populi*."

His eyes lit up brightly. "Fantastic!" He smacked the table with his hand enthusiastically. "You made my day, both of you!" He lifted his tea in a mock toast. "Power to the people!"

May and Ginny both raised theirs. "*Ops Populi*!" May said.

The jubilant Lochridge gave them a brief rundown of the organizational and financial aspects of OP-USA. By making them employees of the foundation, they would be entitled to benefits, especially the umbrella of protection from liability it afforded. It was his plan to purchase annuities for each of them or they could take a lump sum, whichever they preferred.

After breakfast, they went to his office in the turret, where Lochridge gave them keys and codes they would need while he was gone. Then, they sat on the sofa—Lochridge in the middle—to learn how to operate the satellite phone.

"You developed this for the military?" May asked him as they waited for the device to go through its start-up routine. "I don't think I've ever seen one."

The screen was flashing "Acquiring Signal," continuously. "TNOE only authorizes them to combat units, platoon level and higher," he said, then to Ginny's shrug, added, "Sorry, Ginny. TNOE is the acronym for table of organization and equipment, the list of all the manpower and equipment a military unit is allowed to have. The Pentagon has been buying these from us for about 10 years now. We're on the third version, but it's essentially the same as the original."

After a couple of minutes of waiting, he pushed a button that displayed a cryptic alphanumeric list of some sort. "I discovered the automatic satellite signal selection doesn't always work properly in this region of Europe, so you may have to manually select it." He pressed another button continuously to scroll through the list. "This is the one with the best coverage, but when we have a heavy cloud cover, the next one seems to work best."

Once the device had its satellite, it was easy to operate. He pulled open a rubber cover to reveal ports used to connect it to a computer or a standard telephone. The Sat-Phone had many other bells and whistles—GPS, encrypted data transmission, access to real-time meteorology data, even a gunnery computer to compute firing solutions for artillery and mortars—but to keep it simple, he showed them only what they would need for talking to Erik securely.

"When I return, I'll introduce you to Sally," he said. "She's retired—was retired—in Saint Augustine, Florida."

"Any word from Erik?" Ginny asked.

"Nothing yet, but it's only 4 in the morning in Maryland," Lochridge replied, May chuckling in the background.

"Oh, yeah, I forgot," she blushed.

After a lunch of *brotchen* and various meats and cheeses, they returned to the office. Lochridge called Jerome Hunnicutt to have the necessary documents drawn for May and Ginny, and he asked Hunnicutt to fax them as soon as possible.

"They will come directly into my computer," he said when he finished the call. "Let me show you how you can print them if they come in while I'm gone."

While May walked around the room examining the regalia adorning the walls, Ginny sat with Lochridge writing down passwords and miscellaneous instructions to access his computer. There was an older model laptop she was welcome to use, he told her, and Wi-Fi internet connectivity was available throughout most of Burg Segur. May tuned the conversation out when he came to three framed documents hanging below a large photograph of Lochridge standing on the deck of a boat with a man and woman he didn't know, all holding a five-foot hammerhead shark. Two of the documents were a B.A. degree from the University of Virginia and a Juris Doctor from William and Mary. May was surprised to learn of the law degree, but it was the third document and the distinctive eagle badge that captured his full attention. It was a certificate of membership in the Society of the Cincinnati, which was familiar to May as a result of his research into private groups that had influenced public policy throughout American history. Founded near the end of the Revolutionary War, it was not only among the country's oldest fraternal organizations, it was one of the most elite with its membership initially open only to Continental Army officers and some high ranking French officials. He had discovered that twenty-three of the signers of the Constitution had been original members. With an estimated 3,700 or so members at the time he had been conducting his research, May knew Lochridge had been required to prove he was descended from an officer who served in the Revolutionary War to become one of them.

"On my father's side of the family," May heard Lochridge say from behind him. "Killed in North Carolina."

The phone on his desk startled them with the first ring. Lochridge looked up at May, before saying, "Hello, Erik. Any news?"

Enough to warrant the use of the sat-phone, apparently, since Lochridge hung up without saying another word and walked back to the sofa to retrieve it just as it started its peculiar chiming. "We're all here, Erik," he said, pressing the transmit button.

According to Bachman, Erik told them, Army CID was trying to pinpoint Krug's location in Iraq. The FBI was "working on" Prather and Hewitt, who were both currently in the States, although he could not or would not elaborate, and Erik did not feel comfortable pressing him for details.

"I'll be flying to Baltimore tonight for an—uh—appointment," Lochridge said. Ginny and May traded a quick glance of realization that Erik must not know about his condition. "If all goes well, I'll see if I can arrange to see him myself. Get the skinny."

To Erik's delight and unbridled enthusiasm, Lochridge shared the news about May and Ginny being on board with OP-USA. "I never had a doubt," he said about his friend.

"I've made contact with all but one on my list," Erik reported to Lochridge, referring to his part in scheduling the meeting of the group at Burg Segur. "Late June or after the fourth of July seems to be the consensus. A couple of concerns about the long trip over there, but most are happy—and surprised—about the location."

"Good work," Lochridge said. "I'll check in with Sally myself. I want to introduce these two to her before I leave."

They said their good-byes, and Lochridge tapped a button to end the call. He leaned back, rubbing his hands together, and with no outward sign of gloom or despair, he locked eyes with May. "I have my doubts as to whether I will be here in a couple months, let alone at the end of June. I want the two of you and Sally to be ready to run this meeting if I'm not."

CHAPTER 50

Lloyd Fletcher looked with dismay at the pile of paper on his desk, thinking to himself there had to be a better way to do this. He took a swig of his cold, stale coffee to brace himself for the task ahead. Of all the interesting jobs the FBI had to offer, he would spend the better part of a week chained to his desk in his little Washington office looking at computer reports analyzing millions of financial transactions from all over the world, looking for that needle in the haystack that would allow the bureau to nail some crook. This was grunge work, he thought to himself, better suited to someone without his superior intellect and knowledge of the criminal mind.

He flipped open the first binder, glanced at the page, then pressed his intercom button. "Jackson, get in here," he barked.

A few seconds later his office door opened and a meek looking Harvey Jackson stepped through it. "Sir?"

Fletcher leaned back in his chair, placing his hands behind his head and, in the process, displaying his sweaty armpits to his subordinate. "Jackson," he said with a fake smile, "why is it that a senior analyst has to spend almost a week looking at this pile of garbage on my desk, when you and the other juniors," he emphasized the word juniors, "are perfectly capable of sifting through it and presenting me with a nice executive summary?"

Jackson saw it coming. Gravity carried shit down hill, and this pile was about to land in his lap. His instinctive reaction was to deflect it as best he could by stroking the ego of the arrogant ass. "Sir, we annotate the reports as you requested, allowing you to make the executive decision about what transactions are worthy of further investigation."

Fletcher's smile evaporated instantaneously. To Jackson's relief, he lowered his arms, placing his folded hands on the desk before him. "And as the one empowered with the executive authority, I am telling you right now that this is not working to my satisfaction. The chicken-scratch notes are difficult to read and I waste too much of my valuable time on this. I want a better way."

After nearly three months of putting up with this jerk, Jackson and the half dozen other analysts were all convinced this guy was a first-class moron with absolutely zero qualifications for his job. Fletcher's position had been created for him out of thin air when the former director had abruptly announced his resignation, forcing his entourage of hand-picked cronies to scramble for new positions. In just a few weeks, he went from being a glorified bodyguard to analyst in charge of one the most sophisticated and complex financial monitoring programs ever attempted.

"An executive summary would force us to make the critical decisions about what activity deserves your attention, sir." Jackson was doing his best, but, the way it was going, he and his fellow analysts better get ready to slip on the high-topped boots.

Fletcher again flashed his phony smile, reveling in the deference gushing from his subordinate. He stroked his chin while considering the possibility that his juniors would think less of him if he were to delegate this executive-level responsibility to people who were a full three pay grades beneath him. "Perhaps you are right," he said, to Jackson's delight, though Jackson carefully maintained his subservient, stoic demeanor. "Perhaps you and the others should type your annotations, then, and tab the relevant pages of the reports." This was not a suggestion nor did he expect his edict to be questioned.

Did he even realize how idiotic the idea was? Their unit was charged with uncovering questionable activity by analyzing roughly 11 million or so daily financial transactions routed through the Brussels-based international banking consortium known as SWIFT, or the Society for Worldwide Interbank Financial Telecommunication. About six trillion dollars in electronic transactions, domestic and international, involving nearly 7,800 banks, brokerages, stock exchanges, and other institutions worldwide, every single business day. Plus, they sifted through thousands of suspicious activity reports, or SARs, flowing into the bureau from the nation's banks every day. And they were expected to type their notes and tab the reports? Ridiculous, he thought, as he took a deep breath.

"Sir, we have done some things—made some improvements—to the reports to assist you in your crucial analysis." How much longer could he keep this up? "Let me show you."

Jackson timidly took the few steps around his boss's desk, but to his surprise, Fletcher stood and made a hand gesture toward his chair. He was, after all, trying to help make the SOB's life easier. He pulled one of the books he personally compiled for Fletcher from the stacks on his desk and opened it to reveal the familiar tables of small print, columns listing names, dates, amounts, account numbers and codes. He and his fellow analysts used several powerful computer applications under continuous development in partnership with the CIA to sift through the raw data. At no small cost to the taxpayers, the software—designed to apply statistical and quantitative methods to the data to identify patterns which could indicate activity of questionable legality—was far from perfect. Although it did a fairly good job of synthesizing huge quantities of information, the final analysis required human intervention to interpret the results. Before Fletcher's position had been created, the analysts performed this role as well as could be expected under the circumstances, but now they were required to do the work and write it all down so their new boss could take credit for it.

"Sir, if you look at this group of transactions here, you can see why the computer flagged them." Fletcher, who was nearing his 47th birthday, reached for his reading glasses while bending at the waist to look at the book. "Within 4 days, nearly $6 billion landed in this fairly new Swiss account." Looking down through his spectacles, Fetcher put his index finger down right next to Jackson's, close enough to prompt Jackson to flinch and yank his away.

"Jackson, it would be very helpful if you printed horizontal lines to separate all these rows," Fletcher groaned. "I have to use a straight-edge to be able to read these—I sure can't do it while standing up." Jackson jumped from the chair and awkwardly traded places with him in the small space behind the desk. "Yes, registered to OP-USA, Inc., I see," he said when he was seated again.

Jackson gritted his teeth at the snide comment about printing lines on the paper. Yes, it would make the reports more readable, easier to use, but Fletcher knew he had no control over the format of the software's output. What Fletcher apparently didn't know—or didn't care about—was the private contractors who were developing the software were burning through their budget with overtime just to make it perform the demanding tasks required of it. As he and the other analysts struggled with ideas for improving the functionality, making the output look pretty was low on the priority list at the moment.

"Yes, sir, I will pass your request on to the programmers," he said with as much enthusiasm as he could muster. "In any event, we back-traced the deposits into the Swiss account to try determine the source. In the annotation, you can see the cross-reference to the book and page number and the code I used to indicate the relationship." He pulled one of the other books from the stack and opened it about midway, flipping through several pages. Once he found the correct page, he gently laid the book on top of the first. "We are annotating the related transactions in descending order, from the largest to the smallest. This is the largest source deposit—about $1.24 billion from an account in Hong Kong. The annotations show where you can find its source—"

"This is what I'm talking about," Fletcher said in his whiney voice. "This is too damned complicated. My time is too valuable to be flipping through books, trying to decipher sloppy handwriting."

Jackson bit down hard on his lower lip—so hard, in fact, he thought it might bleed. What they were trying to do was too complicated for this buffoon to comprehend. He and the others were working long hours to make him look good. He spent enormous amounts of his own time feeding modifications to the developers to make this job easier. And this was the gratitude. Keep your grip, he reminded himself, self-control.

Refusing to acknowledge his boss's last comment, Jackson continued. "We back-traced the Hong Kong money to several accounts in the Cayman Islands. All registered to corporations that none of us recognize." Sensing that he was rapidly approaching the limits of Fletcher's patience, Jackson condensed the remainder of his analysis. "A large chunk came from this account in Virginia—" he paused, grabbed another book, and opened it—"this one," he said, placing the book in front of his boss.

"I'll be damned," Fletcher mumbled, squinting at small print, "IMSI." IMSI was the lead developer of the software responsible for the report he was looking at. He was pretty sure they were involved in the 2000 upgrade of NCIC, or the bureau's National Crime Information Center, as well, but he didn't want to sound uncertain to his subordinate, so he kept it to himself. "I'll bet they never expected their name to appear on one of these," he said, chuckling at the irony.

Jackson flashed a half-hearted grin to humor the idiot. "No, I don't suppose they did. Anyway, we back-traced this group of transactions to a brokerage house in New York, and—"

"What's the bottom line?" Jackson interrupted, looking at his watch. "You see? A one or two page executive summary on all of this would have saved us a lot of time," he snapped.

Jackson stood up straight, subconsciously clenching his fist. When he realized it, he jammed his hands in his pockets and walked around to the front of the desk, hoping his face was not turning red with the rage he was feeling.

"Large blocks of IMSI stock sold on one day, proceeds wired from the broker through a series of off-shore accounts, all eventually ending up in the account registered to OP-USA. That's why these transactions appear on our reports."

"Okay. I get it, Jackson. Lots of IMSI stock sold, wired to Switzerland. A lot of money, but what's the relevance?" Again, he looked at his watch.

"Sir, I checked IMSI's last SEC filing. The only one with that much stock is Martin Lochridge, the chairman and former CE—"

"I know who he is," Fletcher barked. "And he is certainly not on our watch list, nor is he going to be on the CIA's. He's getting old. Maybe he's calling it quits—cashing in, you know?" He stood, and walked over to the hook on the back of his door and grabbed his jacket.

"It's not just the amount of money," Jackson said to his back, rolling his eyes. "The computer pulled these because of all the inter-account wiring, all the foreign accounts. For some reason, Lochridge is trying to conceal this."

Fletcher put his hand on the doorknob, then let go, and turned to look back at Jackson. Because of his involvement with IMSI, Lochridge would certainly know how to avoid having his own software capture his personal transactions if he were trying to hide something. But his stock broker wouldn't.

"What about the rest?" he asked, looking up at the much taller Jackson. "You said $6 billion, I think. Into the Swiss account."

"I traced the largest chunk of it back to his broker in New York. Lots of stocks and bonds being dumped—all at once. Other than the broker, I think the next largest one was about $700 million that we traced back to LaSalle Bachman Aerospace."

Fletcher put his hands in his pockets and looked down at the floor. "Why? And what is this OP-USA?" He removed his coat and tossed it onto one of his armchairs on his way back to his desk.

CHAPTER 51

After giving Ginny all the passwords and user names she needed to use his computer, Lochridge printed some financial reports to review on the long plane trip to Baltimore. He did not show up for dinner, but stepped in to tell May and Ginny good bye while they ate.

"Anything you need?" he asked them, resting his briefcase on the edge of the table.

"No, you have made us quite comfortable, Martin," Ginny said.

May swallowed the mouthful of food he had been chewing, and added, "We are fine. Is there anything we can do for you while you're gone?"

Lochridge shook his head. "Just think about the meeting, and look out for the fax from Preston. Oh, and feel free to call Sally to bounce ideas off her. If there is one thing I am sure of, it is that she is a good sounding board."

Half an hour into the flight, with his latest financial statements spread out on the table before him, he was fuming. He dialed Jerome Hunnicutt's private line.

"Hello," he answered.

"Dammit, Preston, you told me you were keeping the fund transfers under the Fed's radar. You did $6 billion in less than a week, and you don't think anyone might notice."

"Martin, I just found out about this myself," he said with cowed submissiveness. "I can do nothing but apologize for the blunder."

"Some things cannot be delegated, and this is one of them. From now on, you will handle this personally. Are we clear?"

"Yes," he said simply.

The only reply he received was the click in his ear when Lochridge ended the call.

CHAPTER 52

"Sally? Sally? Can you hear us?" Ginny said into the Sat-Phone, when Sally Sexton's voice began breaking up.

"—have to—witch sat—ssing the—button," her voice crackled.

"Oh, the manual selection thing," she said to herself. May observed as she brought up the menu, checked her notes for the correct satellite to select, then pressed a sequence of buttons. "Is that any better?"

"You're coming in crystal clear now," Sally said. "I wonder if they are ever going to get that fixed."

"We only got a few words of the part about the TV ads," Ginny said. With a click, she reconnected the standard telephone and switched on its speaker.

"I was saying that basically, it is going to be managed by several of the media and communications staff at Jonic—Martin's real estate company. With all the advertising we did, the staff have the expertise and the contacts with the production companies and publicity firms that we'll need. Especially Missy Clark—she's a top notch public relations and communications executive."

"They can work for us and do their regular jobs, too?" May asked her.

"Martin and his hand-picked successor worked that out in their deal when he stepped down. They will be on loan to us for as long as we need them, though they don't know it yet," she said.

"This will be the most important aspect of the whole movement," May said. "Advertisements and the internet piece. I think we're going to need them full-time—and then some."

"Don't worry—the arrangement is to have them working for us exclusively for as long as we need them," Sally said, hearing the concern in May's voice. "Believe me, we spent a lot of time talking through this because of how crucial it is. Martin and I both know these people very well and have absolute confidence in their abilities. With new people, it would be that much more challenging to get quick results. And to achieve the surprise—Martin uses the term blitz—that we need."

"Sally, when is he going to tell people about his condition?" Ginny asked her out of the blue. "His prognosis? He said we are the only ones who know."

The long moment of silence that followed made Ginny think there was a problem with the satellite again. She looked at May, shrugged, and glanced down at her notes, when Sally's voice broke the quiet.

"Ginny, the short answer to your question is at the last possible moment. Maybe never. He hasn't even told his son."

"I saw a picture of him on the wall here," May said, "with Erik. The change in his physical appearance is pretty noticeable—it will be difficult to hide the fact that he is ill. Especially from anyone who has known him for awhile."

Again, a long pause. In the most secure mode—the mode Lochridge advised them to use in his absence—the Sat-Phone functioned like a telephone, with no video, due to the added encryption and scrambling. But when Sally finally spoke, the change in the tone of her voice made it plain she was upset by the current topic.

"I know. He is going downhill faster than I thought possible," she said with perceptible sadness. "He knows his time is short, but I will tell you something—and this goes for both of you. I know your agreement to work with us is giving him a great deal of peace of mind right now."

May felt Ginny's eyes watching him, so he spoke. "I hope I can make a difference," he said, with humility. "It is a great opportunity for me."

"When he found out he was dying, for the first time since his wife was killed, I saw him anguish over a problem."

May and Ginny flashed each other a look of surprise. "His wife was killed? How?" Ginny asked in unabashed fashion.

"I'm not surprised he hasn't told you—if you haven't figured it out yet, Martin is a very private man. He despises awkward and phony expressions of sympathy." Sally let out a sigh. "Lorraine was killed in 1995 by a deputy in Fairfax, Virginia, while he was pursuing a teenager who had run through a red light. He slammed into her in an intersection, killing her instantly."

"God, how awful," Ginny said. "How long had they been married?"

"Hmmm," she mumbled, while she thought. "They married right after he came back from Viet Nam. He's wearing his army dress uniform in their photo. Maybe 22 or 23 years. Something like that."

"Their kids were already grown then?"

"Their youngest was a senior in high school. He had a terrible time—got in all kinds of trouble. Got into drugs, drinking," Sally said, having lived through it with him. "Martin was constantly bailing him out of one thing or another. Funny, though. In some ways, I think it kept him going. He was devastated by Lorraine's death. Quit working, became a recluse."

As though reading his mind, Ginny just put her hand on May's, but said nothing more. He was almost positive Erik would have told Lochridge about his wife's death in a car accident, but like Lochridge, he wanted no pity, particularly from someone he barely knew. Still, that they had the tragic deaths of their wives in common struck him as something more than a random coincidence; in fact, even in the context of the many extraordinary events of late, it was nothing less than profound.

"We're lucky he came through it," May said, thinking how much of an understatement that might come across to her. Damned lucky was more like it.

"In a way, Sean, you were partially responsible for that," Sally said, knowing May would never hear it from anyone but her. "He walked out of the office one day and said he was moving to Maine. He was already wealthy—and Jonic was running itself at that point, anyway. He bought the house in Camden—you both stayed there for a couple of days, right?"

"We did," Ginny answered. "Very nice place."

"Well, he lived there by himself for a year, maybe two, just sitting by the water, reading. He loves history and political science, so he devoured everything he could get his hands on. To stay active, sailed, played a little golf and tennis. Then one day, on a whim, he went to see you speak, Sean. Something you said that day moved him so much, he was back in Virginia, back at work, in just a few days. He had a gleam in his eye

I hadn't seen since Lorraine's death. He became obsessed with making money—working 12 and 14 hour days, buying and selling companies, investing, taking some fantastic risks. He enjoyed some great successes, suffered some big failures, but obviously, he won more than he lost. A couple of years later, at my daughter's wedding reception, he swore me to secrecy and told me what he was up to and why. It was a lot to absorb, but it changed me forever, too—made me stick with him through all those years of long hours and few vacations. I'm not complaining though—I've been on vacation since I was 46," she laughed, "but I promised him I would postpone it when he needed me."

As she subconsciously processed the striking parallel between Lochridge and May—devastated by the untimely death of their wives until having their spirits revived by their shared passion to reform the Constitution—Ginny wondered about the incredible toll all that working had taken on them both. "Maybe he worked too hard," she wondered out loud. "I mean, working so much may have made him susceptible to illness. Do you think that's possible?"

May nodded, while listening to Sally's reply. "I suppose it's possible. He wonders if the chemicals he was exposed to in Vietnam might have something to do with it. You know, napalm, agent orange, all that stuff."

"That thought had occurred to me too, when I saw he was in the infantry," May said. "A lot of vets, especially the combat guys, are getting sick."

"Anyway," Sally continued, "when he found out he was terminally ill, he quit working for good. He already had a plan in place for liquidating most of his assets and transferring most of his money to a foundation for OP, but his mistake, if you could call it that, is he hadn't planned on dying before even starting the movement. Who would be the one to hold OP together until there was a consensus about launching a campaign? For nearly ten years now, it's been him and his single-minded determination to make this happen that has kept everyone's interest. So he needed to find someone with the enthusiasm and drive to keep the pilot light lit and light the fire for him when the time was right."

"A new leader," May said, understanding.

"Exactly," Sally said. "He called me one day. He's talked about you on and off for years, but something made him think of you that particular day—maybe something he was reading—I'm not sure. He said he knew of nobody else with as much passion and commitment to the principle of constitutional reform than you, so we decided he should approach you, try to get you involved."

"I would have been drawn to it like a magnet, sooner or later," May assured her.

"Yes, well Martin was pretty sure you would be interested, but he was not at all certain you would be receptive to…" A sniffle gave away the fact that she was fighting tears, and she paused for a second.

May and Ginny looked at each other, neither knowing what to say, so they said nothing. What little they knew about the relationship between Sally and Lochridge led to the assumption that it was very close, platonic, but emotionally deeper than a friendship. It was forged through years of working side by side, many common experiences and shared values. They waited, supposing Sally was composing herself, while Ginny's feelings of remorse for bringing the subject up in the first place grew with each passing second.

"Marty knows how successful you've been in your career, but he fought back the apprehension about approaching you and asked Erik to help him find you—right around the time you got hurt, it turns out."

"The way this has all materialized—well, it's quite astounding, when you think about it," May said. "Martin probably saved my life. I owe him." He felt Ginny's fingers on the back of his neck.

"Let's hope he will be here to run the meeting himself," Ginny added.

"After all these years—well, you can understand why he can't bear to think of his effort going to waste, just fizzling out," she said, making no attempt to hide her sniffling. "So, Ginny, that is why since his diagnosis in early November, he has struggled with the decision about whether or not to tell anyone. Our conversations about it always ended up the same way: with him concluding there was nothing to gain and everything to lose.

"It's hard to believe OP's existence has been kept secret for almost a decade," May observed. "When will Ginny and I be able to see a list of the members?"

"No one except Martin has the complete list. Everyone agreed it was best for the group as a whole to keep the member list under wraps. And everyone—including me—has voluntarily signed a statement agreeing to confidentiality and non-disclosure. Unless something has changed, he probably will ask you and Ginny to sign one too, particularly before giving you the list."

A moment's reflection was all it took for May to understand the rationale for this. If anyone got loose lips, the potential harm it could cause would be minimized with anonymity. And as long as everyone adhered to it, the non-disclosure would keep OP and its purpose secret until the timing for taking it public was right. Maximum impact to Lochridge's way of thinking would be achieved through surprise—something taught and understood well by the military.

"Makes sense," May said. "Hopefully, we can handle that when Martin returns from the States."

"And we can sit down with him to get his input on the meeting," Ginny added. "Just in case we have to run it."

"To him, this meeting is crucial. If he can get everyone together, he thinks natural momentum will take over," Sally said.

"Still, someone has to provide structure, take charge," Ginny observed, "or it will be a waste of time."

With sadness creeping into her voice, Sally said, "They can choose a new leader if they want, or maybe they will just defer to you, Sean. In any case, Martin's dream will continue—even if he does not."

"To get this far just to have the group fall apart because of his death would be tragic," May said.

May thought for a moment while Ginny asked her about her plans to come to Germany. She would wait until the results of these new tests were in but knew it would have to be soon if she were to have any quality time with him before his death. That it would be the toughest experience of her life, she understood well and had been preparing herself for it for weeks.

May thought it unlikely he would win the instant confidence of a room full of social and political luminaries, so it would fall on one of the members to assume the mantle and chair the meeting. "Sally, Martin has told me enough to assume we will be trying to organize a fairly prominent group of people at this meeting. Do you think we should ask Martin to prepare some instructions, you know, some thoughts about who should lead the discussion, the agenda, that sort of thing?"

"Already done," she said. "He's made several audio and video tapes between Thanksgiving and Christmas. A couple of commercials for radio and TV, too. And he even set up an interview with one of the network news anchors—he would only tell me he was an enlightened journalist." She sniffled. "It was something he wanted to do while he was still feeling good and looking healthy."

To his credit—especially under these circumstances—Lochridge was well ahead of his game. "Have you seen or heard these tapes?" May asked her.

"He's sent me a few, but I haven't seen the message to the OP members or the interview. He just told me about those recently." She sighed before saying, "Well, looks like I'll be there soon. We can watch them all together."

CHAPTER 53

After their somewhat sad, but interesting, conversation with Sally, Ginny and May had Wilhelm take them into Monschau to a bistro Lochridge highly recommended for its food and ambience. Set in the center of the old village among the historic stone and timbered structures, it offered a wide selection of food, not just German, but also Italian and French. Ginny had a craving for pizza, so May gave into her but couldn't resist trying the *Schumpnudeln*, a tasty dish of creamy noodles and sauerkraut mixed together. On their way back to the car, they stopped in a small corner store offering a vast assortment of chocolates, pies, cakes and ice cream. Instead of choosing just one, they left with a bag full of goodies to sample once they returned to the Burg—and had some room in their stomachs.

Before heading to Ginny's room, they went to Lochridge's office in the turret to check for messages. Lochridge had set up voice mail boxes for both of them, at the same time urging caution for the time being against disclosing their location to anyone. Don't risk using the standard telephone to call anyone, he had warned her sternly. It was too easy to pinpoint the location of a call's origination, and he was certain the U.S. was monitoring inbound calls from overseas. Checking e-mail or using the internet was not a problem, though, since his computer was using the satellite IP address masking technology to prevent back-tracing.

"Wonder if Martin made it to Baltimore okay," Ginny said, scanning through pages of e-mail messages.

May shrugged, dialing the access code for their voice mail. "There's a message," he said. "From Erik. Says he's going to meet with Lochridge, but he'll call on the Sat-Phone—two our time tomorrow."

Eyes glued to the computer monitor, Ginny nodded. "I can't believe all the junk that's getting through my spam filter."

May stood and stretched, yawning widely. With Ginny engrossed in her e-mail cleansing, he put his hands in his pockets and wandered around the large turret room looking at some of the art, photos, and other memorabilia he had not yet seen. When he reached the bookshelves, he perused the eclectic mix of titles arranged by subject, including general business, classic literature, history, law, political science, psychology, and science. His own publications were grouped together along with a black binder labeled "May's Dissertation," which he pulled out to show Ginny later, grimacing at the memory of all the work that had gone into it in his last year at GWU. The decision to work on it full time was a good one in hind sight, but at the time, he was constantly nagged by whether giving up his secure federal logistics job was a monumental mistake that he would later regret. As time went on and his savings were exhausted, he considered leaving without writing a dissertation at all and begging for his old job, but thankfully, one forward-thinking member of his dissertation committee pleaded with him to finish it on the basis that it could be one of the rare instances an academic product of political science could actually serve a meaningful purpose. May would have to call Dr. Kriner sometime very soon to tell him he was right.

"I'm almost done with this," Ginny said to his back. "Just paying a couple of bills. You want on?"

"Nope," May said, content for now to avoid any connection with life's responsibilities. "My bills are paid automatically, and everyone that matters knows I'm on military leave, so I have a pass on replying to e-mail right now."

He continued to mosey along the outer perimeter of the room, pausing briefly to push the power button on the stereo. The speakers came alive in the middle of a lively commercial in French. Hearing no protests from Ginny, he rose from his stooped position and backed away, content just to hear something other than her constant clicking and clacking, but, on a whim, decided to occupy himself with scanning for some music.

As soon as he crouched to look for the tuning knob, a plain black frame standing on the bottom shelf of the cabinet caught his eye. In the lower right hand corner of the frame was an old weathered photo partially covering a document. He grabbed the frame with his right hand and stood, now able to see that there was a scrap of paper containing a short poem in the lower left hand corner of the frame. Decorative print across the top of the document underneath read: "Honorable Discharge from the Armed Forces of the United States of America." His eyes quickly returned to the photo, which he held close to his face to study.

"This is interesting," he said to Ginny, turning to walk toward Lochridge's desk without looking up.

May walked around to the rear of the large desk and laid the frame down flat on the desk. Engrossed in her e-mail purge, she reluctantly tore herself away from the monitor to look down.

"His discharge certificate?" she said, not even acknowledging the photo or the hand-written poem.

"No—well, yes it is—but look at this photo."

Ginny shifted in her chair and lifted the frame to have a closer look at the old, faded snapshot. They both took in the image of what they assumed was a Vietnamese soldier in uniform holding a little girl in a tight embrace while standing in front of a train. The little girl had her arms and legs wrapped around the man, her head resting on his shoulder, both with their eyes squeezed, wearing the painful expressions of parting ways.

"Touching," she commented. "Father saying good bye to his daughter? Wonder who it is?" she asked, turning the frame slightly askew to decrease the glare from the overhead light.

May shrugged. "Pretty beat up. I'm guessing he carried it around with him in the field. I'm not a hundred percent sure, but I would also guess that to be an NVA—sorry—North Vietnamese uniform."

"Interesting place for it. Right on top of his discharge."

Then, she read the faded writing on the creased and yellowed paper:

Bivouac of the Dead

The muffled drum's sad roll has beat
The soldier's last tattoo;
No more on life's parade shall meet

That brave and fallen few.
On fame's eternal camping ground
Their silent tents are spread,
But glory guards with solemn round
The bivouac of the dead.

"Looks like feminine hand writing—like it was cut from a letter."

May shrugged, taking the frame from her hand, eyes returning to the mesmerizing photograph that evoked so many poignant emotions. A father going off to fight, saying farewell to his beloved little girl, perhaps never to see her again. His thoughts drifted to his own daughter, the despair and total misery he had suffered through when she had been taken from him with no warning, no opportunity to tell her good bye. With his back to Ginny, he let the tears fill his eyes while he slowly walked back to the built-in cabinet, carefully placing the frame on the shelf were he had found it.

"Oh my God!" Ginny shrieked suddenly.

"Wha—What is it?" May asked as he hurried back to the desk.

"This," she pointed to the computer monitor. She was looking at a news story with a photograph of a man being escorted in handcuffs from a restaurant, his head hung low. May bent at the waist, squinting to read.

Contractor Arrested While Lunching With Congressman

Washington—FBI agents today arrested James Hewitt, a partner in the government contracting firm Krug, Prather, and Hewitt on unspecified charges while he dined with baseball legend and Michigan Congressmen Chester Crum.

A Washington TV reporter and camera crew were waiting outside to interview Crum on his announcement on the House floor earlier today that he would form an exploratory committee on seeking the Republican nomination for President.

The FBI refused further comment on Hewitt's arrest...

May stood, placing his hand gently on Ginny's shoulder. "Interesting. Wonder if Erik knows anything more…"

"Yeah. Could be they are not saying anything until they arrest the other ones."

"I don't think they ever talk to the media, period. But I'll guarantee the media will dig deeper, especially since he was with Crum." He yawned, staring at the monitor blankly. "You think we have problems now? If that idiot gets elected President, I'm going to run away."

"He is popular—all the name recognition." She stretched, yawning. "I'm thinking about the present—like being able to go home without being hunted. At least we're seeing some progress."

"Yeah, bad news is good news for us," he observed, standing upright. "Well, I'm tired. I think I'll call it a day. You coming?"

"No, go ahead. I'm going to stay here a little longer—try to catch up on recent happenings in Washington."

When he closed his eyes for the last time that night, with the anguished visages of the man and the little girl firmly etched in his mind, he wondered about the story behind the photo that Lochridge carried with him. Perhaps a story better left untold, he thought before drifting off to sleep.

CHAPTER 54

It was hard for Preston Bachman to do anything or go anywhere unnoticed. As a senior Senator with powerful committee assignments, there was always attention focused on him, whether it be the media, lobbyists, Congressional staff members or people from the various executive departments and agencies whose finances and agenda he influenced. So, rather than going to his office in the Hart Senate Office Building at all this morning, he had called his chief of staff, who, after confirming there was nothing crucial on the day's schedule, cleared his calendar for the remainder of the day. To slip out of Washington unobserved took a little effort, but for his old friend Marty Lochridge, he was more than willing.

He didn't do it often, but in some strange way, Bachman actually enjoyed the little game of stealth he played to evade whatever prying eyes were on him. As he drove into the 15th Street underground garage, he smiled at the memory of contriving the little scheme over some beers and fried oysters with his long-time friend, Dave Rader, who lived two blocks south and 18 floors above 17th Street. He found an empty parking space and waited a few minutes, listening to talk radio while looking intently into his review mirror.

Satisfied that no one had followed him into the garage—at least no one dumb enough to be obvious about it—he grabbed a small athletic bag and walked into the Crystal City underground, a network of connecting tunnels containing numerous shops, restaurants, professional offices, a metro subway station, even a grocery store. People living here would never have to see the light of day if they chose not to, their every possible need fulfilled in this subterranean maze. He stopped to grab a couple of fresh, hot bagels and coffee, then completed his trek to the bank of elevators below Rader's building.

To ride the elevators above the second floor required a special code which Bachman tapped into the keypad before beginning his ascent. Once in Rader's apartment, he found a note under the car keys that said: "It could use a wash! Have a good time. Dave." Hunger pangs swept over him, so he sat at the small dining table and devoured the steaming bagels without bothering with any toppings, which they didn't need when they were this fresh. Then, to the bathroom, where he exchanged the navy suit for beige chinos and a yellow polo shirt. When he slipped on the brown wig, he grinned at himself in the mirror. With only some wrinkles betraying him, he could pass for a man 20 years his junior, thanks in large part to a well-maintained, youthful physique.

Since Rader took the metro to his Pentagon office, his candy-apple red 2005 T-bird sat mostly unused in the garage below his apartment. In three years, it had not even turned over 6,000 miles, so the ride on the Baltimore-Washington Parkway was as smooth and comfortable as floating on a cloud. One of these days, Bachman told himself, he would have to do this in warm weather so he could put the white convertible top down.

When Lochridge opened the door to his suite at the airport Hilton, the old friends and comrades in arms momentarily froze in openmouthed astonishment at the site of the other; Bachman at the weakened, haggard shell of the man who had won a bronze star partly for single-handedly carrying wounded men several kilometers through territory teeming with Viet Cong; Lochridge at the youthful appearance of the 58 year-old health nut.

"Pretty Boy," Lochridge said, using the nickname first bestowed on Bachman by a cocky drill sergeant in basic training over 40 years before. The men embraced each other warmly. "Living up to your name. Aren't you a sight!"

Bachman reached up and yanked off the wig. "Effective, huh? Good to see you, Marty." He fought back the temptation to avert his eyes from his emaciated friend, but Lochridge knew him too well, seeing the concern in his expression.

Lochridge pulled a couple of beers out of the refrigerator while

Bachman seated himself on the sofa. Every time they got together over the years, they enjoyed a beer and swapped old war stories. This time was different, though, and Lochridge knew he'd better get down to business in short order. Taking a seat in the armchair next to Bachman, they tapped their bottles together as they always had done, saying in unison, "Duty, Honor, Country!" Despite his doctor's orders to refrain from alcohol, Lochridge drained half his bottle before slowly placing it on the end table beside him.

"I'm a goner, Preston," Lochridge said, looking his friend in the eye.

Bachman eyed him just long enough to see the seriousness on his face that confirmed the meaning behind "goner." Taken with the ailing physical appearance that greeted him the moment before, he knew his friend was dying. He felt himself choking up, so he just looked down at his beer blankly, not really knowing what to say.

"Cancer of the pancreas. They want to cut more out of me, radiation, chemo, but I'm done. It's my time."

"How long?" Bachman asked, fighting to keep his composure.

"Who knows? I'm guessing I've got a month or two left. The end won't be pretty."

Bachman just shook his head, still staring at his beer bottle. His eyes were wet now, so he blinked rapidly, but quickly realized it was useless to try to fight back the tears. He looked up, asking, "what can I do for you, old friend?"

Lochridge ignored the question after a glimpse of Bachman's red, teary eyes, instead grabbing his beer and taking another deep drink. "It's okay," he said, "I'm ready. Hell, you know better than anyone I've been on borrowed time for more than 30 years now."

"It's just so—sudden," Bachman said. "Being prepared for your own death is one thing. It damn sure never made anyone else's death any easier to take."

"I know. I know."

They both sat quietly for a moment sipping their beer. Then Lochridge stood and walked to the window overlooking the deserted pool.

"Remember, I bought into David Hume's philosophy that benevolence is the supreme moral good. Help the most people to the best of your ability. That's all I've worked for and all I care about now." He turned to face

Bachman. "The only thing you can do for me is help keep my dream alive. Give the great people of the U.S. a chance to take back some control over their government."

"Like you've always said, all you can do is give them the opportunity.... Well, if there was ever a good time to—"

"Exactly," Lochridge said over his shoulder. "Now is as good a time as any I've seen." He turned to face Bachman before saying, "All we can do is give them the choice. If it's business as usual they want, then so be it. They'll have to watch their country fall apart without me."

Bachman frowned at his beer while Lochridge pulled a burgundy briefcase from beside his chair, placed it in his lap, and flipped open the locks. He removed a thin manila file, which he laid on the chair's thick armrest.

"Before I left Germany, Sean May and his friend both told me they are on board—"

"Damn, Marty!" Bachman exclaimed suddenly, "I almost forgot to give you the good news about May. He's no longer a deserter, just a WIA," he said, using the acronym for wounded in action. "They want to keep him on their computer system a little while longer—until they get to the bottom of all this."

Lochridge raised a questioning eyebrow at his last remark.

In answer to his unspoken question, he continued, "Marty, I think we both know this thing doesn't end with some lieutenant colonel contracting officer." He shook his head. "No, sir, there are some folks inside the beltway who have their fingers in this pie. I don't know the details of what—or who—the bureau is looking at, but somebody pretty high in the pecking order fabricated the desertion thing to get the cops to help find him. I guess they don't want to take it off their crime system before they figure out who is behind it being there in the first place." Bachman scratched his forehead. "You got the law degree, but the NCIC record is part of the chain of evidence, isn't it?"

"Could be," Lochridge nodded. "From the sounds of it, this can of worms could easily become a big smelly bucket." He reached over to pat Bachman's leg. "Thanks, Preston. Thank you for all you did to help them."

"Well, I think we handled this pretty well, my old friend. You were about to tell me something before I interrupted you."

"Oh, yeah. I was asking you for help again," he snickered. He tapped the file folder with his fingers. "But first, while I'm thinking about it, anything I can tell Sean on the problems at Walter Reed?"

Bachman's eyes narrowed. "Every time I think about it, I get mad as hell."

"You and me both," Lochridge said, his face growing pallid, contorting with fury. "It is unconscionable—shabby housing, the bureaucratic run-around, missed appointments—our wounded deserve better!" He formed a fist with his right hand, shaking it as he continued. "Someone needs to be held accountable…"

"Yeah, and the bastards at the Pentagon and even some of our esteemed Congressmen have known about the problems for several years at least."

"You're kidding, right?" Lochridge asked, his tone indignant.

Bachman shook his head rapidly. "I asked around some. Found out from Derek Nelson, the former chair of the Oversight and Government Reform Subcommittee, that they started hearing about the problems as early as 2003, but didn't want to embarrass the army by going public."

"Hell, they need to be embarrassed. For the love of—"

"Childress—Jake Childress from Minnesota, I think—and his pals on Defense Appropriations tried throwing money at the problems, but that obviously hasn't worked. Remember, the Pentagon had Walter Reed scheduled for closure by 2011 before we went into Iraq, so I'm sure they were letting things slide."

In the late 1990s, Lochridge remembered, BRAC—the base realignment and closure commission—announced plans to close Walter Reed and dozens of other military installations to save money. Some had already been closed, but the ongoing occupation of Iraq saw Walter Reed busier than ever.

"When they did an about-face and started shipping in all those wounded GIs, they should have had the place in ship shape," Lochridge scoffed. "So, what are they going to do?"

"As long as the public still has Walter Reed on a pedestal, I think they'll sweep it under the rug as long as they possibly can. Like all the other vet issues they've been ignoring for years. Hell, like a lot of problems." Bachman drained his beer. "Walter Reed still has a great reputation, and you've got to admit, they're doing a lot of good work there. Apparently, it's the outpatient part that isn't working, and outpatient care doesn't get much publicity anyway." He grabbed the hotel notepad from the end table and started scribbling. "I'll tell you what I would do if I were May. I know a couple of reporters at the Post who would eat this one up if someone like May gave them an exclusive."

The anger on Lochridge's face disappeared, replaced by a wide grin. "Once the public finds out, some heads will roll." He nodded. "Excellent. I'll tell him."

Bachman tore off the top page and handed it to Lochridge. "The sooner, the better. For all their sakes. Let him know I'll help anyway I can, but the first move is his."

"I will—and thank you again."

"Sure thing. This really stinks—it needs to be fixed ASAP." He looked at the file folder on Lochridge's armrest. "OP?"

Lochridge nodded, his eyes following Bachman's to the folder. "*Ops Populi* is now officially a corporation and most of what I have is being transferred to its account. Everything is being sold, turned to cash with a couple of exceptions. Sally and Erik are working on getting everyone over to Germany ASAP. Everything is set, Preston—what I need from you is to lead, with May and Sally as your execs."

"Damn, Marty! You worked your ass off for this. This is your baby—and it needs you. Not substitutes."

Lochridge cracked a smile. "Best ones I can find. Besides, you know I was always better at starting something than finishing it."

"I know you made a lot of money doing that," he said, returning a grin at Lochridge's obvious reference to his knack for hatching businesses—including his brother's—then selling out. But he didn't just cash out and disappear, he always kept his stock and a seat on the board to keep involved. All that stock, he knew, was now being sold to finance *Ops Populi*.

From the day they met—he a green buck private fresh out of training, Lochridge, his squad leader in his second tour—he knew there was something very unique about the man. Once they got to know one another, they would sometimes lie awake under the stars, too tired to sleep as Lochridge often said, and discuss politics and philosophy to get their minds off the death, heat, and bugs that defined their existence until they could drift off to sleep. In 1966, Bachman, still only 18, was little more than a baby-faced kid with dreams of becoming a hot-shot lawyer like his fictional idol, Perry Mason, the character created in the 1930s by his favorite novelist Erle Stanley Gardner. He looked up to Lochridge, not just because he outranked him, but for his intellect and his experiences. With three years of college behind him, Lochridge took great delight in the positive, optimistic tone of the university environment, claiming at the time that he would be a student for the rest of his life if he could figure out how to pay for it. He delighted in telling Bachman all about the history of great civilizations and notable figures he had studied, philosophers like Hume, men who had made great and lasting contributions to humanity, had a significant impact on the lives of others. Like himself, Lochridge had wholeheartedly embraced the altruistic ideals espoused by contemporary politicians and pundits that theirs was a lofty mission, to protect the less fortunate Vietnamese people and the rest of the world from the evils of communism. The reason he dropped out of school to volunteer, he said, was summed up well in the old West Point motto: Duty, Honor, Country.

But having been home long enough between tours to see and hear the other side—those in opposition to the war—Lochridge leaked subtle, but unmistakable hints of cynicism in some of his comments, which Bachman not only picked up on, but also vigorously objected to in their many discussions, at least initially. One recurrent theme of conversation centered on Lochridge's assertion that they had been artfully manipulated into blindly towing the party line, volunteering without questioning the underlying rationale for committing their lives to this tiny remote country and its people. For Bachman's part, he had not known any better, nor had his parents ever objected to the war in any way. In hindsight, his own inspiration had been selfless patriotism, combined with a healthy dose of youthful adventure, and as an18-year old, the scope of his reasoning did not extend much beyond. But Lochridge had an advanced education that had trained him to think critically—yet he wavered more, particularly as it became apparent that the U.S. was engaged in a futile effort.

One night after a brutal firefight which cost their platoon 6 dead and 15 injured, Lochridge collapsed to the ground in exhaustion and burst into tears. Something changed for him at that moment, an epiphany that Bachman didn't fully grasp until much later.

"We are being played. Like pawns in the great American foreign policy chess game," he said to Bachman flatly. "I feel sorry for all these guys who don't understand they're being used."

"What the hell is that supposed to mean?" Bachman, who was himself exhausted and frustrated by the turn of events in their long fight, asked in an angry tone.

Lochridge leaned back, closing his eyes and resting his head on his rucksack. "It's one thing to make a rational decision to give your life to the army, quite another to be forced—or conned into it, like we were."

"What the fu—"

Before they could say any more, ordnance started to explode all around them, and they were back to fighting—and losing ground—until early the next morning.

Despite occasionally becoming irritated with the opinions of Lochridge, they remained brothers in arms, united in a single purpose, and most importantly, were committed to each other. As time went on, they shared more and more of their deepest thoughts and aspirations.

One day, while cleaning their disassembled M-16 rifles in the relative comfort of their base camp, Lochridge said something that Bachman never would forget. Indeed, it not only became the key to understanding the psyche of the man, it also guided his own actions from that moment on.

"Control," Lochridge said as he jammed the oiled swab down the barrel of his rifle.

"Huh?" Bachman looked at him quizzically.

"Control over us is what everyone wants. It's the root cause of conflicts like this one. War, elections, marketing, you name it. The more of it you keep, the more serenity you will have. The inner peace we all crave." He stopped his cleaning to look up at Bachman. "Ever notice how much control most of us give to others? You and I handed over a ton of it to enlist, but think of normal, civilian life. We give 8 hours a day to our employers. We give it to our families, and through them, our way of life. When we go into debt, we give it to banks. And on and on. Pretty soon, most of us have very little of it left. We become slaves to others—our lives, an effect of the choices we've made instead of a cause over them."

He looked back down at the pieces of M-16 arrayed before him. "No sir, after this is over, I intend to do whatever I can to keep it—unless it suits my purpose to temporarily give some away."

"Suits your purpose?"

"When I figure that out, I'll let you know," he said, reattaching the stock to the barrel. "Whatever it is, I know I will do it better if I'm free of society's puppet strings."

"But you can't function in society—"

"Yes you can!" Lochridge interrupted. "On your terms, not theirs. Work for someone else? No way, unless I'm starving. Falling into the trap of letting the marketers tell me what to buy? Hell no. I'll buy what I like and need. Go into debt? You bet, but if I do, I'll use lots of their money to make money, not to buy junk. Banks will never own me, 'cause they'll be the ones worrying about getting their money back from me, not vice versa." Bachman remembered vividly the wide grin on Lochridge's face—a grin he hadn't seen before or since. "I'll play their game, but I'll call the shots. And I'll win."

It was within this framework that Lochridge had made his choices ever since. His life was the result of a careful calculus—a cost-benefit analysis—about whether to relinquish control in exchange for some valuable benefit. It was okay to give it up, he said, as long as you were aware of it and the benefit derived was worth it.

After Viet Nam, geography separated them, but they always managed to keep in touch with each other, taking advantage of any opportunity to re-unite. It was at Bachman's wedding that Lochridge got to know his brother, LaSalle, forging a relationship that eventually would lead to their partnership in founding the hugely successful aerospace company, and propel Preston into politics. Neither LaSalle, an aeronautical engineer, nor Lochridge had any desire to run for public office, but Preston, who by this time was running the family insurance agency in Seattle, had followed his father's footsteps into city council, a nice springboard to the state legislature. Within a few years, bolstered by popular good looks, a magnetic personality, and auspicious circumstances, he was poised for something bigger. So it was together one Sunday for a pre-game brunch at the top of the Space Needle, the three of them agreed a seat in Congress was the next step for Preston Bachman. That afternoon, after the Seahawks trounced their archrival, the Raiders, they had their omen; for the following November, Preston soundly defeated a scandal-ridden incumbent to become Washington's newest, and youngest Congressman.

It did not take Bachman long to win influence among his peers and land key committee assignments. As Bachman thrived in Congress, so too did the aerospace company and Lochridge's new real estate company, Jonic Corporation, which was making a great deal of money leasing and managing commercial office space for the burgeoning federal government.

When Washington's senior senator announced his retirement, Preston Bachman threw his hat in the ring for consideration, winning by a landslide against a virtual unknown. The celebration was dampened when not three weeks into his first term, Lorraine Lochridge was killed in a tragic car accident. In less than a month, the distraught Lochridge announced he was done, retiring, moving to Maine.

"I'll never forget the gleam in your eyes," Bachman said after Lochridge handed him a second beer, "when you came back from Maine. A new man—with a mission. This is a raw deal for you, Marty, but yes, I'm ready to step up. But even May and I won't be able to—"

"You two will kick ass," Lochridge interrupted. "When you came to me all frustrated and downtrodden by the Washington political scene and practically begged me to include you in this, that's when I knew I could count on you."

"Now, more downtrodden than ever. The resignation letter is on my laptop, ready to—"

"No!" Lochridge exclaimed with pleading eyes. "Please. You, Senator, are the bridge from the current Senate to the one of the future. We—OP—need you right where you are—your leadership is key."

"May's the expert. You told me that yourself," Bachman said with a modest shrug.

"Yes," Lochridge nodded, "but none of us knows May all that well. He's got the right stuff, but he needs someone with your clout to keep everyone on task, to get it off the ground." He walked over to the sofa where Bachman was seated and sat down next to him. "I will be at peace knowing you're doing this for me," he assured him. "Now, if you're ready to march, let me tell you what needs to happen..."

CHAPTER 55

It was the first time they had talked since Prather's return to Iraq from Germany, where he was overseeing KPH's assumption of primary responsibility for the security of U.S. military installations from the Germans. He, like his partners, had been elated when KPH had been awarded the contract after the German government, in protest of the U.S. occupation of Iraq, had decided rather suddenly to withdraw the roughly 3,000 soldiers it had voluntarily deployed to protect U.S. facilities from terrorists. Worth nearly $140 million, the contract would propel KPH into the big leagues of international private security, but Prather, while managing all KPH operations in the Middle East, was faced with the formidable task of hiring, training and positioning several thousand employees before July. Never one to skirt a challenging assignment, the strain nevertheless was wearing, putting him on a very short fuse.

"People have been asking questions about me," Prather said. "Don't know if they're feds or what, but we need to get that flash drive back and it'd better be soon."

"We haven't been able to locate May or his girlfriend," Krug said. "We're watching their houses, offices, everything. Tailing his friend in Maryland. Checking credit cards, bank accounts. Nothing."

"So they disappeared off the face of the fucking Earth?" Prather screamed into the phone. This thorn in his side was starting to hurt, and now he had to look over his shoulder. "*Someone* knows where he is."

"Someone is paying his freight. Or he's dead," Krug agreed.

They wouldn't be so lucky, Prather thought. Dead wouldn't get the flash drive back in their hands, but it sure would make it less likely that it would fall into the wrong hands. "It's past time to lean on Frese a little, agreed?"

"It seems like our only choice. Other than waiting some more, that is," Krug conceded.

"I'm told we will have to wait—for him to leave his house. The neighborhood cops, the dogs, alarms—too messy to get him at home."

"Figure something out." Krug shot back, impatiently.

"Run it by Hewitt?" Prather asked, detecting, he thought, uncharacteristic stress in his partner's voice. Prather knew the more intellectual of the three partners might point out potential consequences they hadn't considered.

"Hell no. He'll just say 'do what you have to' anyway. Just don't be stupid."

"Roger that. I'll get back to you."

After Krug had returned the receiver to its cradle, he looked down, dejected, at his feet.

The agent wearing the headset nodded. "Got it."

"Nice job," Special Agent Carl Coogle said, returning the nod and looking down at Krug. "Now, wasn't that a lot better than rotting in prison? Let's go," he said, reaching for his handcuffs.

"The U.S. Attorney?" he mumbled as he stood and put his hands behind his back.

"We'll put in a good word," Coogle said, cuffing him. "No guarantees."

Twenty miles away, in downtown Washington at a popular Thai lunch spot, James Hewitt was being escorted to a waiting black SUV by two suited FBI agents. Unfortunately for him, the camera crew that had been following Congressman DeWitt Hill managed to get a clear shot of his face before the agents were able to react.

CHAPTER 56

As much as he hated taking the risk, Erik decided he'd better go to Baltimore. The test results were not good, showing the cancer had metastasized and was spreading quickly, so this might be his last opportunity to see Lochridge alive. Even Lochridge, himself, had warned against any attempt to meet, but he would be careful, he assured Catherine as he kissed her goodbye, following the same convoluted process as before, only this time, using a different neighbor's car.

This time, though, technology gave his adversaries an added advantage, especially the night vision scopes. Eric wore no disguise—didn't think he needed one—

"That's him!" Ricker shouted, almost causing Shackleford to have a painful accident with his coffee. "Right there—in that blue Lexus."

"That's not his car!" Shackleford said back to him in mock excitement. He returned his attention to his music.

"No shit. He's in someone else's car. Go! Go! Go!"

Shackleford put his coffee down and turned the ignition switch, revving the engine as it came alive. He waited for Frese to get some distance, then he hit the gas—too hard, as it turned out—causing the wheels to spin on the wet soil under the car. When the spinning wheels finally hit the pavement, they let out a screech loud enough to draw the attention of the two special agents parked at the subdivision's entry gates.

"There they go," Martinez said into his radio.

"Got 'em," his radio squawked back, as two headlights suddenly appeared from a wood line across the street. "Where are they going? They just got here at six."

"Don't know why they would be following that blue Lexus. Stay with 'em. We've got it covered here."

As Erik made the steep descent from Braddock Heights, he smiled smugly after a glance in his rearview mirror revealed only distant headlights. Next, he checked the gas gauge, which was too close to "E" for his comfort, particularly in a strange car. "Damn," he said to himself. He decided to stop at the I-270 Rockville exit, where there would be lots of activity.

Exit 2 offered about a half dozen gas stations and quick marts, some fast food restaurants and a couple of name brand hotels. He took a quick survey and pulled into the busiest, so busy in fact that he had to get in line for a pump. For a moment, he waited from far enough behind so he could pull into the first available space, but several cars had come in after him and were pulling up behind cars being fueled. He pulled up behind a deserted Buick LeSabre, assuming its owner was finishing up inside. In front of the Buick, he was distracted by a younger woman with long blonde hair flowing from under a cowboy hat, who was dancing and singing while filling her Jeep. Her friends inside were apparently enjoying themselves, too, moving around enough to make it bounce up and down and sway from side to side. When the owner of the Buick finally ambled up to his car, gawking at the girl, Erik realized he would have to back up so he could get out. He put the Lexus in reverse before he checked the rearview, which showed a Mustang GT so close, it was practically sitting on his bumper.

"Perfect," Shackleford said. "Wait 'til he has some gas, then get in. Take him to Catoctin Park. I'll follow you."

Ricker instinctively ran his hand over his holstered Glock. "Time to go to work."

"Remember what Prather said. No messes."

Ricker said nothing as they watched Erik's hand appear from his window, waving at them to back up. A former military intelligence officer with advanced training in interrogation methods, he knew how to handle Frese.

"That's why I'm here," he said dryly, while Shackleford nudged the car back. "Grunts kill people. I know how to make them talk."

With the Buick now out of the way, Erik pulled into the empty space, took a quick look around and got out. The thumping of the music and the merrymaking from the Jeep quickly turned from a mildly interesting distraction to an annoyance while he waited for the pump to accept his credit card.

A clean, late model sedan pulled into an adjacent restaurant parking lot unnoticed, its headlights off, and parked in the relative obscurity of dark shadows created by the brightly lit convenience store.

"It's him!" Agent Thompson announced into the radio and to his partner. "What's he doing in that Lexus?"

"I don't like this," Agent Matthews, his partner said, reaching for the door. "Not one bit." He peered out over the dashboard a moment longer before saying, "Get us some backup. Something's going down."

Thomson radioed their location and a brief description of what they were seeing to Martinez. "This could get ugly," he said urgently.

"Damn! Backup. I'm on it!" the radio squawked.

"Tell 'em to keep it quiet. We don't want to spook anyone into doing something stupid."

"Roger that. Out!"

They both watched another minute, ready to spring from the car. The Mustang's passenger door swung open and a muscular, middle-aged white male emerged, holding a rag or small towel. He stretched while looking around and then walked toward the front of the car. Thompson was at once thankful for and fearful of the bustling activity he observed through the windshield. Too many bystanders to get hurt.

Erik had finished pumping and was replacing the handle in its cradle when the jeep lurched from its spot, freeing the space in front of him. The temporary quiet was interrupted by the roar of the GT's V-8 coming alive to take its place. When he turned to replace the gas cap, out of the corner of his eye, he saw a man standing in front of the mustang with a rag in one hand, the other under his blazer.

"He's going for a gun!" Thompson shouted. "Move!"

They bolted from their car simultaneously, pulling their guns while running toward Erik's car. Thompson took the rear while Martinez ran toward the front.

Not yet aware of what was happening, Erik heard a deep voice say, "Get in the car. Now!"

He looked up to see the tip of a pistol barrel under a rag pointed at him at waist level. The man from the Mustang had cold, steely eyes that meant business. But before he could react, he heard to voices shouting, "Down! Get down!" Both he and the man with the gun instinctively looked up and over the Lexus to find the source of the shouting, but Erik seized the opportunity created by the distraction to raise his leg with as much force as he could in an attempt to kick the gun out of the man's hand. The Glock flew up and to Erik's right, smacking into the pump before falling back to the ground, just beyond the reach of its owner. At the same time they both lunged for the gun, the driver's side door swung open, and two approaching voices shouted "Freeze! FBI!" Erik grabbed the Glock by the barrel, but his much larger opponent clutched the grip and easily snatched it away. Overpowered, flat on his stomach, arms outstretched, Erik did the only thing he could do to get out of the way: roll toward the car.

Blam! Blam! He felt the sting in his shoulder before the weight of the man collapsed onto his torso, pinning him to the concrete. "Don't do it, asshole! Drop it!" he heard someone shout, then looked up to see a pistol fall at the feet of the Mustang's driver. Erik struggled to free himself from the dead weight of the gasping, gurgling man on top of him, but his stronger right arm was immobilized, his hand resting in a puddle of hot, sticky liquid, which he assumed was the man's blood. Intermittent shrieks and screams filled the air with the growing wail of an approaching siren in the background. He lay there motionless, surrendering to the futility of his struggle to free himself.

The shoes and cuffs of the approaching man were all he could see through the space separating the bottom of the car and the concrete where he lay. "Frese. Mr. Frese, are you all right?" He felt the weight move off his torso, then his arm.

"Uh, I think so." The instant he lifted his right arm, he felt a sharp pain in his shoulder and looked with horror at his blood-soaked hand and sleeve before letting it fall to his side.

"Just lie still—don't move. I'm Martinez. Special Agent with the FBI. An ambulance is on the way."

Erik turned his head to look at his shoulder, but in his current position, could not see anything. "My shoulder," he said. "Am I hit?"

Martinez got down to get a closer look. "Think so. Doesn't look too bad—"

He jumped at the sound of screeching tires, as a small army of cops suddenly swarmed onto the convenience store's lot. Martinez looked back down at Erik. "Gotta go talk to the locals for a second. Just lie still. You're going to be OK."

"My wife!" he blurted out to the departing Martinez, who didn't respond. When he tried to get up, his legs buckled underneath him and he passed out.

CHAPTER 57

A feast of fresh pastries from the Manschau *backerei* greeted May in the kitchen at dawn the next morning. His body was finally adjusted to the time, and with plenty of rest and the slow pace of recent days, he was waking at the first glimmer of daybreak. After explaining the Lochridge-initiated tradition of once weekly trips to the town's bakery, Karla gave him a small description of each of the inviting treats before handing him a plate, which he eagerly loaded up and carried with coffee and great concentration up to Ginny's room. She went straight for the *nussecken*—a triangle-shaped cake made with ground nuts and whose edges were covered in chocolate; May was partial to the *apfelkuchen*, a delightfully rich pastry filled with sliced apples, rum-flavored currants, and bread crumbs, topped with a creamy custard.

"Look at what I found on the net last night," Ginny said handing him a small stack of paper.

May unfolded the pages to see a photograph of a smiling Martin Lochridge dressed in a conservative suit standing in what appeared to be a lobby. A decorative logo with the words "Innovative Management Solutions, Inc.," the much larger letters "IMSI" staggered vertically to the right of Lochridge's left arm. It was a *Business Today* magazine article from 2003, featuring IMSI as a leader in internet-based application development for the public sector. Scanning the first page, May saw that the company had been involved in numerous projects under contract with the federal government. Highlighted were several of the larger ones, including the Army's Joint Patient Tracking Application—described by the writer as a web-based, mobile system designed to allow army medical personnel to access records and coordinate medical care for soldiers from the point of injury to the completion of treatment—a human resources system for the Department of Defense, and a major upgrade to the FBI's National Crime Information Center.

May gave her a puzzled look. "OK, he made it big in computer software. I know that already."

"No, just read a little more," she urged, waving her hand.

May obliged, continuing on to the next page.

"The sidebar," Ginny said pointing.

The gray-shading and the sidebar's title, "All in the Family," captured his attention.

"As it turns out, Martin Lochridge is not the first Lochridge to be involved with the FBI's National Crime Information Center. The nationwide system, known by its acronym NCIC, is widely used by federal, state and local law enforcement to promote coordination and serve as a data repository. NCIC had originally been developed in the late 1960s under then-director J. Edgar Hoover and was long overdue for a major overhaul to take advantage of recent technologies. Lochridge's IMSI, known primarily for its defense-related work, nonetheless submitted the winning bid and completed the project in time for its scheduled 2000 release. When I asked him about the sudden switch from defense to working on the FBI system, I was surprised at his response.

"My father came out of retirement to be one of the consulting developers of NCIC. He truly was one of the first computer geeks," he told me with a laugh.

Robert A. Lochridge was one of the internet's pioneers as a project manager for the government's Advance Research Projects Agency ARPANET in the cold war 1960s, which was originally conceived as a communications system that would be impervious to a nuclear attack..."

"How about that," May said, looking up at Ginny. "His dad. Involved in creating ARPANET—the original internet."

"I never knew it was set up to be a defense department communication system," she said.

May nodded. "They considered our telephone system too vulnerable to the nukes, so they came up with this idea of tying a bunch of computers together. If one of the nodes got knocked out in an attack, the others would keep the network functioning." He rubbed his chin thoughtfully. "This explains a lot."

"What do you mean?" Ginny questioned.

"Martin's interest in my dissertation idea."

"I don't follow…"

"He grabbed on to my central theme of using the internet as the backbone for mass participation in calling a constitutional convention—before most people even knew of its existence. His dad's involvement in ARPANET allowed him to see its potential, something only a few people understood back then. We know what happened—a select few of them jumped on the bandwagon and made piles of money." He snickered. "Even my own dissertation committee—with one exception—thought I was flaky for suggesting a huge political movement could be based on a technology that so few understood and had access to."

"Well, I guess you are vindicated," she said with a shrug. "I wasn't even thinking about that when I printed the article—it was just interesting background." Ginny pointed at the printouts. "I found a few more business-related articles, but I am surprised there isn't more. He's managed to keep himself out of the limelight despite his wealth."

"Privacy seems to be very important to him," May agreed with a nod. "Computers, satellites, real estate. Is there more?"

"No, not really. I guess in my own way, I was checking him out—and feeding my online addiction."

As soon as she signed on to Lochridge's computer, a message window popped up notifying her of a new fax from Lochridge's lawyer.

"Here's the stuff from Martin's attorney," she said to May who was once again perusing Lochridge's book collection.

Ginny printed the 34-pages containing the OP-USA employment forms, memoranda of understanding and trust documents for both her and May. She set aside the cover-page, which included a note to Lochridge requesting him to call to confirm receipt and carried the remaining stack over to the sofa where May was leafing through an old book with yellow post-it notes sticking out of the top. Two other books, which appeared nearly identical to the one he was examining, sat beside him.

"What are those?" she asked.

"*The Decline and Fall of the Roman Empire*," he replied. "I've always wanted to read it, but never had the time." He tapped the two books stacked next to him for effect. "You can see why. Over a thousand pages in these."

"They look old," she observed.

He nodded. "I probably wouldn't have noticed them if it weren't for all of these post-it notes sticking out of them. This set is from the 1940s, but I'm pretty sure it was originally published way back in the late 1700s."

"Reading those would probably put me in a coma," she laughed. "What's with the post-it notes?"

"Not sure yet," he shrugged, looking down at the open book on his lap. "But from what I've seen so far, he marked sections and made notes describing things that happened to the Romans he thinks parallel what is happening in the U.S. right now."

She peeled off his part of the stack from the lawyer's office and set the documents on his lap as she sat down beside him. "Well, here's some more reading for you—the documents from Martin's attorney."

They sat reading through the documents in silence by the light of the bright morning sun streaming through the windows. Both of their careers required a hefty amount of reading, so they were each accustomed to scanning written material at a fairly rapid pace.

"Blue streak," May said with a chuckle. "My OP code name."

Ginny glanced at the page May was reading and skipped ahead a couple of pages to catch up to him. This was the heart of the nondisclosure agreement to keep the group's existence secret and protect the anonymity its members. She read aloud, "Hereinafter, you will identify yourself in all correspondence pertaining to *Ops Populi*, whether oral or written, and through all communications media, as *Running Fawn*."

May, already reading through the document labeled "Trust Agreement," acknowledged her only with a single nod. He put the papers on his lap and looked over at Ginny, shaking his head. "Hard to believe. A month ago, I was in Baghdad, you were in Washington. Here we are, together, in a German castle about to be part of history doing something I had all but dismissed as a fantasy and becoming wealthy at the same time. I don't know about you, but I'm still afraid someone is going to shake me out of this dream."

The phone on Lochridge's desk began to ring a distinctive pattern to indicate it was his private line, the line on which Lochridge had set up their voice mail. They both stood at the same time, but Ginny was closer to the desk, so she stepped over to answer it.

"Hello," she said timidly. "Oh, hello Martin, where are—"

She looked at May openmouthed, a pall falling over her expression while she listened intently to what was obviously bad news. He waited anxiously for some clue, but she said little.

"Yes, I will tell him. We will see you tomorrow." She dropped the phone in its cradle. "Erik was injured in a shootout at a convenience store near Rockville last night."

"Oh, Jesus," May said, dropping his head.

"He's going to be okay," she continued. "Martin talked to his wife a little while ago—what is it, about 4 in the morning there? Anyway, it was just a grazing wound. They're keeping him in the hospital—for protection."

May threw up his hands. "What the hell was he doing in Rockville? He told me he was going to play it safe until this KPH thing was over."

She relayed all that Martin had told her. He left his neighborhood in a neighbor's car, was on his way to Baltimore, guilefully planning to swing through Dulles, buy a plane ticket to throw off his tail, then rent a different car for the remainder of the drive. When he had to stop for gas in Rockville, he noticed two guys in a Mustang, one of them pulled a gun on him, ordered him to get in the car. That's when the shooting started.

"Well-dressed guys in a hot, new car. He doesn't know for sure, but suspects they were KPH goons."

"Who else would it be?" May said, visibly shaken. For the first time in many days, he felt aching in his neck and shoulder region. "Sons of bitches!"

Ginny walked over to him to offer some comfort. "He told Martin the agents still managed to tail him, even though he was in a borrowed car. They probably saved his life," she said, leading him back to the sofa.

May plopped himself on to it heavily. "They are running scared—desperate to get that flash drive back. I knew something like this was going to hap—"

"He's okay and safe now, Sean. That's all that matters. Let him rest awhile then give him a call later."

May nodded, rubbing his eyes. "I hope this thing is almost over," he sighed.

"With the arrest of that KPH guy yesterday, we know it's the beginning of the end, anyway," she said to reassure him. "I have a feeling it'll be over soon."

"You're assuming his arrest was related to—"

"I think it's a pretty safe assumption, don't you?"

"I guess so," May admitted. "The FBI, or whoever, needs to get to the bottom of it soon—before anyone else gets hurt."

Ginny let it drop, choosing instead to brighten the mood. "Martin did say he had some good news, but he wants to deliver it in person. He's flying back tonight."

"Ever the mystery man," May said with a dour tone in his voice.

It was easy for Ginny to see how Erik's wounding was affecting May. Although the past few days had been restful and relaxing, the big ups and downs of the past weeks, the accumulated stress, were all taking a heavy toll.

"Let's go do something fun," she said with as much cheer as she could muster. "How about exploring Cologne? It's pretty close."

"I need to talk to Erik," he said impatiently.

"He's probably sleeping. Four in the morning there, remember?"

May let out a heavy sigh, trying to force himself to relax. He thought about going to his room to find the pills he had been given at Walter Reed.

"C'mon," Ginny urged. "Some sightseeing will be good for us."

With a deep sigh, May reflected momentarily. His pragmatic side told him there was nothing he could do other than disturb his friend's rest. Lochridge's assurance that Erik was all right would have to suffice for now. "You're right," he conceded, dismissing the temptation to go for the pills. "You'll like Cologne. Let's go find Wilhelm."

CHAPTER 58

By the time Prather found out about the arrest of his partners, he was surrounded by a squad of military police, though he was completely oblivious to it. Several hours before, while casually sipping his morning coffee, his assistant in KPH's Baghdad office had come across the same internet story Ginny had seen and had immediately called the Virginia headquarters, where he not only confirmed Hewitt's arrest outside a restaurant in DC, but also was told about the feds taking Krug out of his office in handcuffs. When he tried to call Prather, who was at a KPH job site in Karbala, all he got was static from Prather's cell phone. Less than five minutes later, a squad of military police stormed the office, guns at the ready.

"You'd better tell me where he is," the captain in charge said to him in a calm but even tone. "It would be a shame for a young man like you to spend the best part of his life at Leavenworth."

Prather's young assistant, a spoiled nephew of Hewitt's whose father had condemned him to Prather's Baghdad operation as punishment for flunking out of his senior year in high school, readily caved. Panic-stricken, he gave the captain not only the job location—complete with a description and grid coordinates—but a current photo of his boss as well. Prather was accompanied by one other American KPH employee, the job's security crew were Latin American civilians, mostly Chilean. Twenty minutes later, the teenager was thrust into a six by nine cell, quivering in fear.

They assumed Prather would be armed—most contractors operating in Iraq were. The captain had been briefed on Prather, knew he was ex-Special Forces and might violently resist any attempt to detain him. Before leaving for Karbala, he ordered everyone out of their desert camouflage and into civilian clothes in the hopes of being less conspicuous as they approached the site. Several of his highly trained MPs were of Latin descent, so he rounded up hard hats and some tools to allow them to blend in long enough to nab Prather—hopefully without any bloodshed. His instructions were to bring Prather directly to Baghdad International, where he would hand over custody to a group of waiting FBI agents to be flown back to the states.

The captain's temperament made him well-suited for such a mission. Not one to be easily excited or flustered, the fact that his orders had come directly from the commander, Multinational Forces Baghdad was interesting, but not unnerving. He would execute his mission to the best of his ability, flawlessly, if past performance were any indication. The men and women of "Charlie Company," 327th Military Police Battalion, greatly admired their commander, and the feeling was mutual. He could count on them, particularly the hand-picked squad of veterans, to do the job and do it well.

Prather paid no attention to their faces, only caring about getting warm bodies on each job site for the least amount of money possible. And providing security for re-building a large power station required many of them because it was a priority target for disruptive insurgents. Latin Americans fit the bill perfectly: they were cheap. He could hire four for the same money that one American would cost him—almost 3 for the price of an Iraqi—and because the army had taught him Spanish, he could deal with them one-on-one instead of through a translator.

When his phone started to vibrate again, he ignored it. The sooner he could finish going over security plans with the construction foreman and his Chilean detail chief, the sooner he could get on the road to Baghdad and closer to reliable phone service. Most calls from Hewitt's brown-nosing nephew were a waste of his time anyway, since he delegated very little of importance to the spoiled brat. When the phone vibrated yet again, he cussed under his breath as he flipped open the phone, taking a couple of steps back and turning away from the others.

"This had better be important, Frank!" he said through clenched teeth. "I'm in the middle of a meet—"

"Shut up and listen," the cold voice said on the other end. "Your partners have been arrested in the U.S. You are next. Get out while you can."

When the phone went dead, he squinted at the LCD display to try to identify where the call had come from, but before he could bring up his call list, he heard a commotion behind him and then someone bumped into him hard, almost knocking him off his feet. Annoyed, he pivoted to see a couple of the Hispanics in hard hats with pistols pointed at him and the two men he had been meeting with.

"What the fu—"

"Hands in the air! Now!" one of them shouted in perfect English. "MPs!"

The nimble Prather reacted instinctively, dropping in a twisting motion to hit the ground in a roll. With his right arm, he reached for his .45 holstered near the small of his back, while still managing to keep his body in rotation toward the cover of a partially finished retaining wall.

At the same time, his Chilean detail leader, who still had an AK-47 strapped across his back, dropped face-down to the ground while shouting in Spanish to what he thought was a small group of his security men running to the scene, each carrying assault rifles at the ready. Rather than following his command, however, he looked up to see one of them spraying a burst of 5.56 millimeter rounds in Prather's direction, the others training their weapons on him and the still-standing Iraqi foreman. With the AK-47's strap sandwiched between his chest and the ground, he knew it was too late for the weapon to be of any use to him. Knowing the decision to drop would be his last, a smug grin broke across his lips when the sound of Prather's command voice pierced the commotion—just as he squeezed his eyes closed for the last time, wondering if he would even feel the hot lead tear into his flesh.

CHAPTER 59

Ginny found May lounging on the sofa in the living room, flipping through the seemingly endless supply of satellite TV channels. When he saw her appear from the stairway carrying the black binder that contained his dissertation, he let the remote fall onto the cushion, content to let to the thickly accented BBC reporter deliver international sports highlights.

"Doing some light reading?" he asked in a sardonic tone.

"Very funny," she said, plopping down beside him. "I take it there has been no sign of Martin?"

"Not yet." Karla had informed them at breakfast that a sleepy-eyed Lochridge and Wilhelm had arrived at Berg Segur at a few minutes after seven. "The man needs his rest. Don't you remember how tired we were after that flight?"

Ginny nodded. Their excursion to Cologne, while fun and distracting, had somehow reversed their moods. Ginny awoke feeling anxious and edgy, while May appeared to her to be quite relaxed and in good spirits. "Isn't it driving you crazy? This mysterious news he has for us?"

"Here, try this." He handed her the bottle he had been resting on his leg.

"Is this part of your breakfast?" she asked, reading the label. "Grimbergen Dubbel?"

"More like lunch," he said, glancing at his watch. "The bartender at the place in DC you took me to told me the monks made ales like this to provide nourishment during periods of fasting."

"Quite tasty," she said. "Like a good wine."

"How far are you into that?" he asked, looking at the binder.

She took another sip of the Grimbergen while reading the headlines scrolling at the bottom of the television. "Well, to be honest, I've been skipping around a bit. But I've read a good bit of it."

He looked at her face in expectation of some feedback, but she just kept her eyes on the screen directly in front of where she sat. "Well? What do you think so far?"

When she ignored his question, May followed her eyes to the television just as the ticker was scrolling the words "shot and killed by U.S. Army Military Police in Karbala…"

"What was that—" May started.

"It said the Pentagon reported that an American military contractor wanted for questioning was shot and killed in Karbala by the military police."

"Do you think it could be one of them?" he asked without moving his eyes.

"Possible. I'll see what I can find out on-line," Ginny said, eagerly jumping to her feet.

"See you in a few hours," he said with a hint of sarcasm, knowing her proclivity to spend hours on the internet feeding her self-professed addiction, doing what she loved.

CHAPTER 60

As he often did when he was in his office, Preston Bachman yanked the phone out of the cradle on the first ring without giving his staff the time to answer.

"Bachman," he said flatly.

"Good morning, Senator," came the sweet-sounding female voice, just a hint of a Southern accent. "This is Special Agent Dixon. Julie Dixon. I was asked to give you a SITREP on the KPH matter."

For some reason, he always felt a pinch of irritation when he heard acronyms he associated with his military service coming from civilians. Maybe it was just his peculiar hang-up, but when he heard it, he envisioned himself back in the jungles of Vietnam, bullets flying, his radio man by his side, someone screaming a tactical situation report in his ear. It just didn't seem right to be getting a SITREP from this young lady while sitting in his comfortable office in a suit. Get over it, Bachman.

"Yes, go ahead Agent Dixon."

She gave him the scrubbed and stripped-down version of the apprehensions of Krug and Hewitt, whose arrest had already hit the Washington news media.

This was the courtesy call he had been promised whenever there were new developments in the case. Bachman didn't bother asking her for more information because he knew she was under strict instruction to give him just this basics, nothing more. With cheer in his voice, he thanked her, hit the button to disconnect the call, and dialed a cell phone number from memory, let it ring a few times, then hung up. He pulled his own cell phone out of his pocket and waited for it to ring.

Bachman scowled at this little game his son in-law, Mason, had devised—a "system," he called it—to protect the career into which Bachman himself had installed him about fifteen years before. Not that he wasn't qualified for the job; quite the contrary. He had graduated at the top of his William and Mary law school class in 1986. While preparing for the bar exam, he worked odd jobs in Williamsburg for a year while waiting for Emilee to finish her law degree, then was hired by the Richmond firm Davis, Jeffords and Lee. It was not six months before the complaints started, usually funneled through his blunt daughter in her weekly calls home. Mason hated the grueling hours and tedium of a junior associate in private practice, and Emilee disliked the pretentious, closed social society of Richmond. When, at a family holiday gathering, Bachman casually mentioned the Senate had just approved a hefty $1 billion appropriations increase for expanding the Department of Justice—seven thousand new employees, including new lawyers, were to be hired—Emilee pounced on her unsuspecting father. In 1990, Bachman was still one of the junior members of the Judiciary Committee and its Subcommittee on Crime and Drugs, but he nevertheless was able to open doors to DOJ's Criminal Division, giving his daughter and son in-law a fresh start, no more 70-hour work weeks, and a welcome move up to Northern Virginia.

"Preston, you're at it early this morning," his son in-law C. Mason Quick's deep baritone hummed in his ear. "I'm still crawling along the beltway."

"A pleasant young lady named Dixon just called me with a SITREP," Bachman said with a little too much sarcasm. "What's up?"

"I guess they're getting that stuff from Quantico," Quick said as he changed lanes. "Dixon told you we got two of them?"

"Uh, huh," Bachman grunted. "That's all she told me."

"Good. She did what she was supposed to do. Anyway, a squad of army MPs tried to apprehend the third one—Prather—in Karbala, but he and his boys had other plans. According to the report submitted by the MP commander, they killed him in a gunfight."

As much as he hated to admit it to himself, Bachman grinned with pleasure at the news. With a five-minute phone call to the Pentagon, he had been able to learn enough about Prather's military background to understand he was a wild card, and thanks to all the great training he received from the elite Army Special Forces, a very dangerous individual.

"The end of it?" Bachman asked him.

Quick delayed his reply just enough to carefully choose his words. Bachman knew he was crossing an invisible line between what was, or soon would be, public knowledge and what could be the closely guarded secrets of an on-going investigation. Yet, as much as he liked and admired his son in-law, Mason's reticence was damned annoying. Not once had he ever asked Mason for anything; he expected, felt he deserved, a plain-spoken reply.

"Uh, not yet," he said finally.

"Alright." He took a breath while giving Mason enough time to voluntarily elaborate. Maybe he was navigating through a difficult traffic situation, maybe just being a coy ass. "Why not?" he grunted.

"The stink of this thing," he said very carefully, "is spreading. Hewitt's lawyer is angling for a deal, so he's playing his cards close to his chest. But there are more—people—involved."

Speaking of playing your cards close to your chest, Bachman thought. Did he have to drag it out of Mason?

"Like who?" he asked with as much patience as he could manage.

"People inside the beltway, for one thing."

"Oh, for Christ's—" He stopped as it suddenly dawned on him. "Wait a minute. Are you saying people in the administration are involved?"

"No, not the administration," came the hushed reply.

"Congress?" Bachman asked, incredulous.

"You said it, not me."

"Oh, shit!" Bachman looked up to see a member of his staff standing in his doorway looking at him oddly. He usually didn't close his door, but now wished he had. With a wave of his hand, the staffer did an about-face, pulling the door closed behind him. Another scandal. Just what Washington needed right now.

"That's not all. Hewitt says he has proof that KPH has—had—financial arrangements with others, here, in the UK, and in Iraq all the way back to the Coalition Provisional Authority, and with Iraq's interim government."

"Jesus, sounds like a can of worms to me. Anything said about Sean May and Virginia Burress?"

"The bureau definitely wants statements from them, especially May. But until they find the KPH killers, find out who else is involved in this, they are not safe in the U.S. For that matter, they really aren't safe anywhere."

"Agreed." Bachman listened briefly to the background noises coming from Mason's phone. Construction equipment, probably at the mixing bowl. He turned his chair to look out the window. A bright, blue sky, people walking in shirtsleeves, hinted at the arrival of spring.

"I'm thinking WitSec," Mason said.

Another frigging acronym to decipher. Bachman rolled his eyes, unimpressed. Maybe OP should propose an amendment to outlaw government's use of cute little acronyms, abbreviations and jargon in favor of plain English, he mused. Government might just function a little better without them.

"I take it you're suggesting the witness protection program?"

"Well, it's an option," Mason said in an apologetic tone. "If it were me, I wouldn't want to go home until I was sure it was safe for me and my family. And that could take awhile unless Krug and Hewitt give up some names."

It might be the only alternative to hiding out indefinitely in Germany. Thanks to the quick thinking of Martin, Sean and Ginny were out of sight, but their safety was not assured until these animals were caught. "Getting them in—protection—that would have to come from the U.S. Attorney, I assume."

"Normally, yes," Mason said, "but maybe a call from you could get it on the fast-track. The program is handled over in the OEO—uh, sorry—Office of Enforcement Operations."

A gentle knock on the door was the signal that it was time to go to the chamber. Bachman thanked his son in-law, flipped his cell phone closed, and darted out the door—jacket in one hand, a three-page speech in the other—down the stairs to the basement.

In the system of tunnels connecting the congressional office buildings to the Capitol, one could wait to ride on the rail cars, which in the case of Hart and Dirksen were similar to the cars on the Metro, or walk along the parallel pathway. To stay in shape, Bachman always walked wherever and whenever he could, so without a glance to see if there was a waiting train, he set off on the path that ran underneath Constitution Avenue, across First Street, to a fork in front of Russell and down into the north, or Senate, wing of the Capitol. With the exception of an occasional nod of his head to someone he recognized, he kept his eyes fixed firmly to his front as he moved rapidly through the brightly lit tunnel, all the while mulling over Mason's suggestion. Witness protection was a drastic step—new identities, new homes, no contact with friends and family, hovering U.S. Marshals—but, it should only be temporary for Sean and Ginny. At the very least, they would have to remain hidden until the killer or killers, who, for all anyone knew, were still on the hunt for them and the flash drive, were apprehended and safely behind bars. As long as Sean was on the level, knew nothing about the bribes except what he and Ginny had seen on the flash drive, there would be no logical reason for any of the other accomplices to harm either of them once the U.S. Attorney publicly disclosed they had the drive in their possession. May had some value as a witness; Ginny, who was little more than a bystander in this mess, much less so. Erik and his wife were also not entirely safe at the moment, although they at least had some law enforcement protection.

He barely made it to his seat in time for Morning Business, the period at the beginning of the session allotted to introducing bills and resolutions and during which members could request permission to speak about any subject of concern to them. Wearing a sullen expression, he clutched the three folded pages in his trembling left hand, prepared to deliver, brief, but scathing remarks about yet another emergency supplemental war funding request from His Highness's administration. After much cantankerous debate and with skilled parliamentary maneuvering, the House had just approved their $91 billion version; now all eyes turned to the Senate and its $106 billion package—and where opponents over in the House had plenty of company.

Yes, he had said it all before in one way or another; there had been plenty of opportunity. Since the invasion of Iraq, Congress had been presented with $250 billion of such "requests," which, as a practical matter, were demands Congress could not deny. But, once again, he felt compelled to go on record against the administration's cleverly designed scheme to fund a war—for the first time in history—outside the normal appropriations process, depriving Congress of the oversight and scrutiny it provides. Clinging to his conviction that with all the technical prowess of the U.S., all of the sophisticated weaponry and intelligence capability, a couple of platoons of men like Prather could have accomplished the ostensible goal of taking out Hussein, he would vehemently oppose dumping another hundred billion into what had become the bottomless pit of an occupation rife with waste, fraud, and most unfortunately of all, shattered lives. How long would it—could it—continue?

While preparing his remarks, he had opened a recent CRS report sitting on his desk. A smile at seeing the name Virginia Burress listed as a contributing associate was quickly replaced by red-faced anger when he saw the astounding numbers: the war would consume nearly $10 billion per month in the current fiscal year; as early as next year, the total cost could surpass $500 billion, ten times what the administration had initially projected. Congress was writing blank checks the U.S. couldn't cash without the willing cooperation of the likes of Russia, China, the Saudis and other Middle Eastern nations—all of whom were happily bankrolling American extravagance, but any of whom could have a change of heart in the blink of an eye. A disaster waiting to happen. Sadly, the members of the great deliberative body that was the United States Senate had found neither the moral fiber nor the political will to prevent it.

As he surveyed the faces of perhaps thirty of his colleagues now in the chamber, some smiling and joking, others smug in the belief that what they were about to do was patriotic, heroic even, he couldn't help but wonder if some of the many billions they would be forced to approve—that the U.S. would have to borrow—would find its way into one or more of their pockets.

CHAPTER 61

It was after 2 a.m. Sunday morning when they arrived at their Arlington home. Helen Drysdale had to wash her clothes and pack for another trip to New York with her best friend; her husband, Congressman Thomas Drysdale had pricey tickets to see the Wizards-Lakers game Sunday afternoon. So they had decided to take the late Saturday flight back to Washington after a final day of skiing.

He trudged directly up the back stairs with their luggage, intending to go straight to bed. No sooner had he made it to the top of the stairs when he heard Helen shout out.

"Oh my God! We've been robbed!"

Drysdale dropped the luggage and ran back down the stairs. She had gone into his home office just off the foyer to turn up the heat, where she stood aghast, hand over her mouth. At first glance, the general disarray of what was always a neat and tidy room was evident. Behind his desk, he saw the empty spot on the credenza where his computer's CPU had once been, but the monitor, keyboard and mouse were still there. The normally closed and locked closet door was ajar, so he raced over to it, pulling it open wide.

"Shit! The safe. The file cabinet," he exclaimed. He wheeled around to see that the bottom drawer of his desk, which he always kept locked, was also partially opened. "Call the police while I look around at the rest of the house."

The ringing phone froze them both. Helen, who was closer to it, stepped close enough to see the caller ID on its display.

"The Petersons? At this hour?"

An older, retired couple, their neighbors were always happy to keep an eye of their house—a task made easier in the winter by the barren trees—and to take care their two cats. Robert Peterson was a totally laid back, retired orthodontist, interested mainly in crossword puzzles and his fruit trees, while his wife, Michelle, spent most of her time socializing, gossiping and gushing effusively to everyone she knew about their neighbor, the Congressman.

While Ben surveyed the rest of the house, Helen listened in stunned silence to Michelle, who had waited up all night for their expected return, describe the events of Saturday afternoon. It was just after noon, when a convoy of 10 cars and SUVs paraded down the street. There had been as many as 15 vehicles, including a van with a satellite dish mounted to its top and a local locksmith company van, parked haphazardly in the driveway, on the yard and in the street. The agent in charge had presented her with identification, telling her only that it was official FBI business, whereupon many men went into the house for the better part of an hour. When they were finished in the house—Michelle had not taken her eyes off the place during that hour, she assured Helen—they hauled off a computer, a file cabinet, a safe, and several green trash bags whose contents were unknown to her. Then, they all left as quickly as they had arrived. In characteristic fashion, Michelle excitedly embellished, using 3 words when one would have sufficed, so she was still talking when Tom Drysdale entered the room, shrugging.

Helen grabbed a notepad and pen from his desk and scribbled "FBI" on it in large letters while he looked over her shoulder. Without saying a word, he bolted from the room, followed a few seconds later by a slamming door, and the sound of his Porsche revving in the garage. She was sure that Michelle was watching as he tore out of the driveway, although she made no mention of it, choosing instead to continue her verbose report unabated. While half-listening to the chatter, regret descended heavily on Helen. It was she who had insisted they take this short hiatus together—to de-stress, of all things—without the possibility of intrusions. No e-mail, no internet, no cell phones. Certainly, the world wouldn't fall apart in few short days without Tom Drysdale…

Foreboding so filled his thoughts during the short drive to Capitol Hill, he was only vaguely aware of passing the familiar landmarks, almost driving right by the Longworth House Office Building. One of the three buildings occupied by the House of Representatives, Longworth stood prominently between South Capitol Street and New Jersey Avenue in Southwest Washington, a fine example of the Neo-classical Revival style of architecture. With its grand appearance, a white marble facade rising above a granite base and five porticoes supported by Ionic columns, it was hard to miss. But Drysdale wasn't observing his surroundings—in his present state of mind, he was lucky to have made it downtown at all.

With frazzled nerves and a flood of adrenaline coursing through his body, his hands and legs trembled when, just before 3 a.m., he turned the key to unlock the door to his second floor suite. All relaxation afforded by the four-day ski trip to his chalet in the Colorado Rockies was obliterated by fear that had his heart pounding relentlessly. Instead of a leisurely Sunday afternoon enjoying the Wizards-Lakers game he had been so looking forward to, he would have to do everything he could to obscure a lucrative relationship with the firm whose money had been used to purchase the coveted chalet, the Porsche, and many other toys he never dreamed of owning. But without his staff to help him, particularly with finding things on the computers, he was in for a long, long day.

And how would he explain all this to Helen?

In dark stillness, he cast a couple of furtive glances around him, listening but hearing nothing but the steady, low hum of Longworth's heating and cooling system. Even though it was a cold morning, he wiped beads of clammy perspiration from his face with his coat sleeve. "Get a grip," he mumbled, reminding himself how careful he had been in all his dealings with KPH. He grabbed a beer from the small refrigerator in the reception area and leaned back on the desk, while forcing several deep breaths to calm himself. He rubbed the cold bottle on his forehead, neck and all over his face, while struggling to organize his scrambled thoughts, to bring his focus to the present and the task ahead. To cover his tracks would be a delicate job—sorting through records and selecting which ones to delete—demanding a clear head. In reality, there wasn't anything flagrantly incriminating here that wasn't securely locked away in his safe. But there were many documents, computer files, e-mails, and telephone records linking Thomas Drysdale to KPH, some of which, like campaign finance reports, were already in the public domain. The media scavengers would surely latch on to his close association with KPH, but he would have plenty of company for there were many—probably dozens—in Congress whose ties to the firm could be documented. Deflecting attempts to embarrass him that were sure to come in the days ahead would be manageable, but far more unpleasant things awaited him if the truth were exposed.

Feeling a little more in control of his faculties, he set the unopened beer on the desk and walked to the bank of light switches inside the door. With any luck, he could get through this in time to make it to the one o'clock tip-off.

As soon as he opened the door that separated the reception area from the inner office, he saw that he was too late. The anxiety he had just fought back returned with a vengeance as he surveyed the open desk drawers, empty file cabinets, missing computers. He raced to his office, fumbling with the keys in a panic until he finally managed to get the key in the lock. He tore through the spacious office to his desk, where he was once again greeted by empty open drawers and a void where his computer CPU once sat.

He collapsed in his chair, head hung low. No decisions to make now—except, perhaps, whether or not to run. As he looked up at the photo of himself shaking hands with the President, Thomas Drysdale, the rising Congressional star, knew he was finished.

CHAPTER 62

The FBI agreed to their request to be interviewed from Germany, even sending two agents over on a plane rather than opting for a simple, more practical telephone interview. "Our tax dollars hard at work," a chuckling Lochridge had quipped on their drive to Dusseldorf Airport to meet the agents. In their first direct contact with law enforcement since this all began, Ginny and May each went into separate rooms accompanied by one of the agents—they had even sent a female to interview Ginny—and a tape recorder to go on record with their individual statements. Typical of his mistrust of the government, Lochridge had insisted on accompanying them as their unofficial attorney—just to keep everything clean, he said. "Tell them everything, of course" he coached them, "but if they ask you anything that sounds, well, odd, tell me right away. I'm sure they are sending their expert manipulators. Oh, I mean interrogators," he joked.

As expected, May's interview was much longer and more detail-oriented than Ginny's. When he emerged from the small airport conference room almost two hours later, his eyes were red and he looked tired.

When they compared notes afterward, they were disappointed that neither had been successful in getting any detailed information about the investigation, each being given the official brush-off of "we cannot disclose anything until charges are filed." To their surprise, there was nothing said about witness protection, but before leaving that morning, Lochridge had once again gently reminded them to say nothing about what they knew through Bachman, since all of it was gleaned through unofficial communication. At the conclusion of the interviews, the agents thanked the three of them for their time and cooperation, and, always one to seize opportunity, Lochridge had elicited the promise of being contacted before any charges were made public.

Wilhelm drove them into the center of Dusseldorf, his boyhood hometown, to a structure bearing a striking resemblance to the Seattle Space Needle. Ginny was the first to notice the large, digital clock on its shaft, which Wilhelm proudly explained had the distinction of being the world's largest light sculpture. At nearly 800 feet, it stood about 200 feet higher than Seattle's famous landmark, but like the Space Needle, *Rheineturm* housed a revolving restaurant at its top, offering some remarkable views of the city.

"Now that they have your statements, they will wrap everything up in a nice little package and take it to the U.S. Attorney," Lochridge told them at dinner. "I am guessing it will all go through the Eastern District of Virginia, since KPH is based in Northern Virginia."

Erik was discharged from the hospital the following day, which they all took as a signal that he was no longer deemed to be in danger, though he observed more police presence than ever around his home. He had been assured of a quick recovery from the superficial gunshot wound and wanted nothing more than to get himself and Catherine out of Frederick for awhile. Lochridge made the arrangements for them to fly over that Friday.

With Lochridge's old laptop, May parked on the reclining chair in the living room, busily writing an in-depth description of his experiences at Walter Reed to feed to Bachman's reporter friend. Starting with the ride on the stretcher-filled, old white school bus from Andrews Air Force Base, its windows blackened, sirens screaming, he recounted how at the end of the long trip from Iraq through Landstuhl, in pain and groggy from a cocktail of drugs, he was handed a map of the 113-acre installation and told to find his room across post. May was still so outraged by the experiences there that he found it difficult to write objectively, sometimes having to search for comedic relief on TV to be able to continue. Lochridge offered frequent pep talks, constantly reminding May that the sooner he finished writing, the sooner things would improve for what promised to be an endless stream of wounded vets who rode those white busses down Georgia Avenue every day.

Thursday, May skipped breakfast to put the finishing touches on the document. Ginny found him in his room, still dressed in his pajamas.

"Thank you!" he beamed at her when she held out a cup of coffee and a Danish pastry resting on a napkin. "I'm famished!"

"Just returning the favor," she said with a grin.

"Martin told me that Sally is flying in this weekend," she said handing him a cup of coffee.

"Since his health news was not good, I am not surprised," May replied, running his fingers through his hair. She followed him to the small table where he had been working. "I'm done with this thing—finally!"

"I know you're happy to have it behind you—having to re-hash all these awful experiences is no fun. Let's hope some good comes from it."

With a mouthful of Danish, he just nodded. They sat, listening to the morning news in the background while May devoured the warm, sticky treat. When he was finished, he picked up his coffee and sat down next to her.

"I'm ready to move on. To put all this unpleasantness behind me and start this new adventure," he said brushing a hand across his unshaven face. "You?"

"Absolutely. I signed on just like you. I'll be right at your side," she said with a wink.

"That makes me very happy, indeed." He looked at his watch, then stood and stretched, ready for a shower. With all the legal documents signed, Lochridge asked them both to join him in his office at ten so they could spend the remainder of the day together reviewing the *Ops Populi* materials. "In just a couple of hours," he tapped his watch with his index finger, "we're going to get the ball."

Ginny grinned at the sports analogy. "And run like hell."

CHAPTER 63

The safe was in the wall behind the same group of shelves where May had discovered the three-volume set of *The Decline and Fall of the Roman Empire*. May and Ginny both watched intently as Lochridge had pulled the two built-in shelves open from the center with no more effort than opening a cabinet. Supported by heavy hinges concealed behind the decorative molding, as the shelves swung out from the wall, castors fell from the bottom, allowing them to easily roll on the floor. In less than a minute, Lochridge had dialed the combination, pulled down the lever, and opened the thick steel door displaying its contents.

"I need to apologize to both of you. My attorney faxed you the blank signature page for our manifesto, but I forgot to pull it out of here before I left for Baltimore. Would one of you give me a hand, please?" Lochridge asked over his shoulder.

"Surely." May rose and walked over to the wall. With both hands, Lochridge retrieved a couple of small boxes, roughly shoe-box size, which he handed to May.

"We decided to keep the signature pages separate to protect everyone's anonymity, but obviously, I wouldn't expect you to sign something you've never read." He placed the boxes in May's outstretched hands. "Careful, the one on the bottom is heavy," he warned.

"We signed it anyway, Martin" Ginny admitted. "Sean said we had a three-day right to rescind."

They heard Lochridge chuckle while he retrieved several accordion style file boxes. May carried his two boxes over to the end table, wondering what occupied the heavier one, and how an object of such density and mass could possibly be relevant to *Ops Populi.*

"Now let me explain the two boxes I handed to Sean first," Lochridge said, taking the much lighter top box from the table while taking his armchair seat. "Hopefully, you will never need them, but just in case."

He removed the lid and handed the box to Ginny, who was closest. Her eyes grew wide as she beheld the stacks of currency inside—dollar and Euro notes—banded together in separate denominations. She looked up at Lochridge—who was removing the lid from the second box—while passing the box of money toward May. Again, using both hands to support the weight, he held the box out to Ginny.

Her mouth fell open, her eyes suddenly grew very wide. "Is it gold—a gold brick?" she stammered.

May, who was studying the different Euro notes, nodded in understanding to himself about the box's disproportionate weight. He had taken enough science to know that gold was a very dense metal, much heavier by volume than most others. When Ginny placed the box on the sofa next to his leg, he felt the cushion compress under its weight and looked down in amazement.

"It is called an ingot," Lochridge said to Ginny.

"It must be worth a fortune," May breathed as he lifted it. Inscribed in its center was a circular logo containing the letters UBS horizontally, SBG vertically with the B in the circle's center. Underneath the circle, on separate lines, were Union Bank of Switzerland, 999.9, Fine Gold, "This thing must weigh about 20 pounds."

"Twenty-five," Lochridge corrected him. "400 Troy ounces."

May did some quick math using information he had heard just two days before: a BBC report on the recent upward trend in gold prices, which that day had spiked to over $700 per ounce in London. Over $280,000 worth of gold sat in his lap.

"For an emergency," Lochridge said, taking the currency from May's hand. "You may think me overly cautious, but my faith in the world's banking system is waning daily."

"No doubt a U.S. constitutional convention will cause some instability in the markets," May observed.

"Very true," Lochridge agreed. "But my concerns are not based on what may happen, but rather on what has happened over the past several years. The entire system is poisoned with bad debt, most of it unfortunately in risky U.S. mortgages. It's a house of cards and there are signs in the U.S. that a strong breeze is starting to blow."

"Mortgages?" Ginny asked, wanting to understand.

"Yes, risky loans made primarily in the U.S. and then split into pieces before being sold off to investors throughout the world. Many of the owners of these loans are banking institutions at home, here in Europe and in Asia. Problem is, most don't have a clue what they own due to some clever shenanigans from the cagey folks on Wall Street."

"I have stock in a couple of banks through my TSP—thrift savings plan—at work," Ginny said with a perplexed expression. "My impression is that the banks are doing very well. Interest rates are low, and everything related to real estate seems to be booming, especially around Washington."

May nodded in agreement with her. "One of my neighbors in Granville quit his job and is making a fortune in buying and selling houses in Columbus. Flipping, I think is what it's called." On this topic, he was certainly no expert, but stories of newly-minted real estate millionaires were being told all over, even in Iraq.

"There is no doubt that many, myself included, have made a great deal of money in real estate in the last few years," Lochridge said with authority. "The problem lies with the financial structures that have been put in place to ensure the money keeps flowing." He glanced at both of them to try to gauge their level of interest, for he didn't want to bore them with too much intricacy. As one who had been immersed for years in the so-called secondary market of buying and selling whole mortgages, he was somewhat of an expert on the subject, though he would not profess any expertise in what he deemed the underhanded methods of slicing and repackaging loans for maximum profit. "During the past decade, they have become, well, very complicated. More importantly for making my point, these structures have allowed banks to engage in reckless lending, creating an insanely over-inflated housing market in the U.S. and in some parts of Europe. Prices have reached levels that can't be supported by the underlying fundamentals in their economies."

"A bubble," May said. "I'm old enough to remember the S and L crisis in the mid-eighties and—"

"Oh, this is quite different, Sean," Lochridge said raising his hand. "In those days, banks made loans to people based on a reasonable expectation they would get paid back. They had to be somewhat cautious because those loans were held on the bank's books until they were paid off. Now, the loans are chopped up and sold as securities—like stocks—shortly after they are made, so the banks are off the hook for the money." He made a sweeping motion with his arm for emphasis. "Now they are irresponsibly lending hundreds of thousands of dollars to people with bad credit, no down payment—no job even—without worrying about the consequences. Speculation has overtaken common sense. As long as it is someone else's money, it's someone else's problem."

May leaned forward, resting his elbows on his knees. "I'm no economist, but the market should correct itself, right? Then there's foreclosure to deal with people who don't pay."

"That happened to a friend of mine in Texas. The lender just auctioned off the house and she and her family were evicted."

Lochridge shook his head, sympathetically. "Yes, there is the foreclosure process and you're right, Sean, a market correction will occur—very soon. But, unlike the savings and loan crisis, this will have huge repercussions for the U.S. and probably the world. You see, so many people have borrowed enormous sums of money with little or no down payment. These borrowers have, as they say, no skin in the game. Many more have taken out 100 percent equity loans using today's inflated values. What do you think will happen when a lender tries to foreclose and the house is worth less than what is owed?"

"They'll have to eat the difference," May said understanding where Lochridge was headed.

Lochridge leaned back in his chair, briefly looking up at the domed ceiling. "Let's say, hypothetically, that on average an investor loses $20,000 foreclosing on a borrower who owes more than the house is worth. If that were to happen, say 1 million times—"

"20 billion," Ginny said almost instantaneously.

"Exactly." He leaned forward and began replacing the lids on the boxes. "To make matters worse, when the securities are created, an insurance company issues a policy guaranteeing their value to perspective purchasers, so they are on the hook, too, if the underlying loans go into default. But, the most pernicious hazard is the widespread multiple leveraging of these securities."

"Multiple leveraging?" Ginny asked with her head cocked to the side.

"Yes, simple really." Lochridge snatched a piece of paper from the table and handed it to Ginny. "Let's say this is a security you bought as an investment. It is a sliver of a big pie cooked up by a Wall Street investment bank and insured by a brand name insurance company. Safe, right?"

Ginny nodded on cue.

"Wrong! Because unbeknownst to you, the pie's main ingredient is a pool of risky mortgages made to people with bad credit, no verifiable income, no down payment. But everyone is under the same delusion as you, thinking it is worth at least what you paid for it, perhaps more because the only direction real estate is headed is up, right?"

Again, she played along with a quick nod.

"Well, one day, something happens and you need some quick cash, but you don't want to sell your valuable security outright. So you take it to a brokerage which agrees to loan you half its value. You get your cash and still own the stock. With me so far?"

A nod from May and Ginny.

"Mr. Broker finds himself in a slump, so he needs a little money to tide him over while business is slow. He takes a batch of securities—yours included—to his friendly banker and pledges them as collateral for his loan. And on and on, *ad infinitum*, until your security stands behind loans 20, 25, even 30 times is nominal value. That, my friends, is multiple leveraging."

Ginny rubbed her chin thoughtfully. "And if the mortgages behind my security go bad?"

"You have a mini disaster," Lochridge said, his eyes shifting between the two of them. "Unfortunately, we have poisoned the world financial system with over-leveraged, degraded paper. So the potential losses could easily be hundreds of billions—perhaps in the trillions—because it won't just be the value of the defaulted mortgages impacting the economy. It's the insurance company and all the companies and institutions in the chain who will feel it."

"A weak chain," May remarked. "This is legal?"

Lochridge nodded somberly. "No laws or regulations to stop it. Only the inevitable change in the direction of real estate prices will expose this fraud. And in the most overheated markets—places like California, Florida, Arizona, and, yes, DC—the pain will be particularly acute. When the financial sector wakes up and realizes what a mess they've created, the investors whose money has fueled it will get spooked. With less money to buy mortgages, lenders will have to curtail their lending. Undoubtedly, many will fail altogether. Fewer loans, means lower demand, which in turn should lead to further drops in values."

"A collapse," Ginny observed.

"Indeed." Lochridge sighed and folded his hands, his expression grim. "Inflated housing and bad mortgages are just a part of the rot spreading through the system. Credit card debt is rapidly approaching a trillion dollars while personal income growth is anemic at best. Meanwhile, Uncle Sam is borrowing over a billion a day. It simply cannot continue."

May sat back, folding his hands behind his head. As he had been listening to Lochridge, he came to the disturbing realization that his time on active duty with the army had caused him to lose touch with the subtleties of the social and economic climates to which he would have normally been very attuned as a professor. The news bites that had made it to the Middle East painted a picture of an economy in high gear, much of it, of course, attributed to the booming housing market. Awash with cash from the paper wealth it created, people were on a consumption binge, creating more businesses and jobs in the process. Government economic statistics he had seen had on balance been very positive, although the mushrooming federal deficits and the looming shortfalls in entitlements, especially the huge Social Security and Medicare programs, were largely being ignored by a swaggering Washington elite.

"You wouldn't know there is anything wrong by listening to the media," he observed.

"Most of the public are masterfully manipulated by the highly controlled, selective bits of information they are fed, oblivious to what is really happening around them and *to them*," Lochridge said as he reached down and began to lift the largest of the accordion files from the floor. "Now, in here—" He suddenly winced as he began to lift it, and he grabbed his right side below the rib cage. Ginny and May both jumped to their feet when he moaned, his face contorted in a pain-inflicted grimace.

Ginny, who was closer, reached out to put her hands on his shoulders. "Martin, are you alright?" She shrieked.

Lochridge, still slumped from his attempt to pick up the file box held up his left hand. "I'm OK," he breathed. "It will pass in a moment."

Ginny looked down on him for a moment then shot a furtive look of concern at May, who remained standing, his expression one of helplessness. After a half minute or so of silence, Lochridge finally sat up straight, wearing a forced smile.

"You see? It comes on suddenly, then it's gone. My unusual movement must have brought it on."

May sat down while Ginny lifted the file box off the floor and rested it on the arm of the chair. A seemingly recovered Lochridge pulled it into his lap.

"Thank you, Ginny," he said softly. "I was about to say that there are several interesting reports in here," he tapped the file box, "a few from the Congressional Research Service, in fact, that cast some doubt on the data being fed to the media by the White House."

Ginny slowly sat, not taking her eyes off of Lochridge. "Definitely. Whether it's the administration's case for warrantless wiretapping, which we found to be blatantly illegal, or the blank checks for war funding, there's plenty of questionable information coming from the administration."

"Ginny, what a stroke of luck to get you on our team," Lochridge said to her with a wink. He sat back in the chair, trying but failing to conceal a grimace. "Soon, I expect the financial sector to implode, to be followed by a general world-wide economic calamity that could last for years. As I've already told Sean, it will make for a receptive audience to *Ops Populi* and its aims. We will be ready," he said with a glance at the boxes containing the gold and the currency.

"It's hard to reconcile what you are predicting with all the prevailing optimism I've seen in the financial markets," Ginny said. "They seem to think everything is just peachy."

"False optimism," May said, looking not at her, but nodding in deference at Lochridge. "Economics is a complex discipline, but the simple fact is the American consumer is two-thirds of the U.S. economy. If they can't borrow money—if the banks won't lend—they can't buy. If they don't buy, business takes a hit, tax revenues fall, people lose their jobs, and so on. If you're right about this, Martin, we could be about to see an economic meltdown unlike anything since the depression."

"Not a matter of if, Sean, just a matter of when," Lochridge said, gingerly massaging his abdomen. "If you two read some of the more recent reports and correspondence with other OP members—a compilation of some of the finest minds in the country, I believe—you will see that I am not just some lone, paranoid crackpot. Sean is right, though, about the magnitude of the coming crisis. In an economy that depends on credit, meltdown is a good term for what will happen when the banks begin to collapse. Massive sums of money will vanish into thin air, businesses will fail, state and local governments will be paralyzed by sinking revenues and a surge in demand for social services."

"Ugly," Ginny said, shaking her head, while also casting a quick glance at May to see if he had noticed Lochridge's obvious discomfort. She read in May's expression the same guarded concern she knew was reflected in her own.

"Somewhere in these boxes, you will find documents that expose the fraud that is our central banking system. It is shocking, really, yet we were fairly warned of its evils long ago by many of our brilliant Founding Fathers," Lochridge said with a smug grin belied by his straining voice. Yet, he continued, "If the machinations of the bankers are ever laid bare for the world to see, the U.S. will be the scorn of all civilized society, exacerbating the ire and contempt of many nations to the point of retribution, I fear, particularly if this progresses to the point we are forced to repudiate our national debt." Both Ginny and May saw the reflexive twitch followed immediately by another wince, but he persisted, "We must," he started, weakly, "If we are to restore some semblance of an honest and ethical comportment—" he gulped air, struggling mightily now "—the, the U.S. must renounce the bankers' schemes…"

Lochridge lurched forward as another wave of acute pain shot through the middle of his body, this one proving almost unbearable. He clenched his teeth and struggled to his feet hoping for relief, but it grew worse. His arms jerked and he started to sway unsteadily, so they both jumped to their feet to assist.

"Let me help you, Martin," May said, hurrying to his side.

"I'm sorry," he said, draping his arm over May's shoulder for support. "Wilhelm is on his way to Dusseldorf to pick up Sally, so—"

"No apologies necessary," May said. "To your room?"

Nodding, Lochridge looked down at the file box. "I had planned to spend the rest of the day going through everything with you. But right now, I really need my medication and rest." With his free hand, he grasped his side and squeezed his eyes closed in quiet agony. "I am running out of time, I'm afraid."

"We'll get started without you. It'll be fine."

As they walked toward the elevator, Ginny impulsively said, "Don't worry about anything, Martin." She regretted all she had to offer him were her words, a feeble attempt to reassure a dying man she barely knew, but one whom she truly believed stood as the epitome of a modern day American patriot.

CHAPTER 64

May stepped out of the elevator frowning.

"He told me to tell you he was sorry." He tossed a piece of paper onto the sofa, where Ginny sat surrounded by neatly arranged manila folders.

She shook her head. "Sorry? Is he okay?" she asked, while unfolding the paper.

"As okay as can be expected, I suppose. When we got to his room, he swallowed a handful of pills, said he'd be okay. I did all I could."

Ginny looked at the paper. "A bunch of numbers?"

"Codes, combinations. Before he handed that to me, he said he has great faith in his instincts." He looked down at the boxes containing the money and gold bullion. "He told me he trusts us implicitly. The fifth one is the combination to the safe, written backwards. I think the first thing I want to do is put those boxes away—all that money sitting there makes me nervous."

"Oh, yeah," Ginny said. "Here are the computer passwords. Too bad we don't have the coding system for these file folder labels."

"Well, have you found the manifesto? Or a list of OP members?" One glance at the labels and he knew what she meant. The first label read "B-2000-001."

She shook her head. "Not yet." She nudged one partially empty file box toward him, two others remained unopened exactly where Lochridge had left them. "It's here somewhere. Look through these, and I'll keep going through this pile. Most of what I have seen are old letters, reports, stuff that we can read later."

May grabbed a handful of folders from the open box and plopped down in the arm chair, subconsciously rubbing his hand across his neck. "I remember how it felt to be ambushed by a wave of excruciating pain. I honestly don't think he's going to be around much longer."

"I know," she said sadly. "I hope he's got some strong drugs for the pain."

"I don't know what he took, but it seemed to start working fast. I helped him get comfortable the best I could."

"Good." As Ginny stood to stretch, she looked down at May, whose saddened expression and distant stare were as gloomy as the gray late winter sky. "How about a little music?"

"Sure. I'll see what I can find," he said, snapping back to the present. "I was just thinking about what I would do if I found myself in Martin's situation. Are we morally obliged to fight death at any costs? Submit to painful, debilitating treatments and surgeries? Or accept the inevitable? Enjoy the time you have and just try to stay as comfortable as possible?"

"My mother had cancer. She fought it," Ginny asserted. "Bought herself almost another seven years."

With his back to her, hunched in front of the stereo system, he asked, "But what if you were told it was terminal? What would you do?"

She looked out the window in thought while May used the tuner's scan function to find something uplifting. "My rational side says to do what Martin is doing. At my age, would I feel guilty for not fighting? Hoping for some miracle?" She turned to see May standing behind her, snapping his fingers and bobbing his head at the beat of a Dutch rock tune. Surprised by the sudden change in his mood, she couldn't help but smile.

"No more morbidity," he announced, playfully dancing around in front of her. "Music always worked miracles for me." When she started laughing out loud, he made a coltish bow to her and fell into the chair, head still bobbing.

It was an odd moment for her, having allowed her mind to wander into the chasm of dread that always accompanies the contemplation of one's own mortality. She had to force herself, as she was sure May had, to pull away from the confrontation with the unknowable—from thoughts her instincts compelled her to avoid—and back to the reality of the present.

"Let's see if we can find that manifesto we signed without reading," she said, resuming her seat amongst the carefully arranged folders.

May nodded, skimming through a small stack of documents in the open file on his lap. "Martin's room is huge—larger than the first floor of my house."

"I don't remember him ever showing us his room. Is it like ours? Modern?" she asked curiously.

"No, not really. It's down on the ground level in the eighteenth century part, I think. Full of relics and antiques—his bed is this beautiful, ornately carved burled walnut—well, anyway, it's dark in there, almost spooky."

"Parts of this place are creepy. Then you walk through a door and you feel like you're inside a new house."

May pulled his batch of folders from the floor and set them on his legs. "This experience has been full of stark contrast. Very old, thoroughly modern. Extreme joy, intense sadness. Life, death. Love, hate. An American constitutional convention launched in a German castle." He scratched his head, as he scanned a yellowed, handwritten document. "Do you feel that way, too, or am I just weirded out?"

"I hadn't thought about it in those terms exactly, but no, you're—wait! Here we go," she said looking down at a newly opened folder.

He glanced at the document and saw the large, upside-down type at its top. "The manifesto?"

She nodded, lifting the surprisingly thin document—just a few paper clipped sheets—from the folder. May stood, carefully moving the sorted folders from the cushion beside Ginny to the floor so he could sit next to her.

"Let's have a look," May said, squeezing in close, his neck craned, so they could read it together.

Printed in large letters on the title page:

Manifesto

Ops Populi—United to Save America

We hold these truths to be self-evident:

That all men are created equal; that they are endowed by their Creator with certain unalienable rights; that among these are life, liberty, and the pursuit of happiness; that, to secure

> *these rights, governments are instituted among men,* ***deriving their just powers from the consent of the governed; that whenever any form of government becomes destructive of these ends, it is the right of the people to alter or to abolish it, and to institute new government****, laying its foundation on such principles, and organizing its powers in such form, as to them shall seem most likely to effect their safety and happiness. Prudence, indeed, will dictate that* ***governments long established should not be changed for light and transient causes****; and accordingly all experience hath shown that mankind are more disposed to suffer, while evils are sufferable than to right themselves by abolishing the forms to which they are accustomed.* ***But when a long train of abuses and usurpations, pursuing invariably the same object, evinces a design to reduce them under absolute despotism, it is their right, it is their duty, to throw off such government, and to provide new guards for their future security.***

"Justification lifted directly from the Declaration of Independence," Ginny observed.

"Nobody said it better than good 'ole Tom Jefferson," May quipped with a gentle nudge in Ginny's side.

"And look at these…." Ginny said as soon as she had flipped to the second page, where a group of quotes were set off by themselves.

Ginny read aloud:

> *"The basis of our political systems is the right of the people to make and to alter their constitutions of government."—George Washington*
>
> *"Happy for us that when we find our constitutions defective and insufficient to secure the happiness of our people, we can assemble with all the coolness of philosophers and set it to rights, while every other nation on earth must have recourse to arms to amend or to restore their constitutions."—Thomas Jefferson*
>
> *"This Constitution had been formed without the knowledge or idea of the people. A second Convention will know more of*

the sense of the people, and be able to provide a system more consonant to it."—George Mason

"This country, with its institutions, belongs to the people who inhabit it."—Abraham Lincoln, 1861

"All power is originally in the People and should be exercised by them in person, if that could be done with convenience, or even with a little difficulty."—James Wilson

"Who is James Wilson?" she asked when she had finished reading the quotes. "He's the only one I don't recognize."

Though not surprised by her question, May nonetheless felt a tinge of annoyance—annoyance he tried mightily to conceal by not looking at her—at the pervasive ignorance of what he considered basic American civics. Ever increasing mass indifference to the actions—or inactions—of the government, its history and, most importantly, its principles had deeply troubled him for many years. As he looked down at the *Ops Populi* manifesto, he knew overcoming apathy meant the difference between success and failure.

"He signed the Declaration of Independence, and, along with James Madison, of course, was a major force in writing the Constitution," May said, squinting to read the smaller print on the second page. "And, he was one of the six original justices Washington appointed to the Supreme Court. Unfortunately, he gets little credit, but his contributions were huge."

"Humph!" she exclaimed, eyebrows raised. With a modest shrug, she turned her eyes back to the manifesto.

We, the undersigned members of Ops Populi—United to Save America, Inc., organized and chartered under the laws of the State of Virginia, do hereby subscribe to and affirm the following:

That we are citizens of the United States of America who revere and avow our allegiance to the fundamental principles as set forth in both the Declaration of Independence and the Constitution ;

That, because of the aforementioned reverence and allegiance, we believe it is our sacred responsibility as citizens to not only uphold those principles but to provide for the perpetuation of our great republic;

That we must both acknowledge and endeavor to correct certain structural defects and anachronisms in the supreme law of our country;

That the institutions and mechanisms otherwise available to the sovereign citizens of the United States for correcting defects and anachronisms are impracticable;

That as such, the government cannot be held accountable to the people from whom its consecrated power is derived and for whom that power is exercised;

We resolve therefore,

To propose that the American people assert their constitutional prerogative to petition the Government to convene at the earliest possible date a constitutional convention in accordance with the provisions of Amendment I, which states:

"Congress shall make no law respecting an establishment of religion, or prohibiting the free exercise thereof; or abridging the freedom of speech, or of the press, or the right of the people peaceably to assemble, and to petition the Government for a redress of grievances."

And;

To consider for inclusion, the amendments enumerated in the briefing document and incorporated herein by reference.

Notwithstanding the inclusion or exclusion of any or all of these suggested amendments, we invoke the eloquent words and the very spirit of our Founding Fathers to underscore a fervent resolve to our principal objective: to provide the opportunity for the sovereign people to freely examine their government and to revise it as they see fit.

"As the people are the only legitimate fountain of power, and it is from them that the constitutional charter, under which the several branches of government hold their power, is derived, it seems strictly consonant to the republican theory to recur to that same original authority…whenever it may be necessary to enlarge, diminish, or new-model the powers of government."

And, to this end;

"…with a firm reliance on the protection of Divine Providence, we mutually pledge to each other our Lives, our Fortunes, and our sacred Honor."

"Short, but sweet," May said.

Ginny turned to him, with a puzzled look. "I thought your whole premise was to base a convention on Article V. Your dissertation says—"

"I know," he interrupted, "and you're right, but when I was a naïve student, I assumed that Congress would obey the law and call the convention when they received the petitions from the states." He pointed to the document as he spoke. "Congress has chosen to view Article V as optional, which is why this says the institutions and mechanisms otherwise available are impracticable."

"So, where did the First Amendment idea come from?"

"A judge—the judge Martin clerked for after law school. He told me his name…it starts with a 'B '—Bremer, Bremen—something like that. He told me there are some letters…" May started thumbing through the piles.

"Here," Ginny said, reaching for a shoe box labeled 'Breslin' on the cushion beside her. When she pulled the lid off, she saw it was full of envelopes. She looked at the return address before handing the stack over to May. "Does Hugh J. Breslin, Jr. ring a bell?"

"Yeah, that's him." He took the box from her and placed it on the arm of the empty chair. "Not before Martin told me about him. He was a district judge in Portland when Martin graduated from law school. Then, he was on the First Circuit Court of Appeals in Boston until he retired. He's pushing ninety now."

"A retired federal judge," she said to herself, shrugging. "I'd imagine an appellate judge would have to know the Constitution pretty well."

"No question. It will be interesting to read through those later."

"I wonder if he's a member of OP?" she wondered aloud.

"Let's find out," he said. "There's got to be a list in here somewhere."

Ginny placed the manifesto face down on the sofa cushion and picked up the remainder of the stack on her lap. "I also want to find that briefing document. To see the specifics."

"I am under the impression from Martin it is very similar to what you read in the dissertation. In fact, he offered me a blanket apology for any plagiarism."

Ginny chuckled. "The best form of flattery, ay?"

They both looked up in surprise as the elevator doors opened. Off walked a sprightly, bespectacled, middle-aged woman, followed closely by Wilhelm. May and Ginny both rose as the woman's tanned face registered palpable disappointment in not seeing Lochridge anywhere.

"Sally?" Ginny asked as the woman's eyes settled on the two of them.

"Sean and Ginny, I assume?" Sally said with a smile, as she walked over to them.

Anticipating the question, May extended his hand in greeting, while saying, "Martin is not feeling well. He's resting."

Sally refused his hand, instead quickly embracing each of them as her eyes wandered to the window and its breathtaking view. "It's every bit as beautiful as he said." She surveyed the room a little more slowly, with a quick glance at the open safe, then the many neatly-arranged piles of documents on the sofa and the floor. "Fabulous!" she exclaimed, as she unbuttoned her knee-length wool coat.

May stepped over to help her with the coat, while Wilhelm excused himself to check on Lochridge.

"Is he okay?" Sally asked with a tone of palpable concern.

May, who was standing behind Sally, looked over her shoulder to see

Ginny's grim expression. As he slipped the heavy coat from her frame, he was reminded of Lochridge's description of their relationship, mutual affinity and closeness rivaling that of a long-time, albeit platonic, marriage. Instinctively, he gently placed his free hand on her shoulder.

"I don't want you to be surprised when you see him—he's not looking very well at all, and he's in a lot of pain," he told her, "but, his spirits seem pretty high when the pain is under control."

Sally's eyes filled with sadness. She just nodded, evidently not surprised by May's assessment, and looked down at the floor.

"We were meeting to go over these files, and he suddenly was overcome by pain," Ginny added. "I'm sure seeing you will make him happy."

Sally walked over to Lochridge's desk and touched the polished wood lightly with her fingertips. "His wife bought this for him as an anniversary gift. After watching the grief he suffered when she was killed—and now this." She turned to face May, still standing with her coat draped over his arm. "I just need to help him any way I can. And be positive. I owe him that."

"That's all any of us can do," Ginny agreed. "Let me get some of these papers out of the—"

The elevator door opened to reveal the stunned face of Wilhelm. He leaned unsteadily against the steel frame. May lurched toward him.

"He's...he's dead."

CHAPTER 65

Only the sound of shuffling papers and an occasional cough or clearing of the throat broke the silence in the dreary, windowless conference room. After more than five hours reviewing files forwarded to them by the nation's numerous intelligence gathering agencies, they were all anxious to depart the confines of Washington's Bolling Air Force Base in time to beat the awful Friday afternoon traffic and begin their weekends.

While their new building was under construction at a not-so-well-kept secret site near Tyson's Corner, they utilized the secure, if drab facilities, personnel, and resources of their Defense Intel host at Bolling. The deputy directors and assistant deputy directors of the Office of the Director of National Intelligence, or ODNI, as it had come to be known, had only one task in their twice monthly meetings: to sift through and prioritize for the Director potential national security threats identified by the 15 civilian and military intelligence-gathering agencies in the field. As the statutory leader of the intelligence community, the Director was charged with the daunting responsibility of coordinating, collecting, analyzing and disseminating a constant deluge of information. He met regularly with the heads of the other agencies, all of whom were members of the President's Information Sharing Council, and with their help and the assistance of his own staff, reported to and advised the President.

Despite the fatigue felt by all at this point, ODNI's senior staff had unanimously rejected the suggestion of their leader, Associate Director and Chief of Staff Charles Cave, that they meet more frequently to shorten the duration of the meetings. Though no one had said it, they all knew the White House was pushing harder than ever for coordinated, reliable intelligence in the war on terror, and the ever-increasing volume of information flowing to them would quickly transform the shorter weekly meetings into all-day affairs. More frequent meetings were inevitable anyway; they were willing to wait until they became mandatory.

"Why are we looking at this?" Cave asked his assistant in dry monotone. It was his way of getting a verbal synopsis of the file without having to wait for everyone to read and comprehend the hodgepodge of documents sent to them from the field.

As usual, Assistant Deputy Director Holsten was ready with a synopsis. "This came to us from FBI SWIFT unit," he said looking at his notes. "Actually, this is one very unusual file," Holsten said.

"Aren't they all," someone mumbled in the back of the room, followed by several snickers.

By this point in the day-long meeting, Holsten was de-sensitized to any snide commentary from his peers. He flipped the switch of the projection unit attached to his laptop. "In your file is a handwritten letter I found difficult to read, so I transcribed it for everyone." In an instant, the transcription appeared on the large projection screen.

"Go on," urged Cave, watching the tired eyes around him focus on the screen.

"Our subject is Martin Lochridge, a U.S. citizen with dual citizenship in Ireland, who currently resides in Germany. The Bureau SWIFT unit picked up on some very large wire transactions flowing through several offshore accounts in Hong King, the Caymans and Antigua into a Swiss account registered to something called OP-USA, Inc.—"

A whistle rang out in the background. "A lot of loot," a female voice everyone recognized as belonging to Heather Burns, ODNI's financial expert.

"Billions," Holsten said without looking up.

"I can see why SWIFT picked these up—it was all the off-shore transfers—but what's the relevance to national security?" a male voice asked impatiently.

Thomas Gibson, the Deputy Director for Analysis, sat with elbows on the table, chin resting on his folded hands. "It's a stretch in my opinion, but FBI sent it up so we will look at it."

"Please continue, Jim," Cave said to Holsten.

"OP-USA is actually a fictitious name. The corporate charter is to *Ops Populi*—United to Save America, Inc., whose manifesto you see in the file along with several letters from Lochridge to John Collier—"

"Who?" someone asked before Holsten could finish. He looked up to see a few nods of recognition, others who looked at him blankly.

"The media mogul, right?" Andy Ward, another assistant sitting next to Cave, asked.

Holsten inadvertently let out a heavy sigh at the interruption but as soon as he had, he forced a smile and a nod at Ward. If everyone would shut up, they might have a chance to get home in time for dinner. "Collier is—was—like our Mr. Lochridge a—" he paused to search for the term he wanted, "a multi-faceted businessman who built one of the country's largest cable companies from scratch, owned several magazines, some newspapers, a few radio and TV stations and some prime real estate. He and Lochridge were close—they lived together for awhile when they were in law school at the University of Virginia, then had several business relationships throughout the years." He looked up at the screen. The letters, as you will see, are strongly worded affirmations of Collier's membership in the OP-USA organization, whose mission is to promote a constitutional convention—"

Cave looked up at that instant, peering over his reading glasses to observe the reaction, which, as expected, was a mixture of blank stares, dismissive shrugs, and a few astonished expressions of disbelief in what they had just been told.

"A what?" someone asked incredulously. A low hum of murmuring arose all around the room.

"Constitutional convention. You know—to re-write the Constitution."

A couple of muffled laughs were heard among the dull chatter.

"I think we all know what it is, Jim," said Public Affairs Director Deborah Redding, "we just can't believe you said it."

"All right, everyone," Cave said, trying to keep them moving. He, like Gibson had disregarded this file as a waste of time when he first saw it, but now was having second thoughts. "Go on, Jim."

Holsten nodded, unflustered by the commotion. "The bureau got this manifesto and the letter in early January from Collier's son, who was trying to cut a deal with the U.S. Attorney's Office in Denver on a narcotics charge." He held up a folder. "I have copies of statements, court pleadings, transcripts, and so on if anyone wants them. Basically, junior was miffed at his old man for giving most of the family fortune to this OP-USA after he collapsed and died of a heart attack on his airplane New Year's Eve. So he gives this letter and manifesto to his lawyer, who asserts that junior went off the deep end because this subversive fringe group of crackpots manipulated his father into giving away his client's inheritance."

"Sounds pretty lame," Ward said, catching an annoyed look from Cave for the interruption.

"Even though he had priors for drugs, his lawyer got the charge reduced," Holsten said, ignoring Cave's obvious irritation. "As you can see, though, OP-USA itself didn't get any serious attention—these documents were filed and forgotten—until now."

"I'll give everyone a few minutes to read, then we can talk about it," Cave said, slipping his reading glasses over the bridge of his nose.

Although he had read and re-read the letter, Gibson found himself drawn to it again. Despite the snickers from the staff and the lawyer's unflattering characterization of the group, he was not quite ready to reject it out of hand as the whimsy of a nut case. In fact, he found both documents persuasive and eloquently written, but the letter, in particular, appealed to the long-submerged sense of civic pride and duty of his youth.

September 18, 2005

"We must be contented with the ground which this Constitution will gain for us, and hope that a favorable moment will come for correcting what is amiss in it."

Thomas Jefferson—1788

Dear John,

It has been a long time since I penned a letter by hand, but I find myself without the modern conveniences of electricity and telephone service—and the many distractions they bring to my life—compliments of a powerful nor'easter that slammed into the coast yesterday. No severe damage here, just minor inconveniences that pale in comparison to the horrendous damage and awful suffering along the Gulf coast. So, until I can resume my preparations to return to Europe, I am taking advantage of the lull to consider whether Jefferson's "favorable moment" is at hand.

When we last met at our UVA law reunion, we agreed that the ongoing decline of the U.S. would be accelerated by the reckless and irresponsible invasion of Iraq. Well into the third year of profligate squander of American life and treasure—and most recently, with the abysmal response to the Gulf hurricanes—it is evident we are on the cusp of a ground swell in public antipathy for our government unlike any in modern times. You may have seen Gallup and other public opinion polls that ostensibly measure satisfaction with the President and Congress in a free-fall, while satisfaction with the general state of the nation has plummeted to historically low levels. The opportune time for action is nearing, and we must be prepared. "Lock and load," to use the old army term, but, from a strategic perspective, I recommend we leave the safety on for a just a bit longer.

The elements are now in place, heralding the coming implosion for those of us whose vision extends beyond the present euphoria: our enormous public and private debt is the powder keg; the match that will ignite the fuse is a crash in the U.S. housing market; the catalyst is none other than the unrestrained avarice of the secretive banking syndicate many of our Forefathers warned would put our country in peril. Indeed, it has.

Cloaked in its benign public façade, a largely private enterprise, the consortium of greed and deceit we know as the Federal Reserve, is presently engaged in perpetrating the most egregious fraud ever devised by mankind. It has carefully projected a mirage of cohesion, reliability, and prosperity through loose credit, while at the same time conspiring to mastermind what most certainly will be the most prodigious plunder of wealth from the unwitting masses in the history of civilization. If unchecked, I fear the consequences will be great human privation and suffering, anarchy, and perhaps even cataclysmic world war, which, as the annals of history tell us, has all too often been the unhappy result of tyranny bred of desperation.

I am persuaded that our chances of achieving success will only be improved by a progressive onslaught of widespread malaise, a trend I expect will accelerate in the coming months. In fact, I believe the "state of the nation" will deteriorate to a level not seen since the Great Depression within the next year, perhaps two, due to an impending economic collapse I will explain below. Were we together in the same room, I would not be at all surprised by your vehement objection, since my outlook is contrary to the prevailing optimism about the prospects for the U.S. economy—although it remains to be seen whether it endures in spite of the damage done by Katrina. So, indulge me if you will, for since I now have more leisure time than you, I tend to delve a little deeper than before, trusting not the government-generated economic statistics and rosy projections of the market pundits (no offense intended to those whom you employ), but rather my own instincts and the acumen of those whose impartiality is truly beyond reproach.

John, what I see on the horizon is actually the convergence of several different phenomena that will unfold to shake the very foundations of the world's financial edifice and devastate the U.S. economy in its wake. At the epicenter is an astounding level of accumulated debt—both in the private and public sectors, much of which has been leveraged many times over by cunning investment bankers.

As one who has been focused primarily on real estate since "retiring" from government contracting, I have watched in utter amazement the complete disintegration of rationality in all aspects of the industry. Powered by artificially low interest rates (encouraged by the feds and made possible by the constant infusion of foreign money), astonishingly reckless lending practices, *and a co-opted media, prices have risen to unsustainable levels. Mortgage borrowing in the U.S. has jumped from $386 billion in 2000 to $894 billion in 2004, much of it of poor quality at best, fraudulent at worst. Nominally, this is a huge increase over a brief period, but to make matters worse, the debt has been used as collateral by unrestrained bankers to borrow huge sums, many times greater than the actual principal owed. So, even though a house produces nothing real, earns nothing real and actually loses utility with each successive year of its existence, the debt against it could be multiples of its full, artificially inflated value. Add to that the fact that Americans have (so far) borrowed nearly $700 billion against their fictional wealth—while also amassing another $700 billion in credit card debt since 2002.*

Our government—by definition, a consumer of and not a producer of wealth—meanwhile is borrowing over a billion per day, and its tab will soon surpass $9 trillion. Spending like a drunk at the bar, Uncle Sam has run up a tab that he can never hope to pay, so he is technically insolvent.

Economic growth in this decade has been a fallacy, created by a debt-fueled consumption binge, not business investment, employment growth or increasing incomes. When the rate of personal savings turned negative this spring—for the first time since the Great Depression—the private sector officially joined Uncle Sam at the bar, spending more money than it makes.

John, the tipping point is near. Investors throughout the world are holding worthless paper, deluded by guileful, if not criminal, Wall Street bankers into thinking it is secured by a tangible asset. When these investors begin to realize they have been hoodwinked, planted firmly at the base of a fantastic pyramid of greed, a chain of events similar to the following will set in motion the great unraveling:

1. *Investors holding worthless or under-secured U.S. mortgage bonds demand their money (recourse to the bond insurance companies or government agencies who guarantee them),*

2. *Insurers seek re-purchase of the mortgages from the investment bankers who issued the bonds. Highly-leveraged bankers can't absorb re-purchase demands, nor can assignees or the original lenders, so they declare bankruptcy, many exit the business. Bond insurers and government agencies tighten standards for guaranteeing future mortgages.*

3. *Fewer lenders, tighter credit reduce demand for houses. Prices begin to decline. As values fall, homeowners who purchased at or near peak prices with small (or zero) down payments find themselves in negative equity.*

4. *Interest rates on adjustable-rate mortgages reset. Homeowners who cannot meet the higher payment obligation, cannot refinance because of tighter credit standards or negative equity, default.*

Although admittedly over-simplified, I believe the above will become cyclical, repeating an indefinite number of times, destroying trillions of dollars of wealth—primarily, real estate and stock equity—and precipitating waves of bankruptcies and foreclosures. Credit will surely be curtailed, and what remains will be harder to obtain and more expensive. Without easy access to credit, guess what will happen to the ordinary American consumer whose wages are stagnant, who is spending more than he earns, and whose standard of living depends on borrowed money? He must reduce spending, thereby starting a parallel cycle of recession, with each cycle exacerbating the other as we spiral into a full-fledged economic disintegration.

The government, meanwhile, itself insolvent, can do nothing other than borrow and print money, both of which devalue it, thereby furtively stealing from everyone who holds dollars or dollar-denominated assets. It cannot increase taxes on a insolvent, recession-plagued public without worsening the implosion. Moreover, if inflation rears its ugly head—which I think is probable given the trend in energy prices—the value of the dollar will plunge, causing a cash-strapped public to further reduce consumption. Interest rates will spike as creditors demand more dollars in return for lending money.

In this scenario, a tidal wave of massive default—public and private—is certainly plausible—I would maintain inevitable—and if it comes to fruition, it will precipitate a global crisis in confidence of catastrophic proportions, ultimately bringing about worldwide collapse of a flimsy foundation built largely upon the tenuous "full faith and credit" of the United States of America. Hundreds of billions, if not trillions, of dollars in paper wealth will abruptly evaporate, many state and municipal governments, particularly those which depend on consumption and real estate for revenue, will fall into insolvency, taking with them the pension plans of countless public-sector retirees.

The federal government will be compelled to intercede, which will likely take the form of knee-jerk responses to stimulate consumption and "rescues" (bail-outs) of large institutions, particularly those that have strategic significance. At best, these palliatives will slow the implosion, since their attempts will be financed by ever more debt and economic plunder. Uncle Sam will not only return to the bar as a remedy for his hangover, he will jovially buy rounds for the house. But the only way to pay the enormous tab is with counterfeit, or at best watered-down paper money whose real value declines with every drink. Ten-dollar loaves of bread or gallons of gasoline could very well become reality in the not-too-distant future.

The public, impaired by faulty information, is destined to watch in bewilderment as all of this unfolds, not understanding why their dollars are becoming worth less (worthless?), but justly outraged at the same time.

So, my optimistic friend, I leave it to you to persuade me I am wrong. I can assure you, convincing me will require more than media sound-bites, most of which I have learned are contrived by Uncle and his lieutenants to beguile us into a false sense of security with spurious economic data and hollow reassurances. On the other hand, as I confessed earlier, mine is a minority opinion, so I would understand if you and the others decide not to wait for events you deem unlikely. Certainly, I can find ample current justification for proceeding immediately, if that is the consensus.

Impending financial crisis or not, the U.S. has crossed the line, I believe, from a self-sustaining republic to a nation dependant on foreigners for capital, oil, and manufacturing, all so vital to our prosperity if not our very survival. Not since the Revolution have we been so vulnerable to the whims of foreign governments—many of which hold the U.S. in low esteem, with more than a few of questionable stability. Infused with hubris but no longer in control of so many essential elements of national survival, our administration's recourse to imperialism to ensure our viability is the path to inevitable ruin. For if we stay on the path, the United States will, like the old Roman Republic on which so much of our system was modeled, lose its democracy to a domestic dictatorship. The aggressive usurpation of executive power by our President is an ominous portent and a warning to us all.

Roman history holds some interesting lessons for the United States. Not unlike colonial Americans, the early Romans of the republic held moral values typical of a conservative agrarian society. With a foundation of strong family bonds, they were industrious and self-reliant, prudent and frugal, ethical and committed to their personal and civic responsibilities, and steadfast in the face of adversity. Over time, Rome, too, became dependant on foreigners for the essentials of food and money. Not only did it undertake costly military ventures abroad, but its demise was hastened by the same internal decay we are witnessing in America today—apathy, complacency, too much self-indulgence, and moral and ethical depravity. Gradually, Rome lost its dedication to humanitarianism and its commitment to the revered principle of virtue, later adopted by our own Founding Fathers. Courageous and selfless action on behalf of the people and the republic were replaced by self-interested expediency, insatiable greed and self-aggrandizement.

Our government is presently engaged in a vicious assault on our most cherished liberties, the prodigious waste of life and treasure, and complete paralysis with respect to confronting our most urgent national issues. True to your prediction, in the aftermath of 9/11, the administration shamelessly exploited the fears and fury of the American people to surreptitiously alienate our "inalienable" rights by subjecting us to all manner of unprecedented intrusions into our privacy—all in the name of the nebulous concept of national security. You may recall that egregious abuses of project Echelon—the secretive global surveillance network my father's work helped bring to fruition in the 1970s—began the wholesale erosion of our civil liberties causing those of us who were aware of it great consternation. For years, I have been appalled at the perversion of my father's efforts into a weapon used by our government against its citizens. Now, I am burdened by much regret that, through my own work, I have unwittingly enabled new, more pestilent encroachments. Yet, I remind myself often that had I not followed my father's sage advice—"Don't become a scientist," he told me firmly, "unless you want very little control over your professional life. Instead, learn all you can about business and the law then hire the best scientists you can find."—you, LaSalle and I would find ourselves in vastly different circumstances, perhaps powerless to do anything except watch on the sidelines as the United States plunges headlong into ruin.

Ironic though it is, satellites and the internet are the instruments used to impinge on our rights, while at the same time providing us the means to give Americans the ultimate gift: choice and control over the destiny of their country. As Professor May, whom you know has had a profound influence in my thinking, explained so eloquently, the American political system is rife with irony, starting with its founding by a small group of its most elite citizens, whose basic design remains brilliant but whose barriers to reform and widespread active participation are archaic. That such a carefully orchestrated, monumental effort is required to break out of the constitutional prison we find ourselves in is perhaps the saddest irony of them all.

Insidious decay, both physical and moral, is evident all around us, though it is marginalized by our elected leaders and—I say without intending to directly indict you—the mainstream media, upon which the public depends to maintain its vigilance over its leaders. Regardless of whether my dismal prediction for an apocalyptic meltdown manifests in whole or in part, I will wager my last worthless dollar that the people, especially the great American middle class—the very engine of our country and, arguably, the ones with the most to lose—will rise to the challenge if given an opportunity. Thanks in large part to your wisdom, financial support, and media resources, they shall have it; I must now defer to your wisdom as to when.

Our great country has blessed us with much, and we have the means and obligation to save it. The great patriot Edmund Randolph said, "When the salvation of the Republic was at stake, it would be treason to our trust not to propose what we found necessary." Ultimately, we can only propose, the onus is on the American people to recognize their opportunity and to seize it. They must take great care to find leaders possessing high morals, virtue, character and fortitude, and with great care, set about the crucial work of reconstituting our Constitution. We, of course, have pledged to defer to their collective wisdom as to whether and how they do it. I must defer to your wisdom as to when we make that critical opportunity available to them.

In the end, John, when you and I turn out the lights for the last time, we will not be judged not by what we had, but rather in what we did with what we had. I cannot think of anything of greater import to all of humanity than the perpetuation of the United States of America, can you?

As Abraham Lincoln said in his first inaugural, "This country, with its institutions, belongs to the people who inhabit it." It remains to be seen if they will take it back, but I fear for its survival if they do not.

With utmost regards, I remain,
Sincerely yours,
Marty

When he had finished reading the typewritten version of the letter, Gibson looked around the room to survey the expressions of the others. Some were still reading, others were fidgeting with their electronic devices, looking at their watches, patiently waiting to move ahead with their agenda. While he waited for the others, he flipped through the few hastily compiled pages of Lochridge's dossier. It contained quite a bit of biographical data, most of which likely came from his army "201" file. But the more recent information was a little vague, particularly the estimate of net worth which was expressed as a range of just over $5 billion to $22 billion. With so much uncertainty in the net worth estimate, he wondered how much confidence they should place in the rest of it. Surely, if Lochridge was worth upwards of $20 billion, he would have expected, at the very least, to have heard something about him in the media, yet he couldn't recall a single thing. Decorated veteran, two-year clerkship with a Federal District Judge in Portland, Maine following law school, then a variety of business interests which were broadly categorized as "science/engineering/technology" through the 1990s, though the dates often overlapped or contained gaps. Several of the listed companies were heavily involved in government contracting, most of it related to the military, but the only one he recognized was the publicly traded LaSalle Bachman Aerospace, which had been in the financial news on occasion. From 2000 to the present, Lochridge had been an officer and director in the privately held Jonic Corporation, categorized on the report as "Real Estate." The final section, the public records search, revealed very little for a man of his age, wealth and breadth of business activity, not even any real estate titled in his name. As one who made his living in the intelligence field, Gibson knew Lochridge was a man with a penchant for privacy.

"Any thoughts?" Cave's voice boomed through the low hum of mumbling whose crescendo generally suggested the group had finished reading.

"A waste of time," said the tired Lester Allgood, throwing the file on top of a stack in front of him. A computer scientist by training, he typically contributed little to the discussions, but his pragmatic, black and white approach typically led him to quick conclusions. "Thousands of people are saying stuff like this on the internet all the time. If we had to look at every knucklehead who…"

"Knucklehead?" Deborah Redding interrupted. "This guy doesn't strike me as a—"

"Flake?" Ward hooted, spurring muffled laughter around the room.

"All right," said an annoyed Cave. "Does anyone have anything intelligent to say? Intelligence is our business, remember?"

Earl Hunsley, a nerdy, but intellectual former CIA analyst brought into ODNI for his expertise in world history and international politics, crossed his arms across his chest as he spoke. "I basically agree with Lester," he started with a nod to Allgood, "but not just because our subject has unconventional views. Conceptually, a constitutional convention is so far fetched—there are so many legal and practical obstacles—I would rank it right under impossible on the scale of likelihood."

"Like people flying jumbo jets into New York sky-scrapers?" Paul Pickard's voice erupted with sarcasm.

Gibson looked around the room to see many were following Allgood's lead, tossing the file on their completed heaps, others already looking at the next one on their agenda. A scant few pondered the letter on the screen or quietly reflected as they listened to the discussion.

"I know we are all tired, ready to go home," Gibson said. "But, in my opinion, we shouldn't be too quick to dismiss this—"

Ward slapped his open palm on the table. "How do you justify using American intelligence resources on some ex-pat Viet Nam vet who started a Constitution club? He probably doesn't even have all his oars in the water!"

Cave glowered at Ward, but Gibson continued in a level tone unaffected by the interruption. "Maybe you're right, Andy. But my impression is that our subject is quite rational."

"And well-financed," Burns added.

"Exactly." Gibson pointed at her, happy for the reinforcement. He shot a Glance at Cave, who inclined his head toward him in encouragement. "Need I remind everyone why we are here? Paul's remark was right on. The U.S. was blind-sided by what happened on 9/11, because using commercial jets as missiles was too *far fetched.* Our subject may be eccentric, but this letter," he pointed at the screen, "this was written with conviction. And, I think, it shows the will—the determination of someone with, as Heather pointed out, the means to act."

"But how is a const—" Ward started.

"Let me finish, Andy" he said firmly. "Yes, a constitutional convention is improbable, but this organization can make a lot of noise with billions of dollars. Perception could very well be the main threat. Look what happens just when we have elections. People the world over get antsy. Financial markets get the jitters. Now imagine the level of apprehension if a well-financed, well-organized movement introduces the *possibility*—however remote—of altering our entire system of government. The resulting instability could pose a grave threat to our national security, not to mention all American interests world wide." He shook his head while saying, "It would be a mistake to ignore this."

Cave, whose self-defined role in this open forum was moderator, normally reserved his own opinions until the end of the discussion to avoid influencing or impeding the free exchange of ideas. He had reached the same conclusion as Gibson, but his own anxiety went beyond concern for ODNI's national security mission, piercing deep into the core of his American psyche. National security threat or not, in his view, this man's intention to tinker with the country's most revered document—to which he, like everyone in the room, everyone in the government, swore true faith and allegiance, to support and defend against all enemies, foreign and domestic—was tantamount to treason. Yet, he found it quite unnerving that, unlike the hundreds of files they had poured through, this contained no implied or overt threat to American citizens or property by foreigners. Lochridge was an American citizen—a war hero at that—who appeared to be motivated by genuine patriotism, and whose "threat" was actually very nebulous, theoretical, certainly not well-substantiated, but possibly as destructive to the country as any they had ever considered.

There were too many things about this, too much abstraction, to allow him to make a definitive recommendation to his boss. In the most technical sense, Mr. Lochridge and his *Ops Populi* might not constitute what they understood to be a threat to national security, but when the huge sums of money it was accumulating were taken into consideration, it could, at the very least, cause significant problems for the government, the country, perhaps the world. Uncomfortable with his ambivalence, one look a the weary faces of his staff sealed the decision, one he had never had to make before.

"I'm taking this one up to the director with no recommendation," he announced with authority. "He can decide himself or take it to the President."

CHAPTER 66

Even though he tried to talk her out of it, Sally insisted May show her to Lochridge's bedroom suite. Her somewhat subdued reaction to Wilhelm's pronouncement struck both May and Ginny as odd until she explained how Lochridge had given her the grim test results from his recent trip to the States. His pain was constant, he had told her, particularly acute after eating and even the slightest exertion. So, when May described his observations of debilitating pain, apparent intolerance of food, and lethargy, she seemed more relieved than grief-stricken. She just wanted to sit and hold his hand for a few minutes, she said through a few tears, while Wilhelm summoned the authorities.

Sally began to sob openly as soon as they saw Lochridge's body. Lying curled up in a fetal position, the huge antique bed exaggerated his withered and emaciated appearance. She sat gingerly beside him, as though not to disturb his slumber, transfixed by what no doubt was the shock at his abrupt metamorphosis into a gaunt shell of what he had been just months before. It was May who spotted the nearly empty prescription bottle—which just hours before had been almost full—on the nightstand on the far side of the bed. When he walked over to retrieve it, the folded paper that had been obscured by the bedpost became visible. If Sally took note of him removing the note and the pill bottle, she said nothing.

"I'll wait outside the door," he told her.

A partial nod was her only acknowledgement.

May sat in one of the two Chippendale chairs adjacent to the doorway. Little white triangular shaped pills rattled in the plastic bottle when he turned it right-side-up to read the prescription, which he saw had been filled at Johns Hopkins just two days earlier. The medication was something called "Dilaudid," with "hydromorphone" in parentheses, which meant nothing to him, but which he assumed was something much more heavy-duty than what he had been given at Walter Reed. What was clear, however, was that Lochridge had consumed many times the prescribed dosage of the 8-milligram pills in the span of several hours.

When he unfolded the single sheet of folded paper, the first thing that struck him was it was not handwritten as expected, but prepared with a word processor sometime before today. It was not dated, addressed to anyone in particular, nor was it signed.

> *I think it was Mark Twain who said, "The fear of death follows from the fear of life. A man who lives fully is prepared to die at any time." Well, I have certainly lived a full life and I have been mentally prepared to die since stepping off the plane in Viet Nam. Fortunately, providence saw fit to give me some extra time, for which I am grateful. Theologians will no doubt deem my actions a sin, but I have never given much credence to their opinions about morality anyway. As you know, Sally, I discovered long ago sanity is rooted in control over ones life, so why would a sane man surrender control over his death?*
>
> *My worldly affairs are in order. I am comforted by the knowledge that those who will read this are both willing and capable of taking the reins, and for that, you have my eternal gratitude.*
>
> *Do not mourn, rather, let my death sow the seeds of permanence for the country I love.*

Sally emerged from the room 15 minutes later, her composure intact. May rose and handed her the note and the pill bottle without saying a word.

She held the bottle in front of her, showing no perceptible surprise at what it signified: Lochridge's death was obviously a suicide. When extending her arm failed to bring the small print into focus, she handed it back to May. "My reading glasses are in my purse. Whatever it is, he told me the doctor just doubled the strength." She opened the folded note, glanced at it long enough to know she would not be able to read it either, and held it out to May. "Would you mind?"

May read it aloud, folded it, and handed it back to her.

"Please don't think less of him," she said. "It was his way."

"I understand," May said to her quietly, reflecting on whether he could—would—take his own life under similar circumstances. He recalled reading about the controversy surrounding assisted suicide, his moral dilemma eventually resolved as it always had been in matters of personal choice. "And I respect his right to make the decision for himself."

"He would be happy to know that," she said looking not at him, but at the carvings on the closed door to his left. "You are one of the few whose opinions he truly valued."

"He spoke very highly of you as well, Sally."

For a moment, neither spoke. Then, she stiffened slightly, clutching the note in both hands. "I can't feel sorry for myself—you know, for not being able to see him one last time. That would be selfish, wouldn't it?"

May suddenly felt awkward, could not think of anything to say that would not sound inept. Did she expect an answer or was this just her thinking out loud?

Sally must have sensed he was uncomfortable, because she inclined her head—a half-nod in silent answer to herself—then shifted her eyes to May. "Well, I should go back up to his office. I've got quite a few phone calls to make."

CHAPTER 67

A tired, jet-lagged Sally devoted the remainder of her first day in Germany on the telephone in Lochridge's office, several hours of which were consumed by figuring out the logistics of getting his body released for transport back to the U.S. With Wilhelm nowhere to be found, Karla offered her help with translation, while May and Ginny excused themselves, each taking an armload of the OP files to Ginny's suite to give Sally privacy. Every hour or so, one of them checked in with her to make sure she was all right.

By mid-afternoon, she confessed to Ginny with a strained voice and bloodshot eyes that she was emotionally and physically spent. Ginny suggested an early dinner, a hot bath and a good night's sleep were just what she needed.

"He wants to be cremated," she announced while sipping a glass of wine after dinner. "His ashes scattered in Camden Harbor. His son, Andrew, is making the arrangements."

May shifted in his chair at the mention of Lochridge's son.

"Nice final resting place," Ginny said, raising her eyebrows. "He didn't say much about Andrew"—she glanced at May, whose face betrayed indifference—"I think he mentioned him just once."

"I'm not surprised," Sally said. "Andrew was the biggest disappointment in Marty's life. I couldn't believe it when Jerome told me he was executor."

Good wine seemed to temporarily relieve the effects of Sally's fatigue and any lingering inhibitions she may have felt, for she openly proclaimed her new freedom to speak candidly to someone other than her husband about the man for whom she had kept many business and personal secrets over their years together. It was apparent to her early on that he took extraordinary measures to protect his personal privacy—if there was a way to keep his personal information out of the public eye, he did. Working for him, she soon came to understand how essential the exercise of discretion was in business—particularly so in the fields of technology and real estate—but equally important in her role was keeping his confidence, which required his absolute trust in her silence.

"His self-described failure as a parent was his ugly scar," she told them. "I saw him lose, but he always told me not to worry, it would make him stronger. But Andrew—what happened to him—he felt completely powerless."

"What *did* happen?" Ginny asked.

A frown settled over her face as she began to describe how 13-year old John and the 11-year old Andrew had been splattered by their mother's blood and tissue when her car was smashed broadside by the speeding police cruiser. John lost a leg, and suffered multiple internal injuries, including permanent brain damage. He died in the hospital a couple of months later. Andrew recovered—physically, anyway—but had severe emotional problems through adolescence, did poorly in school, eventually turned to alcohol and drugs and got in trouble with the law. Unable to cope with the complex problems himself, Lochridge tried every technique, treatment, and school he could, but temporary improvements were quickly reversed by setbacks. Nothing seemed to work—he simply could not deal with his anger and recalcitrance, nor could anyone else. Andrew placed the blame for his problems squarely on the shoulders of his father's lousy parenting, and after telling him off, moved to Phoenix, where somehow he managed to put himself through trade school when he was not in rehab. Lochridge had not spoken to him in years.

"Normally, you hear success begets success, but this is a case of tragedy begets tragedy," May said to her when she had finished the story.

"Awful," Ginny agreed.

Sally poured herself a little wine, but didn't drink, instead she just studied the amber liquid as she swirled it around in the glass. "Now you understand why he didn't talk about his family. With all of his accomplishments, all his money, his personal life was a tragedy. He felt totally humiliated by Andrew."

"Yet, he made Andrew executor," Ginny said.

"A gesture to his only living blood relative, I suppose. I don't know. He didn't tell me he was doing it. But most of his assets were transferred to a trust for *Ops Populi*, so what's left of the estate is what he wanted Andrew to have."

"I assume Andrew is not involved in OP?" May asked her. Lochridge's personal affairs were none of his business, but *Ops Populi* certainly was.

She shook her head while fighting back a yawn. "Oh, no. Definitely not. I doubt he knows much of anything about what Marty has done in the last ten years."

May had one more question he wanted an answer to before Sally excused herself. "We have been looking in the files for a membership list—you know, for OP, but we haven't been able to find one. Do you know—"

"There isn't one," Sally interrupted, "not on paper anyway." She saw May and Ginny trade a puzzled glance. "You've seen the manifesto, right?"

They nodded.

"Well, to protect the identities of everyone in the group, Marty had Jerome—Hunnicutt, his lawyer—prepare a blank signature page. After he got them signed, he scanned them onto an encrypted CD, destroyed the originals. Every member was also assigned a code name—"

"We have one, too," Ginny told her with a nod.

"We all have one. Marty's was 'paper tiger.' Anyway, the code name is all we—Marty, Erik and I—ever used to refer to them. Supposedly, there is a cross-reference list on the same CD, but I have never seen it."

"You don't know their real names? Even the ones you've talked to personally?"

"No—well, I have an idea about who a few of them are and I think Erik has figured out one or two of his. Then there are the ones Marty handled himself." She ran her fingers through her hair as she measured her words. "I have a couple of suspects, you might say, but I am certain of only one—and that's because he died."

"John Collier?" Ginny asked her. "I saw an obituary."

"Yes, that's the one," she said in surprise. "We—Marty—worked with him off and on for years. Marty named his son, John, after him. I wondered, but I never knew. Until he was dead."

"I haven't seen any CD, have you?" May asked Ginny.

She shook her head. "We haven't been through everything yet, though. And there's the box of letters from that judge, too—"

"Ah, good old Judge Breslin," Sally interjected, with a chuckle. "Refused to play by Marty's security rules. Drove him nuts. No technology, just good old-fashioned letters."

"Maybe he stuck the CD in one of the other boxes."

"I'll help you look for it tomorrow," Sally said, squelching a yawn. "I know it's encrypted." She stood, steadied herself with both hands. "First, we need to find—he told me last fall that he was going to make a list of his security codes—"

"Got it!" Ginny said.

"Good. Having that list certainly will make our lives easier."

"Martin gave it to me this morning," May told her, standing up. "Are you OK?"

"Fine," Sally assured him. "Just tired, that's all."

As they walked through the living room toward the stairs, May stopped near the shelf holding the framed photo of Erik and Lochridge, "Sally, have you seen this before?"

She walked up to his side, and her face betrayed deep sadness as she took the picture in her hand. She shook her head in response to May's question. "That's the Marty I remember. God, I'm going to miss him!" she cried out.

With the color suddenly draining from his face, May hung his head in shame. "I'm—I'm sorry, Sally. I didn't mean to—"

"No, no, it's okay, Sean. My nerves are a wreck." She wiped her eyes on her hands while looking at the photo. "I don't recognize it. Probably one of the commercial projects in Cleveland or Northern Virginia they were working on together when my husband had his heart attack." She put the photo back on the shelf. "That was October 2004. I never came back—I retired, and we moved to Florida."

"Did you talk to Erik today? He is supposed to be flying over here Friday." May asked her.

Sally nodded. "We just spoke briefly. Of course, he was shocked by the news, so I let him go as soon as I told him."

"I'm sure he was," May said, following her and Ginny to the stairs.

"Let's get a fresh start in the morning. It's going to be a very busy day."

CHAPTER 68

"You look like hell," Ginny said to May when she sat down to breakfast. The smells of temptation wafted in from the kitchen. She hesitated momentarily, contemplating waffles, sausage, eggs, but forced herself to grab an empty bowl and the *muesli*, determined to resist.

"Thanks," came the sardonic reply.

"Didn't sleep?"

"Just a couple of hours. I got engrossed in all the files from Martin's safe." May laid a thick maroon file folder he had been reading from onto the table beside his placemat and reached for the coffee pot.

"Must be some pretty interesting stuff to keep *you* awake. You've been out by ten lately."

"Definitely interesting enough to get me through my "almost-all-nighter." This morning, he was very appreciative of Karla's usual hi-test brew, but he carefully filled only half of Ginny's cup knowing full well most of the other half would be used for cream and milk. "I know a lot more about Martin than I did yesterday, that's for sure."

"Such as?" Ginny asked intrigued as she sliced a banana into her cereal.

"Ever heard of a government program called 'Echelon'?"

"Doesn't ring any bells. What is it?"

Simultaneously, they both started as Sally bounded energetically into the room, obviously refreshed and energized. "Good morning!" she chimed. "I feel like a new woman."

"Morning," Ginny replied, frowning at the tiny puddle of spilled milk caused by the jolt Sally's entrance had produced.

May had risen in his chair as his well-ingrained manners had programmed him to do. "Slept well?"

"Like a baby!" came her energetic reply. Sally took the chair at the end of the table next to May where Lochridge had normally been seated every morning. With an apologetic countenance, she glimpsed at Ginny who was wiping the table with her napkin, while May sat down and moved the file he had been reading out of her way. She helped herself to coffee and mulled over the tempting platter of fresh pastries, which, Ginny explained, Wilhelm dutifully brought in from the village bakery every Thursday, today being no exception despite his obvious distress.

"These look wonderful!" Sally exclaimed as she studied.

May chuckled, tapping his stomach. "They are—believe me."

She settled on a cherry tart, which she bit into with obvious delight. "I do now!" she exclaimed, reaching for her coffee.

May followed her eyes to the age-yellowed paper in the file.

"What's that?" she asked casually.

"From Martin's safe," he said. "I was just asking Ginny when you came in if she had ever heard of something called 'Project Echelon.'"

"Oh, you discovered Echelon, did you?" Sally asked with an expression of instant recognition. "The bane of Martin Lochridge. I've never seen anything in writing, but I've heard plenty."

"Unbelievable stuff here," he said while lifting the file. "As I told Ginny, it explains a great deal about his—well, um—"

"Paranoia?" Sally finished his sentence.

Ginny stopped eating and glared expectantly at both of them, waiting to be let in on the knowledge they shared. "His bane?" she asked, her tone and face both pleading for elaboration.

Before speaking, May glanced at Sally, who was for the moment apparently more interested in savoring her tart than talking. He had read enough to describe Echelon and Lochridge's connection to it. Echelon was the National Security Agency code name for a U.S.-led multi-national surveillance program dating back to the early 1970s, whose original cold-war objective was to protect the national security interests of the five participating countries. Lochridge's father, Robert, who at the time was working on the FBI's ambitious National Crime Information Center computer project, was one of few scientists in the country with expertise in both computers and satellites. NSA eagerly recruited and handsomely paid Robert to work on Echelon's development, which included the deployment of a complex network of satellites, erecting massive ground-based antennae and microwave towers to intercept and relay communications across the country, even secretly sending divers into the oceans to install devices to tap into transcontinental telephone cables.

"As a scientist," Sally said when May paused to sip his coffee, "Robert, was accustomed to taking meticulous notes. Marty told me his dad was always in his recliner in the evenings and on weekends writing things down—something NSA probably wouldn't have approved of—but as far as he knew, the notes were never seen by anyone, except Marty, himself."

Done with her food, Ginny listened intently while sipping from a tall glass of orange juice. "I'm surprised Martin didn't follow in his dad's footsteps. Most of the boys I knew—especially the ones with successful fathers—did. Or at least tried to."

"Well, he did—sort of." Sally told her. "Robert convinced him how lucrative it could be to carry on, not as a scientist, but as the owner of a government contracting company employing many scientists. He knew NSA had carte blanche to spend whatever it took to build and maintain Echelon and with a little help, he could give Marty the keys to the government vault."

May smiled at the simplicity of it all. A scientist with proprietary technical knowledge gives it to his entrepreneur son, who, armed with business and law degrees and a team of scientists, sells it to a federal agency with a virtually unlimited budget and no congressional oversight or public scrutiny. If he played his cards right—which in hindsight he obviously had done—Martin would become vital, if not indispensable, to NSA's tenacious pursuit of intelligence with no clearly defined limits and an endless cycle of refinements and upgrades. Cold war or not, the U.S. would always have the need to keep its watchful eye on others who it perceived as potential threats to American interests.

"Talk about good job security," he said.

"Absolutely. Nothing like free-flowing money and a secret budget," Sally agreed. "With Robert's help, Marty was able to build a successful company, and when Ronald Reagan was elected, he saw the opportunity to parlay his success into building several defense contracting companies.

In the early eighties, the U.S. began spending huge sums of money on defense-related technology, and Marty, with his affable way, his education, status as a veteran, good war record, was in the right place at the right time."

The conversation came to an abrupt halt when Karla walked in with a fresh pot of coffee. With three sets of penetrating eyes on her, she took the clue and made a quick exit without saying a word.

The eighties and early nineties were very prosperous years for Lochridge, Sally explained, not only with government contracts but also the budding media empire of John Collier, who in the early eighties, and with the sage advice of Robert, figured out how to use the broadening distribution of satellite transmissions for entertainment. While his small but growing army of scientists took care of the government's ever-expanding list of wants and needs, Lochridge helped his friend build a cable television conglomerate. At the same time, he was investing heavily in LaSalle Bachman Aerospace in anticipation of the explosion in demand for private satellites, which throughout the sixties and early seventies had been monopolized by NASA.

"John Collier drove Marty crazy," Sally said with the certainty of someone who had been an eye-witness. "Every time he got ahead financially, he would risk it all to buy something else—a newspaper or a magazine or something." She rolled her eyes in mock disdain. "He once bought a film company and was immediately rewarded with a series of total flops. Marty tried to get him to focus—to concentrate on one thing—but he was too eager, too restless to stay focused on the slow, tedious process of building a cable system almost from scratch."

"How did Martin manage all this?" Ginny asked incredulous.

"Simple, really. He hired good people to work for him. He delegated. And he worked—a lot."

Wearing a hesitant expression, Karla entered once again with an empty tray and began to clear the few breakfast dishes. This time, Sally smiled warmly at her, and while May gathered the plates and glasses, complimented her on the pastries and engaged in some polite chit-chat.

When Karla had gone, Ginny leaned forward with an intent gaze at Sally, and rested her chin in her hand. "You said this project—Echelon—was his curse, but it sounds like it was a gold mine for him."

"It was both of those," she said with resolve. "Anyone who knew him would have told you he had the perfect life—money, good looks, a beautiful and engaging wife, a business bonanza, you name it, he either had it, or if he didn't, it was because he didn't want it. On the surface, he was raking in tons of money, most of which was coming from the taxpayers, at least until later. But he was not motivated by avarice: He was very proud of the work he was doing for the government, believing that he was still a soldier fighting the cold war to protect his country, his way of life. But—to use his words—the grand illusion started to unravel in the late eighties."

As Sally was talking, May had taken the file from the table and started searching through it for something he had read. When he found it, he held it in one hand while carefully placing two small stacks back onto the table, so as to preserve its place.

"What's this?" Sally asked when he held it out to her. She took it and read the title aloud. "*An Appraisal of Technologies of Political Control.* Published in January 1998, by the European Parliament in Luxembourg." With no discernable recognition, she held it in front of her, casually flipping through the 60 or so stapled pages.

May looked down thoughtfully at the thick open file. "This file is full of reports, letters, copies of news clippings—like Martin was researching for an Orwellian spy novel or something. It is hard for me to understand how this all ties together, but from what I've seen so far, it looks like he's compiled a case *against* Echelon."

In less than a minute of scanning the report, she began nodding. "Yes," she said sliding it on the table to Ginny, "when this came out, he was livid."

For a moment, Sally struggled with the dates and the sequence of events, but her recall was soon clear and vivid. The long unwinding of his self-described grand illusion had started in 1988 during the first of several trips to the largest overseas U.S. satellite and communications station, known as Menwith Hill, near Harrogate in Yorkshire, England. Congress had just approved tens of millions in funding for "Project P415," a U.S. initiative to vastly expand Echelon's capabilities. At the time, Menwith Hill employed some 1,200 people, two-thirds of them American, most NSA and other government workers, some American contract employees. One of the American contracting firms was LaSalle Bachman Aerospace, which, thanks in no small part to Lochridge, had been a key player at Menwith Hill for years and figured prominently in Lochridge's proposal for the Project P415 expansion. An LBA employee—a woman Sally believed was named Patricia Dupree—who had been promoted and moved to Menwith Hill in early 1987, recognized Lochridge from an LBA company Christmas party he had attended just before her transfer to England. She approached him, and according to the way he had remembered the encounter, practically demanded they meet for dinner or a drink, at least, while he was there.

"Out of nowhere, this woman he doesn't recognize boldly asks him out," Sally chortled. "Now, Marty wasn't an unkind man, but on a trip as important as this, he would not want any distractions, particularly a strange woman coming on to him. So when he politely refused her invitation, she winked at him, and whispered she wanted to finish what they started at the Christmas party!"

"A cue of some sort?" Ginny surmised. "Either that, or she was a crackpot"

"Exactly!" Sally was impressed with Ginny's perception. "In a place like Menwith Hill, a private conversation was out of the question, so she tried this absurd overture, which I think was pretty clever of her. He took the bait and met her at a pub next to his hotel after work."

Despite being in an English pub, Dupree presented herself very formally, still dressed in her business suit, with a firm handshake, apologies for her tactics, and effusive gratitude for agreeing to meet with her. She was quite uneasy at first, constantly looking around at the pub's patrons, shifting in her chair, and so forth, which, in turn, made Lochridge uncomfortable. But after downing a half-pint or so, she settled down enough to tell him the story of one day being ordered to eavesdrop on a telephone conversation of a prominent U.S. senator, whose name she did not immediately divulge to him. Lochridge was skeptical at first, but Dupree went on to describe a routine of sitting at her desk wearing earphones, listening—in real-time—to phone calls involving U.S. citizens, many of whom were high-ranking politicians and business executives. She feared repercussions from discussing this with anyone at work, and of course, dared not reveal anything in an overseas phone call. So she was taking this enormous risk to confide in him in the hopes that he would relay the information to her boss. He assured her he would carry the disturbing message to LaSalle himself, not to worry, he would be discreet.

Neither he nor Bachman wanted to believe any of it, for if true, the system they built to protect Americans was being perverted and abused to spy on them illegally. Though initially incensed that one of his employees would violate propriety, if not the law, and tell such an incredible story to someone outside the company, Bachman honored his promise to Lochridge of no retaliation and brought Dupree back to the U.S. Lochridge, convinced by Bachman that Dupree's allegations were unlikely, put the whole affair out of his mind, went about his business, ultimately winning a major role in Project P415 for himself and LBA. With hundreds of millions of dollars in taxpayer money, they put up more satellites, upgraded existing facilities, and built new hi-tech stations, one of which Sally was sure was just south of Monschau, in the Taunus mountains near Wiesbaden.

Bachman, meanwhile, handled the Dupree matter poorly. Back at Fort Meade, Maryland and with access to the computers she still managed at Menwith Hill, Dupree continued to observe what certainly was an NSA program of deliberate spying on U.S. citizens. But he stubbornly rebuffed her persistent complaints and eventually fired her.

"One day, Marty opens up the newspaper and finds the whole story staring him in the face," Sally told them. "Not only was he mad that LaSalle had fired her, but he was astonished by her accusations, which by now, not only included monitoring telephone calls, but intercepting and sifting through the growing volume of internet traffic—using software and hardware his company developed!"

May looked down at the open file, remembering the article, but not having understood its relevance when he started to read it. Now he did.

"Was anything done to stop it?" Ginny asked.

"Not a thing," she replied. "Everyone in the government denied it. Even Senator Pierce—"

"Pierce?" May interrupted. "He was a loyal supporter of the administration, probably helped get the money for Echelon. Why would they spy on him?"

Sally shrugged. "His only public comment was that he didn't believe

Dupree, was not concerned, so the story was just swept under the rug. The Democrats—including Preston—called for an investigation, but without Pierce, it went nowhere."

"So Pierce discredits Dupree publicly and they write her off as just another disgruntled former employee," May observed. "Her word against a senior Senator's."

"Didn't anyone follow up with Dupree?" Ginny asked. "You know—to try to get more details?"

"I don't know, but I'll bet Preston remembers more—"

Sally was cut off by the deafening screams of sirens, which startled her more than May or Ginny who had heard them once before.

"Intruder alert system!" May shouted over the noise. "We have to go to up to Martin's office to shut it off!"

They didn't know it yet, but this time it wasn't just an animal that had broken through Lochridge's virtual perimeter.

CHAPTER 69

By the time they got to Lochridge's office, a sulking Wilhelm was there waiting. With his help, they were at least able to turn off the sirens, but for the moment, none of them could figure out how to access the complex system of sensory equipment comprising the virtual perimeter to determine what had breached it. Probably just wildlife, they agreed. Ginny fiddled with the computerized controller for a few minutes but soon gave up, fearing she might inadvertently damage the system, or worse, set off the confounding sirens again. With all that they had to do—first and foremost, dealing with the disposition of Lochridge's body and coordinating arrangements with his son, Andrew—the incident was easily forgotten.

A private and modest man in life, the last wishes of Martin Lochridge left no doubt that he wanted no grandiose observance of his death: nothing more than a small memorial service at his adopted home of Vienna, Virginia, and the scattering of his ashes in the peaceful and lovely Camden Harbor.

What should have been relatively straightforward was complicated by German bureaucracy and language barriers, on the one hand, and a drunk, recalcitrant and grief-stricken Andrew Lochridge on the other. As the named executor, his cooperation was required to get the body home, but instead, Andrew had decided to go on a binge. He sobbed profusely to Sally, who, with the patience of a saint, listened as he alternated between blabbering about his many regrets for the way he treated his father over the years, and ranting incoherently at the indignities of growing up with no mother and a patronizing father who, in his judgment, was a poor excuse for a parent. When she had finally had enough and told him so, demanded he sober up, he hung up on her, shouting obscenities. It took the intervention of Jerome Hunnicutt, who somehow managed to coax Andrew into relinquishing his powers of executor, to finally resolve the issue.

"The kid has problems," Preston Bachman consoled her later that afternoon. "It's a damn shame, too. You know Marty loved him."

"That's why I put up with him as long as I did," she said with a sigh.

"Did Hunnicutt say anything about Sean and Ginny? He's supposed to be working on their situation."

"No, not yet," she said.

"I'll find out what's holding him up from my end. Is there anything—anything at all—I can do for you here?"

"Not really. We'll let you know the details on the memorial as soon as they are finalized," she assured him. "You know…" Her voice trailed off as an idea popped into her head.

"No, I don't know. What?"

"Why didn't I think of this earlier—can you hold on a second? I want Sean and Ginny to hear this."

"Sure."

"I'm going to put you on speaker. There, can you hear me?"

"Yes—hello, Sean, Ginny. How are you?"

"Hello, Senator. Fine, thanks." May answered.

"Great!" Ginny said.

"I want you two to hear an idea that just popped into my mind out of the blue a minute ago," Sally announced. "Preston, you know Marty detested funerals, wakes, and such."

"Thought they were a waste of money. He would tell us to have a party—drink some beer, eat some good barbecue," Preston said, with a deep belly laugh.

"Exactly. So let's have a short memorial service for the benefit of Andrew and any of Marty's non-OP friends, then immediately have the OP pre-campaign meeting. And throw in a party in his honor!" Sally bellowed.

May looked at her in disbelief. How could they possibly organize this meeting in just a few short days? They didn't even know who would be coming, let alone what it was they were supposed to do. Ginny, who leaned forward with both elbows on Lochridge's desk, didn't appear the slightest bit troubled by the idea. He opened his mouth to protest but at the last second, decided to keep his opinion to himself—at least for the moment.

For a moment, Bachman was quiet—they could hear the squeaking of his office chair as he moved. "I like it," he said finally. "What better way to honor his memory than to march on with OP business and throw him a party in the process. Question is, is it even possible? It's pretty short notice, and—"

"What do you think he would say?" Sally interrupted.

"Make it happen!" Bachman said in a gruff tone to simulate Lochridge's command voice. "Suck it up and drive on!"

Sally grinned widely, knowing that Bachman had been on the receiving end of it in Vietnam, like everyone else who ever worked under him. As if reading his mind, she looked directly at May before saying, "Not a bad imitation, Preston. I heard it a thousand times—along with 'No thanks, I don't like whine.'

Thankful he had kept his mouth shut, May nevertheless squirmed uncomfortably in his chair.

Sally picked up a pen and looked down at the notepad she had been scribbling on since yesterday. "Let's talk about this for a minute. A funeral is usually on short notice, right? I'm going to assume that a majority of the OP members are people Marty knew fairly well, and that many of them would attend his memorial service on short notice anyway. So if I am correct, we may have most of the group in Virginia very soon."

"Sounds reasonable," Ginny said, still staring blankly at the phone.

"I can't speak for Erik—or Marty, of course—but I would bet most would prefer to meet in Virginia instead of coming over here." She looked around, stopping to fix her gaze at the window and the scenery it displayed. "Don't get me wrong—this place is stunning. And safe. Marty made sure of that. But we have his house and the Jonic building which are both very secure—"

"Have it at his house—the place is a fortress and plenty big," Bachman said. "Plus, a small memorial service will serve as a good excuse for everyone to come together there," Bachman added.

"Right. And since Marty is going to be cremated, we have a little extra time."

"If you think you can pull this off, I'll do whatever I can to help. It's the only reason I'm still sitting in this office," Bachman said.

Sally turned her hopeful eyes first to Ginny, who nodded as she lifted her elbows from the table, then to May, who also gave her a quick, though tentative, affirmative nod.

"Okay," Sally said with determination. "All we can do is give it our best shot. We'll get an agenda over to you to look at by tomorrow."

"You know…all that is really required at this point is a formal vote on the—what did he call that thing?"

"Briefing document?" Ginny guessed before Sally could swallow the last of her coffee.

"That's it—the *briefing document,*" Bachman said, adding emphasis. "Why he called it that, I don't know. But you would think after working on it and passing it around for almost five years, there should be consensus, unless anyone has had a sudden change of heart."

"You would think," Sally agreed. "But there was a reason it took that long to—"

"I know," Bachman interrupted. "Good 'ole Marty wanted it to be perfect. Well, I think it's damn good. We should put it to a vote as is, deal with the budget later."

May now regretted he had become so engrossed in the intrigue of the Echelon file, assuming up until this very moment he had ample time to study it later. As he stood to go look for it, he silently agreed with Bachman: it was an odd name to give such an important policy and implementation document.

"Why the *briefing document*?" Ginny asked the question May had been thinking. "Sounds—you know—media-oriented."

"Simple, really," Sally answered. "One document. A single document containing the group's suggested changes to the Constitution—which is the meat of it and why it took as long as it did to get agreement—and the broadly worded action steps to carry out OP's core mission. It is media-oriented in the sense that the members will use it as a reference when they publicly comment on OP. But Marty didn't want the members to get bogged down in the minutia of execution, so it specifically delegates the details to staff, that is, us. We have a lot of discretion, and a lot of responsibility to go with it, I might add."

"But they—the members—have to approve a budget?" May asked.

"Technically, yes," Sally said. "To formally authorize the trustees to release the money from the trust account."

"We can do it by fax, later," Bachman said. "Besides, the money's not even all there yet." Bachman had yet to transfer any of his money to the relatively new trust account and assumed, correctly, none of the others had either.

"Agreed," Sally said, noticing May was holding the thick Echelon file next to his waist. "Preston, guess what Sean found in Marty's safe?"

"God only knows. What?"

"A pile of his Echelon stuff. I told him what I could remember—"

"He kept all that?" Bachman cut her off. "Good! I can't wait to see what's there—all together in one place. What do you think, Sean?"

"Pretty amazing. Very disturbing."

Bachman snorted loudly. "That's an understatement. I was ready to resign from the Senate until Marty begged me—"

"Didn't get that far," Sally cut him off. "That crazy alarm system went off and—."

"Alarm? What triggered it?" Bachman asked with concern.

Sally explained what had happened, that they were unable to determine the cause.

"Glad it wasn't anything more serious," he said, suspicion forming in the back of his mind. "See if you can get a look at that video, you know, just to be sure it was an animal."

"Maybe, if we can find a book or something," Ginny mumbled.

Loud ringing bells suddenly erupted from the phone's speaker.

"Time to vote," May observed. Those who visited the Senate learned about the system of bells used in the Capitol and Senate Office buildings to signal votes and quorum calls.

"Right you are, and this is an important one—the President's supplemental war funding," Bachman said hurriedly. "Sean, I'll buy you a beer and tell you a little more about Echelon when you get here. In the meantime, I'll find out what the hell's taking so long to get you and Ginny taken care of. Call me the same time tomorrow, OK?"

"Will do," Sally replied, but he was already gone.

As he took his second row seat near the center of the Senate chamber, Bachman's eyes narrowed and his jaw tightened when he looked up at the rostrum where the Vice President would soon be seated. Echelon. Marty had been right all those years ago, but he stubbornly refused to believe it. He was a junior Senator in his first term, still full of idealism and energized by the opportunity to make a difference. Until that day he threw that thick pile of documents Sean was now reading down on his desk and said, "don't look now, but the bastards are watching you."

Well, Marty, he thought, so your lawyer screwed up your money transfer; if the bastards are watching now, they are too late. And, thanks to Sally's idea, they will be barking up the wrong tree, wasting their time watching the wrong place, spying on a man who is no longer there. But your spirit is here, with all of us who really care, as you did.

Up in the gallery, he zoomed in on the busts of John Adams and Thomas Jefferson, two of many such busts lining the wall that honored former presiding officers of what should be, but no longer was, an honorable institution. No doubt, they would roll over in their graves if they could see what a shambles their beloved country—for which they sacrificed everything—was becoming. No, we will not allow your sacrifices to be in vain—squandered, wasted—lost forever. We, too, will sacrifice what we must. "God has favored our undertakings," said the Latin *Annuit Coeptis* inscribed over the east entrance through which he passed every day. It was true 230 years ago; with his fists clenched, his eyes squeezed tightly closed, he silently prayed, it would be true now.

CHAPTER 70

"Where could it all be?" Ginny said in exasperation after going through the piles of paper for the third time.

She and May were sitting on the floor of Lochridge's office, in what was now apparent to them both a hopeless quest to find the briefing document and the CD-ROM holding the secretive information on the other OP members. Other things seemed to be missing, too. Neither of them had seen OP corporate documents, bank account information, or any of the marketing literature Lochridge had told them about.

"Damned if I know," May said with obvious disgust, "if they're not here, not in the safe, and not in his desk—are you sure there is none of it on his computer?"

"Absolutely" she rolled her eyes. "I know what I'm doing with PCs, you know!"

"Sorry. I know you do."

They just sat there, sipping from their mugs, not sure what to do next. A morning of futile searching had stumped them both.

"Maybe Erik or Bachman know something," May suggested weakly.

"Maybe, but I wouldn't count on it." She glanced at her watch, shook her head. "In a few hours, we can ask—it's just after five o'clock their time."

May yawned, and lazily rose to his feet. "I'll go see how Sally's doing with the Germans."

They knew Sally was suffering her own frustration with the peculiar way the Germans dealt with death, particularly that of a foreigner who died on their soil. Neither Wilhelm nor Karla could offer much assistance beyond translation, so through a series of awkward phone calls, and finally a call to the U.S. Embassy in Cologne, she finally knew what had to be done. Since Lochridge died in a private residence with no attending German physician, she first had to call a *Notarzt* to issue the German death certificate, which then had to be sent to the embassy for an American certificate of death abroad. Sally found a Dusseldorf funeral home—evidently one of the few in the entire country—authorized by the German government to handle the remains. Until recently, only the German government could collect, embalm, bury or cremate the deceased, whose remains had to be interred in a state owned cemetery. There were strict procedures for transporting a foreigner's remains to the country of origin. Even if cremated in Germany, private citizens were not permitted to handle the ashes, so special arrangements would be required to ship them back to the U.S. To her great relief, the funeral home would handle all of it—once they had the body, that is—but first she had to arrange for the body to be taken there. For the emotionally strained Sally, it had been a trying experience.

Before May had even reached the elevator, the door opened and an exhausted Sally walked out carrying a briefcase and a small wooden box.

"Thought you might appreciate this," she said, handing him the intricately hand-carved box.

"Thanks," he said, as he opened the lid. It contained his old army decorations, insignia, and patches. But for the moment, he was more interested in the contents of the briefcase both he and Ginny had completely forgotten. Was it possible he had taken the missing items with him on this last trip to the U.S.?

Sally placed the briefcase on the only remaining uncluttered spot on the desk, then collapsed in the armchair, rubbing her eyes. "It's locked. You have the list?" she asked Ginny, who had it last. "We could break it open, I suppose."

"Right here." May slid the list from under the mouse pad and quickly stooped to perch on one of the chairs in front of the desk. For a few minutes, he turned the yellow dials rapidly with both thumbs as he worked down the list. Sally watched him try and fail a few times before a flashing red light on the copy machine caught her attention.

"Some of them are reversed, remember?" Ginny said. She took the list and sat down beside him.

Oh, yeah. Right." Ginny read numbers aloud while he worked the dials. It wasn't long before the locks sprung open with a snap. "Bingo!"

"Good work," Sally said, her back to them, struggling mightily to pull the copier away from the wall. "Now, if I can just slide this out without breaking it."

Instead of giving into his urge to start rummaging through the briefcase, he slid it toward Lochridge's chair and stood to help Sally.

Without hesitation, Ginny had the lid open and was picking through its contents before May had even made it to the corner of the desk. First, she unzipped and flipped through the black CD-DVD case, which true to Lochridge form, contained several cryptically labeled CD-ROMs, and interestingly, two identical DVDs, which stood out because of their gold patina and professional imprints. She looked closely at the logo of an eye superimposed over a movie camera, a computer monitor, and a pamphlet, all arranged over a silver image of a compact disc. Interestingly, when slightly tilted, the words "EyezOn Media" appeared along the top edge. "a division of Fostoria Production Co., Great Falls, VA" along the bottom. She set the case aside, confident one of the CDs was the one they had been searching for, then took several manila folders into her hands and sat back, crossed her legs, and began perusing them.

"I think it's all here," she declared almost immediately and without looking away. "What do you know—all this time, he had it with him."

A hunched-over May pulled a long, black tube from the center of the copy machine as Sally looked down at him. "See any bank account info?" she asked.

"Uh, huh," Ginny mumbled as she thumbed through the third file. "CDs, the briefing document, corporation documents. All here." Since Sally and May were busy behind the desk, and with no easy way to reposition the computer, Ginny decided to hold off on the CDs for now. Instead, she placed all but one of the folders back in the briefcase, and began reading through the briefing document.

Out of the corner of her eye, she saw Sally walk to the bathroom and back to May with a roll of paper towels. "Oh, you got it on your pants," she heard Sally say to him, evidently referring to the copier's toner.

Ginny guessed the briefing document to be under 100 pages, perhaps 60 or 70, which was far fewer than she had expected. The first section was titled "Suggested Amendments," with each of them set off in bold print, followed by several pages of explanation and justification.

"Sean, didn't you have almost a couple of dozen amendments in your dissertation?" she called out to an open closet, where he and Sally were apparently in search of a new toner cartridge.

"Twenty-one exactly," he called back as he stepped out of the closet with a long rectangular cardboard box. Sally turned off the light and closed the door behind him. "Why?"

"There are," she counted, while turning pages to be sure, "only seven in this briefing document."

"Huh?" He walked over to look over Ginny's shoulder. She turned the pages, pointing to each one, as he read them aloud:

"An Amendment to Revise the Methods and Procedures for Amending the Constitution of the United States of America,

"An Amendment to Limit Consecutive Congressional Terms of Office,

"An Amendment to Reform Campaign Finance,

"An Amendment to Abolish the Electoral College,

"An Amendment to Limit Presidential War Powers,

"An Amendment to Limit Federal Judicial Terms and Impose a Mandatory Retirement Age,

"An Amendment to Require the President to Submit a Balanced Budget to Congress."

He stood the toner box on the floor, then gently took the briefing document from Ginny and began leafing though the pages, his face betraying astonishment. Most of the document was devoted to implementation—the media "blitz" strategy and direct mail campaign, the contents of the OP web site, selecting state delegates—with just a quarter, perhaps 25 pages, of suggested amendments, discussion and justification.

"Seven. I don't understand," May said to Sally, who was stooped over the desk, reading the copier's spiral-bound instruction manual.

Sally looked at him over the rims of her reading glasses. "You expected more?"

His forehead wrinkled as he stared blankly at the open copier manual under Sally's face. "Martin led me to believe that all, or at least many, of the proposed amendments in my disser—" He looked down at the document. "It's just—well, I expected to see more suggested amendments."

Sally lifted her head and leaned back in the chair before saying, "It took Marty a long time just to get everyone to agree to the ones you are seeing there," She looked alternately at both of them. "Some members believe there are still too many."

"Too many?" Ginny asked. "I don't understand—even I can see there are a lot of issues not even mentioned."

"Marty ran into a lot of philosophical resistance to suggesting most any amendment for consideration." Sally explained. "Too many amendments would bog down the process, you know, distract people from OP's core mission of providing the opportunity to have a convention in the first place." She held up her index finger as she continued, "Four of the members—the 'gang of four,' as he called them—wanted one, and only one, amendment."

"Really?" May looked astonished.

"Which one," Ginny asked.

"The first one—revising the method used to amend." Sally pulled her reading glasses off, dangling them in front of her face while she thought a moment. "I wish he was here to explain it; he could do a better job. But a small minority of the members—only one in my group that I know of—argued tirelessly to keep the convention very narrowly focused. They maintain there's a higher probability of success if the delegates leave the Constitution mostly untouched, and frankly, I see their point. Part of me agrees with them." She leaned forward, resting her elbows on the desktop. "You see, if you can increase the odds of successfully adopting that one and, in the process, arouse the American public from its lethargy towards the Constitution, to take back the ownership of it..." Her voice trailed off as she struggled with how to phrase the rest of her thought.

May nodded, as though understanding her unspoken words. "Make it changeable through an orderly process accessible by the public directly."

"Yes, exactly," she gestured with her hand. "Get people engaged, give them a meaningful, practical way to take control—to use Marty's cherished word—but leave structural reforms off the table for now."

May leaned back, looking up at the ceiling while he paraphrased. "A limited convention. Let the public choose how and when to make specific changes, but through regular amendments, not through a convention."

"Right."

"So Martin convinced you and the others to add these others?" Ginny asked.

"Took him years, but yes. And the convincing has been made easier—I certainly became more receptive—by the war in Iraq. He and Preston talked constantly about how urgent it was to correct the systemic problems now, before it is too late." She frowned as she looked down at a list by the phone, not at all ready to resume the unpleasant phone calls. In Maryland, she knew, Erik would be busy working his way through his own.

"Surely, some of them wanted more," May said with inflection that suggested both a question and a statement. "All of the changes I proposed had a great deal of public support at the time."

"Oh, yes," Sally said as she looked toward the sitting area, dust particles flittering in the streams of sunlight. "Somewhere in those piles over there, you will see references to many others that were discussed, debated at length. Equal rights, abortion, gun control, flag burning, school prayer, the death penalty—you name it. And Marty suggested one you didn't include, Sean: privacy."

"It would be there if I were writing my dissertation today," he assured her. Starting in 1965 with the case of *Griswold v. Connecticut*, the U.S. Supreme Court began to carve a constitutional right to privacy from the Bill of Rights' provisions for freedom of association and protection of security of home and person. Then in 1973, the Court used that tacit right as justification in the controversial *Roe v. Wade* abortion decision. Yet, despite test cases involving wiretapping and eavesdropping, dissemination of personal information over the internet, access to government information and others, the Court had not extended privacy as a constitutional right significantly since. As Lochridge and most students of the Constitution knew and understood all too well, as a practical matter, such a right did not exist, and laws aimed at protecting privacy were wholly inadequate.

"Well, even though there are just seven, every branch of the government is affected by these," Ginny said, the document resting on the edge of the desk. "They appear to be well-supported, but like I've said before, Sean, I have to believe there will be some disagreements over them, too."

May looked at her thoughtfully, reminded that she had never really taken a position or asserted a firm opinion about any of the proposals he made in his dissertation. She seemed indifferent, somehow, neither supporting nor opposing, just content to play the devil's advocate role. Did she, as someone who had not spent a career thinking about these issues in depth, find these seven proposed amendments desirable, agreeable? With her above-average education and intellect, was she even a reliable barometer of how they would be received by the public? If the people were as indifferent as she seemed to be, *Ops Populi* would surely fail. Of one thing he was certain: Only by overcoming the pervasive apathy, by inspiring patriotic passion among the public at-large, could they ever hope to achieve the momentum required for a convention.

"Sure, they are all debatable, certain to be opposed by some," May said to her, "but they are all needed. The question is whether the American people agree."

"It really doesn't matter," Sally reminded them. "Our first job is to capture their attention. Then, to offer some crucial revisions for their consideration. It is at that point we have fulfilled Marty's wish for OP and we again assume our place among all other citizens, whose prerogative it is to formally propose and adopt changes to the Constitution."

May smiled as he remembered writing in his dissertation something similar to what Sally had just said. In making his case for the legitimacy of popular control over government—whether through ballot initiatives, constitutional conventions, or proposed amendments—he had concluded: "In a democratic system, legitimacy rests with the people—if they propose it, see it, and vote on it, it is, thereby, legitimate."

CHAPTER 71

Two Days Later…

Lochridge's Falcon made a smooth landing at Dulles International Airport early Saturday morning. They were escorted to a windowless room where a group of five people were waiting. Sally's face lit up in joy at the instant recognition of the older man, flanked on either side by suited men wearing very serious expressions.

The older man was none other than Preston Bachman himself, whose salt and pepper hair, trim athletic frame, and slightly weather-beaten face presented an image one might expect of a rancher or a construction worker, and one surely younger than his 58 years. After exchanging a long hug with Sally, he warmly introduced himself to Ginny, embracing her as though he had known her for years. Finally he came to May, who, with bags in both hands, received a friendly squeeze on the upper arm. The men with suits stood by patiently at a comfortable distance while Bachman made some idle conversation about the flight, whether they had slept, eaten and so forth. Then, with a quick nod, one of the suits approached them, producing the distinctive badge of the U.S. Marshals Service.

Delighted to be back on American soil, both May and Ginny expressed their gratitude to Bachman, who had pulled the strings, called in the favors, and twisted the arms necessary to get them home. But at the moment the Marshal handed them new passports, the impact of assuming new identities hit them both forcefully; talking about it had been one thing, seeing their pictures beside different names, with strange Social Security numbers and addresses was something else entirely.

Just two days before, when the Justice Department's Office of Enforcement Operations had authorized their admission to WitSec, more commonly known as the Federal Witness Protection Program, they had been asked to select their new names. Keep your same first name if you want, they were told, but if you decide to change it also, keeping the same initials was advisable. So, in a matter of hours, Sean May and Virginia Burress became Samuel Mullins and Victoria Barnes, at least for the foreseeable future. They would not go home, return to their jobs, or have contact with friends or family, and though Samuel and Victoria had no intention of completely severing ties with each other or Erik, all future contact would be carefully orchestrated. Family and friends were aware that they were safe—something of greater importance to Ginny than May—though their whereabouts and new identities must be withheld to ensure it remained that way. They, of course, declined offers of help with obtaining employment or a monthly stipend, but they would accept assistance with finding suitable housing in their new hometowns—Stafford, Virginia for Sam; Annapolis, Maryland for Vicki.

For the first time in many days, May felt dull pain where he had been injured weeks before. Perhaps it was lack of sleep—always impossible for him when traveling—but he was also well aware of his own apprehension about this homecoming and all the near-term uncertainty that it entailed.

No, the present circumstances were not ideal, but were they ever really? Virginia Burress and Sean May were resigned to the fact that they had to disappear for a time to finally put an end to their ordeal. Precisely when they could safely go back to being Sean and Ginny was uncertain for now, but in the grand scheme of things, considering all that they had been through, all the adaptations they had made, each of them knew they would re-emerge stronger, better than before.

"You realize we won't be able to attend Martin's service or the OP meeting, don't you?" May said to Ginny the day before yesterday, once Bachman's news had sunk in.

"Why not?" She asked in surprise. "The rules I heard were: No contact with unprotected family, former friends and associates, check in with the Marshals Service once a month. I don't think you, Sally, Bachman, or anyone in OP fit that defin—"

"Think for a minute," he interrupted. "Our names will be different. How do we explain who we are, why we are there? And later—soon, I hope—how do we explain that our names have changed? Oh, and I'm sure everyone would be happy if we brought the U.S. Marshals along. I know they probably have better things to do than follow us around everyday, but what if they do follow us there?"

"Yeah, I guess you're right," she said in a way that suggested a touch of self-pity. "I'm not sure what I am supposed to do, other than keep away from people who know me."

"What you and I have done all along," May replied looking up at her. "Go with the flow. It's either that or stay here, and I, for one, am ready to move on."

"Move on to what? That's the question. We won't be us anymore, so what *are* we supposed to do exactly?" She said, hanging her head. "They're even splitting us up, so I guess I'll just stay home and learn to knit!"

May took a deep breath, remembering how much she had helped him through his bouts of tortured sadness and anxiety. Although briefly disheartened by being relegated—at least for now—to a faceless role in OP, he was looking beyond what was just another in a string of unforeseen twists and turns along this improbable pathway he and Ginny had landed on just a few weeks before. "We're being split up on paper, but there is no rule preventing us from seeing each other." Leaning toward her, he continued, "Look, I am disappointed, too—I was looking forward to meeting all these people, watching the dynamics of how everyone interacts. But we still have plenty to do, even if it's behind the scenes." He laid his outstretched hand gently on the side of her head. "Maybe the cops will wrap this up quickly and it will be over, you know?"

She smiled, reached up to her head, took his hand in hers. "You're right, of course," she said clutching his hand tightly. "I just needed reminding that this is almost the end—and the beginning of something really awesome."

And so, in an unspoken pact, they each forcefully suppressed their anxiety about returning to the U.S. as unknowns, strangers having no past, no connections, no roots. When they boarded the Falcon at just before ten that night, they were in good spirits, ready to go home, and looking to the future with optimism and enthusiasm.

While Ginny and Sally slept, May, condemned to a long, restless ride across the Atlantic, used the time to continue reading the correspondence taken from Lochridge's safe. Notes, letters, articles from magazines, journals, and newspapers, all added historical context and clarity to the evolution of OP into its present form.

Over time, the simplicity of the briefing document became more appealing to May, whose youthful idealism had been tempered by the cautious practicality of middle age. For a relatively small group of twenty committed individuals to take a concept so immensely complex and distill it into two fairly brief documents was remarkable. Not that their brevity made the task ahead any easier, but their elegant simplicity stood in stark contrast to the ambitious, if not quixotic, process envisioned in his 294-page doctoral dissertation. His notion of a modern convention undertaking governmental reform while also tackling complex and controversial social issues was fantasy, doomed to hopeless stalemate. As it was, if they were to adopt the suggested reforms, the delegates were not only bound to have substantive disagreements among themselves, they would operate in a media fish bowl, under continual scrutiny and enormous pressure, not the closed-door isolation of the first convention that made possible essential compromise and conciliation among often deeply divided delegates. This time, hordes of special interests and power elites were certain to descend on the delegates like vultures: Only highly principled people of great character would be able to resist their incessant attempts to influence, or worse, manipulate the final outcome. Part of his job, as he understood it, would be to make that abundantly clear to the state conventions who would choose the national delegates.

After the commotion of Lochridge's death had subsided, the three of them focused on removing the shroud of secrecy that he had artfully placed over the identities of the people behind the movement itself. Once Ginny managed to open the encrypted CD, with the excitement of children on Christmas morning, the three of them had huddled together, peering intently at the monitor, eager to end the mystery.

For May, just knowing their names, seeing their photos, learning just a little about them, gave substance to what up until now had been only a nebulous vision of a group of faceless people. Two, including Lochridge and his close friend and business partner, John Collier, were dead. Of the remaining 18, he recognized only a couple of the names besides Sally's, Bachman's, and, of course, Erik's, whom Lochridge had added as the last "original" member.

Lawrence Bucklew, who had won the Nobel Prize in economics when May was in graduate school, was one of the many sources cited in his Ph.D. dissertation. Bucklew challenged the prevailing macro-economic theory, known as "supply-side"—or more accurately, "Reaganomics," since what was put into practice in 1981 was in fact a cherry-picked perversion of supply-side—which held that lower taxation and reduced government spending would stimulate economic growth through private investment, leading to higher revenues over the long term. The problem with Reaganonmics in Bucklew's view—one largely adopted by May himself, and evidently, also by Lochridge—was that the administration, to the delight of Congress, proposed steep tax cuts for affluent Americans and large corporations but failed to balance reduced revenue with corresponding reductions in spending. This resulted in more than doubling the national debt in eight short years. Although the eighties were considered by many Americans to be prosperous years, Bucklew assailed Reaganomics as nothing more than a great hoax perpetrated on the masses of American people who not only failed to benefit from the policies, but were actually hurt by them. Slowly but surely, the middle class, so vital to the social and economic health of the country, was being ravaged by the loss of manufacturing jobs—which were mostly replaced by lower paying service sector jobs—inflation, the erosion of benefits, and an ill-conceived tax policy that actually increased the taxes of a large swath of Americans. Embraced as gospel by subsequent Republican administrations, Reaganonmics—the quintessential "free-lunch" dogma, according to Bucklew—when combined with absence of fiscal discipline in Congress, spelled inevitable social and financial disaster for the U.S. Writing after the invasion of Iraq in late 2004, Bucklew convincingly argued the continuation of this pattern of reckless tax cuts for the wealthy, accumulation of a public debt rapidly approaching $9 trillion, de-regulation of many industries accompanied by relaxed environmental and safety standards, loss of manufacturing capacity, and a burgeoning military-industrial complex were altogether a burden America could not bear indefinitely, and if not checked, would eventually lead to the demise of American prosperity. That Bucklew would be attracted by an opportunity to make reforms he believed so crucial to the viability of the United States came as no surprise to May.

The other familiar name, Eban Townes, had achieved some notoriety as a professional football player in the late seventies before a career-ending neck injury crippled him for life. Then, in the late-eighties, he suddenly appeared on the national scene again, this time as a trail-blazing African-American cable entrepreneur supposedly worth hundreds of millions of dollars. But it was in 1990, when he became the outspoken, though unofficial, spokesman for a growing black Republican conservative movement, that he captured the national media spotlight and the attention of May. He championed views that, though not truly orthodox Republican, were nonetheless so antithetical to the traditional liberal-leaning, democratic orientation of mainstream black America, he caused a media sensation. He threw his influence, media prowess and money into supporting like-minded African-American political candidates and the conservative black nominee to the U.S. Supreme Court, Clarence Thomas. For this, he was rewarded with the support of many whites, while drawing the ire of most black leaders. After finding himself on the receiving end of several death threats in the early 1990s, he toned down his public rhetoric somewhat, choosing instead to channel his efforts through a non-profit corporation of his creation, as well as several political action committees.

Ginny did not seem to be bothered in the least by not recognizing any of the names; rather she zeroed in on the four other females on the list and eagerly read through the dossiers Lochridge had compiled to acquaint herself with them. Sally knew quite a few, having met, or at least talked to some of them on occasion throughout her years as Lochridge's assistant. Since she and Erik used only code names when communicating with OP members, she expressed some surprise that she had not identified a couple of the voices belonging to people whom she had seen off and on throughout the years. Clearly, though, Lochridge had strategically divided the list among himself, Sally, and Erik to protect their anonymity—and he had been successful.

The dossiers revealed that most of the unfamiliar names were business leaders—several of whom May would have probably have heard of if he had been more attuned to financial news and investing—a couple of physicians—including an award-winning Johns Hopkins medical school faculty member who had treated John Lochridge when she was a practitioner—a former Maine governor, and a retired NASA flight director. Curiously, the dossiers contained little information on political affiliations or activities, but as May reflected further on this, he concluded that in light of OP's nonpartisan mission, political ideology was less important than a fervid commitment to basic democratic principles and structural reforms. Partisanship and polarization were certainly a large part of the problem—manifested primarily by the gridlock immobilizing Congress—but did not have any healthy role in the solution.

During a self-imposed lull in Sally's marathon phone calls, May showed her the bundle of hand-written letters from Judge Breslin.

"I had just started reading these when you arrived," May said. "Do you know Judge Breslin?"

"Oh, sure. Never met him, but I sure know who he is. Why?"

"Just wondering why he isn't an OP member. He sure seems to have had plenty to say about it," May said, looking at the hefty stack on his arm.

"Well, I can only tell you what Marty thought," she said, "because I've never even talked to him. He told Marty he was too old—I think he's around 90—too tired. He has some health problems evidently. But Marty thinks," she squeezed her eyes closed, before correcting herself, "thought the real reason was fear. Fear of a runaway convention."

It had been lingering in the back of his mind ever since he learned what *Ops Populi* was, what it was trying to accomplish, and it was as certain as the sun rising in the morning that this was the fear opponents would play on to try to prevent a second constitutional convention from ever occurring. Pedantic warnings from political elites and many of his fellow academicians would be heard on talk shows, accompanied by predictions of an impending apocalypse designed to instill popular terror that a convention might decide to trash the whole Constitution, start over, threaten the cherished protections guaranteed by the Bill of Rights.

It was a tired old argument, based on antiquated and elitist notions of mass ignorance, intolerance, majority tyranny and repression, primacy of self-interest over patriotism and statesmanship. In their own runaway convention of 1787, in which their charge to revise the Articles of Confederation was promptly scrapped in favor of starting over, there was enough disagreement among the Founding Fathers over how the new Constitution would be changed—something all of them accepted as inevitable—to produce Article V, which though creating formidable obstacles, explicitly provided for a convention method of amendment. This, in a predominately agrarian society with no universal education, no mass communication, no internet, spoke volumes to those of more egalitarian leanings, and in modern times rendered the old notions obsolete, the fear, illogical.

Why should the American people, with all the advantages afforded them by affluence, education and technology, not trust themselves to reform and modernize their own government? To be sure, there could be no guarantees of the outcome, but neither were there guarantees the people they entrusted to run the country would not strip away their rights, squander their prosperity, plunge their nation into ruin—all of which ample evidence and observation suggested was well underway. When given this opportunity, would the people doubt their wisdom to correct errors in their government enough to continue to accept the reality that Congress has an unrestricted power to propose amendments while claiming that the people have no power at all? Or that nine elites in black robes sit as a kind of perpetual constitutional convention, with as few as five of them making—and, in at least 100 instances, reversing—what John Marshall declared to be the law of the land? Should Americans ask for guarantees about the convention that do not exist either in the Court or the Congress?

No, May thought, Judge Breslin and others of his ilk were ensconced in the status quo and would not budge without assurances that are impossible to have on any serious constitutional question. If the people wished to trash their Constitution, it was theirs to trash, but it certainly would not be done in a vacuum of ignorance or under the same shroud of secrecy that existed in Philadelphia nearly 230 years before. And there was no reason to assume a modern convention would choose to reinvent the wheel, to discard what for 230 years was proven to be essentially a sound system of governance. Just as the Founding Fathers had boldly assumed the prerogative of correcting the errors in their government, so too should modern Americans, assured by the bedrock of the existing

Constitution and confident in the knowledge their actions are no more hazardous than the perpetuation of the status quo—ownership, and awesome responsibility, but no direct control.

Through the interior walls that separated them from the hangar, they could hear the echoes of male voices talking, car doors opening and closing, the low, vibrating hums of several motors.

"You OK?," Ginny asked May when she saw his hand on the back of his neck. She held out a cup of coffee. "Thought you could use this."

"Oh, yeah, just a little tired. Didn't sleep." With a grateful smile, he carefully took the hot cup from her hands. "Sleeping on planes doesn't seem to be your problem," he remarked in a wry tone.

Bachman, who had been chatting with a visibly energized Sally, started walking toward them.

"You two," looking first at Ginny, then at May, "have been through quite the experience. These fellows are going to take you down to Quantico until you get your housing squared away."

May looked at the two Marshals still in the room. The others were getting their belongings off the Falcon and into the waiting SUV. "Are you coming down, too?" he asked Sally.

"No, I'm going to get a rental car and follow Preston over to Marty's place. Get settled in."

"Sure you don't want to stay with me?" Bachman asked her. "I have plenty of—"

"No, no, I'll be fine there," she assured him. "As long as you can get me through his security system."

"Not a problem." He looked at the Marshal, who was apparently ready to go. "Don't worry about a thing. They're going to give each of you cell phones, some money, credit cards, IDs—everything you need." He reached into his pocket, producing a couple of business cards. "I wrote my cell number on the back and the number to Marty's place. Once you get down there, give me a ring, OK?"

Ginny nodded, while May took another sip of coffee. Another handshake, and a quick hug from Sally and they were off to Quantico, and they both hoped, food and a hot shower.

CHAPTER 72

A friendly FBI agent named Ann Largent greeted them in the Crossroads Inn lobby. Although located inside a military installation, the 78-room Crossroads offered an impressive appearance and all of the comforts expected from a modern hotel. Food was the first order of business, since neither of them had eaten in nearly 18 hours. By the time they walked into Mulligan's, it was already after ten o'clock, so they had the restaurant mostly to themselves. May worked on a stack of pancakes and sausage links, Ginny, a ham and cheese omelet. While they ate, Ann unpackaged two new cell phones, installed the batteries and tested them. She apologized for not being better prepared, but their case had just been handed to her the previous afternoon. No time to do much of any of the normal advanced "in-processing," so they would stay here as guests of the Department of Justice until drivers licenses, credit cards, money, cars, and housing could be arranged. All she needed them for today was photographs for the drivers licenses and the required paperwork for starting the processing, which she confidently predicted would be done by Wednesday, perhaps as early as Tuesday. By eleven-thirty, they had their rooms, quick showers, photographs, cell phones and $250 cash. Ann produced two folders—each labeled with their new names—containing available rental listings and community information—thanked them for their time, and looked forward to seeing them in the lobby at nine tomorrow morning to talk to them about their housing.

May spent most of the day in bed, while Ginny called Bachman, who suggested they get together at seven for dinner at a favorite of his, *Der Biergarten*, just a little south of Quantico's main gate on the left side of

U.S. Route 1, or Jefferson Davis Highway, as it was commonly known. I know you might be tired of German—they have American, too, he told her. Just tell one of the inn's desk clerks where you need to go; they'll handle the transportation.

The civilian desk clerk informed her that a special tour of the base had been arranged by Senator Bachman's office. Within 20 minutes, the thickly built FBI Academy instructor, Don Anderson, was guiding her through the sprawling academy, proudly pointing out places the public would never see. After the tour, she rode a shuttle bus to the National Museum of the Marine Corps. From separate exhibitions on the Corps boot camp experience, its roles in World War II, Korea, Vietnam, and the war on terrorism, to the "Leatherneck Gallery," featuring a 210-foot ship's mast, with two Corsairs, a Curtis Jenny and a Harrier suspended from the ceiling overhead, she found herself thoroughly enjoying the experience more than she had expected. On her way to the reproduction of Philadelphia's famed Tun Tavern where the Marine Corps was first organized in November 1775, she strolled through a long hallway where many of the museum's several thousand paintings, photos, prints and sketches lined the walls.

Just before seven, Ginny and May walked into what appeared from the outside to have once been a large private home, resting atop a thickly wooded knoll at the end of a narrow gravel driveway. A cheery hostess costumed in traditional Bavarian garb greeted them with a furtive glimpse at the thick folder May carried under his arm. When May gave her their new names, she flittered an odd expression at them, as though she sensed deception, but instantly reverted to her sunny disposition. May saw Ginny's slight shrug out of the corner of his eye as the hostess turned to lead them into the dining area. They followed her through two large rooms separated by a staircase and a stone chimney into a spacious but cozy corner room where a solitary table set for four awaited them. They had been in their seats only a minute or two when the approaching sound of Bachman's robust baritone announced their arrival.

"Just one more German meal," Bachman declared with a broad smile when he entered. "Is it too much to believe that this little place happens to be one of my favorite restaurants between DC and Richmond and it's right outside Quantico?"

Looking refreshed and feeling better, May took Bachman's outstretched hand in his, with a chuckle. "Senator, I don't know if I believe you or not, but I'm sure this will be the first time I've had *schnitzel* for breakfast," he quipped,

"You were in the army, so I know you've had worse breakfasts," he said, laughing.

"I saw him drink beer for breakfast one day," Ginny cracked.

"Ale," May corrected. "It's nutritious, remember?"

"Marty and I ate here a few times," Bachman said, his eyes scanning the room. "They have some good imports here." As he took his seat, he looked at Sally, who was not a beer drinker, and said, "Good selection of wine, too."

"Lorraine hated sauerkraut, banned it from her kitchen," Sally told them all as they looked through the menu. "So yours truly accompanied him to every German restaurant he could find."

"How did you find this place?" Ginny asked Bachman.

"It was Marty who found it," he said with a grin at Sally. "When he had the contract to upgrade the FBI's computer system, he did all the testing at the academy, so he spent a lot of time down here." Knowing May would be living here, he looked up at May and said, "He loved Chinese, too—discovered one of the best Chinese places I've ever eaten at just a few miles down the road in Aquia. If you like Chinese, it's called Beijing Palace, I think."

They ordered, and for the next hour, they ate and drank merrily, while engaging in casual conversation. A relaxed Bachman skillfully probed Ginny and May to learn more about their backgrounds, of which he knew only what Lochridge had told him. As the evening wore on, Bachman and May naturally gravitated toward telling war stories, each interested in the other's experiences, though May downplayed his own in favor of the more interesting combat experiences of Bachman and Lochridge in Vietnam. To Ginny's relief, Sally managed to distract them with vivid narratives of an African safari she had taken in 2002 with her husband, Gene, and a more recent trip to Australia, which included excursions to Tasmania, New Guinea, and New Zealand. The war stories, it seemed, would have to wait.

Their waitress was met with murmured grunts and groans when she placed a tray holding an assortment of tempting desserts on the table, gleefully describing each in her thick German accent. She flashed a polite smile when, after a quick visual survey revealed hands on stomachs and shaking heads, Bachman declined for them all.

"What's that?" he asked May when he lifted the bulky file from the floor by his chair.

"Martin's Echelon file," May answered. "You told me you wanted to look at it."

"Jeez! How many trees did this kill?" Needing both hands, he took the file from May and perused it while Sally gleefully described her custom-built retirement home on St. Augustine beach. Anytime you want to explore the oldest city in the nation or relax on a beautiful white beach, she told them, come on down. We have plenty of room.

With his peripheral vision, May saw Bachman shake his head and turned to see he was leafing through *An Appraisal of Technologies of Political Control* wearing a mildly disgusted expression.

"Disturbing, isn't it?" May asked in a muted tone.

"Damn right it is." Sally stopped talking mid-sentence, as she and Ginny looked over at Bachman. He slid the file back to May. "You hang onto this, OK? If I see much more, I'll get depressed."

"Sure," May nodded.

He directed his comments to May, but Ginny craned her neck in Bachman's direction in a hint to Sally that she might be more interested in what he had to say than in the multifarious tourist traps of St. Augustine.

"By the time the European Parliament released this report, Marty was winding down his government contracting and focusing on real estate." He looked at Sally quizzically. "I think—wasn't it around 1998 when he started Jonic?"

With unmistakable scorn, Bachman told them of Lochridge's intense bitterness and resentment—by his tone of voice, evidently felt by Bachman himself—which were made more poignant as stinging revelations from all over the world exposed the government's misuse of spy technology, the very systems Lochridge and his father had helped create. Americans were oblivious, their complicit government and its intelligence agencies in complete denial, but the European Parliament, at least, was now asking whether the Echelon communications interceptions violated the sovereignty and privacy of its own citizens and those of other countries.

It was not long after the Dupree story broke that the President issued a special executive order promising jail time for anyone in the intelligence community who divulged information about sensitive operations. Without Senator Pierce's active support, there was no way their investigation would ever get inside the iron fence surrounding NSA.

"So Marty and I decided to conduct our own little inquiry to see what the hell was going on. Between the two of us, we had enough contacts to do some careful prying. And Ginny, he even hired someone from CRS—a very sharp fella, who come to think of it, was actually retired—to help us out. When you came along and agreed to work with OP, he was absolutely thrilled."

Ginny smiled, but didn't say anything.

"What about your brother?" May asked. "Was he on your side in this?"

"No, still in denial mode, and making money hand over fist. Don't get me wrong, LaSalle is a good man, just has a hard head sometimes," he tapped his own head with the heel of his hand for emphasis. "So, anyway, Marty flew to Charleston, South Carolina to talk to Dupree in depth. This time, though, he left the conversation believing every word she said." Not long after that, in the early nineties as best as Bachman could recall, the CRS researcher found an article published in a London newspaper containing confidential quotes from several former officials of the British General Communications Headquarters, an intelligence agency better known as GCHQ. These unnamed officials raised concerns that Echelon was being used for political purposes—to monitor the communications of peaceful organizations such as Amnesty International, Greenpeace, and the American mission organization, Christian Aid. A few months later, a former employee of the British Joint Intelligence Committee admitted that the Prime Minister had personally ordered the monitoring of several individuals and organizations that posed only political threats.

"In his spare time, Marty turned Echelon into a hobby," Bachman said, looking at the file. "He would get busy, forget about it for awhile, then a news story would break, or someone would tell him something to get him fired up again."

"Some of what I read in there is pretty frightening," May said, following his eyes. "Cell phone interceptors, hidden RFID chips, pinhole size cameras, remote-controlled spy planes."

"That's just what we know about—there's surely more, much more. You see why he was so cautious?"

"I think I was happier not knowing any of this," Ginny said, lifting her beer.

"Me, too," May agreed. "And a secret federal court?—not in any political science text book I've ever read."

"Ah, the Foreign Intelligence Surveillance Court," Bachman groaned. "A real piece of work, compliments of the United States Congress." Gesturing with his right hand, he continued emphatically, "It was put there to protect our civil liberties, but it became the patsy of the intelligence agencies."

While scanning through the stuffed folder, May's attention was drawn to a two-page type-written summary of a federal court nobody ever talked about, whose existence was virtually unknown even among serious students—and teachers—of American government. In 1978, Congress had created this secret court as part of the Foreign Intelligence Surveillance Act, which was intended to prevent unlawful or abusive eavesdropping of Americans by executive agencies—particularly the FBI and NSA—by requiring them to obtain the court's approval before conducting electronic surveillance. In 1995, Congress granted it additional power to authorize clandestine entries into buildings. Its eleven members, who are federal District Court judges appointed by the Chief Justice of the U.S. Supreme Court, operate in secrecy behind closed doors on the top floor of the Department of Justice building. The summary's author noted the scarcity of public information about the court's activities; non-government personnel are not allowed entrance nor are its files available for public inspection. In fact, not even Congress' own intelligence oversight committees review these special cases on a regular basis.

"Is this court subject to any review at all?" May asked.

"Once a year we get a report from the Attorney General telling us how many applications were submitted, approved and rejected. That's it. And of more than 10,000 applications received, precisely zero have been rejected."

"Hmm. A court that rules in favor of one side one hundred percent of the time. Sounds a little fishy," May said.

"Sounds like a rubber stamp to me," Ginny said.

"You got that right, lady." Bachman snorted. "FISA's courtroom advocacy is decidedly one-sided, of course, since no one outside the government is allowed in to argue against the government's applications. No opposition, no review process to prevent legal and factual errors, no appeals. Nice setup, huh?"

The waitress popped her head in the door to ask whether they needed anything. Three more hefeweizens and coffee for Sally, the designated driver.

According to the summary in Lochridge's file, despite the misgivings of some and its patent inability to regulate the court's activities, Congress continued to support its existence. After 9/11, the Patriot Act and subsequent revisions gave the court additional powers, which in effect allowed it to authorize surveillance of persons without showing probable cause to believe a crime had been committed. Though not a constitutional lawyer, it was clear to May the normal constitutional protections against illegal searches and seizures, enforced by every other court in the country, didn't apply to this one.

"Why doesn't Congress do something about it?" Ginny asked. It seemed like a logical question, since it was doing exactly the opposite of what Congress had intended when it was created—to be a watchdog for the constitutional rights of the American people against domestic surveillance.

"No guts." came the sharp reply. "Some of us have asked for hearings, but there is a lot of hand wringing and complacency. And in my opinion anyway, lack of courage. You can't be a coward to take on the intelligence agencies. And since no one outside really knows what is going on, there is really no constituent pressure to do anything."

Lochridge was amassing what for him and Bachman was a convincing, though circumstantial, case of flagrant perversion and misuse of Echelon. But the pivotal events came in the mid 1990s, starting with a casual conversation Bachman had with his older brother, LaSalle at a holiday gathering.

"I'll never forget," Bachman told them, "we were sitting around after dinner watching a football game, and one of his foreign-owned competitors ran a commercial about all the good things they were doing for U.S. defense. He told me LBA had been contacted by a federal agency he had never heard of called the National Economic Council to offer intel—intercepted communications—LBA could use to its advantage to win a deal on some Japanese project they were both bidding on."

Bachman and Lochridge found out what they could about the newly created National Economic Council. A brainchild of the Clinton Administration, its sole purpose was to enhance U.S. competitiveness in the increasingly intertwined global economy by feeding intelligence to select companies. In the course of their investigation, they discovered yet another agency, this one called the Office of Intelligence Liaison under the Commerce Department, which also was forwarding data gathered by U.S. intelligence agencies about pending international deals to American firms.

"Echelon was being used for corporate espionage?" Ginny asked.

"No question about it. But then all hell broke loose when a Baltimore newspaper reporter confronted Roger Montague, who at the time was a congressman from Idaho, with verbatim transcripts of several telephone conversations he had with a staff member while in the Balkans."

May scratched his head as he listened. "How did a reporter get them?"

"She said they came from the White House. Apparently, Montague was stepping on someone's toes, and they were trying to discredit him. LaSalle did a complete and sudden U-turn, and by this point, we were all pretty well convinced Echelon was being misused. And if they were spying on Congress, you could bet your sweet a—" he paused, cleared his throat, "sorry, ladies. There was little question in our minds: no American—in fact, no citizen of any country in the world—was immune from the prying eyes of Washington."

May placed the palm of his right hand on the file. "I remember reading some quotes in here taken from people in other countries—Britain, Canada, Australia, New Zealand—most of them former intelligence operatives. They were talking—"

"A guy from New Zealand wrote a whole book about Echelon," Bachman interrupted. "I remember when Marty bought it."

"NSA has never admitted Echelon exists, has it?"

"Never. But it doesn't matter, really. When NSA admitted publicly it had intercepted phone conversations in its files on Princess Diana after she died, the whole world found out what the U.S. was doing with its spy toys."

"But he and your brother kept enabling them with new and better tools to spy on us," Ginny said. "That's what doesn't make sense to me."

"They stayed in the game because it was the right thing to do," he said with conviction. "For Martin, it was a two-edged sword. This technology had also done a lot of good for the country—it helped bring down the Soviet Union, right? When the U.S. was attacked on nine-eleven, we all decided to stick to it a little longer—me in the Senate, them in defense technology—believing we were doing much less harm to the country than good, both in the short-term and by building up to a second convention. It wasn't about power or money, for any of us."

As was plainly clear to them all, the choices made were the right ones. Lochridge, the Bachman brothers, indeed all of the members of OP possessed uncommon patriotic fervor that would bring them to the precipice of an event with implications for all Americans, if not the entire world. They shared a vision of a government of principled and ethical statesmen and women, under the control of and responsive to the needs of its people, not beholden to special interests; one that upheld rather than subverted the sacred liberties enshrined by the Founding Fathers, who in their great wisdom, both feared the very monster that the federal government was becoming, and provided a way to tame it.

May raised his glass in a toast. "To *Ops Populi*," he said looking at all of them. "And the patriots who made it possible."

"To the United States of America," Bachman said in riposte.

"To Martin Lochridge," Sally added.

"Hear! Hear!" Bachman said before he tipped his glass.

For the remainder of the evening, they quietly discussed their near-term plans, frequently glancing at the door to make certain no one was within earshot. As soon as they were settled into their new homes, Sam Mullins and Victoria Barnes would take the lead in setting up the advertising, bringing the OP web site on-line, and coordinating member interviews and media appearances once the advertising began. For the time being, they would have to be back-office staff with no face-to-face contact with the public. One day soon, though, Sam and Vicki would have to be unceremoniously dismissed and OP-USA, Inc. would proudly announce the addition of Sean May and Virginia Burress to the staff.

"I don't have any experience in advertising or web sites," May said looking forlorn.

"Me neither," Ginny said.

"Thanks to Marty, we have advertising and a web site ready to go," Sally said.

"We do?" Ginny asked in surprise.

Sally and Bachman both nodded. "Remember the DVDs—in his briefcase? He and Missy Clark have been working on a few ads, to have some ready to go."

"And the web site?" May asked.

"It's a work in progress, but we have one we can put on-line," she assured them. "He was making changes right up until—well, that's why he had all that stuff with him on his trip," she said with sadness creeping into her voice. "Missy has been handling it for him."

"All we have to do is get a host account, upload the files, and we're in business," Bachman said, "but first we need to have people to follow up with anyone who fills out the form. Sally has the lead in setting up the office, hiring people to answer the phones, send out mail, et cetera."

May and Ginny were both shocked as they learned how much planning and preparation had already been done.

"Marty has been working on all of this for years," Bachman reminded them. "With lots of help," he added, nodding deferentially at Sally. "I think he was so sick—and with all the chaos over the last month or so, he didn't get to lay it all out for you the way I'm sure he would have preferred."

"Chaos is pretty accurate," Ginny said in agreement.

"When you two get established, we'll get you set up with computers, phones, and faxes," Sally said. "You'll be up to speed in no time."

"Make no mistake, that wasn't the Martin Lochridge Sally and I knew. He despised chaos, did anything to avoid confusion and being caught unprepared."

"He was constantly planning something," Sally said. "I found a detailed security plan for the castle in his briefcase. And proposals from several security companies to have people patrolling the property during the meeting. I guess the virtual perim—"

"That reminds me," Bachman perked up. "Did you find out what triggered the alarm the other day?"

May shook his head. "We couldn't figure it out ourselves, and the company is in Cologne. They couldn't get a tech person out until next week."

Bachman scratched his head. "Hmmm."

"What are you worried about?" Sally asked. "He said animals set it off all the time."

"I know," he said. "Something Marty told me when I saw him last week, about the money transfers. His lawyer screwed up, transferred too much money into the OP bank account at one time. He was pretty sure it would catch the attention of the snoops."

"Snoops?" Ginny asked.

Bachman gave them all a quick synopsis of SWIFT and the FBI-Department of the Treasury financial monitoring program. "Wire transactions of this size and the use of off-shore accounts were certain to draw attention," he told them.

"Uh, oh," Ginny mumbled.

"You think maybe someone was trying to set up surveillance on Martin?" May asked.

Bachman's eyes narrowed perceptibly, as an uneasy pall swept over his face. "It's certainly possible—I wouldn't put anything past them, would you?" He turned toward Sally, and added, "No, we need to find out what is on that security video as soon as possible."

What they could not know was the information supplied by John Collier's son had brought the existence of *Ops Populi* to the attention of men who would not look too kindly on its ambitions once their potential implications were fully considered and evaluated. One such man was the Director of National Intelligence, whose judgment would determine whether OP would be a topic of conversation the next time he visited the Oval Office.

CHAPTER 73

Gnawing trepidation was hidden beneath the weary faces of the three men as they entered the private conference room some 850 feet above the streets of downtown Charlotte. For two days, they and thirteen of their peers had been barraged with sobering statistics, economic modeling and gloomy projections across nearly all sectors of U.S. commerce. Then in the final hours of the day, they were hit by a gut-wrenching assessment of the flimsy condition of their own industry. A storm was brewing, they were warned, and it very well could develop into a devastating monster unlike anything they had ever encountered.

Nearing ten o'clock, the vast majority of the 60-story tower's occupants had long since departed, leaving the dim lighting and still quiet of inactivity behind. Their heads hung low, not a word was spoken on the ride up the elevator. Only the squeaking leather of their expensive shoes, muted whirs and hums of drowsing office equipment, or the occasional chirp or two of a distant phone disturbed the tranquil silence of the abandoned executive suite. The relatively youthful Charlotte host led his older, forlorn guests—the eldest from New York, the other, from Los Angeles—to the polished wooden double doors of his office, where he waved a plastic card in front of a box mounted on the wall. A faint buzz followed by a metallic click caused the doors to slowly swing inward in unison, revealing the darkened, but expansive and richly adorned office of the president and chief executive officer. The man holding that title took several steps to the side, allowing his guests to behold the gleaming lights of the city below through the transparent outer walls, but they were evidently neither impressed nor interested, so he turned on his heel abruptly to lead them to their destination, through another door and into the conference room. The two guests stood by the table while the host simultaneously flipped several switches, assaulting their tired eyes with the sudden, piercing brightness of overhead fluorescent lights.

"Gentlemen," Charlotte said as he walked up to the table, placing his briefcase on the floor next to the closest chair. "Can I offer you anything to drink?"

"No," New York grumbled with obvious impatience. "The sooner I'm on a plane out of here, the better."

"I understand," Charlotte said quietly in sympathetic reply, looking to the opposite side of the table where LA was carelessly tossing the jacket of his $4,000 Armani suit onto the table. He too declined the drink offer with a quick shake of his head before dropping heavily into his chair. "Having talked for most of the last hour, I need a little water. I'll be back momentarily."

While he walked the short distance to the small bar to get a bottle of water, he thought very carefully about his next words to the two men whom he had just hours before informed by a hastily scrawled note of this impromptu meeting. He had the unpleasant task of delivering still more bad news, but at this point, given their fatigue and eagerness to be on their way home, he saw no need to sugarcoat it. They were the big boys, and Charlotte's two guests were the biggest of the big. Cloaked in a veil of esoteric mysticism, they exercised raw power through money and their control over it, while also projecting more subdued influence in the shadowy fringes of politics.

Ominous though the grave warnings and prognostications of the previous two days had been, the endemic hubris infecting all but a few of them produced the collective "wait and see" response he had anticipated. After all, his haughty peers continually stressed in their peremptory speeches, they had at their disposal a vast arsenal of flexible weapons that could be deployed swiftly and decisively as they had so many times in the past. But judging by the facial expressions and body language he had observed this afternoon, at least a few of them believed they had gone too far too fast—had waited too long to make "adjustments"—and that this was the beginning of the end of their reign of world dominance.

Only time would tell, but of one thing he was certain: they had no ready-made weapons for the problem that was the topic of tonight's conference. Confounding in its singularity, its ramifications were arcane. Containing it was far beyond their extensive sphere of influence, but without question, its potential consequences were enormous and likely to be quite menacing. In fact, New York believed one probable effect would be the destruction of the fragile, delicately balanced global political and economic stability that underpinned their very existence.

Charlotte twisted the cap off his water bottle as he walked through the door to the conference room, where the two newly vulnerable titans sat waiting in uncomfortable silence, fidgeting, anxious. The irony was never too far removed from his conscious thought; bitter enemies they were in their daily lives, yet compelled to work together to manipulate and maintain a healthy competitive environment. His advantage was in his youth, he knew. For although he enjoyed the power, wealth and prestige of his position—each of which had increased immensely in the preceding five years—and would defend what he had with all his strength and tenacity, he was adaptable, flexible, resilient enough to rebound from even the most severe blows. His two elder peers, on the other hand, but most especially New York, though wielding far more power and influence than he, were much too complacent and too rigid to accept anything other than the status quo, and therefore, in his eyes at least, were most likely to fall fast and hard, taking the accumulated wealth of multitudes with them.

Despite being somewhat comforted by these advantages, at least in a relative sense, he nonetheless felt strangely isolated from them, as though they were privy to some special knowledge or intelligence of strategic importance that they were deliberately withholding from him. When he had candidly asked New York in a private moment why Martin Lochridge's group posed a threat of any great consequence, he was given a rather curt but intriguing reply: "The last time I saw the man," New York had said with gravity, "he made no bones about his disdain for us and everything we represent. If he has his way, he will destroy us." And so, Charlotte concluded, there was indeed something they knew that he did not—historical context he would never have—and it had evidently given rise to this formidable detractor whose animosity engendered quiet terror in men who, until now, had feared very little.

"During the lunch hour today," he began, remaining on his feet with his right hand resting on the back of the chair at the head of the table, "I was informed that Mr. Lochridge has died—"

"Good," New York interrupted coldly and LA breathed a sigh of relief.

"However," Charlotte continued, "this group—this *Ops Populi*—survives him."

"Perhaps it will fizzle and die without his leadership—and money," LA said hastily, hopefully.

"We still don't know who belongs to this group?" New York muttered in a half question, half statement fashion.

Charlotte took a quick sip from his water bottle, while his eyes shrewdly appraised the expressions of his two guests, both of whom were shrewdly appraising him in return. "No, we do not know the composition of the group, nor are we certain there are any other living members of it at all, for that matter."

LA looked up at him with strain in his bloodshot eyes, then said, "Certainly, it is reasonable to assume there are others."

"Certainly," Charlotte said in acknowledgement to LA. "But it is apparently a well-guarded secret."

Looking down at the table, Charlotte briefly recalled with a twinge of angst the Monday morning a week before: that he had arrived at the office very early to prepare for a board meeting, was greeted by the security guard at the front desk—curiously, a man he didn't recognize—who handed him a plain brown envelope with his name hand-written in large, block printed capital letters across its front, told him it had been delivered just minutes before by courier, wished him a good day; how he had casually tossed it into the pile of mail awaiting him on his desk and set about the task of preparing for his meeting; and how the next day, sorting through the now imposing stack over the trash can, he had come so close to tossing it along with all the other junk, but at the last minute was moved by curiosity to open it; and finally, how the yellow post-it note affixed to the side of the manifesto had admonished him simply with a single word—again hand-written in capital letters—"HEED."

When he had looked at the letter, he instantly recognized the addressee's name, John Collier, as the renowned media mogul and famed real estate guru, but not the letter's writer, Martin Lochridge. New York, he learned in a conference late that afternoon, did have some familiarity with Lochridge—knew quite a bit about him, in fact. "Do not mention this to any of the others," came his stern admonishment, "until we determine whether these documents are credible or just another hoax. But if Lochridge's organization is legit, we will present it to the others only when we have a plan to deal with it. The last thing we need right now is knee-jerk irrationality." To his offhand question of how much Lochridge was worth, New York had no definitive answer other than "billions."

"We must squelch any remnants of this organization," New York said in a surly tone, ending Charlotte's moment of reflection. His wrinkled face took on a menacing countenance as he continued, "We must know who they are if we are to destroy them."

"Our investigators have found no other names, no other documents, little more than a few unidentified faces coming and going from Lochridge's home in Germany," Charlotte said. He glanced at LA who was wearing an expression of equal intensity as New York's, but not feeling it himself.

"Find them!" New York barked with an almost desperate impatience.

Charlotte's eyes narrowed slightly, but otherwise he kept his patient composure. "More than likely, they are servants, but the investigators are working on identifying them, which, as you might expect, is complicated by their location, particularly the language barrier. But—"

LA froze in mid-yawn, his arms stretched above his head. New York sat forward attentively, resting his elbows on the table in eager anticipation of Charlotte's next words.

"—our investigators in Virginia discovered there was some substantial activity at his home in Vienna recently."

"Oh?" New York asked. "What sort of activity, exactly?"

"A gathering of some sort. Quite a few people, formal dress. Perhaps a meeting," he suggested, "but that is only my speculation. The investigator talked to a neighbor who was passing along second-hand observations made by her husband, who was working in his yard, but who, unfortunately, is out of the country on a business trip and cannot be questioned directly." He paused for another sip of water, while New York and LA absorbed this new information. "She thinks her husband saw a senator—Preston Bachman—leaving the, uh, event."

"Bachman?" LA asked reflexively.

"Hmmm," New York rubbed his chin thoughtfully. "Yes…yes! I remember seeing Bachman's name on some documents in our files on Lochridge. But not *Preston* Bachman. *LaSalle* Bachman. I'm pretty sure they were in business together. Interesting. Very interesting," he said, more calmly now.

"LaSalle Bachman Aerospace," LA mumbled. "I know the company well. From Seattle."

"That's the one," New York replied. "Preston Bachman is also from Washington, so I'll wager they are related. I'll be damned—the connection never even occurred to me."

"In any event," Charlotte interjected, "his is the only other name we have at the moment. Whether he is part of the *Ops Populi* organization is anyone's guess—"

"No guessing," New York said flatly as he stood, and LA stood as well. "We cannot afford to be wrong." He cleared his throat as he collected his briefcase and turning toward the door to leave, he abruptly drew back, casting a sinister glare with his narrowed eyes to each of them in turn. With perceptible gravity in his voice, he added, "I don't care if you have to hire an army. Find out who these people are. We've got to have a plan to stop this before it gets off the ground. Before we tell the others."

They were already too late. The wheels of *Ops Populi* were already in motion.

CHAPTER 74

Two Weeks Later…

It wasn't that she didn't like Annapolis, Ginny confided in Ann, it was a wonderful place to visit. She had been there many times. What she didn't tell Ann was that it would take her several hours to get down to May's new house in the gated community of Aquia Harbor, which was the first and only place Ann had taken him to see the day before. With 3-bedrooms, 2 full and one half bath, 1,800 square feet, it was a steal, Ann told him. Good, I'll take it he said. After playing along with Ann, looking at several rentals in Annapolis, Ginny began to express doubt that she would find anything desirable within the government-allotted price range—a restraint which, unbeknownst to Ann, Ginny exploited in finagling her way into a location nearer to May. Living on the water was what she really wanted if she were to live here, she told Ann after seeing and rejecting a newly-built 2-bedroom, 2-bath townhouse, but waterfront in Annapolis was out of the question, Ann replied. How about Fredericksburg? Ginny offered casually. Ann would have to get approval from her superiors at OEO at the Justice Department. But Ginny had a better solution: a phone call to Bachman. Two days later, she found a nice 2 bedroom, 2 bath duplex on Caroline street, just a few blocks away from the train station.

After a few days of settling into their new homes, they got to work. They set up shop in one of May's spare bedrooms, which offered ample space and natural light. The furniture was all rented, the computers and copier were the first equipment purchased by OP-USA, Inc. Government-provided cell phones were not to be trusted, so a second set of cell phones, fiber-optic broad-band internet access, cable, and, of course, sat-phones connected them to the world.

May's Granville house was up for sale, his belongings moved into a storage unit. Ginny's Georgetown apartment was also empty. They had both mysteriously vanished into thin air.

As far as they knew, multiple investigations were on-going, a killer or killers, still at large. That prosecutors were cutting deals, analysts were poring through financial records, and people were being watched—all part of an expansive effort to determine the extent of the rot—did not concern them.

The little flashing red light on both sat-phones indicated a live connection to a satellite somewhere overhead. They checked and re-checked, tested and re-tested until they were satisfied they were working properly. Now, they waited, engaging in all manner of possible distractions, for the audible signal of an incoming call.

"Six-thirty," May said throwing his keys on the counter. "They've been at it all day long."

Ginny helped him with the sauce—and grease—splotched brown paper sacks holding their Chinese food. "Sally said people were lingering—Sean, they couldn't just kick them out. Sorry but you have to leave so some of us can have a secret meeting," she said with exaggeration.

Ginny started unpacking the food while May grabbed plates and silverware from the drying rack in the sink. "But they started the memorial at ten," he grumbled.

"A lot of these people probably haven't seen each other in awhile. They had food, too. You know how people like to congregate around food," she said with a snicker as they both hovered over the open boxes of Chinese.

He tore open a package of duck sauce with his teeth. "Wonder if Andrew showed up. Hopefully, he was sober if he did."

"Yeah, that's a sad situation. Kid's screwed up."

"That *kid* is older than you, almost as old as me," May said, parking himself on the recliner.

No sooner had Ginny sat down on the sofa, than sat-phones started their distinctive low-tone chirping. May, already chomping on an egg roll, started to rise, but Ginny held up her hand, and dashed down the hall to the bedroom office.

"Erik! How are you?" Having expected Sally to call, Ginny was surprised to hear his voice on the other end. "What happened? Wait a second to answer until I hand Sean a handset."

Ginny returned to the family room with May's handset to witness him stuffing half his second egg roll into his mouth.

"What do you know?" he said into the speaker, still chewing.

"What a day!" he exclaimed. "It's done—we got a unanimous vote. But there was some lively discussion about the timing. And removing some amendments."

"Timing," May muttered. As soon as he had heard Erik say the word, May thought back to the conversation with Bachman at the German restaurant outside Quantico. Apparently Ginny had too, because she had picked up a pen and scribbled something on her napkin. When she held it up, he saw "Snoops?" scrawled across its front. Had Bachman told anyone other than them? He and Ginny both shrugged while Erik gave his synopsis.

The discussion about the timing centered on Lochridge's prediction—shared by most, but not all the members—that a housing market collapse was imminent, would bring down the financial services sector, and eventually the U.S. economy with it. Should they not wait? Surely the shock value of the OP media blitz would be greater and the public would be more receptive in a period of economic distress. On the other hand, what if it were just a mild correction or didn't happen at all? Statistics painted a mostly positive picture for the state of the economy. Gross domestic product was increasing at a healthy clip, the Dow had topped 11,000 in January for the first time since June 2001, the NASDAQ had its best close since February 2001. Unemployment was low, real estate was still humming, though not at the blistering pace of 2005. If they delayed, they might miss the opportunity that was at hand.

"Martin was pretty convincing," he said as he fumbled with the chop sticks, watching Ginny out of the corner of his eye effortlessly manipulate hers. "Said the banks were really out on a limb with their lending."

"Yes he was," Erik agreed. "You should have seen everyone gaping at the screen when his video message was playing. It was eerie in a way, but it served its purpose. Right after the video, the economist, Larry Bucklew, asked to be recognized. He wore a bow tie, reeked of pipe tobacco—nice guy, though. Anyway, he gave us all something to think about," Erik said. "Definitely a pessimist. Sent shivers down my spine."

"So was Martin," Ginny said, nibbling on a vegetable in her pepper steak. "Probably where he got it."

"Was he for or against delaying?" May asked.

"Neither, really, at least not that I could tell. Things are bad now and going to get worse very soon." May and Ginny heard the sound of crinkling paper during the brief pause. "This guy was so good, I even took notes. He said, get this, 'American society has abandoned the virtue of ascetic self-discipline in favor of impatient and unrestrained acquisitive lust.' And it gets better. 'We along with our public and private institutions have created the illusion of sustainable prosperity and progress by borrowing massive amounts of foreign capital. Some of us who are watching closely see the cracks beginning to appear in its delicate shell. When it inevitably shatters, nothing less than a world economic crisis as consequential as the Great Depression will occur.' The cracks he talked about were things like declining real incomes, loss of manufacturing jobs, negative personal savings for the first time since the Depression, and so on. You could see gloom on everybody's face."

Ginny shrugged again. So far, evidently, Bachman had said nothing and she and May were both keeping their mouths shut for the moment. If, after a few beers, Bachman had revealed something confidential to the two of them that he wasn't sharing with the rest of the group, then they would play dumb now, ask questions later.

"Sounds like a case for waiting to me," Ginny said.

"That's the direction my thinking was going. But then Eban Townes—you know, who he is?"

"Uh, huh," May answered. "We read the bios."

"Oh, yeah, right. Anyway, he told us that from a media-marketing perspective, starting now with a consistent message would plant a seed in the minds of the public—branding is the term he used—so if and when the economy started to unwind, the concept of reforming government would already be firmly implanted. Kind of the 'build it and they will come' mentality."

"Done all the time in advertising," Ginny said. "You may not think you need it now, but when you do, you'll remember that XYZ brand they drilled into your brain."

"Right," May said. "The blitz is one thing, but it's not like this is a one-shot deal. It'll probably take years to build up enough moment—."

"Yeah, Erik interrupted—"somebody—um, Louise Bond, I think—used the civil rights analogy. It grew in its appeal over time, got stronger as more people were drawn to it. But then, she said something interesting that questioned the whole premise of waiting for the economy to unravel."

May stopped chewing, his curiosity aroused. He remembered his interest when he read Lochridge's dossier on Bond, an ACLU board member, who had risen to become a highly respected constitutional law scholar, an accomplishment all the more impressive for a black female from a generation noted for pervasive racism and sexism in the legal field. "Really? What?"

"She asked everyone to consider the implications of holding a convention in a period of national distress. Her basic point was that people might be inclined to act out of irrational fear and, you know, make bad decisions."

"That thought had crossed my mind once or twice," May said. "History is full of examples of newly minted dictatorships during times of mass chaos and panic. People are more receptive to appeals from extremists, willing to cede civil liberties in return for promises to restore order and economic prosperity. Anyway, democratic institutions tend to be most vulnerable during times of political instability."

"You just summed up the whole discussion, my friend," Erik said. "It took us most of an hour instead of a minute, unfortunately."

"So, how did you all resolve this?" Ginny asked still pecking away at her food. "With a vote?"

"No—there was only one vote at the end. I stood up and told everyone what I told Martin a few months ago. In stocks, real estate, if you wait for a bottom to buy anything, you'll never get in the game. Everybody kind of nodded their heads. Then while I was still standing, somebody," the sound of cackling paper interrupted as he consulted his notes, "John Ritzert said, "We've been waiting almost ten years, so what's another year? That's when Preston walked into the room flipping his cell phone closed, and said, 'I'll tell you why we can't wait another year—or even another month!'"

Bachman prefaced his remarks with a caveat about the classified nature of the information he was about to disclose, not out of any concern for himself, but to protect the jobs of the people—his son in-law, in particular—who gave it to him. He proceeded to describe the SWIFT program and how Lochridge was fairly certain that his lawyer's wire transfers into OP-USA's corporate account would be detected.

"He announced to us all he had just learned from 'a trusted source' that the Justice Department was in possession of certain documents from an organization calling itself *Ops Populi*—United to save America, though his source did not know, or would not reveal, precisely what documents they had or how they had been obtained," Erik paraphrased. "We were all stunned."

The existence of OP had been compromised, Bachman warned in no uncertain terms, and it was very possible that it was being scrutinized by analysts somewhere deep in the bowels of Washington's highly sophisticated intelligence labyrinth.

"Amazing," May said, without having to feign surprise, for Bachman had said nothing at their dinner about any OP documents in government hands. "Wonder what they have?"

"And where it came from?" Ginny added.

"I don't have a clue," Erik admitted. "But that was the last thing said about the subject, before Governor Walsh brought up the tired issue of the number of amendments."

Erik told them about the re-hashing of the debate about how many amendments OP should put forward for consideration, the proverbial dead horse they had been beating on and off for years. Walsh was one of several steadfast advocates of a single-purpose convention to open up the Constitution to publicly-initiated amendments in the future. He personally agreed with the current list—in fact, favored a slate of broad reforms that would expand it—but as a matter of sound constitutional principle, all of the systemic reforms should be handled in an amendatory process, not a convention. They should be considered separately, subject to individual scrutiny and debate, not as a package.

"Sally came to our rescue," Erik said. "She stood up so everyone could see her serious expression and then proceeded to remind everyone that the convention would ultimately do what it damn-well pleased. We are suggesting only those changes that we believe are critical for the survival of the country. They may throw our ideas in the garbage if it pleases them, or perhaps, they will come up with even better ideas."

"I think she hit the nail on the head," May said. "Besides, if there is going to be a meltdown as bad as Martin predicted, as a country, we don't have the luxury of waiting to consider the others one at a time anyway. OP's suggestions are at least a starting point."

Ginny had abandoned chop sticks for a fork, which she now waved in front of her as she said, "Martin made it clear—to me and Sean—he wanted only to offer Americans the chance to have a convention, something they could choose or decline. Yes, he thought it was necessary, crucial even, for the survival of the country, but I think he was humble enough to recognize he didn't have all the answers."

"Let's face it," May said. "Whatever changes a convention proposes for ratification will be scrutinized ad nauseam. The media will make sure of that, I'm sure."

"In the end, we agreed to disagree on the question of timing and the agenda we're offering," Erik said. "When the ideal time will come—whether we should propose one, two, five, or twenty amendments—nobody really knows. But Ginny is right: It is providing the opportunity itself that was most important to Martin, because he knew, after 230 years of status quo, there was little chance that it would ever happen otherwise."

"I wish I could have been there," May said, looking at his empty plate. "Maybe when I'm Sean May again, I'll get to meet them all."

"They are good people. Their hearts are in the right place," Erik said, with a yawn.

"Tired out, huh?" May asked.

"Tired and hungry—but relieved this is over."

"How was the service?" Ginny asked. "Sally was too rushed to say much when I talked to her earlier."

"It was good, as these things go," Erik replied. "Bachman gave a moving tribute. Then Sally. Then Andrew."

"He showed, huh? May asked. "Sober?"

"Yeah. He and Sally seemed to have a good long talk. She gave him the urn, told him he could take the Falcon up to Maine."

"Good," May said. "How about you? Are you still a prisoner in your own house?"

"It's not that bad, really," he said unconvincingly. "The cops just follow us wherever we go. Bugs Catherine more than me."

"Did they follow you there today?" Ginny asked.

"You kidding?" Erik snickered. "I rode the 15 miles to the closest car rental company in the back of one of my neighbor's SUV, covered in garbage bags stuffed with newspapers. They'll get a real kick in the teeth when Catherine picks me up there tonight."

CHAPTER 75

For anyone who had seen Lochridge in the last days of his life, the video was a poignant lesson in how swiftly and ferociously aggressive cancer could ravage a human body. The Eyezon logo above a date stamp of "11/30/05" was the first thing May had seen once the DVD had initialized. It had the polish of professional production—high quality audio and video, well-chosen camera angles, and a studio setting. The DVD actually contained two different productions: one, a monologue format that showed Lochridge in a charcoal gray suit, seated behind an ornate mahogany desk, hands folded, American Flag stanchion to his left rear; the other, an interview featuring the retired network news anchor, Lou Jenkins, asking scripted questions answered by an outwardly healthy, enthusiastic, energetic Martin Lochridge. The videos could stand alone or be edited for use in advertisements, newscast, or in any number of ways they had not yet thought of.

May fumbled with the new remote control, pressing buttons until he managed to get to the section containing the interview.

Jenkins: "Mr. Lochridge, *Ops Populi*—United to Save America has aroused the passions of many Americans. For those in our audience who may not know, OP-USA is a private, not for profit organization recommending a second U.S. constitutional convention. If you can, please tell us a little about your organization's goals and philosophy."

Lochridge: "Thank you, Lou.

"We want to offer Americans an opportunity for a convention but only if the American people agree with us that it is necessary. We obviously believe it is—in fact, we think it is long-overdue and critical to the long-term viability of our nation.

"Our philosophy is simple: Government of the people, not the elite career politicians who currently dominate Washington; by the people, not the special interests, lobbyists, or the corporations; and a government for the people, not adverse to their rights or well-being. We do not assert that government is a panacea for all of our ills, only that it should be part of the solution not the problem. It is time to go back to the basics envisioned for it 230 years ago, things we cannot do for ourselves, such as providing our national infrastructure and defense."

Jenkins: "You said it is critical. Why?"

Lochridge: "It is absolutely crucial. We fear the United States has been brought to the brink of an implosion by the unmistakable extravagance, recklessness, and negligence of our own political leaders and institutions of government. At this point, it is quite clear they lack the will to act prudently or make the tough choices required to ensure our continued viability.

"The United States is abandoning the very bedrock maxims that serve as the foundation of our liberty, that distinguish us from other nations, all in the name of 'national security.' Without our principles, we are no different than those nations we are fond of condemning as backward. It is sheer hypocrisy to proclaim ourselves as champions of human rights and individual liberty, yet disavow the Geneva Convention, torture our war detainees and deny them basic procedural rights. Our government is currently committing egregious violations of constitutional principles against its own people. The door to tyranny and despotism is open. We must close it now—before it is too late.

"Only the American people, by seizing control of what is rightly theirs, can stop our headlong plunge into ruin. Fortunately for us all, the Founding Fathers gave us a way to accomplish that peacefully."

Jenkins:— "OP-USA has been the target of harsh criticism by many, both from within our borders and abroad, who have been using words like subversive, seditious, even treasonous, to describe it. Among the most outspoken critics are some very influential politicians—including the current administration—business and religious leaders, and academics alike.

What is your reaction to their…well, accusations, and more importantly, are you and your group advocates of overthrowing our government?"

Lochridge: "Overthrowing the government? Hardly. We do not reject the Constitution, its fundamental principles, or the basic structure of our system. Rather, we will urge our fellow Americans to work within its existing framework, beginning with a petition of the people under the provisions of the First Amendment."

Jenkins: "Isn't Article Five the prescribed method for calling a constitutional convention?"

Lochridge: "Yes, it certainly is. But Article Five requires Congress to issue the call for a convention upon receiving the applications of the legislatures of two thirds of the states, something it has stubbornly—and illegally, I might add—refused to do in spite of that requirement having been satisfied long ago. In fact, 49 states have submitted more than 550 requests, but the sovereign voice of the people has been squelched, ignored by arrogant politicians, who have denied them their only recourse to make substantive changes to what is rightfully theirs. Frankly, the American public cannot afford to stand idly by while it waits for Congress to obey the law any longer.

Jenkins: "So, OP-USA is asserting a right of the people "to petition the government for a redress of grievances" as the legal basis for a publicly initiated convention?"

Lochridge: "To peaceably assemble and to petition, absolutely. But it is not just our right. It is our sacred duty as Americans to reassert our supremacy over the establishment, pro-status quo elitists who have turned our republic into a plutocracy dominated by those of wealth and privilege. To be sure, our founding fathers created an enduring document that has withstood the test of time, but they were not so naïve to believe it would last forever. So they made it possible to change it peacefully, without having to resort to a violent revolution as they had.

Lou, to our critics, all I would say is they either do not understand our intentions, which as we see them, are altruistic, or they fear the possibility of losing their power and influence if we are successful."

Jenkins: "As you know all too well, the American public is not known for its fervor in participating in government. The statistics on election turnout—the basic form of participation available to us as citizens—I think could be fairly characterized as mass indifference to government. Even our Presidential races are lucky to attract half of eligible voters to the polls. How does OP-USA intend to overcome this, something it surely must do to accomplish its goal?"

Lochridge: "I agree that we have quite a challenge in front of us. Much of the public is numb when it comes to electoral politics. But based on some of the approval numbers I've seen recently, I think it's more than indifference—I would call it revulsion. Scandals, corruption, incompetence, all have actually driven people away rather than just making them not care. We want to bring them back into the fold as active participants in the democratic process. We think the words 'of the people, by the people and for the people' have to mean more than going to the polls once in awhile, where more often than not, we are asked to choose from among undesirable alternatives. That is, if given any choice at all.

We want to re-awaken patriotism, energize the public with the spirit of populism. Our forbearers have given us liberties and individual dignity that are the envy of the world. And I would like to encourage people to browse through a section called 'the quest for freedom' on op-usa.org where they can gain a true appreciation for the meaning and value of our many blessings, dreamed about throughout the ages by great philosophers, such as St. Thomas More, Selzhenitsyn, Antigone, Galileo, Montesquieu, Rousseau and Locke. Our freedom is like any other treasured possession: we have to protect it from harm, jealously guard it from thieves—take care of it.

Our one and only purpose is to plant a seed. Once the movement gains traction, I am confident its own momentum will sustain it. The combined energy of OP-USA and the funding our members have provided will be the spark, if you will, hopefully providing enough of a catalyst to overcome the public and institutional inertia that has the public in its apathetic stranglehold."

Jenkins: "If the constitutional change OP-USA proposes is so desperately needed, why has it taken so long for people like you to champion the cause.

Lochridge: "Lou, make no mistake, OP is not the first or only group advocating a convention to reform our government. Many smart minds are available and willing to help us navigate through this uncharted territory. But to be frank with you, it is only OP's substantial financing that promises a reasonable chance to overcome 230 years of inertia.

"In direct answer to your question, several things come to mind. Public furor has been averted in large part because of the actions of the Supreme Court, which has assumed unto itself a *de facto* role of the perpetual nine-member constitutional convention. With two exceptions I can think of—the Civil War, being the main one, and Civil Rights, the other—it has prevented violent upheaval of the disaffected public. Of course, Congress threw in 17 new amendments of their own along the way for good measure.

"Another reason is that the established political elite have a vested interest in maintaining the status quo. They constantly appease us with promises they cannot or will not keep. Instead, once elected, they join the select Washington club whose mantra is 'business as usual.' Setting aside the majority of Americans who choose not to participate at all, there are enough of the remaining 'attentive' people swayed by the 30 second sound bites and the illusion of control created by the voting machine to avoid anything more than a few letters and some grumbling at parties.

"The last thing I would mention is what I call the 'brainwashing effect,' which is nothing more than unwarranted fear of all sorts of contrived scenarios of gloom and doom if we, the lowly public, have the audacity to take control of what belongs to us. I'm afraid we are about to be inundated with crafty rhetoric from many persons and groups desperately clinging to their power who will issue dire warnings of a "runaway convention"—something they will assert we should fear just as much as another terrorist attack. They will claim the people cannot be trusted with such an important responsibility, that we might stupidly erase 230 years of proven success by tearing up the Constitution to create a new one instead of fixing what we already have. They will try to persuade people that a convention could destroy their cherished, constitutionally protected rights and freedoms. Throw the nation into chaos and destroy our renowned political and governmental stability.

Jenkins: "No doubt a United States constitutional convention would cause some pretty significant anxiety here and abroad."

Lochridge: "I would agree with that—but only to the extent that the convention's purpose and intentions remain in doubt. An orderly, coherent convention process with a defined agenda, reported accurately by you and your colleagues in the media, should go a long way towards alleviating it."

Jenkins: "But journalists cannot control the content of the messages sent out by the opponents you alluded to before. Their campaign—if you can call it that—will have a de-stabilizing influence."

Lochridge: "We can only hope in the end, that the American public and the rest of the world will distinguish reality from attempts to beguile and deceive.

Lou, I would argue the existing federal enterprise has already done these things that opponents of a convention will tell us we are supposed to be afraid of—which is precisely the reason a convention is needed. Although the United States has enjoyed a stable political system for most of our history, the price we have paid is enormous, and continues to grow rapidly. Our supposed financial stability is a delusion—our total outstanding public and private debt is approaching $50 trillion—our political culture, one of corruption, lies and deceit. We have an imperialist administration that hides behind a cloak of national security, while the executive branch systematically dismantles our constitutional protections and perseveres in a foreign policy that has alienated our traditional allies and exposed us to ridicule for our hypocrisy. I could go on, but the point is, our present situation is not at all stable. It is very tenuous and destined to become a severe crisis. The longer we wait to take corrective action, the greater the potential for chaos, even, God forbid, violent upheaval.

The tactics opponents will employ are nothing more than fear mongering from the established elite who are terrified of losing their status and power. And, when you stop and think about it, messages such as these are very patronizing, implying that we the people are idiots who would recklessly squander our most precious asset, the best country the world has ever known."

Jenkins: "A 'runaway convention,' then is not something to be feared?"

Lochridge: "Only if you believe Americans are so utterly ignorant as to throw away 230 years of proven success. The more important question to ask is whether some 300 million citizens will stand pat while 536 political elites wreck their country and everything they hold dear.

"Many people may not know—or have forgotten—that our first and only constitutional convention actually ran away. Our Founding Fathers were sent to Philadelphia to reform our first government under the Articles of Confederation. What we got instead is the Constitution, a brilliant document—the greatest democratic achievement in the history of mankind.

"An important thing for us all to remember is the work of a people's convention will have to be ratified to have the effect of law. Consequently, the types of cataclysmic changes envisioned by the alarmists would almost certainly be rejected by the public. Meanwhile, the existing government will continue to function as normal, so any real disruption should be minimal, at most.

Jenkins: "Your web site—op-usa.org, which I would like to invite everyone to visit—"

Lochridge: "Thank you."

Jenkins: "You're welcome. I saw some quotes from our Founders on your web site that support your position."

Lochridge: "There are many, but Thomas Jefferson said it best, I think, right in the Declaration of Independence."

Jenkins (reading from notes): "'Whenever any form of government becomes destructive to these ends—life, liberty and the pursuit of happiness, that is—it is the right of the people to alter or abolish it.'"

Lochridge: "That is the one.

"Lou, there is no ambiguity about what the Framers envisioned. They knew the Constitution would have to be revised and changed from time to time—in fact, Jefferson thought it advisable once every generation—to accommodate developments they could not foresee. But I'm certain they didn't expect what has happened—that the Supreme Court, with its lifetime appointees, would end up being the primary instrument of that change. In the crystal clear language of Article Five, they provided for a convention as a method for proposing amendments to circumvent Congressional refusal or inability to make needed adaptations. As I said previously, despite the explicit language in Article V compelling it to call a convention when two-thirds of the states submit applications, Congress has obstinately refused. I don't think the words 'shall call a convention' can be construed any other way, and neither did Alexander Hamilton when he wrote *Federalist No. 85*, which, by the way, can be read in its entirety on op-usa.org."

Jenkins: "Give us a description of the OP-USA process."

Lochridge: "On this point, I want it to be very clear to your audience: We don't define the process, we don't make the rules. All I and the other OP members have ever wanted to accomplish is to provide the opportunity for a publicly-initiated convention. We offer the web site, op-usa.org, to exchange information, collect signatures, and host meetings and forums, some staff support to assist with organization, and, finally, a sustainable advertising and marketing campaign, which has been something lacking—a big disadvantage when trying to overcome widespread apathy—in similar efforts. If it occurs, it will be a people's convention; they will define the process and run it the way they see fit.

"Having said that, though, I would expect some form of local organization, be it based on counties, census tracts, Congressional districts, or some other geographical criterion, for the purpose of selecting delegates to attend the national convention. Obviously, the Framers chose the states as theirs, and it is the states that under the Tenth Amendment retain the powers not explicitly granted to the federal government, so I would expect them to have a central role in a convention."

Jenkins: "So *Ops Populi* is taking an egalitarian stance in this. Who will lead?"

Lochridge: "We are absolutely in favor of a process that shuns domination by established elites. Granted, our current Constitution was created by men who were in the upper echelon of society, but in the context of eighteenth-century America, there was no alternative. Today, the evolution of technology has made it possible to collect and synthesize information from the mass public, making possible something closer to a true democracy more practical.

There is a distinct difference between elitism and leadership, and I truly hope to see leaders emerge who are as committed to the Framers' ideals and principles as we are. OP-USA has some wonderfully talented people—constitutional scholars, a Nobel Laureate, business leaders—people of power and influence, to be sure. And we want to contribute—to participate as other citizens—but we do not intend to lead.

Jenkins: "You do, however, propose some Amendments you feel are essential to the long-term health of our country."

Lochridge: "I think it was Edmund Randolph who said, 'When the salvation of the Republic was at stake, it would be treason to our trust not to propose what we found necessary.' We are proposing only those we believe are crucial, but make no mistake, there may be many more worthy of consideration in the future."

Jenkins: "Let's spend the few minutes we have left on these. I know some of these are fairly involved, so I encourage people to visit op-usa.org for detailed descriptions."

[List on screen]

"First, an Amendment to revise the methods and procedures for amending the Constitution of the United States of America and providing for citizen-initiated legislation."

Lochridge: "Lou, we believe this Amendment is central to everything a convention should undertake, because without it, the people would be subjected to having to organize a convention for every future constitutional change, no matter how minor, or every law that Congress refused them.

"To begin with, we suggest that the existing Congressional-initiated Amending provision be left intact, only that the majorities of each house of Congress required to propose them be lowered and the number of states required for ratification be reduced to more reasonable percentages.

"A new method would replace the existing state-based Article V requirements with a process that would require Congress to either propose an amendment for ratification or call a convention within 90 days of receiving certification from half of the states that at least one-quarter of its eligible voters want the particular Amendment or convention.

"We suggest a similar process, organized by state, for the people to propose legislation directly, which would have to then be accepted by a majority of the states to become law."

Jenkins: "Next, OP proposes an Amendment to limit consecutive Congressional terms of office."

Lochridge: "To make Congress more accountable and responsive to the people, we recommend imposing limits on consecutive terms for both the House and the Senate. For the House, we are suggesting 3-year terms instead of two, so a House member can spend more time as a representative, less as a candidate."

Jenkins: "These days, being a candidate is prohibitively expensive for a qualified, but otherwise ordinary American. Your next suggestion: an Amendment to reform campaign finance."

Lochridge: "This is an immensely complex issue, Lou, and one made even more so by potential conflicts with First Amendment free speech rights. At its very core, though, is the integrity of our politics and the corrupting influence of money, particularly the enormous sums now required for Congressional and Presidential elections. OP does not claim to offer the one definitive solution to the problem. We do maintain, however, that the needs of 99.9 percent of the public for elections beyond reproach outweigh the needs of the fractional percentage who insist on an unfettered right to spend their personal fortunes to win public office. Wealth was never a legal criterion for holding public office, and lack of money should never bar an otherwise qualified person from serving.

"Our suggested Amendment would place a cap on the total expenditures for a campaign, including so-called "soft money," or independent spending, based on a formula for each office—President, Senate, House of Representatives—mandate public financing, and require a substantial portion of a House candidate's funds be derived from persons or groups located in the district the seat represents.

Jenkins: "This next one, an Amendment to abolish the electoral college, should appeal to the democratic purists among us."

Lochridge: "Our electoral college is an eighteenth-century relic whose existence is no longer justified. We cannot tolerate a system that allows our President to be chosen by a minority—or worse yet, by a single Supreme Court Justice, as was the case in 2000. Instead of handing our precious votes to an elite group of electors who we have no role in selecting and who may arbitrarily choose to cast aside popular will to vote for another candidate, we should each have an equal say in who becomes our leader and the most powerful person in the world."

Jenkins: "An Amendment to limit presidential war powers would take some of that power away."

Lochridge: "It is assumed power, never legally conferred upon the

President, and as our current situation attests, has had devastating consequences for the United States. Our Constitution explicitly gives the power to declare war to the Congress, and certainly, when it comes to committing our life and treasure to preemptive or imperialist wars abroad—when there is no immediate or direct threat to the safety and security of Americans—there should be firm constraints on this prerogative assumed by recent Presidents.

"As the commander in chief, the President must have the authority to take swift and prudent action when the country is faced with an imminent threat, but Americans need to have the benefit of more than one person's judgment to spend hundreds of billions of dollars on military actions that might destroy the lives and property of many thousands of people as a matter of foreign policy. This is not only achievable; it almost certainly has broad support among the American public given the way the experiences of Korea, Vietnam, and Iraq have touched so many generations."

Jenkins: "As we proceed through the list, I can see your recommendations affect every branch of the government. The next one, an Amendment to limit federal judicial terms, would take away lifetime appointments, I assume."

Lochridge: "Yes, we believe life tenure for federal judges has on balance become more of a detriment to our interests than a benefit. The principal reason for life tenure is to insulate our judiciary from political pressure, which arguably is desirable, since a crucial function of federal judges is to secure our fundamental rights against overt attacks by and negligence of other public and private entities. Appointment without possibility of renewal for a fixed term of years would achieve the same goal, while insuring some predictable turnover. Yes, some good judges would be forced out, but so would bad ones, who we currently have to tolerate until they choose to retire or die.

Lou, as you know, the Supreme Court gets the most public attention, but our appellate and trial judges also are vitally important to the proper functioning of our society, and our system for nominating and confirming them is in the stranglehold of partisan politics. We think eliminating lifetime tenure would lower the stakes enough to fill the many vacancies that are crippling our judicial system.

We think our plan to give each President at least two Supreme Court appointments strikes a good balance between judicial independence and insuring the Court is not dominated by permanent, out of touch ideologues."

Jenkins: "I am old enough to remember the movement for and spirited debate that accompanied your last one: a balanced budget amendment."

Lochridge: "There were quite a few nuances among all the different proposals being debated back then, but I remember it, too. Ours actually reads: an Amendment to require the President to Submit and Congress to Enact a Balanced Budget. A budget is nothing more than a plan, and our elected officials need to responsibly plan to balance expenditures against revenues as a matter of course.

"We chose this wording carefully, because in the reality of the twenty-first century, globally entwined economy, unforeseen events will undoubtedly occur that will require the government to borrow money. We don't want to hamstring our national government by outlawing deficits, particularly in legitimate emergencies, but we do believe a *planned* deficit should be explained to the satisfaction of the public who would have the power to refuse it. Unfortunately, future generations of Americans will be paying dearly for the profligacy of our current officeholders, but perhaps, we can put a stop to it."

Jenkins: "You mentioned the importance of technology earlier, and op-usa.org goes into great detail on the subject of using the internet to conduct political business. Critics allege the internet is too prone to fraud and hacking to allow citizens to vote on-line.

Lochridge: "If the internet is secure enough to handle trillions of dollars of on-line transactions each and every day, it can certainly be made safe enough for political participation and voting. The technology exists right now and it will only get better over time."

Jenkins: "On op-usa.org, there are references to Congress' previous attempts to define procedures and regulations for future constitutional conventions, which may strike some in our audience as somewhat ironic given your comments about its intransigence in calling one. Do you expect Congressional interference?

Lochridge: "I fully expect Congress to attempt to assert its presumed authority to regulate a convention, but it has abrogated its constitutional obligations under Article Five, and by doing so, surrendered any control it—and the courts, I might add—might have claimed over the process.

"Our position is rooted in the very fabric of our American constitutional law. Congress has committed an act of tyranny against the people, forcing them to take extraordinary measures to reassert their sovereignty. To give Congress control over the process would be absurd.

Jenkins: "And if the government tries to resist? With the police and or the military?"

Lochridge: "That, sir, would be an act of unspeakable despotism—and, need I say, foolish, given the fact that we have an armed citizenry."

May stopped the DVD, and clicked over the latest version of OP-USA web site, which sat on a secure intranet server at Eyezon somewhere in California. As soon as the finishing touches were complete, the interview he just saw would be shown to millions of people, broadcast to millions more over the radio. He thought it was well done. But his opinion was just that, one opinion. What really mattered now were the opinions of the other 300 million or so that OP-USA hoped to reach in one of the most ambitious and expensive public outreach campaigns ever attempted.

He read the quote Ginny helped him find and that he had asked Missy Clark at Jonic to have added earlier today—an old favorite of his, also from Thomas Jefferson, but one Lochridge and all the others who had worked on the web site's prototype had missed. In 1788, Jefferson had written:

> "We must be contented to travel on towards perfection, step by step. We must be contented with the ground which this Constitution will gain for us, and hope that a favorable moment will come for correcting what is amiss in it."

Lochridge had nailed it, dead on, in his interview. It was no accident, and not empty rhetoric, that the Constitution began with the words "We the People," because the Founding Fathers knew from history that democratic governments failed when citizens abandoned their role as guardians of their freedom and succumbed to demagoguery. The result, as in the case of Rome, and others, was the replacement of a republic with an authoritarian regime that denied the people the right to govern themselves. Americans were about to be given the chance—perhaps their only chance—to ensure that would never happen in the United States.

As he shut down the computer and turned off the lights, he thought back to his days in graduate school, the energy and excitement that surged inside him when he dreamed of the possibilities that now loomed large. Then, his youthful zeal was extinguished by naysayers who convinced him his vision was a hopeless fantasy. So many times he had warned his young students against "excessive idealism" and impatience for change. Lower your expectations, he warned them, or you will become disillusioned, then bitter, and finally, indifferent toward your government. Today, he knew he was wrong.

Today, he felt that excitement and energy surging inside him once again.

CHAPTER 76

By seven on this warm, spring Monday morning, the West Wing was already bustling with the activity of White House workaholics. Highways in and around the capital were snarled, made worse by a steady rain. This Monday was a happy occasion for the few; for the many who trudged wearily to their offices, it began another long week of toil at jobs they really didn't like too much, but had to endure.

Press releases had been distributed to all major media outlets during the weekend. Full-page print advertisements appeared in all the major metropolitan morning papers. The national television ads were scheduled to begin airing during the morning network news shows, and radio spots would be heard by afternoon commuters in cars throughout the country. Internet ads would soon be plastered on the web's most heavily visited web pages and popular search engines. Major cable operators would roll out the same national commercial to local markets, starting with the biggest—New York, Washington, Boston, L.A. and Philadelphia—gradually expanding to blanket the entire country by mid-week. A massive direct-mail campaign was to begin within a few days, and targeted computer-generated phone calls to key organizations and individuals were on tap for later in the week as well.

After a restless night, May was up and out the door by 5:30 a.m. to hunt for cappuccino and pastries, the mutually agreed upon celebratory breakfast to mark the occasion. By 6 a.m., May and Ginny were multi-tasking in the bedroom office, watching several TVs, listening to the radio, and browsing the web on her computer. Missy Clark had told them to be patient, not to be disappointed at the lack of instantaneous results, particularly from the press releases and the internet ads. But even though verifying ad placement was her responsibility, they were eager to see some results of all the planning and coordination, watch it all unfold for themselves.

May's monitor displayed the status of the op-usa.org web servers in the organization's new Northern Virginia operations center about 30 miles to the northwest. They ignored the paltry number of hits registered since midnight, which barely budged when he clicked on the browser's refresh button to update the display. Between sips of cappuccino and bites of a chocolate croissant, he kept one eye on Ginny while he leafed through the morning newspaper. Minutes seemed like hours, as nothing seemed to be happening, until Ginny suddenly bellowed, "Found One!" Then another, and another. Slowly the hit counter came to life, registering several hundred views of the home page by 6:30, a few thousand by seven, when the network news shows started.

John Russell normally arrived at his West Wing office by six, but a wife with the flu and the lousy weather's effects on traffic flow put a damper on his routine. One of the few who, despite the high stress environment, loved his job and its promise of a lucrative career after the 2008 election, Russell was part of a small army, paid handsomely by the taxpayers to watch TV, listen to the radio, read newspapers, magazines, and follow the opinions expressed in cyberspace. The army's mission was to monitor national and world events, with special focus on the administration's image as it was perceived and portrayed by countless critics, who—so it seemed to them, at least—were increasing exponentially. Still damp, but with coffee in hand, he plunked down behind the massive stack of paper that awaited him, refusing to be distracted by the bank of TVs mounted in the wall flickering wildly in front of him. First things first: log onto the computer, check e-mail. Other media soldiers were covering the morning news shows at the moment.

Monday morning e-mail was brutal, especially if it was neglected all weekend. As usual, his e-mail was jammed with multitudes of irrelevant messages interspersed with the few he had to read, all of which claimed his careful attention to sort through.

"John! Look at number six!" someone shouted, startling him.

After four years on the job, he knew number six was the TV tuned to NBC. His eyes hit the screen as the camera panned at a wide angle, displaying two trains on a single track that circled a mountain, one above the other, but obvious to the viewer they were closing on one another toward an inevitable collision neither could see coming.

"I can't hear—turn it up a little," he commanded.

"It is up," came the reply.

Indeed, the only audio was a distant rumble of the engines and the steady metallic clackety-clack of the rolling wheels, interrupted by an occasional screech or hiss. The camera zoomed in on the top train to show its engine, a stock photo of the White House superimposed on an American flag painted on its side. As the trailing cars rounded a bend, the viewer saw the sides labeled in large letters: "Debt," "Social Security," "Poverty," "Crime," "Healthcare," "Greed," "Deceit," "Scandal," "Eavesdropping." A quick switch to a second camera showed the lower, ascending engine, chugging furiously as it struggled in its climb, engine emblazoned in red, white, and blue, pulling cars labeled "Liberty," "Freedom," "Justice," "Equality." Clever animation work, Russell thought. Cut back to the first camera, which pulled back from the top train to show both trains on their imminent collision course, the top one appearing to careen uncontrollably, headlong toward the bottom of the mountain. At the point of impact, the screen goes black, no sound. A second later, the words "It's Your Country," flash in bold white letters, fade to "Do Something." The final image displays for about five seconds: "www.op-usa.org."

"What in the hell…who is…?" Russell muttered as his fingers hit the keyboard.

In the operations center, Sally Sexton's elation was fleeting as she watched the screen cut to the next commercial. She crossed her fingers, hopeful the 23 people waiting in the cubicles outside her office door would somehow manage the expected onslaught of calls.

"Nice!" She exclaimed to May and Ginny, who exchanged a hi-five hand slap.

"That was great," Ginny shrieked.

"Here they come," Sally announced. "Time to muddle through—"

"Hang in there!" May interjected encouragingly. "You'll be fine." He felt somewhat foolish, given that they all knew the operations center was woefully understaffed. Sally's staffing plan called for 100 to man the phones, another 20 for mail, and a full complement of professional and technical staff to round out what amounted to a medium-sized company. But there had not been enough time to implement her plan with any semblance of order; for now, she would grab as many warm bodies as she could from the temporary agencies, interview permanent candidates from dawn till dusk, and, to use her words, muddle through.

As the morning wore on, the networks ran the spots, the newspapers were read, the web site's traffic numbers soared, and the phones began ringing non-stop. The small staff fielded as many calls as they could, but it quickly became apparent that the public's response was more enthusiastic than any of them had ever imagined it would be.

Twelve hours later, op-usa.org had logged over 3,500,000 visitors, with over 3,000,000 requesting immediate registration packets. Thousands of e-mails sat on the mail server, with phone calls pouring in even faster than they had earlier in the day. They all worked non-stop, barely pausing long enough for a quick bite of a sandwich or a bathroom break all day.

NBC was the first network interview request followed quickly by CNN, FOX, ABC and CBS—even BBC had picked up on it—all of which were asking for on-air exclusives. It wasn't long before Sally was pleading for help, begging other OP members to agree to news and talk shows interviews all over the country, with even some foreign media outlets clamoring for their time. Podcasts and streaming audio and video presentations of the group's mission, goals and strategic plan were made available to the general public over the internet.

"We understand that the op-usa.org web site has enjoyed resounding success in its first day," the talk show host said from her Washington studio. The radio station had a news-talk format and was broadcast on three separate frequencies throughout the region surrounding the nation's capital.

"Yes we have. It has been tremendous." May answered, his voice slightly trembling. He knew he would get better at this with a little practice, just as he had adjusted to giving college lectures. No cameras—for now, at least. "America's citizenry, I believe, is ready to consider some meaningful change in their government."

"Mr. Mullins, some of the early reaction from politicians and corporate leaders is dismissing your organization's cause as outrageous, with some even going as far as to label it anti-patriotic, since your main objective is to circumvent the normal practice of amending the Constitution, calling for a general convention that could fundamentally alter our country's system of government." She paused briefly for effect. "How do you respond to this criticism?"

Although he had rehearsed his response to this kind of question in his mind for days, he was surprised that it had come this early in his very first interview. He found himself unprepared for the onrush of emotion, as the image of Lochridge appeared in his mind's eye. He remembered the words of the man whose fervid love of his country had rekindled idealism that lay dormant for so many years, given his life new meaning, new purpose. But it was so much more than just the revival of latent academic and intellectual interests, or even patriotic fervor: It was a spiritual reincarnation after years of emptiness, as his soul lay buried in the graves of his wife and daughter. How improbable but fantastic it was to once again experience genuine passion and the hopes and dreams of a promising future. Hope, he now understood, makes life worth living. Hope is nourishment for the soul.

He looked up at Ginny, who had been standing at his side, her hand resting on his shoulder. He reached up to take her hand in his. Their eyes met in a moment of tacit realization that fate had chosen to irrevocably link them. The past was just that—past; yet, the future, though rife with uncertainty and more than a little trepidation, was nevertheless filled with hope. Hope for their new lives together. Hope for their country.

So, he cleared his throat, choked back a few nascent tears, and spoke the words he had last spoken in concluding what he believed was an insignificant lecture to a little group of ordinary people in Camden, Maine a decade before:

"A people's convention is not only sorely needed, it is the most authentic, genuinely patriotic thing any American citizen could ever do." He smiled broadly at Ginny and squeezed her hand tightly before saying, "Even though *Ops Populi* translates to 'power to the people,' for every American, its true meaning is hope."